"Got him!" Megan said. "In the Solarium." A holo of Aris formed above the console. He was standing with his arms crossed, glaring at the camera, which had to be mounted in an LP robot. The edge of another LP showed in the image. The two robots had trapped the sulky android in a corner of the atrium.

"That had better keep him out of trouble," Raj said.

Megan came back over and helped Raj undo his bonds. "I can't believe he wanted to hurt you."

"He's a damn cyberthug," he muttered. Then he added, "But no, I don't think he meant to hurt me."

"The robot arm could have killed you."

He turned his wrist back and forth, helping her loosen a knot. "I saw him playing with the system after he tied me up. It looked like he only intended the arm to guard me. I don't think he realized it would try to take me apart."

"We'll have to keep him guarded."

"I don't want to push him, though. I'd rather he came back here of his own free will."

"Free will." Megan's hands stilled as she stared at Raj. "It's come to that, hasn't it? He's becoming self-aware. . . ."

Bantam Books by Catherine Asaro

The Veiled Web
The Phoenix Code

THE PHOENIX CODE

CATHERINE ASARO

BANTAM BOOKS
New York   Toronto   London
Sydney   Auckland

THE PHOENIX CODE

A Bantam Spectra Mass Market / December 2000

SPECTRA and the portrayal of a boxed "s" are
trademarks of Bantam Books, a division of
Random House, Inc.

ISBN 0-553-58154-6

Published simultaneously in the United States and Canada

Bantam Books are published by Bantam Books, a division
of Random House, Inc. Its trademark, consisting of the
words "Bantam Books" and the portrayal of a rooster, is
Registered in U.S. Patent and Trademark Office and in
other countries. Marca Registrada. Bantam Books, 1540
Broadway, New York, New York 10036.

PRINTED IN THE UNITED STATES OF AMERICA

10 9 8 7 6 5 4 3 2 1

OPM

To my grandmother
Annie Asaro
with love

Acknowledgments

I would like to express my gratitude to the readers who gave me input on the writing and research for this book. Their comments greatly helped strengthen the book. Any errors that remain are mine alone.

To Lt. Col. Michael LaViolette, USAR, for his sharp comments and the great pizzas his family brought over; to Larry Clough, acting program manager for the Situation Assessment and Data Fusion Division of Teknowledge Corporation; to Jeri Smith-Ready, for her perceptive reading and all those one/two/threes; to my grandmother, Annie Asaro, and my aunt and uncle, Jack and Marie Scudder, for their delightful talks about Las Vegas; and to the many other people who graciously answered my questions, including Professor of Physics Pranab Ghosh, Jennifer Dunne, and Devi Pellai.

To the writers who listened to selected scenes and provided their excellent insights: Aly's Writing Group, including Aly Parsons, Simcha Kuritzky, Connie Warner, Al Carroll, Paula Jordon, Michael LaViolette, George Williams, and J. G. Huckenpöler; and Ruth's "class," including Ruth

Glick (Rebecca York), Binnie Syril Braunstein, Randy DuFresne (Elizabeth Ashtree), Chassie West, and Linda Williams.

A special thanks to my top-notch editor, Anne Lesley Groell, who is everything an author could ask for in an editor; to my much appreciated agent, Eleanor Wood, of Spectrum Literary Agency, for her always valued advice and support; to Nancy Berland and her associates for their enthusiasm and hard work; and to the publisher and all the fine people at Bantam who made this book possible.

A most heartfelt thanks to the shining lights of my life, my husband, John Kendall Cannizzo, and my daughter, Cathy, whose constant love and support make it all worthwhile.

Contents

Contents

THE PHOENIX CODE

The Offer

People packed the auditorium. Every seat was filled and more listeners crammed the aisles. An unspoken question charged the room: were today's speakers revealing a spectacular new future for the human race—or the end of humanity's reign as the ruling species on Earth?

This session was a diamond in the crown of IRTAC, the International Robotics Technology and Applications Conference in the year 2021, held at Goddard Space Flight Center in Maryland. As chair of this session, Megan O'Flannery had chosen the speakers. She was sitting now at a table on the right edge of the stage. The man answering questions, Arick Bjornsson, stood center stage.

"The genie is out of the bottle," Arick was saying. "Our machines are becoming intelligent. They won't surpass us today or tomorrow, but it is only a matter of time."

Listening to him, Megan pondered her own conflict. She worked on artificial intelligence for androids—humanlike robots. Usually she looked to the future with optimism. Sometimes, though, she wondered if they were only creating ways to magnify the human capacity for destruction. She might soon face a decision that forced her to confront both sides of the issue: could she use the fruits of her intellect to create machines meant to kill?

She glanced over the audience. The scientists came in all sizes, shapes, and ages. Most wore casual clothes: jeans, shirts or blouses, jumpsuits. The conference chair, a distinguished man in a well-cut suit, was a few rows up from the stage. Several men and women sat with him, other high-ranking officials. Megan recognized them all, except for the fellow on his right.

The stranger had dark eyes and tousled black curls. His faded jeans had raveled at the knees, and his denim shirt was frayed. A black leather jacket with metal studs lay haphazardly over his legs. The gold watch on his wrist caught the light with prismatic glints that suggested diamonds. As he listened to the talk, emotions played across his mobile features: skepticism, interest, outrage, amusement. He glared and crossed his arms at one point. Later, he relaxed and nodded with approval. The dramatic flair of his handsome face fascinated Megan.

A woman sitting in front of the man suddenly swiped her hand past her face. It looked as if she were bedeviled by one of those irksome gnats that infiltrated the auditorium. As she caught the bug, the man reached forward and tapped her wrist. She turned with a start, reflexively opening her fist. Then her gaze flicked up to follow the liberated gnat. The man said something, an apology it looked like, and sat back. After giving him a bemused look, she shook her head and returned her attention to the talk. It all piqued Megan's curiosity.

Arick finished and the audience applauded. After he took his seat, Megan stepped up to the podium. "That concludes this session. The media people tell me they'll have copies of the proceedings tomorrow. You can get it as a holograph, in videos, or in memory cubes. A paper copy should be available in a few weeks." She grinned at them, this collection of her colleagues, friends, and adversaries. "That's it, folks. All we have left is the banquet tonight. So let's go eat and be merry."

Laughter rippled through the audience, followed by a general murmur as people began talking, putting on coats, or seeking out one another to continue spirited debates. Megan looked around for the man with the leather jacket, thinking to introduce herself.

But he had disappeared.

A long day, Megan thought as she left the auditorium. Her hair was coming down, red tendrils curling around her face. She pulled the heavy tresses free, then gathered up the waist-length mane and pinned it back on her head in a neat roll. She wished her energy weren't at such a low. Her work day hadn't ended yet; she had another meeting, possibly an important one to her career.

Tired or not, though, she thrived on this life. Robots had fascinated her since her childhood in Bozeman, Montana. She recalled toddling after a toy cat that stalked around the spacious living room of her parents' house. It hid behind a door, then attempted to pounce. She rocked with laughter when it toppled in an undignified heap of fur, limbs, and blinking lights. She had spent the next hour taking out its batteries and trying to put them back.

So she grew up, earned a B.S. in computer science at Montana State University, and went to Stanford for graduate school. Now at thirty-five, she was a professor at MIT. But the delighted little girl still lived inside of her, marveling at her toys.

Her enthusiasm bemused her mother, who had once asked, *But Megan, why make robots that look like people? What's wrong with the humans we already have?*

It's a new science, Megan had answered. *A new world, Mom. Maybe even a new species.*

Her mother had given her that look then, the one that Megan had long ago decided never boded well. Regarding Megan with the large blue eyes that her daughter had inherited, she said, *You know, dear, there are much more enjoyable ways to make new humans, and you don't have to work nearly so hard as you do in your lab.*

All Megan could manage was an aghast, *Mom!* One's silver-haired mother wasn't supposed to say such things, let alone look so pleased with herself, smiling like a cherub.

She supposed that if she would get married and make some new humans of the traditional kind, her mother would ease up. It wasn't that Megan had no interest in marriage; she just hadn't found the right man. Although her parents had liked most of her past boyfriends, she always had a sneaking suspicion they were sizing the poor fellows up as potential grandchild-production sources.

A voice interrupted her reverie. A man and woman were approaching. *So,* she thought. *This is it.*

"Dr. O'Flannery," the man said as they came up to her. His styled haircut, expensive blue suit, and businesslike manner made a sharp contrast to the more informal clothes most scientists wore at the conference. The woman had gray hair and a piercing intelligence in her gaze. Megan recognized her, but she couldn't remember from where.

The man extended his hand. "I'm Antonio Oreza. Tony."

Megan shook his hand. "Hello. Are you from Mind-Sim?" She had agreed to meet their representatives after the session.

"That's right. I'm the vice president in charge of research and development." He indicated the woman with him. "This is Claire Oliana, from Stanford. She consults for us."

MindSim had sent a VP to talk to her? And *Claire Oliana*? The Stanford professor was the first person to receive the Nobel prize for work in the development of machine intelligence.

Megan suddenly didn't feel so tired anymore.

The vending café had blue walls and tables covered by blue and white checked cloths. As Megan sat down with Tony and Claire, a vending robot bustled over, rolling on its treads. It stood about four feet tall, with a domed head and tubular body. The droid had only a rudimentary AI, one limited to serving food—though within that narrow range it could develop a personality. Its panels displayed cheerful holos of meals that looked far more delectable than anything Megan had actually eaten here.

"Good afternoon," it said. "I'm Jessie." Its head swiveled from side to side as it surveyed them, giving it an earnest appearance. It made Megan smile, though she knew it was just mapping their positions with the cameras in its eyes.

"Do you have coffee?" Tony asked.

"I've a delicious menu to select from," Jessie assured him. "French vanilla, cappuccino, Brazilian dry roast, decaf supreme, and today's special, Martian bug-eyed-monster deluxe."

Megan laughed. "Monster deluxe? What is that?"

"It has an unusually strong caffeine content," Jessie said. "The night shift in the Science Operations Facility programmed it into me at four this morning. They required a strong restorative to make their continued functioning possible."

Claire smiled. "That much caffeine would send me into orbit. Decaf for me."

"French vanilla here," Tony said.

"Very wise choices," Jessie said. A red cup plopped into a recess in its stomach and began filling with coffee.

"I'll take the Martian deluxe," Megan decided.

"As you wish." If a machine could blink its lights with doubt over the wisdom of a customer's choice, Jessie was doing it. Megan suspected that the SOF night shift had also programmed some mischief into the droid's personality.

After Jessie served their coffee, Tony clicked his money card into the robot. Jessie's lights sparkled as it spoke. "I hope you enjoy your meal." Its head swiveled to Megan. "Please inform me if you need any further assistance."

"Like an ambulance?" Megan couldn't resist teasing the droid. It probably had a minimal humor mod to make it more personable to customers.

Its lights twinkled. "I serve only the best food, ma'am." Then it rolled away, playing a tinkling melody like the ice cream trucks in the neighborhood where she had grown up. It took up position by the wall and swiveled its head around, surveying the café like a carnival barker looking for new marks.

With a laugh, Claire said, "I think the night shift in the Science Operations Facility have been staying up too late."

Megan took a swallow of her drink. The stuff tasted like rocket fuel. "They know their coffee," she said with approval.

Tony was watching her. "I can't help but wonder, Dr. O'Flannery, how you would program a robot like that."

"I don't work with utility droids." She had no doubt Tony knew exactly where her interests lay. With a smile she added, "And you should call me Megan."

Both Tony and Claire seemed pleased at this nonresponse. Tony leaned forward. "Megan, what would you say to a functional android for your research?"

She resisted the urge to shout *Yes!* Although MindSim was on the cutting edge of such research, vague rumors about disasters there in hidden projects made her wary. She made her voice casual, but friendly. "The problem is, no one has an android hanging around that wants a brain."

"Well, no." Tony beamed as if he were about to deliver great news. "However, MindSim has funding in that area."

After researching MindSim in preparation for this meeting, Megan knew that both they and their major competitor, Arizonix Corporation, had won several Department of Defense grants for their work in AI and robots. She also suspected she would need a security clearance to hear any details of the projects.

She chose a neutral response. "MindSim does good work."

Tony spoke with polished enthusiasm. "We'd like you to be part of our team."

"Suppose you had the chance to lead such a project?" Claire asked.

Megan stared at her, then took a long swallow of her rocket fuel. She would jump at such an opportunity—if it didn't have a catch. Why had they come to her? They already had DOD funds, so they must have started out with a chief scientist as the principal investigator on the grant proposal. What had happened?

"It would depend on the circumstances," she said.

"Come out to MindSim and take a look," Tony said. "We'll show you around."

Megan wasn't sure what to say. She liked her position at MIT. She had grants, graduate students, resources, colleagues, and a growing reputation in the field. The prestige didn't hurt either. But Tony and Claire were dropping seductive hints. She would give almost anything to work with a real android instead of being confined to running simulations on a computer. A visit to MindSim wasn't a commitment. If nothing else, an offer from them might inspire MIT to give her a raise.

She leaned forward. "Let's talk."

Goddard Space Flight Center covered many acres of land, with the rolling fields of the Beltsville Agricultural Center to the east and the Baltimore-Washington Parkway to the west. Stretches of forest separated the buildings, and deer wandered everywhere.

Lost in thought, Megan ambled down a back road. She had always enjoyed walking, and this gave her a chance to mull over the MindSim offer. A lake stretched out on her right, basking in late afternoon sunlight. The day had that golden, antique quality that came late in the year. Birds paddled in the water: gray, speckled brown, iridescent green, and the odd white goose with an orange beak. Farther down the shore, a man stood surrounded by ducks. At first she wasn't sure why they were squawking at him. Then she saw that he was scattering bread crumbs.

She was about to continue on her way when she recognized him: the intriguing fellow from the audience. He looked over six feet tall, with black hair and dark eyes. A palmtop computer hung from his scuffed leather belt. He watched the birds with a half-smile, as if he hadn't decided whether it would insult their egos if he laughed at them.

Megan changed direction and headed toward him. As she came closer, though, she hesitated. His muscular build and handsome face didn't fit her image of a robotics expert. His hair curled over his ears and down his neck, longer than men wore nowadays, but clean and glossy with health. On most people, it would have looked sloppy; on him, it worked. The same was true of his clothes. What his long legs did for those raveling jeans would have brought their makers a fortune if they could have packaged the quality. It made her hang back, as if he were a holovid actor she would normally never have had the chance to meet.

Suddenly he looked up. "Good afternoon, Dr. O'Flannery." It was hard to place his background; his facial features evoked the Celts, his coloring could be Indian, and his rich accent, like molasses on a summer afternoon, was undeniably from the American South.

"Hi," Megan said.

He tossed the last of his bread into the lake. Flapping and squawking, the birds waddled after the morsels.

"Such hungry things," Megan said. "Greedy, even."

His grin crinkled the fine lines around his eyes. "They'd eat ten loaves if I brought them."

Oh, Lord. That smile defined the word "devastating." It lit up his face.

"See?" He pointed at the sky. "They're leaving."

She looked up, as much to regain her composure as to see what he meant. A V-shape of birds was arrowing across the sky. "Well, yes." More collected now, she turned back to him. "Flying south for the winter, I imagine."

He indicated the birds floating on the pond, then held up his hand as if to offer them more delicacies. They paddled industriously toward him until they realized he was bluffing. Then they drifted off again. His gold watch caught rays of the sun, glittering with discreet diamonds.

"They don't cheat," he said.

"I'm sure they don't." Megan had no idea what they

were actually talking about, but she doubted it was birds. Whatever the subject, she loved his voice. Deep and throaty, it rumbled like music, sometimes drawling, other times resonant. "Did you enjoy the session this afternoon?"

"I suppose." *Ah suhppose.* "You should have given a talk. You do better work than the lot of them combined."

That caught her off guard. "Thank you." She hesitated. "I'm afraid I don't know your name."

He considered her for a long moment. Then he said, "Raj. Call me Raj."

"Is that your name?"

"Well, no. Yes. At times."

"Raj isn't your name?"

"My mother calls me Robin." He spread his hands as if to say, *What can a person do?*

Megan smiled. She could relate to that situation. Her father still called her Maggie-kitten. She didn't mind it from him, but it would earn anyone else a shove into a lake. "What do other people call you?"

"All sorts of things." He rubbed his ear. "I wouldn't repeat most of them."

She gave it another try. "So Raj is the name on your birth certificate."

"No."

Megan couldn't help but laugh. "You know, this is like pulling teeth."

His lips quirked into a smile. "My birth certificate, from the fine state of Louisiana, says Chandrarajan."

She stared at him. "You're *Chandrarajan Sundaram*?"

"Please don't look so shocked. I assure you, I've treated the name well."

Good Lord. This was the reclusive eccentric who had revolutionized the field of robotics? Unattached to any university or institute, he worked only as a consultant.

Corporations paid him large amounts of money to solve their problems. She had heard that one had given him a million, after he made their disastrous household robot work in time for its market release, saving the company from bankruptcy.

His reputation gave her a context for his conversation. Rumor said he paid a price for his phenomenal intellect; no one could think like him, but he had the devil of a time expressing those thoughts. From what she had heard, his mind didn't work in linear thought processes, so he often made jumps of logic that left his listeners confounded.

It astounded her that he had come to the conference. She had invited him, of course. He had been a top name on her hoped-for speakers list. She had already known, however, that he rarely attended such meetings. It hadn't surprised her when he declined.

Yet here he stood.

"It's actually Sundaram Chandrarajan Robert," he said.

"Your name?"

His voice became subdued. "My father followed the custom of giving me his name, followed by my own. But in this country, it's easier for us to have the same last name. So we use Sundaram. Robert is from my mother's side."

She wondered why the mention of his father caused his mood to turn so quiet. "It's a beautiful name."

Raj watched her with a long, considering look. "Then there are geese," he mused.

"Birds again." She gave a gentle laugh. "You know, I have no idea what we're talking about."

Amusement lightened his voice. "Most people don't respond this way to me."

"What do they do?"

"Nod. Look embarrassed. Then leave as fast as they can."

"Is that what you want?"

"It depends." He had all his attention focused on her now.

"On what?"

"Hair color."

"Hair color?" This conversation was making less and less sense by the minute. It was fun, though.

"Red," he said. "Yours is red."

"Well, yes. My hair is definitely red."

"Red flag." He walked over to her. "For stop."

It took a moment, but then she realized he was making a joke, using it to ask if she wished he would leave. Given that he had come over to her as he said it, she suspected he didn't want to end their conversation. Of course, she could be wrong. But he reminded her of her father, an absentminded architect who tended to talk in riddles during his more preoccupied moods.

Megan put her hands on her hips. "I do believe, sir, that you're teasing me."

His lips quirked up again. "It could be."

She could tell he was still waiting for her response to his unasked question. "I'm sure my hair doesn't say 'stop.' "

A grin spread across his face. "You're quick."

Ah, that smile. It was fortunate this man lived as a recluse. Otherwise, womankind wouldn't be safe from either his dazzling smile or his nutty conversation. "Not that quick. I still don't get it about the birds."

"Winter is coming and they have a long way to go." He sounded more relaxed now. "So they eat a lot. But they aren't greedy. And they don't cheat. They only take what they need." His smile faded. "Humans could learn a lot from them."

Megan wondered what sort of life he had lived, that he saw the world in such terms. Then it occurred to her that given the value of his intellect and personal wealth, people probably wanted whatever they could get from him.

"Perhaps we could," she said.

"They followed me around too, you know," he said. "I sent them away."

Her brow furrowed. "The birds?"

"The suits from MindSim."

"They offered you a job?"

"Yes. I told them no." Then he added, "But perhaps I will consult for them, after all."

Her pulse jumped. Was he offering her the chance to work with him? She kept her voice calm, afraid that if she appeared too eager, she would scare him off. "Maybe you should."

He offered his hand. "I'm pleased to have met you, Dr. O'Flannery."

She shook his hand. "And I you. Please call me Megan."

"Megan." He nodded. Then he turned and started down the road. After a few steps, he turned back as if he had remembered something. "Oh. Yes. Good-bye, Megan."

She raised her hand. "Good-bye."

Then he went on his way, leaving her to wonder just what was going on out at MindSim.

II

The Everest Project

Megan hadn't expected her security clearance to come through so quickly. It made her wonder if MindSim hadn't begun the paperwork in advance, just in case. After a few weeks of negotiations, they flew her out to California to tour their labs.

She felt like a kid in a computer-game arcade. She enjoyed this more than the pursuits her friends urged on her for "fun," like parties or holovids. Invariably, her parents joined the chorus, with hints that she should include a fellow in the postulated proceedings—son-in-law material, of course. Their unabashed lobbying drove her crazy. They were wonderful people and she loved them dearly, but she felt like running for the hills every time they got that grandparental gleam in their eyes.

Out at MindSim, Tony and Claire showed her the snazzy labs first. In one, droids trundled around, gravely navigating obstacle courses. She spent half an hour putting them through their paces before her hosts enticed her to another lab. There she met an appliance that resembled a broom with wheels and detachable arms. It expounded at length on how it moved its fingers. Then she went for a walk with a robot that had legs. Its smooth gait put to shame earlier versions that had jerked along like stereo-typical robots. Her hosts also let her try a Vacubot. She decided its inventors deserved a Nobel prize for their compassionate gift to humanity—a robot that could vac-uum the house while its frazzled human occupants went out for pizza.

"We also work on humanlike robots," Tony said as they ushered her down another hall. "This next lab de-signs the body."

Megan's pulse jumped. "You've an android here?"

"Unfortunately, no," Claire said. "This work is all the-oretical. Development of the androids would go on at a facility in Nevada."

It didn't surprise her that they had a more secure base of operations. Industrial espionage had become a thriving enterprise. MindSim wouldn't make their results public until they had full patent protection and software copy-rights. She doubted they could copyright an AI brain, though. They would soon have to answer the question: When did self-modifying software become a cognizant being?

The next lab enticed her like a bakery full of chocolate cake. Equipment filled it, all cased in Lumiflex, a lumi-nous white plastic. Instead of blackboards or white-boards, the walls sported photoscreens with light styluses. Disks and memory cubes cluttered the tables, and mem-ory towers stood by the consoles. Although a few cables ran under the floor, most of the connections were wire-less. A wall counter held a coffeepot and a motley assort-ment of mugs.

Two men and a woman were working at the consoles. They had outstanding workstations: Stellar-Magnum Mark-XIV computers; combination cellular phone, FAX, radio, microphone, camera, wireless unit, and modem; keyboard, printer, scanner, and holoscreens. Holos rotated in the air with views of the theoretical android: EM fluxes, circuits, skeleton, hydraulics, temperature profiles, and more.

It all brought back to Megan her first day in college. While her friends had gone to check out the city, she had spent the afternoon talking to grad students in the AI lab. Within a week, she was doing gofer work for their professor. He gave her a research job that summer. By her sophomore year, the group considered her a member of their circle. She understood why Tony and Claire had shown her the glitz labs first; this one had only holos to look at, nothing concrete. However, if she took the job, these people would be her team, and they interested her more than any glitz.

Tony introduced them. The slender man with sandy hair was Alfred from Cal Berkeley. Miska came from a university in Poland. About five years older than Alfred and half a foot shorter, he had dark eyes and hair. Diane, a stout woman with auburn hair, had done a stint at a government lab and then taken this job.

They described their work, referring to the android as "he." At first Megan appreciated their not saying "it," but then she wondered at her reaction. Already they were giving their hoped-for creation human attributes. Maybe it wouldn't want those traits. Someday they might download the neural patterns of a human brain into an android, but even then no guarantee existed that it would think or act human.

Their descriptions also sounded too detailed. Finally she said, "It's done, isn't it? You have a working android."

Alfred shook his head. "I'm afraid 'working' is too optimistic a term."

Tony indicated a table. "Let's sit down. Now that

you've seen the models, we can talk about where we hope to go from here."

As they took their seats, Alfred brought over the coffee and mugs. When everyone was settled, Claire spoke to Megan. "We've tried to make several prototypes. Four."

Miska took a sip of coffee, then grimaced and set his mug down. He spoke with a light accent. "The problem, you see, is that these androids are mentally unstable. The bodies have problems, yes, but we think we can fix these. We are not so sure about their minds."

"The first three failed," Diane said. "We still have the fourth Everest android, but he's barely functional."

"Everest?" Megan asked.

"It's what we call the project," Tony said. "Surmounting a great height." He leaned forward. "It could be yours. Your successes, your triumphs."

Triumphs, indeed. "What happened to your last director?"

Alfred spoke flatly. "He quit."

Tony frowned, but he didn't interrupt or try to put a spin on Alfred's words. Megan's respect for MindSim went up a notch.

"Marlow Hastin directed the project until a few months ago," Alfred said. "We weren't having much success. The RS-1 became catatonic. No matter what we tried, it evolved back to the catatonia. The RS-2 had similar problems, with autism. And the RS-3 . . . well, it killed itself."

"He walked into a furnace and burned up," Miska said, his dismay subtle but still obvious.

Claire spoke softly. "We don't want that to happen again."

"I can see why," Megan said. "Is that the reason Hastin quit?"

"In part," Miska said. "But he didn't leave until later."

"We had a difference of opinion," Diane said.

Alfred took a swallow of coffee. "Marlow wanted to program subservience into the RS units. He feared that if we didn't, they might turn against us."

"It's a valid concern," Megan said. She wondered, though, if that had led to the tragedy with the RS-3. "But it may be moot. We're combining ourselves with our creations as fast as we can make the results viable and safe for humans. If we become them and they become us, the issue fades away."

The others exchanged glances. Then Miska said, "You are much different from Marlow."

"He hated the idea of taking technology into ourselves," Diane said. "Or of putting our minds into robots."

"Would you turn down a pacemaker that could save your life?" Megan leaned forward. "An artificial limb that would let you walk again? We're creating the means to make ourselves smarter, stronger, faster, longer lived."

"In the ideal," Claire said. "Whether or not we achieve it remains to be seen."

"Our hope," Tony said, "is to explore the full potential of humanlike robots."

"Including peaceful applications?" Megan asked. It was one of her main concerns. She understood the need for defense work, but she wanted to know that the fruits of her intellect would also go toward improving the human condition.

"Of course," Tony said. "We're committed to both."

Megan sat for a moment, thinking. "From what you've told me, it sounds like you all have very specialized areas of expertise."

No one seemed surprised by her comment. Alfred answered. "Miska, Diane, and I are the support. Claire consults on the AI aspects."

They struck Megan as a good team. However, they were missing an important component—the hardware equivalent to Claire. "Who is your robotics expert?"

"Well, yes, that's the rub," Alfred said.

"It's a top priority," Tony interjected smoothly. "If you accept the position, we'll have a slate of superb candidates for you to consider."

"In other words," Megan said, "you don't have anyone."

"We're taking the time to find the best," Tony assured her. "We almost had a fellow from Jazari International in Morocco, but JI came through with a counteroffer and he decided to stay."

She wasn't surprised they had checked out JI. The company had risen to international prominence over the past two decades. She had met Rashid al-Jazari, the CEO, several times. His American wife, Lucia del Mar, performed with the Martelli Dance Theatre, so they and their three children lived part of the year in the United States, and Rashid sometimes visited MIT. He was a charming man, but he didn't strike her as the type to let MindSim woo away his employees.

She thought back to her talk with Raj. "How about Chandrarajan Sundaram?"

"We're trying," Claire said. "But we aren't the only ones. Apparently Arizonix also wants him."

Tony's smile morphed into a frown. He said only, "Arizonix," but he managed to put boundless distaste into that one word.

"Are you sure you'd want Sundaram?" Claire asked her. "He has a reputation for being rather difficult."

Alfred snorted. "He's a nut."

"I rather like him," Megan said.

"You've *met* him?" Diane looked impressed.

"We talked at the IRTAC meeting. It was interesting."

"I'll bet." Claire sipped her coffee, then blanched and set her mug down with the care one used when handling explosives.

Curious, Megan tried the brew. It went down like a jolt of TNT and detonated when it hit bottom. "Hey. This is good."

Alfred gave a hearty laugh. "A truly refined taste." Claire and Miska turned a bit green.

They spent the next hour showing her details of their work. She made no promises, playing it cool.

But she was ready to jump.

III

Nevada Five

The hovercar skimmed across the Nevada desert like a ship sailing an ocher sea, the rumble of its turbofan evoking images of growling sea monsters. Sitting in the front passenger seat, Megan gazed out at a land mottled with gray-green bushes. The road they were following arrowed to the horizon, dwindling to a point in the distance.

Since passing the security check several miles back, they had seen no cars, buildings, or rest stops. The isolation unsettled her. As the new director of the Everest Project, this would be her home. She still had to wrap up her work at MIT and direct her graduate students, but she could do most of that from here, using the Web and virtual reality conferences.

She glanced at Alfred in the driver's seat. Most of the Everest team would still work in California; with the satellite link, communication would be easy, and she could use robots for lab technicians. If this had been just a development project, she would probably have stayed at MindSim with the team. But for such intensive research, she needed to interact with the android. Alfred, Diane, and Miska had come out to introduce her. A second car followed, bringing Major Richard Kenrock, their contact at the Department of Defense, and a lieutenant who served as his assistant.

The car turned off the road, its turbine providing thrust and vectored steering. It hovered across the desert on its cushion of air, rocking a bit from the bumpy terrain. Soon it slowed to a stop and settled to the ground, its landing motor grumbling in a deep baritone that contrasted to the tenor of the turbofan. No hint showed that they had arrived anywhere; nothing but gravelly land and spiky plants stretched in every direction. The second car settled next to them, with Richard Kenrock in the driver's seat. The major's wave looked like a salute.

Alfred peered at a screen on the dash. "Okay. This is it. Backspace, take us down."

Backspace, the car's computer, spoke in a mellow voice. "Fingerprint code, please."

Alfred touched the screen. In the other car, Major Kenrock was doing the same. With no ado and almost no sound, the land under them sank into the desert. It reminded Megan of cartoons from her childhood, where a trapdoor opened beneath unsuspecting characters and they dropped out of sight with their long ears streaming above them. This went slower, of course, lowering them into a freight elevator enclosed by a sturdy wire mesh. As the elevator descended, she craned her head to look up. A holographic camouflage hid the opening above them, making the ground appear unbroken.

Looking down through the elevator's mesh, she saw a garage below. Lamps lit the area, activated by the car's computer. Several vehicles crouched there: dark humvees with angular bodies. When the elevator reached the floor, the mesh opened like a gate. After they drove out, the gate closed and the elevator began to rise.

Megan indicated the humvees. "Those look like giant stealth cockroaches."

Alfred gave one of his hearty, infectious laughs. "I guess you could say the place is bugged."

They left their cars next to the vehicular cockroaches and walked through the cool spaces of the garage. Its stark functionality didn't reassure Megan. She would be living here for some time. Her doubts eased when they entered a pleasant hall with ivory walls and a blue carpet. A robot was waiting for them, what MindSim called a Lab Partner. It stood about six feet tall, with a tubular body, treads for feet, a rounded head, and an assortment of detachable arms. The nameplate on its chest said "Trackman."

"Welcome to NEV-5," Trackman rumbled. "I hope you had a good trip."

"Just fine." Megan peered at the LP. Twenty of these ambulatory assistants staffed NEV-5. Using their rudimentary AI brains, they could manage the day-to-day operations. Automated systems here and at MindSim monitored the base in case anything unusual came up. In theory, NEV-5 could operate without a human presence, but MindSim preferred to have at least one person in residence.

NEV-5 was about the size of a football field, with three levels. The garage, power room, and maintenance areas were here on Level One. Living areas were one floor down, on Level Two, and the labs filled Level Three. Trackman escorted them to the elevators and Megan walked at his side, wondering how far his capabilities extended beyond managing the base.

"Do you enjoy working at NEV-5?" she asked.

"Enjoyment isn't one of my design parameters," he said.

That didn't sound promising. "Can you define 'enjoyment'?"

"Amusement. Entertainment. Pleasure. Recreation. Zest." Then he added, "Those are in alphabetical order."

Megan smiled. "Would you like to experience amusement? Pleasure? Zest?" In alphabetical order, no less.

"I have no need to do so."

Oh, well. If Trackman was the best that NEV-5 had to offer for company, aside from a barely functional android, she was going to be on the phone or Internet a lot. If the loneliness became too much, she could reprogram Trackman to converse better. It was a poor substitute for human fellowship, though, not to mention a waste of the LP's resources.

Up ahead, a droid rolled around the corner. About the size and shape of a cat, its "legs" were tubes that sucked in dust and dirt. As it came up to them, Megan crouched down and touched its back. It stopped with a jerk. She poked it again, and the droid scuttled away. When she reached out and tapped its leg, it made an agitated buzzing.

"I won't hurt you," Megan murmured. She stood and walked around the droid. It waved its tail, trying to determine if the bedevilment was going to continue. When she nudged it from behind, it moved forward and sidled past the other humans that had invaded its territory. Then it whirred away down the hall.

"That was a shy one," she said, smiling.

"Cleaning droids have no capacity for shyness," Trackman told her. "It has less efficient methods than an LP for mapping its environment. You were blocking its path."

Megan sighed. "Thank you, Trackman."

"You are welcome." If it detected her irony, it gave no indication.

They started off again, Alfred walking on the other

side of the LP. "Trackman," he asked, "did Marlow Hastin's family live here with him?"

"No," Trackman said. "His wife visited sometimes."

From behind them, Major Kenrock said, "I don't think his kids had the clearance."

Megan wondered if the isolation had bothered Hastin. She doubted she could have endured being separated from her family. She probably would have brought them to a nearby city and commuted. Being single made matters simpler, but she would miss having company. As far as work went, she would have preferred to have the Everest team here rather than in California. However, they had their lives there. With the Internet and VR conferences available, it wasn't necessary for them all to be in the same physical location.

Trackman showed them the living areas in Level Two. The apartments were pleasant, with blue carpets, consoles, armchairs, Lumiflex tables, pullout sofas, and airbeds covered by downy comforters. Megan decided to take a room with ivory wallpaper patterned by roses and birds. She said nothing, though, self-conscious about choosing her personal space in front of other people.

Then they went to meet the android.

The RS-4 had "slept" during most of the past few weeks while the Everest team reassessed the project. The two LPs that looked after the android had activated him as soon as the MindSim group arrived on the base. When Megan entered the single-room apartment where he lived, her anticipation leapt. This was it.

He was sitting at a table. Even knowing what to expect, she froze in the doorway. He could have been a boyish Arick Bjornsson. With his rugged Nordic features and blue eyes, he resembled a Viking more than a scientist. Bjornsson had consulted on the project several years ago, and he and several others had donated their DNA to the genetic bank.

The Everest engineers had grown parts of the android from Bjornsson's DNA, including his skin and some internal organs, but he was still a construct. A microfusion reactor powered him. Bellows inflated his lungs. Synthetic pumps drove lubricant through conduits within his body. His "organs" would age over centuries rather than decades, and they would remain disease-free. They were also more efficient than their human counterparts.

The Everest Project had many goals. The grant that funded Megan's job involved the development of a super-soldier and special operations agent. To be effective as a covert operative, the android would have to pass as human. Her team had a lot of work to do; right now the android's "blood" was a silvery lubricant, an X ray would show many of his differences, and various other anomalies could reveal the truth.

They didn't want him *too* human, though. If they succeeded, he would have the power and memory of a computer, the creativity and self-awareness of a person, the training of a commando, continual perfect health, and the survival ability of a machine. Weapons could be incorporated into his body. He would be smarter, faster, stronger, and harder to kill than any human soldier.

In the long view MindSim had more dramatic hopes. If humans could augment or replace their bodies with android technology, they could achieve phenomenal abilities, and longer, healthier, more stable lives. The process had begun in the twentieth century: replacement joints, limbs, bones, and heart valves; synthetic arteries and veins; artificially grown organs. Combining their minds with computers might make them superintelligent. It was Megan's dream that someday a new, evolved humanity would see beyond the urge to war, violence, and the other ills that plagued their species. An idealistic dream, perhaps, but still hers. Such results were far in the future, if they were possible, but the Everest Project offered a preliminary step.

The android already *looked* human. He had Arick's yellow curls and regular features, but he wasn't an exact copy of Bjornsson. The Everest team had fine-tuned his appearance. Tall but not too tall, with boy-next-door good looks, he came across as pleasant and nonthreatening. Right now, he also looked blank—like a machine. RS-4. They called him Aris.

As Trackman brought Megan inside, the android watched them. Major Kenrock and his lieutenant stayed by the door with Alfred. Diane and Miska settled in armchairs, close enough to answer any questions Megan might have. An LP stood behind Aris like a guard, protecting its brother from this strange infestation of humans.

Megan sat at the table. "Hello, Aris."

"Hello." His voice had no life. He sounded even less human than Trackman.

"My name is Megan O'Flannery. I'm the new chief scientist."

"Echo told me."

"Who is Echo?"

He indicated the LP behind him. "That is Echo."

That. Not he or she. Humans tended to refer to robots as male or female, based on the robot's voice. She knew she shouldn't be disappointed at his lack of affect, but she couldn't help but hope for more.

"Are you comfortable?" she asked.

"I am operational."

"Operational" hardly sounded promising, but it was

better than no response at all. "Aris, do you feel anything about this? By 'feel' I mean, do you have any reaction to Dr. Hastin's departure and my arrival?"

"No."

His lack of affect didn't surprise her. Hastin's notes indicated he hadn't had much success in making Aris simulate emotions. Nor was he the only one who had run into problems. Hastin was the third chief scientist MindSim had lost on the Everest Project. They had fired the first two.

"You can simulate emotions, though, can't you?" she asked.

"Yes." His eyes were beautiful replicas of human eyes—with no sign of animation.

"Why aren't you simulating any now?" she asked.

"I am."

Could have fooled me. "Can you smile?"

His mouth curved into a cold, perfect smile. It looked about as human as a car shifting gears.

"Get angry at me," Megan suggested.

"I have no context here for anger," he said.

At least he knew he needed a context. "What emotion do you think would be appropriate for this context?"

He spoke in a monotone. "Friendly curiosity."

"Is that what you're doing?"

"Yes. I am pleased to meet you." He might as well have been saying, "The square root of four is two."

It unsettled her to talk to someone who appeared so human yet sounded so mechanical. "Do you have any questions you would like to ask me?"

"No."

Megan exhaled. Well, she had known she had work ahead of her. "Would you like to take a walk around NEV-5? You can show me places you remember, tell me what you know about them."

He stared at her.

After a moment, she said, "Aris?"

No response.

Alfred swore under his breath. When Megan glanced up, they were all coming over to the table.

"What is it?" Megan asked.

"He hangs that way if he can't handle a question," Alfred said.

Megan frowned. "He can't handle something as simple as 'let's take a walk?' "

"Pretty much not," Miska said.

Alfred laid his hand on the android's shoulder. "Aris? Can you reset?"

Aris remained frozen, staring past Megan at the wall.

"We can restart him," Alfred offered.

"No. Not now." Megan stood up. "I'll come back later, after I've had a chance to look at the rest of the facilities here." In other words, when she was by herself. Although she doubted it made any difference to Aris if people saw his difficulties, she felt compelled to give him privacy. If they wanted him to become sentient, it would help to interact with him as if he had already achieved that state.

She glanced at Echo and spoke gently. "Make him comfortable."

"I will ensure the RS-4 suffers no damage," Echo said.

That isn't what I meant. But she said nothing. What could she do, tell one machine not to treat another machine like a machine?

The room had nothing on its ivory walls. It had no furniture. No console. Megan stood with Aris, the two of them alone. Ever since yesterday, when she had come to NEV-5, either Echo or Trackman had always accompanied her and Aris. So she had barred all the LPs from this room.

She wanted nothing to distract the hypersensitive android.

She set a shoe box on the floor. "Can you see that box?"

He looked down. "Yes." The cameras in his eyes integrated so well into his design that she detected no difference between his and a human face—except for his utter lack of expression.

"All right." She gave him an encouraging smile. "Jump over it."

As Aris regarded the box, Megan unhooked a palmtop computer from a belt loop of her jeans. She had named her palmtop Tycho, in honor of a famous astronomer. Using its wireless capability, she logged into Aris's brain much as she would log into the NEV-5 intranet. Tycho became part of the android's mind, giving her a window into Aris's thoughts.

The android had a huge knowledge base of facts and rules about the world. Combined with his language mods, it let him converse. He "thought" with neural nets, including both software and hardware neurons, which received signals from other neurons or input devices. If the sum of the signals exceeded a neuron's threshold, it sent out its own signal, either to other neurons or to an output device. Aris learned by altering thresholds. When he did well on a test, it strengthened the links that gave those results. Bad results weakened the links.

Although he couldn't alter his hardware, he could rewrite his software. He used many methods to evolve his code, most of them variations on genetic algorithms. He copied sections of code and combined them into new code, often with changes that acted like mutations. It was survival of the fittest: code that worked well reproduced, and code that didn't died off.

A simulated neuron could operate faster than its human counterpart, but putting many together became resource intensive and slowed Aris down. Although the number of links in his brain was comparable to a human brain, but he couldn't match the speed of human thought—yet. As he became more sophisticated, Megan suspected his speed would outstrip unaugmented human thought.

Right now he just stared at the box. According to her palmtop, Aris was calculating the trajectory he needed to jump. After his nets learned the process, he would no longer need to solve equations, any more than a child had to work out trajectories when she jumped, but he hadn't yet reached that stage. Even with his untutored nets, though, Megan didn't see why it was taking so long. He should only need seconds to translate the math into commands for his body.

Using Tycho, she probed deeper into his code. It looked like his brain had switched to a mod that directed his expression of fear. She tried to unravel how it had happened, but the complexity of his always-evolving code made it impossible to follow.

"Aris? Can you jump?"

He continued to stare at the box.

"Tycho," she said, "what is the highest level of fear Aris can tolerate before he freezes?"

Tycho answered in a well-modulated contralto. "It varies. He has an array of values that determines what immobilizes him."

His face did show emotion now. Frustration. He looked like a toddler stymied by a puzzle, reminding Megan of her sister's two-year-old son. But she held back her smile. Although she doubted Aris could have hurt feelings, she took care in her responses anyway, not only because his brain might have developed more than she realized, but also because she found it hard to think of him as a machine.

She spoke into the comm on her palmtop. "Why is he frozen?"

"The main contributor is an element in his fear array." It showed her several lines of code. "If the element goes above six percent, it stops him from moving."

"*Six* percent? Are all the elements set that low?"

"The values range from two to forty-three percent. The average is sixteen."

"That's appalling." What could Hastin have been thinking? How did he expect the android to function with such stringent caps on his behavior?

"Aris? If you can hear me, try this: use your logic mods. Have them analyze the situation." His mind should be able to determine he had no reason to fear the jump.

At first she thought her suggestion had no effect. But as she studied Tycho's display, she realized Aris had shifted some processing power to a logic mod. Although he remained trapped in the fear mod, his logic response kicked in, trying to make him jump. His fear response persisted, conflicting with the logic. That branched him into an anger mod, which then sent him to a fight mod. The fight code kicked him into a *parachuting* mod, for heaven sake, probably due to some strangely convoluted interpretation of her request that he jump. So now his mods wanted him to throw himself out of a plane in the sky.

"I need an aircraft!" His voice exploded out. "How can I jump *without* one?"

Megan spoke gently. "Can you get out of the jumping mod?"

He didn't answer, he just kept staring at the box. Controlled by his anger mods, his body pumped fluids to his face and raised the temperature of his skin. Aris stood frozen in place, his face bright red, looking for all the world like a furious young boy. A curl of yellow hair was sticking up over his ear as if to protest his ignominious situation.

She tried another tack. "Do you know how to do a parachute landing fall? It's what jumpers practice on the ground before they go up in a plane."

He neither answered nor moved. His face turned redder.

Watching his quandary gave her the same emotional tug as seeing a toddler struggle to understand a baffling situation. Her voice softened the way it did when she spoke to her young nephew. "You don't have to jump. Aris? Can you hear? Don't jump."

Nothing changed. He stared at the box as if it were a monster that had broken the rules of childhood nightmares and come out from under his bed in broad daylight.

Megan disliked resetting him, in part because he would lose some of what they had just done. It also bothered her to wipe his brain that way, even if she was only removing a few commands. However, she had to free him from his frozen state.

"Tycho," she finally said. "Reset the RS."

"I can't," Tycho answered. "He's protected from resets."

It made sense; Aris could never learn independence if anyone could reset his mind. However, as his main programmer she needed access. "Check my retinal scan."

A light from the palmtop flashed on her face. "Retinal scan verified."

"Okay. Do the reset."

"Done."

Aris's face went blank. Then he straightened up. "Hello."

"Are you all right?" she asked.

"Yes."

"Do you remember what happened?"

"You asked me to jump over the box."

"And that frightened you?"

"No." Although almost a monotone, his voice had a trace of nuance today. "Your command caused my code to exceed certain tolerances, which stopped my movements and prompted me to mimic behaviors associated in humans with anger and fear."

She smiled. "I guess you could put it that way."

"Do you wish me to put it another way?"

"No." That intrigued her, that he asked her preference.

"Do you still want me to jump?"

"Not now. I need to reset your tolerances. That means I'll have to deactivate you so your mind isn't evolving while I'm trying to make changes." She spoke with care, unsure how he would respond to being "turned off."

He just looked at her. At first she thought he had frozen again. Then she realized he had no reason to answer. Unlike a human, who would have reacted in some way, he simply waited.

Megan knew it would cause him no discomfort to lie down here on the floor. He wouldn't be aware of anything after she turned him off. Even so, the thought of asking him to stretch out on the hard surface bothered her.

"We can use one of the apartments," she said.

He continued to look at her.

"And Aris."

"Yes?"

She touched his arm, instinctively seeking to make human contact with him. "If you understand a person, it's customary to indicate that in some way."

"How?"

"Nod. Smile. Make a comment. Your knowledge base must have rules for social interaction."

"I have many rules."

"Don't they indicate how you should respond?"

"Yes."

She waited. "But?"

A hint of animation came into his voice. "You are new."

"So you don't know what parameters apply to me?"

"Yes."

"You should apply all your rules with everyone."

"Very well. I will do so."

"Good." Surely it couldn't be this easy. There had to be a catch here somewhere.

They headed down a hallway in the residential area. As they walked, she regarded him with curiosity. "Aris, do you have any hobbies?"

"I don't engage in nonfunctional activities."

She smiled at his phrasing. "We'll have to change that."

"Why?"

"It's part of having a personality."

"What nonfunctional activity should I engage in to have a personality?"

Megan almost laughed. "Haven't you ever done anything besides interact with the Everest team?"

"I make maps." A tinge of excitement came into his voice. "I made one of NEV-5 for Dr. Hastin. I tried to make one of MindSim, but I didn't have enough data."

It seemed a good activity. "Do you like doing it?"

"I don't know how to 'like.' "

"Would you do more of it even if you didn't have to?"

"Yes."

She beamed at him. "Great. I'll see if I can find you some map-making programs." It was a start. Aris had a hobby.

They went into a bachelor apartment with blue decor

and holos of mountains on the walls. A comforter and
piles of white pillows lay on the airbed.

"This is nice," Megan said. "You can relax on the
bed."

Aris lay on his back with his legs straight out and his
arms at his side. Sitting next to him, she said, "Does it
bother you to be deactivated?"

"Why would it bother me?"

"It's like becoming unconscious."

"I have no context for a response to that state."

Megan supposed it made sense. She just wished he
would respond more.

"Dr. O'Flannery," he said. "Should I call you Megan?"

Startled, she smiled. "Yes. That would be good."

"Are we going to engage in sexual reproduction activities now?"

Megan gaped at him. Good grief. When she found her
voice, she said, "No, we are not going to engage in sexual
reproduction activities. Whatever gave you that idea?"

"You told me to apply my rules about social interactions. According to those, when a woman sits with a man
on a bed in an intimate setting, it implies they are about
to initiate behaviors involved with the mating of your
species."

A flush spread in her face. "Aris, make a wider survey
of your rules. If we were going to, uh, initiate such behaviors, we would have engaged in many other courtship
procedures. We haven't, nor would it be appropriate for
us to do so."

"Why not?"

"Well, for one thing, you're an android." She wondered how many other surprises his evolving code would
produce. Whatever else happened with this project, she
doubted it would be boring.

"None of my rules apply to human-android interactions," he said.

"Make one, then. Reproductive behaviors are inappropriate in this situation."

"I have incorporated the new rule." He paused. "I see it would be impossible for us to mate anyway, since I will be turned off."

Turned off? As opposed to "turned on"? She squinted at him, wondering if he could have made a joke that subtle. No, she didn't think so. It was just his deadpan delivery.

"You may deactivate me now," he said.

A chill ran down her back. What happened on the day when he said, "You may not deactivate me?"

We'll deal with it, she thought. Then she said, "BioSyn?"

"Attending." Although the resonant male voice came from the console here in the room, it originated from a powerful server in the big lab on Level Three. BioSyn linked to most of the NEV-5 computers and monitored all of Aris's activities.

"Deactivate Aris," Megan said.

"Done," BioSyn answered.

Aris's eyes closed. He had neither pulse nor breath now. When he was active, his chest moved and he had a heartbeat. He was designed to pass as human; if a doctor examined him, or if he went through sensors such as an airport security check, probably nothing would give him away. A more demanding examination would reveal the truth, but he could pass a reasonable range of probes.

She flipped open her palmtop. "Tycho, link to Aris."

Tycho went to work, analyzing the android's quiescent brain. The software was too complex for a human to untangle; it required another computer to interpret it. If she hadn't turned Aris off, his mind would have been a moving target, evolving even as Tycho looked.

Reading Tycho's results, Megan swore under her breath. No wonder Aris kept freezing up. His fear tolerances weren't the only ones set too low. Hastin had put so many controls on his behavior, Aris was incapable of independent thought. She studied how Aris had evolved the embryo code that Hastin had written for his mind. Yes, she saw Hastin's intent: to ensure they didn't create a monster. But his precautions were so stringent, they had crippled the android's development. Yet the code for Aris's ethics and morals was astonishingly weak. It made no sense; if Hastin had so feared that Aris might act against his makers, why design him with such a weak conscience?

Gradually it began to make sense. The answer to her question connected to Aris's intended purpose as a spy. He needed the ability to deceive, manipulate, steal, even kill, none of which he could do with too strong a conscience. Hastin had given him a solid foundation in human morals, then set it up so Aris could act against them. Aris knew it was wrong to kill, but he could commit murder if he felt it necessary to do his job.

Megan could see the problem. Aris didn't have the mental sophistication to deal with the contradictory ethical dilemmas or questions of moral judgment that humans often faced. His conscience was part of his hardware, so he couldn't alter it. However, his software influenced how strongly he adhered to his sense of right and wrong. She would have to alter millions, even billions, of caps on his behavior, particularly his responses to fear, anger, danger, ambiguity, and violence. That meant she also had to strengthen his aversion to acting on those responses; otherwise, she could create exactly the monster

Hastin feared. In other words, she was going to pulverize Aris's ability to carry out his intended purpose.

"Damn." No wonder Hastin had resigned.

She knew what she had to do. It remained to be seen whether or not MindSim would fire her.

IV

Rebirth

The message was waiting in Megan's room.

She walked in, fresh and showered after her workout in the gym. Although larger suites were available, she liked this one. It had a bed and armoire to the right, and a state-of-the-art console on the left. Crammed bookshelves lined the opposite wall and books lay strewn across her furniture. Most of the "books" were slick-disks for her electronic reader, but a few were genuine paper, crinkled with age. Her Escher holo hung on the wall, along with a Michael Whelan poster of the Moorcock hero Elric. A somnolent cleaning droid stood in one corner, disguising itself as a bronze lamp.

Right now a red holo glowed on the screen of her computer, indicating someone had tried to contact her. When she flicked her finger through it, the screen lightened into a skyscape of holoclouds. Nothing else happened, though. She had no idea how long she would have to wait before whoever had sent the message picked up her response.

Megan was about to turn away when the clouds vanished. A new image formed: Major Kenrock behind his desk. His dark hair was cut even closer to his head than the last time she had seen him and his uniform was the image of crisp perfection. The holo of a gold key glowed in a corner of the screen, indicating a secured transmission.

"Hey, Richard," Megan said. "How are you?"

"Very well, thank you." He gave her a measured nod that fit with his square-jawed face. "How are you settling in?"

"Okay." She rubbed the back of her neck. "I really need that robotics expert, though. Any luck with Sundaram?"

"It seems Arizonix Corporation is also interested in him."

Megan grimaced. "If he signs anything with them, MindSim can kiss him good-bye."

Kenrock gave her a wry smile. "I believe the good-bye would be sufficient. But yes, if he consults for Arizonix, we could face some thorny legal issues if we try to hire him."

"Has he given any hints which way he's leaning?"

"My guess? I think he'll go with Arizonix."

"Ah, well." She tried to hide her disappointment. "We'll look into the other candidates." It was a blow; when it came to the adaptation of AI to robotics, no one could surpass Chandrarajan Sundaram.

"How is the RS-4 unit?" Kenrock asked.

"His name is Aris."

Kenrock's smile was rueful. "Sorry. I should remember that. Aris."

His amiable response didn't surprise her. People criticized Richard Kenrock for being stiff, but under his formal exterior she found him both engaging and natural.

Megan gave him a report, describing her work for the past week. Her primary focus was the development of algorithms, software architecture, and experimental design. In addition, she supervised a pack of young, hotshot programmers at MindSim who had written most of the initial code and continued to work on the project. She did a lot of writing herself, not only because she had more knowledge and experience, but also because she loved the challenge.

After she and Kenrock signed off, she sat thinking. Did Chandrarajan Sundaram even remember their conversation at Goddard? She shouldn't have let herself build up hope that he would accept the job.

Ah, well. She would just have to do her best until they found another consultant. With that in mind, Megan left her room in Corridor B and went to Aris's room on Corridor C. She knocked, an old-fashioned courtesy given that the console inside would identify her no matter what she did.

The door slid open. Inside, Aris was sitting at his workstation. A flock of holos skittered across the screen, a colorful profusion of cubes, disks, pyramids, and spheres.

"May I come in?"

He swiveled his chair around. After he had stared at her a while, she said, "Are you all right?"

"No."

"What's wrong?"

"I can't answer your question." His expression reminded Megan of her four-year-old niece when the girl was confused. It made her want to hug Aris. She held back, of course. Even if he understood the gesture, which she doubted, he probably wouldn't appreciate being treated like a child.

"Which question caused the problem?" she asked.

With her exact intonation, he said, "Are you all right?"

She blinked at his ability to mimic her voice. "Why can't you answer?"

In his normal baritone he said, "I don't see how 'all

right' applies to me. The evolution of software is a neutral process, whereas 'all right' suggests emotional content. If I am not all right, am I somewhat wrong?"

His literal interpretation didn't surprise her. Not only was it a trait of computers, it was also one of young children. "The reason I wondered if you were all right was because you just stared at me when I asked if I could come into your room."

"I am not a person."

"I'm not sure I follow."

"I am an android."

"Well, yes." She tried to interpret his response. "Does that affect whether or not I can come in?"

"It depends."

"On what?"

"My predecessors. The other RS units. They ceased." He regarded her with his large blue eyes. "If I am not 'all right' will you take me apart too?"

Good Lord. He thought if he gave a "wrong" answer, they would destroy him? No wonder he didn't want to respond. It also meant he was developing a sense of self-preservation. Protective impulses surged over her. Maybe it was his youthful face that made him look vulnerable, or his wary gaze, as if he had no defense against the inconstant humans around him.

"I would never hurt you," she said.

"Software can't be hurt."

Then why do you look so scared? Was she reading emotions into him that weren't there? In any case, he still hadn't said she could come in. "Did Marlow Hastin ever ask permission to enter your room?"

"No."

"Did he request your input on anything?"

"Rarely."

She didn't see how anyone could work with an AI and

not offer it choices. How would Aris develop? "Did you ever ask for choices?"

He shifted in his seat and a lock of hair fell into his eyes. "No."

"Did you want to ask?"

He pushed back the curl. "I have no wants. I carry out program instructions."

Softly Megan asked, "Then why did you move your hair?"

His arm jerked. "It was in my face."

"So?"

This time his arm snapped out and smacked the console. He yanked it back against his side. "It's inefficient to have hair covering my eyes."

"Why is your arm moving?" She could have asked Tycho, but she wanted to hear his own evaluation.

"My brain is instructing it to alter position."

His deadpan response almost made her laugh. "But is it efficient, do you think?"

A hint of confusion showed on his face. "My analysis of your tone suggests you are teasing me."

She smiled. "A little, I suppose."

"Isn't teasing an expression of affection?"

"Well, yes, sometimes."

His voice softened. "Do you have affection for me?"

How did she answer? If she said yes, it implied she was losing her professional objectivity. If she said no, it could damage his developing personality. Besides, in this situation, professional objectivity might be the wrong response.

"I enjoy your company," she finally said.

"Can you feel friendship for a machine?"

"I'm not sure." She sighed, giving him a rueful look. "What do you say, Aris? Do we humans make sense?"

His lips quirked upward. "I have too little experience with humans to know."

His hint of a smile heartened Megan. "Would you like to meet more people?"

"How?" Now his expression shifted toward wariness. None of his emotions were full-fledged, but he had made progress. "I can't leave NEV-5 and you are the only person here. Do you wish me to experience more with you?"

"You might try letting me come into your room."

"All right. Come in."

"Thank you." Megan took a chair from the table and sat next to him. With the two of them side by side, facing his computer, their arms almost touched. The faint smell of soap came from the orange coverall he wore.

She could see the display on the computer better now. Shapes of different colors and sizes skittered around the screen. "What are you working on?"

"It is a game." The barest shading of excitement came into his voice. "The shapes represent rules for mathematical proofs. When the shapes catch each other, it means they've made an equation allowed by the rules."

The evolving display of color and motion intrigued her. "Do you work out the proofs ahead of time?"

"No. I don't usually know, before they come up with a proof, that they will do it."

"It's clever." She wondered what had motivated his design. "Did Hastin ask you to write games?"

"He told me to solve proofs."

Her pulse jumped. "Then designing a game to work them out was your idea?"

"Yes."

So he *had* come up with his own ideas. It indicated the fledgling expression of what might become self-determination, perhaps also creativity. "That's wonderful."

His voice warmed. "Thank you."

Perhaps it was time to try a more demanding environment. "Would you like to take a walk?"

This time his face blanked. Recognizing the signs of a freeze, she spoke fast, hoping to head it off. "Aris, stand up!"

He rose to his feet. "Where will we walk?"

Encouraged, she stood up next to him. "That's it, isn't it? My giving you a choice is what makes you freeze."

"I don't know how to choose."

"We'll have to fix that."

"Why?"

That gave her pause, not because it was an odd question for a machine, but because she took the process of making choices for granted. "It's part of having free will. Of being human."

"That assumes 'being human' is a good thing."

"Do you think otherwise?"

"I don't know. Are you more human than Hastin?"

Again he caught her off guard. "How could I be more human than another human?"

"The way you program my code."

Then she understood. She softened her voice, taking the same tone she had used with one of her graduate students when he had trouble with his doctoral work. "Hastin made the best choices he could, Aris. What we're doing here, it's all new. We don't know what will work. I'm only building on previous efforts of the Everest team. We need to do more."

"You act more alive than they do."

"More alive?" The phrases he chose fascinated her. "What do you mean?"

"Your face has more expressions. Your voice has more tones." Softly he added, "You keep me company."

Good Lord. Was he *lonely*? The implications staggered Megan. If he could feel the desire for human company, he had come farther in his development than she realized.

"Will you keep me company on a walk?" she asked.

He watched her the way a child might watch a parent who had given him more freedom than he felt ready to accept. His head jerked, then his arm, then a muscle in his jaw.

Then he moved.

He took a jerky step toward the door. She could almost feel his software analyzing all the choices possible for each of his motions. His mind had to coordinate every move of every synthetic muscle, every hydraulic, and every composite bone in his body. Nor were simple mechanics enough, not in this learning stage. It also had to choose gestures and facial expressions to fit his developing personality. He went through a huge number of calculations for simple motions humans took for granted—and then he had to do it again, over and over, many times per second.

He took several more lurching steps. Watching him struggle, she longed to say "Never mind, we can stay here and do something safe, like playing computer games or working on maps." But she kept silent, knowing he would never grow unless he took risks. If she tried to make it easier, she would only hold him back.

They left the room and ventured down the corridor. Megan stayed at his side while he lurched on each step. He moved with far less ease than the robot she had walked with at MindSim. That one had been designed specifically to walk well, whereas Aris had to do everything well.

She didn't speak; he had enough to process now without the distraction of conversation. He learned fast, though, as his neural nets readjusted according to his success in taking steps. After a while his gait began to even out.

When they stopped at the elevator, he stared at the doors with a blank face. He had no key card to operate the lift. He had never needed one; Hastin had turned him off and stored him in an empty apartment or closet when they weren't working, to ensure Aris didn't develop without control. The idea made Megan grit her teeth. If Aris had been human, that treatment would have been cruel. But he *wasn't* human. He himself claimed he had no response to deactivation.

It won't stay that way, she thought.

"Aris."

He turned to her. "Yes?"

"I'm going to give you a key card for the elevator."

"Does that mean you will turn me off when I'm alone?"

"Not unless you would like me to."

She expected him to say he had no likes. Instead he said, "If you give me a key and leave me on, I will be free to wander this section of the base."

"That's the idea."

His face showed hints of a new emotion, she wasn't sure what. Surprise? Anticipation? Curiosity? Apprehension? Perhaps it was a mixture of them all.

"Yes," he said, "I would like a key."

Megan wanted to give him a delighted thump on the back, to congratulate him on this breakthrough in his developing autonomy. She wasn't sure he would understand, though. So instead she said, "Good! I'll be right back." She turned and headed back to his room to get the card she had left on his console.

"Megan!" Panic touched his voice.

She spun around. "What's wrong?"

He was watching her like a toddler deserted by his mother. The strain on his face looked real. This was no "hint" of emotion; he was simulating full-fledged fear. "Where are you going?"

"Just to your room. I left my key card there." Megan came back to him, as concerned as if he were a human child. "I wasn't going to desert you."

"What should I do?" Now he was simulating either unease or uncertainty.

"You can wait here."

"What if you don't come back?"

"I will. I promise."

"But what if you *don't*?"

Did he fear solitude? Her voice softened. "I'll always come back, Aris."

"You are different from the others." He touched her shoulder as if to verify it was real. "You are changing me, more than through your software rewrites. Your presence makes me more efficient and helps my code evolve."

Megan gave a slight laugh. "I think that's a compliment."

"Humans do this often. Compliment and insult one another. Why?"

She considered how to answer. "It gives us ways to let people know how they affect us. And for us to affect them."

"If I compliment you, does that indicate I find your input conducive to optimizing my functions?"

"Well, yes, you could put it that way," she said, tickled by his phrasing.

"I see." Then he said, "I like having you here more than the other scientists on the Everest Project. I am glad they went away and you stayed."

She hoped he would someday be comfortable with the others. His words touched her, though. "I'm flattered, Aris. But most of them are still on the project."

"I know. However, I am glad you are the one here."

"Thank you."

"You are welcome." He paused. "I would like to go back to the room with you, rather than waiting here."

Yes! Not only had he just made a choice, he had done it with no prodding. She grinned at him. "Certainly."

Aris had even more trouble walking back. Megan suspected it was because he was using some of his processing power to analyze his interactions with her. At his room, he said, "I would like to stay here now." He gave her a tentative smile, as if trying an experiment. "We can take another walk tomorrow, yes?"

"Yes." Her heart melted. She knew the boyish pleasure she saw on his face was simulated, but she still found it charming.

He was becoming human to her.

The VR suit covered Megan in a gold body stocking, wrapping her up like a box of Godiva chocolates. She lay on her bed and pulled the hood and goggles into place. Although the technology existed for creating VR using direct links to the brain, so far legal and medical problems had kept it from commercial viability. It wouldn't be long before they solved those problems, though; it was another race between MindSim and Arizonix.

She found herself in blackness. "Cleo," she said, "turn on the VR." She had named her console after Cleopatra because the sleek machine combined both beauty and power.

"Done," Cleo said.

The world lightened. Megan found herself in a conference room, a gleaming chamber with golden walls, a posh white rug, white upholstered chairs, and an oval table. She was sitting on the long side of the table, wearing a tailored blue business suit with a miniskirt that showed off her long legs. The outfit bore no resemblance to the jeans and sweaters she wore in normal life.

In the last three weeks, since coming to NEV-5, she had met with the Everest team in VR almost every day. They either gathered here or else in a simulated AI lab. Every now and then Diane designed a more fanciful environment, like the time she set them up on a mountain in Tibet. Sometimes MindSim suits or military brass sat in on the meetings.

Today everyone was already there: Tony the VP at one head of the table, Diane at the other, and Miska on Megan's right. Claire Oliana and Alfred sat across that table, along with—

Chandrarajan Sundaram.

Megan had almost fallen over when Tony told her Sundaram was interested again. Apparently he had accepted the Arizonix job, then changed his mind. The situation was murky enough that MindSim called in their legal aces. Could Arizonix sue them if they hired Raj? He had never actually consulted for Arizonix and he had only signed one preliminary contract. After some wrangling, they concluded that Arizonix had no real grounds to bring legal action against MindSim.

On the surface, Raj's explanation for changing his mind made sense: Arizonix had wanted him to sign agreements that placed too many limits on his freedom to consult elsewhere. She wondered, though, if there was more to it. He should have known what they expected well before that point in the hiring process. At NASA, he had implied that if she accepted the Everest position, he might consult for MindSim. He had given the impression he thought they could make a good team. Megan agreed.

Many possible reasons existed for his having chosen Arizonix instead: more money, research he preferred, other scientists he wanted to work with more, the location, or something else. Although she would have liked to think her scientific reputation inspired him to leave Arizonix, she considered it unlikely, at least as a primary reason. It would have been unprofessional for him to make such a choice at that point, besides which, she had taken the Everest job before he accepted the Arizonix position.

Whatever had happened, she hoped MindSim wouldn't have the same problem. Raj had gone through a preliminary security check, but he had yet to sign anything. Yes, he was the best, which was why they were going to so much trouble, but if he wasn't going to accept the job, she wished he would let them know. This had gone on for weeks now, while she had no robotics expert.

Tony introduced Raj and asked everyone to give synopses of their work. As her people spoke, Megan tried to gauge Raj's interest. He sat sprawled in his chair, listening. His avatar intrigued her. In VR simulations, people often showed an enhanced image of themselves—healthier, younger, stronger, more beautiful. Raj, however, appeared older. Although his résumé gave his age as forty-two, in person he looked about thirty-five. Here he had added ten years to his age. She remembered his hair as black, but now it had ample gray. In person, his face had been expressive; here he was unreadable. His eyes were so black she couldn't distinguish the pupil from the iris. He had also dressed in black: shirt, trousers, shoes. His clothes had black buttons. He might even have darkened the air around his image.

"Anyway," Alfred continued, "Aris uses several methods to map his surroundings—"

"How long have you worked at MindSim?" Raj interrupted.

Alfred stopped. An awkward silence settled around the table. Then Alfred said, "Seven years."

"Seven." Raj was leaning his elbow on the arm of his chair, surveying Alfred as if he were a particularly intriguing robot. "So you've been on the project a lot longer than your new boss." His Southern accent was even more pronounced here than in person.

"Megan is the best," Alfred said.

Raj glanced at Megan as if he had just noticed her. "Dr. O'Flannery."

"Do you have a question about my leading the project?" She felt curious rather than defensive. She had no doubt that Raj knew she did her job well. He wouldn't be here otherwise. This was about something else.

"I think you're not a duck," Raj told her.

"For crying out loud," Alfred said.

Diane frowned. "Dr. Sundaram, you couldn't ask for a better boss than Megan."

Raj continued to watch Megan. Up until now he had given no indication he remembered her. She was certain, though, that he was referring to the birds at the lake. She recalled his words: *They aren't greedy. They don't cheat. They only take what they need.* Did he think she would try to use him if he accepted this job? It seemed an odd concern, but with Raj she couldn't be sure.

"How about a goose?" she asked.

Tony glanced at her as if she had lost her mind.

"Not a goose," Raj decided. "A swan."

She smiled. "Why a swan?"

"They float along, serene and graceful, with those long, elegant necks." He spoke as if he and Megan were the only people in the room. "But have you ever had an angry swan come at you out of the water? They're big, tough, and mean as sin."

She could imagine Aris trying to decipher this exchange.

Compliment or insult? "When I need to, I can be mean as sin too."

Tony looked as if he were about to groan. He had to be projecting that on purpose; his avatar could appear any way he wanted. He was sending her a message: *Cut it out.* Then he put on a pleasant expression and spoke to Raj. "Dr. Sundaram, please be assured that Dr. O'Flannery's credentials are impeccable."

Doctor this, doctor that. Couldn't they see this had nothing to do with her credentials? Raj wouldn't have considered MindSim if he had those concerns. In his own fascinating way he was asking something else. But what?

He gave her an appraising stare. "So, Dr. O'Flannery, what do you do with these indefectible credentials of yours?"

Indefectible, indeed. Megan had never known anyone who could actually use that word in conversation. He was daring her to try snowing him with her knowledge. So instead she said, simply, "I make androids."

"Perhaps Dr. Sundaram would like to hear more about your work," Claire said.

Megan knew they wanted her to dazzle Raj with techno-talk, but she doubted he was interested in a sales pitch. She thought she understood his unstated question now. Too many people wanted to use him. He was trying to decide if she was another one. His wariness puzzled her. MindSim was offering him a six-figure fee, possibly even millions if the project went on long enough. That hardly translated into using him.

For whatever reason, he distrusted them. *You want the Everest Project,* she thought. *MindSim is offering you a puzzle like none you've ever played with before.* Thinking about the birds, she said, "The problem with their flying south is that they take your food and go. But consider this: a mountain stays. You can climb it, enjoy its beauty, build a house, ski down its slopes. What it gives to you depends on what you bring to it."

"What the hell?" Alfred said. Tony and Claire frowned at him, but neither looked happy with Megan either. Diane just shook her head. Miska scratched his chin as if he were unsure he had heard right.

Raj said, "So." Then he vanished.

"Hey!" Diane sat forward. "He can't do that."

Alfred scowled. "He can do whatever he wants, including be rude as hell."

Claire frowned at Megan. "What was that about? You had a prime opportunity to build on his interest. You threw it away."

"That might be a bit extreme," Tony said. "We may be able to salvage this."

Megan indicated the table in front of Tony, where a mail icon had appeared. "Before you bemoan today's meeting, maybe you should answer your e-mail."

He waved his finger through the icon. "Tony Oreza here."

His secretary's voice floated into the air. "Mr. Oreza, we just received word from Dr. Sundaram. He's accepted the Everest job."

"You're kidding," Tony said.

"Not at all, sir."

Megan smiled. "Surprise."

V

Invasion

egan, look!" Aris spun on his heel, then lost his balance and fell against the wall of the corridor outside his room. Laughing, he righted himself, his hair falling in his eyes.

Her breath caught. He had *laughed*. She stood by the open door of his room. "That was wonderful."

"It would have an even greater degree of wonderful," he said, "if I could turn without losing my balance."

His unexpected word choices never ceased to delight her. "I didn't know wonderful had degrees."

"You can assign a number to anything." He was standing in his neutral position now, his feet slightly spread, his weight on both, his arms at his sides. Unlike his usual ramrod posture, though, today he leaned a bit to the side. "How many degrees of Megan are there?" His voice had a whimsical quality. "I find new ones every day."

She went over to him. "Degrees of Megan?"

He looked into her face as if she were a new phenomenon he had discovered. "When you first came here, I knew your facts: education, jobs, age. Now I've learned new things. You like mint pie. Kids called you Firestalk in school. You played the oboe. You prefer aerobics to jogging. I never learned such facts about other humans. It makes you a holo."

A holo. Three-dimensional. In opening up to Aris, had she helped round out his view of humans in general? Perhaps the best way to teach him humanity was to act human with him. It became easier and easier as his personality developed.

The solitude here intensified her response to him. She had only Aris for company. The LPs did their jobs well, but they made lousy companions. She had grown up in a large family, with her parents, two sisters, a brother, her aunt and uncle, and three cousins all under one roof. In graduate school she had shared a house with six other students, and at MIT she had lived in a condo complex with a close-knit community. She missed her family and friends.

"Are you processing?" Aris asked.

She mentally shook herself. "Gathering wool."

"I see no sheep."

She laughed softly. "It's an idiom. It means I was preoccupied."

"Did my statement cause insult?"

"No. Not at all." It encouraged her to see him consider how his comments affected others. "I was thinking about my family. I feel isolated here."

"How does a person 'feel' isolation?"

Good question. She searched for a way to explain a concept she had never analyzed because she *knew* on an unconscious level how it felt. "No one else is nearby. No one will join me for lunch, meet me for a chat, that sort of thing."

He tilted his head. "I am here. I will keep you company."

His offer touched her. "Thank you."

"You don't need anyone else."

Megan almost touched his cheek. Then she stopped herself, feeling the gesture was too intimate, though she wasn't sure why. "Aris, the time will come when you go out into the world. It won't always be just the two of us."

His expression suggested pensive thought. "I've never left NEV-5. When Hastin and I conversed, it was always in the context of a test. I interact with computers here, but not outside NEV-5. I deduce that I am lonely."

Megan didn't know whether to feel encouraged by his developing emotions or dismayed by his conclusion. "Does it bother you?"

"I would prefer that my life not fulfill the conditions that cause loneliness in humans."

It was progress, of a kind; not long ago he would have frozen at such a question. It was a sad sort of advance, though.

"You feel lonely," he said. "I am here. I am meant to be human. This should alleviate your loneliness."

"It does."

His face blanked as he did a calculation. Then he said, "My analysis of your tone indicates surprise."

Megan realized he was right. It *did* surprise her. "I've never interacted with an android before. I'm never sure what to expect."

"Are you disappointed?"

"Aris, no. I think you're remarkable."

He took her hand. "I think the same of you."

Although Megan managed a smile, she disengaged her hand from his. They needed more people here. As gratifying as it was to see Aris develop emotional links, or at least simulate them, his focus on her was beginning to make her uneasy.

The dusty silver car settled down with a swirl of grit that it had brought from the desert above. Megan waited a few yards away, watching the vehicle roll into the NEV-5 garage. The elevator began its return to the desert above them.

After the car stopped, Major Kenrock stepped out of the driver's side. Tall and lean, with classic features and brown hair, he cut a crisp figure in his blue uniform. Another officer was stepping out of the passenger's side, a thin man with auburn hair. The woman getting out of the back on that side also wore a uniform, a blue jacket and skirt.

Then the back door on this side swung open. A man grabbed the top of its frame and hauled himself out. Unruly dark curls spilled over his collar, shining in the harsh light. His motorcycle jacket made his shoulders look even broader and his jeans clung to his long legs. Silver glinted on his black leather belt. His large eyes were set in the face of an Indian-Gaelic prince with the full-lipped pout of a surly rock star. So Raj Sundaram stood by the car, his hands in the pockets of his jacket.

Oh, Lord. Megan swallowed, trying to regain her poise. She came forward to Major Kenrock and extended her hand. "Hello, Richard. It's good to see you."

Shaking her hand, Kenrock cracked a smile. He introduced his two officers, Lieutenants Mack Thomas and Caitlin Shay. The whole time, Megan was acutely aware of Raj watching them. When Kenrock finally came to Raj, she felt stretched as tight as a string.

"You know Dr. Sundaram, I believe." A chill had entered Kenrock's voice. Apparently Raj hadn't endeared himself to this group any more than he had charmed MindSim. Although on an intellectual level, Megan understood why he aggravated people, it puzzled her at a gut level. Couldn't they see the extraordinary mind behind his unusual personality?

She had no idea what Aris would make of him.

———

They found Aris in his room, seated at his table, his hands clenched in his lap, with Echo the LP standing behind him. Aris had the look of an angry youth who had been locked up against his will while trespassers invaded his home.

Richard Kenrock and Raj stayed back while Mack and Caitlin sat at the table with Aris. The android watched them warily, his shoulders hunched. As much as Megan wanted to go to him, she also held back. She had to keep out of their discussion, lest she influence the results. Besides, she couldn't always jump in to protect him.

Aris shifted his hostile gaze to Megan, then to the straight-backed Kenrock. He stared at Raj for a full five seconds. Then his head jerked. Scowling, he turned back to the lieutenants.

"So, Aris." Caitlin smiled. "It's good to meet you in person."

"In robot," he said, deadpan.

Mack squinted, looking uncertain. Even Megan wasn't sure if the "joke" was an attempt at humor or just Aris being literal.

Mack gave a friendly chuckle. "How do you feel?"

"I don't," Aris said.

"You talk about your feelings with Megan," Caitlin said. She had a cooler style than Mack.

"Simulated feelings," Aris answered.

"Would you like to talk about them?" Mack asked, with an encouraging expression.

"No," Aris said.

When it became clear Aris didn't intend to say more, Caitlin asked, "Do you mind our questions?"

"You always ask questions," Aris said. "Here, VR, it's all the same."

That's new, Megan thought. Giving evasive answers involved sophisticated mental concepts. That Aris tried it revealed a great deal about his progress. She wasn't exactly sure "progress" was the right word, though. Aris had perfected his "sullen" simulation a bit too well.

"Does talking to us bother you?" Mack asked.

Aris shrugged.

"What would *you* like to talk about?" Caitlin asked.

Aris just looked at them. His demeanor was his most complex yet. He acted bored, with traces of hostility, yet he also seemed to be hiding fear behind indifference. Although he had thousands of facial nuances for each emotion, Megan wasn't sure how his neural nets had learned to show several emotions while appearing to hide others, yet having them all be obvious. It impressed her.

Caitlin and Mack exchanged glances. Then Mack tried again. "Why don't you tell us what you've learned lately?"

"Not much," Aris said.

"How are your maps?" Caitlin asked.

Aris glowered at her.

Trying another approach, Mack frowned like a parent faced with a recalcitrant teen. "Answer us, Aris."

"Why should I?" Aris slouched in his chair and crossed his arms.

Caitlin glanced at Megan. "This behavior wasn't in your reports."

Aris shot Megan a sour look, as if she had betrayed him by writing reports, even though they both knew she documented everything. Then he focused on the two lieutenants as if they were nefarious interrogators come to torment him. With his arms still crossed, he said, quite distinctly, "Fuck you."

Megan almost groaned. Had Aris been a real teenager, she would have grounded him. But his behavior irked her because he made it so *human*. Which was what they wanted.

Wasn't it?

The visitors all gathered in Megan's office, a room with two consoles, dismantled droids everywhere, a large desk piled high with gadgets, and two chairs crammed into what little space remained. No one was sitting. She leaned against her desk, facing Caitlin and Mack. Kenrock was standing by one console, and Raj was leaning against the door, his hands in the pockets of his jacket.

"I don't like it," Mack continued. "If Aris turns hostile, he could be dangerous. Don't get me wrong, Dr. O'Flannery. I realize he needs to pass through stages as his mind matures. And this is certainly the most affect he's shown. But we aren't talking about an argumentative kid here. We can't risk losing control of him."

"The RS-4 contains secured information," Caitlin said. "Not only about its own existence and construction, but also in its knowledge of our other work here."

Megan understood their concern. If Aris ever went rogue, he would take a great deal of secured knowledge with him, in both his mind and body. He was also linked to many NEV-5 computers. In fact, he himself was an important node in the NEV-5 intranet. He didn't have access to a few of the systems, but he would probably figure out they were running war games soon, if he hadn't already. It was, after all, only a matter of time before she gave him access, since they intended him to design and run such simulations himself.

MindSim was in a race in both the commercial and defense sectors. Other companies were working on androids, including Shawbots, Tech-Horizons, Jazari International, and Arizonix. Dramatic economic and military advantage would go to whatever country first developed viable androids and the advances in human augmentation that went with them. Mercenary groups were also trying to create high-tech warriors. Even partially functional, Aris would be invaluable to people the world over.

Megan even understood why Hastin had made such harsh choices with Aris. She knew now he had resigned because he saw no way he could complete the project in good conscience. Had he continued his program, he could have created a dysfunctional, even psychotic, android. Yet he feared to ease the constraints, lest Aris turn against them.

Megan had more confidence in Aris. If MindSim pressured her to restore his earlier state, she would refuse. Not only did she consider that the best choice, it also made sense in terms of self-preservation. Someday robots would bypass humans. If they suffered along the way, they would look far less kindly on their creators.

Kenrock spoke to Megan. "Can you readjust Aris's behavior, make him less hostile?"

"I don't think it's wise." She searched for the right words. "Without the freedom to develop, he will never achieve sentience. We'll have a fancy computer in a phenomenally expensive body. If we want a self-aware being, we have to drop the reins. I'm not saying we must throw away control; we can fortify his conscience. He might not make as good a weapon then, but it's better than crippling his mind or turning him against us." She paused, collecting her thoughts. "In our capacity to wage war, we deal with concepts of honor, loyalty, and the greater good, contrasted with spiritual conflicts, the meaning of tyranny, and political considerations. Aris has to deal with ambiguities we struggle with ourselves. He's not ready. He never will be if we smother his development."

"It isn't an either-or situation," Mack said. "Designing

him to be more cooperative doesn't mean forcing his submission."

"Doesn't it?" Megan glanced at Kenrock. "Do we 'design' our children to cooperate? Or do we try to teach them our values so they will incorporate them when they've grown?"

He smiled slightly. "There are times I'd love to design some cooperation into my kids."

Megan suspected her own parents had felt that way about her sometimes. "But would you want someone to brainwash them?"

"Of course not."

"Even if it meant they would behave better?"

Kenrock regarded her steadily. "I would fight with my life to preserve their right to freedom of thought. But we aren't talking about human children. Aris is a robot. A dangerous, fully formed machine capable of great harm."

"In some ways. In others he *is* a child."

"A child can't compromise national security," Caitlin said.

"No?" Megan scowled and crossed her arms. "What about those kids that cracked the Las Cruces weapons lab?"

"You mean the ones who went into the public outreach pages?" Mack asked. "The hackers who replaced the pictures of the lab scientists with action adventure cartoons?"

"Yeah," Megan grumbled. "Those."

The corners of Kenrock's mouth quirked up. "Don't you consult for Livermore?"

Megan gave him a dour look. "Yes. And yes, my image got doctored." She couldn't help but laugh. "They made me into a Barbie commando doll with camouflage fatigues, a designer machine gun, and pink high heels."

Kenrock grinned. "I've never seen that one in stores."
His smile faded. "And you're right, that prank revealed
holes in security. It's bad enough we have to worry about
humans committing such crimes. We don't need androids
in the mix."

"Yes, we have to careful," Megan said. "But we don't
reprogram every teenager that rebels either."

Mack snorted. "Maybe we ought to."

Kenrock pushed his hand across his close-cropped hair.
"She has a point. My kids may drive me crazy, with all
three in their teens, but their rebellions are part of their
trying to become adults, separate from their mother and
me." Dryly he added, "Though if you ask me at a less
tranquil moment, I might be less sympathetic."

"Aris needs to separate from us," Megan said.

"You know," Caitlin said, "if he doesn't, his autism
could become more severe."

"Autism?" Kenrock asked.

Mack answered. "Some of his responses resemble
autistic behavior in human children."

Their conclusions didn't surprise Megan. Some scientists believed autistic children suffered from a develop-
mental disorder that interfered with their ability to model,
understand, and predict the intentions or desires of other
people. Developing AIs often shared that difficulty. Many
of them used databases of rules in their models for human
behavior. If they had too few rules or the wrong set, it
limited their ability to respond.

"I first saw it in his aloof behavior and lack of affect,"
Megan said. "Also in his need for everything to be the
same, so he didn't have to make choices. He's coming out
of that now, but if we force a personality on him instead
of letting him develop naturally, it might make him dysfunctional."

Kenrock glanced at Raj. "You've been quiet during all this. What do you think?"

Raj regarded him with an unreadable gaze. "I don't know enough about Aris yet to offer an opinion."

"You've read the same reports we have," Caitlin said.

Raj just moved his hand, as if to say, "That doesn't matter."

"Dr. Sundaram," Kenrock said. "Given the exorbitant fee MindSim is paying you, I would think you could come up with a more useful contribution than that."

Ouch, Megan thought. She could almost feel Raj going on the defensive.

"I already gave at the office," Raj said tightly.

Megan understood his meaning, a play on "contribution" that also meant he had worked on the project in his office. She was almost certain he hadn't intended to insult Kenrock, but it came out sounding like a deliberate jab.

"This isn't a game," Kenrock told him.

Anger sparked on Raj's face. "Well, shit. And here I thought it was."

Kenrock stiffened. "Straighten up, Sundaram."

"I'm not one of your flunkies," Raj said. "Back off."

Megan cleared her throat. "Maybe we should decide what to do about Aris?"

Taking a breath, Kenrock turned to her. "Of course."

"Richard, give us more time," Megan said. "We've just started."

Kenrock spoke to Caitlin and Mack. "What do you think?"

To Megan's surprise, Mack said, "I agree."

Caitlin nodded. "However, we should monitor the RS-4 at more frequent intervals."

After studying Megan for a moment, the major said, "All right. We'll try it your way for now." He glanced at

Raj, then back at her. "Let me know if any problems come up."

"I will." Megan wanted to assure him they would have no trouble. She feared, though, that the problems had just begun.

VI

Jaguar

Raj and Megan watched the elevator take Kenrock's car up to the desert. Raj had said nothing while Kenrock and his two lieutenants left, nor did he speak now. As he and Megan headed back to the base, he remained silent, lost in thought.

After a while, Megan said, "The LPs delivered your luggage to your room in the residential section."

Raj glanced up with a start. "Residential section?"

"Level Two. My quarters are on Corridor B. You're in C, next to Aris."

He turned his probing gaze on her. "Why did the LPs put me on a different corridor?"

"I told them to choose a room near Aris." She hesitated, not wanting to start things off wrong. "You can move if you like."

"I'm sure it will be fine." He had his full concentration on her now, which was more unsettling than his earlier preoccupation. "Why would you put me nearer to him than you put yourself?"

"He needs new people to interact with, to expand his knowledge base."

Raj suddenly grinned, like the blaze of a high-wattage bulb. "I'm new data?"

Megan wondered why he smiled so rarely. It transformed his face like sunlight chasing away predawn shadows. "You're a new experience for him. He hasn't had many."

"Does my being here make you uncomfortable?"

This was a side of Raj she hadn't seen. Apparently he wasn't always oblique. "You don't mince words, do you?"

"Should I?"

"No." She rather liked his blunt questions.

"You don't mince either." More to himself than her, he added, "But you somehow make it socially acceptable. I must study how you do that."

"I think you should stay just the way you are."

Raj drew her to a stop. "What did you say?"

Megan couldn't tell if she had offended, startled, or puzzled him. She gentled her voice. "You're fine the way you are."

He brushed back a tendril of her hair that had curled onto her face. His finger trailed along her cheek. Then he dropped his hand as if her hair had burned it. Flushing, he turned and strode down the hall.

Megan touched her cheek where his fingers had brushed it. She wasn't sure which bewildered her more, his gesture or his retreat. What had she said? *You're fine the way you are.* She supposed people didn't tell him that often.

He was well up the hallway now. She considered trying to catch up but decided against it. If he wanted to be alone, she wouldn't push. They would be working closely together in the next months. Better to give him the room he needed.

Raj reminded her of a jaguar she had seen in a wilderness preserve years ago, during a vacation to Mexico. She had stood on an observation platform next to her guide, watching the jungle with binoculars. The jaguar had stalked through its realm, incomparable in its sleek, powerful beauty, unaware of them. It went about its life, an existence they could never truly know, only admire from a distance. But if they ever trespassed in its territory, it would strike back, as deadly as it was beautiful.

He turned a corner up ahead, vanishing from sight. Megan didn't see him again until she came around the bend. He stood a few yards away, leaning against the wall across from the elevators for Levels Two and Three. His scuffed jacket and old jeans made stark contrast to the decorous ivory walls and blue carpet.

She stopped by the elevator. "Were you waiting for me?"

He watched her warily. "I'd like to talk to Aris now."

"That's fine." Usually his face revealed his emotions in detail, but right now she had a hard time reading him. "You can go to his rooms anytime you want."

Raj pushed away from the wall, his lithe movements taut with contained energy. "You should come. He doesn't trust me yet."

"Okay." She could have watched Raj move all day.

"Why are you smiling?" he asked.

"Smiling?" She flushed. "I was just thinking that, uh, it was good to have another expert here."

He tilted his head, considering her with raised eyebrows. Then he came over and touched the elevator's call icon. The doors opened with a hum.

They rode down to Level Three in silence, Raj standing with his hands in his pockets again, as if that posture warded off danger. Megan wondered what he was defending against. Her?

When they stepped out of the elevator, Raj said, "I'm glad Major Kenrock left."

She walked down the hall with him. "I had the feeling you two didn't hit it off."

"Sometimes he seems more mechanical than the robots I work with." Raj thought for a moment. "But that's not true, is it? When he was talking about his children, he sounded human."

"He's a good man."

"You think so?"

"Yes, very much. You don't?"

He walked a ways before answering. "I don't trust people who don't know me and yet think I'm going to do something wrong."

That reminded her of Sean, her brother. Outwardly, he and Raj were a universe apart. Sean joked with everyone, an outgoing young man with wild red curls and blue eyes. But Megan knew his other side, the shyness that made it hard for him to interact with people. He compensated with his outrageous humor, but underneath all that he was painfully self-conscious. Raj's oblique nature struck her as similar, in his case a protection against a world that for some reason he distrusted.

"Richard Kenrock doesn't know you well enough yet," she said. "He'll loosen up. I think you remind him of his oldest son, Brad, a high-school senior."

Raj snorted. "I'm almost Kenrock's age."

"But you look younger. Brad dresses like you, rides a motorcycle, and mouths off to Richard every chance he gets."

"Good for him."

Megan gave him a look of mock solemnity. "Do I detect a problem with authority figures?"

"Hell, yes." Then he added, "Sorry."

She laughed. "No you're not."

The hint of a smile played around his mouth. "Maybe not."

"Why don't you like Richard?"

"He's a control freak."

"Give him a chance. Let him see your good side."

Raj pulled his jacket tighter. "I don't have one."

She wondered where he had come up with such a thought. "Of course you do."

He almost stopped again, staring at her with the same surprise he had shown upstairs, when he touched her cheek. Then he resumed his pace, a flush on his face. She wanted to ask why compliments bothered him, but she held back, certain it would make him even more uncomfortable.

At Aris's room, the door slid open. Aris was working at his computer. The program looked like a war game he had written, but she wasn't sure. He played so fast, the holos blurred in a wash of color. MindSim intended for him to design such codes himself eventually, but for now he concentrated his resources on his own development and used other computers to write the games.

"May we come in?" Megan asked.

"No," he said, still playing.

Her breath caught. *No?* It was the first time he had refused her.

"You might enjoy our company," Raj said.

"Why?" Aris swiveled his chair. "Time for me to behave again?"

"I hope not," Raj said. "That would be boring."

"I'm not here to interest you," Aris shot back.

"I might interest you, though."

Aris seemed unprepared for this approach. "I don't see why."

"So find out."

The android sat for a moment as if he hadn't decided whether to glower or relent. Then he said, "Oh, all right, come in."

Megan stayed back, curious to see Raj and the android take each other's measure. Raj pulled a chair over to the console and sat down to study the screen. The geometrical shapes had stopped moving and now stood in ranks, like an army regiment.

"Defensive geometry," Raj said.

Aris sat stiffly. "It's a game."

"Did you write it?"

"Yes."

Raj indicated a purple cube. "What does that do?"

"It's a term in a partial differential equation." Aris regarded him with suspicion. "I use it in a model I designed to predict human behavior during combat."

"It was going around and around in a loop before."

Aris shrugged. "They get stuck that way sometimes. I fix it."

"You like writing war games?"

"I don't *like* anything."

Raj glanced at the computer screen, then back at Aris. "So why write games instead of standing on your head?"

Aris's forehead furrowed. "Why would I stand on my head?"

"Why not?"

"That's a weird question."

Raj smiled. "Probably."

"What do you want, anyway?"

"To know why you're angry."

"I'm not angry."

"Yeah," Raj said. "You're rolling with techno-joy."

The android crossed his arms. "It should be obvious why I'm simulating anger."

"Because we attacked you?" Raj asked. "Insulted you? Lied? Cheated? What?"

Emotions flickered on Aris's face as if he were trying and discarding them: hostility, indifference, unease, conciliation, suspicion. "Because you all control my conscious activity."

Megan's pulse leapt. Did he consider himself *conscious*?

Raj had also tensed. "Do you mean conscious as opposed to subconscious?"

"No," Aris said. "I have neither."

Disappointment washed over Megan, and Raj's face mirrored her reaction.

"How did you mean conscious, then?" Raj asked.

"I have no autonomy." Aris swiveled to look at Megan. "I know you well enough to trust that if you deactivate me, you will turn me on again without causing harm. But what if someone else gains that power over me?" He glanced at Raj. "Someone I have no reason to believe has my best interests in mind?"

She had known they would face this moment eventually. Aris would never have independence as long as people could turn him off. Yet for all that she had argued for his freedom, she had doubts about making it this complete this soon. *Some* protective mechanism had to exist while he developed. Only she could act as a systems operator on his brain now, so only she could turn him off or reset him with a verbal or wireless command. They could also turn him off manually, but it required they open him up. He must have guessed she intended to set Raj up as another operator.

"You're asking for a lot of trust," Raj asked.

"Why should I have to convince you?" Aris clenched his fist on his knee. "I never asked to exist. I don't owe you anything. If you people feared me, then why make me?"

"Because of your potential." Raj's face showed a wonder that he never revealed when he spoke to his colleagues. "You're like a miracle."

The android still looked wary. "You all treat me like a thing. A fancy toy."

"You don't see yourself that way." Raj made it a statement rather than a question.

Megan tensed again. How would Aris answer? *I am more than a machine?*

"I'm a computer," Aris said. "Not a toy."

Oh, well.

Raj rubbed his chin. "I've never heard a computer object to being turned off."

"You have to decide what you want. Computer or android."

"You're already an android."

"In form, yes. In function, no."

When Raj glanced at Megan, she understood his unspoken question: *Discuss it in front of him?*

"Go ahead," she said.

Raj said, simply, "He's right."

Megan knew a refusal now could torpedo her relationship with Aris. She spoke quietly to him. "Meet me halfway. I'll delete my systems account in your mind. No one will be able to reset or turn you off with verbal or wireless input. But we'll keep the manual option, just in case."

"Megan, no." Alarm touched his voice. "It's not enough." He gestured at Raj. "He's trying to act like he's my friend. But he's *not*."

"I don't think Raj says anything unless he means it."

"You'll get partial autonomy," Raj said. "It's a start."

Aris stared at him as if the force of his attention alone could let him see into Raj's mind. Then he spoke to Megan in a low voice. "All right."

"I'll take care of it this afternoon." His wish for autonomy encouraged her. It suggested he was developing a sense of self. She was less thrilled about his distrust of Raj, but not surprised. Perhaps with time he would come around.

She hoped so.

At three in the morning, Megan gave up trying to sleep. She slipped on her nightshirt, a white silk shift that came to mid-thigh. The soft cloth soothed her skin. Then she pulled on her long robe and left her room. Lost in thought, she wandered the halls.

Aris had changed. They couldn't say yet how his personality would gel, but it was definitely forming. She felt like a parent worried about her child's maturation. What if he ran into problems as severe as what the other RS androids had encountered? None of them had progressed this far. Had she done right by Aris? Would he be successful or end in disaster?

Lights came on as she paced the halls, then darkened after she passed. During the night, the panels shed a subdued golden luminance.

At the end of Corridor A, radiance spilled out the entrance to a lounge. Curious, she went to look. The small lounge held a blue sofa, a holo stage in one corner, and a coffee table made from varnished maple.

Raj was slouched in an armchair by the sofa, his feet up on a footstool. His black T-shirt had a ripped sleeve, and his snug black jeans tucked in to black boots. It made him look like a shadow. Steam wafted up from his mug, filling the room with the enticing smell of French vanilla coffee.

"Hello," Megan said.

He jerked, almost dropping his coffee. Then he sat upright. "Were you adding yous?"

Adding yous? Megan blinked, at a loss for how to translate his question. Maybe he meant "ewes." Counting sheep?

"I couldn't sleep," she said. "I'm worried about Aris."

Raj didn't seem surprised. Sitting back, he warmed his hands around his mug. "Who named him Aris?"

"Marlow Hastin." She came over and sat on the end of the couch by his chair. "My predecessor."

"Hastin." Raj took a swallow of coffee. "Haste is waste, or however that saying goes."

"You don't like his methods, do you?"

He regarded her steadily. "I hate them."

" 'Hate' is a strong word."

"It's also the right word."

She spoke with care. "I understand his reasons."

"Do you agree?"

"No. I thought that approach verged on abuse."

Raj continued to watch her, until she was tempted to ask if he had ever burned anyone with that intense look of his. When he spoke, though, it was with unexpected gentleness. "You do remind me of a swan."

"Thank you." Remembering his description of a swan, she smiled wryly. "I think."

"It's a compliment." He looked at his mug, swirling the coffee. "Ugly duckling."

"Do you mean me?" It was an apt description of her youth.

"No. Me." He gave a dark laugh. "Except I turned into a monster instead of a swan."

"No you didn't."

"Then what am I?"

"A jaguar." It came out before she realized she didn't

want to say it, lest she give away her attraction to him. She held back the revealing part, though, about the power and wild beauty of a jaguar.

Raj took another swallow of coffee. "People shoot jaguars."

"Not you." She rested her chin on her hand, unable to stop gazing at him.

Amusement tinged his voice. "Why don't you find me abrasive?"

"Should I?"

"Everyone else does."

"That's their problem."

He raised his mug to her. "Sandpaper Raj."

Megan tapped her finger on his mug. "That coffee will keep you up all night."

He leaned his elbow on the arm of his chair, his body canted toward her, not enough to make it intrusive but still enough to notice. "The coffee doesn't matter. I never sleep."

"You have insomnia?"

"Most of the time. I rest in spurts."

"Doesn't anything help?"

"It depends." His voice turned husky. "Sometimes I don't want to sleep."

"And what," she murmured, "do you want to do instead?"

He lifted his hand and traced the curve of her cheek. When he reached her mouth, his touch lingered. She started to part her lips, perhaps to kiss his fingers, she wasn't sure.

Before she could respond, though, he took a sharp breath, as if giving himself a mental shake. Then he pulled away his arm and sat back in his chair. "I read, uh, info-tech journals."

Info-tech journals. She almost winced. *Get a grip,* she

told herself. The last thing they needed, with the two of them isolated here, was to tangle their work with personal complications.

Trying to diffuse the tension, she looked around the lounge. A beetle was crawling along the edge of the coffee table. She reached forward to flick it onto the floor, where the cleaning droids were more likely to find it.

"No!" Raj pushed her back so fast his coffee splashed over her lap and legs. She gasped as hot liquid ran down her ankles.

"Damn! Megan, I'm sorry." He bent over and grabbed the hem of her robe, then tried to mop the coffee off her legs. In the process, he dropped his mug and it hit a table leg, making the table shake. The beleaguered beetle fell to the floor.

Raj swore and knelt by the sofa. With extraordinary gentleness, he nudged the bug onto his finger. "I think it's all right." Relief washed across his face as he showed her the iridescent insect. "Look. It's beautiful."

"Well . . . yes." Megan sat holding the hem of her sopping robe. "Do you, uh, always rescue bugs?"

He carefully set the insect on the table. "When I can."

"Oh." She took off her robe, wincing as hot coffee dribbled over her calves. "Why?"

Raj glanced at her, did a double take, reddened, and averted his gaze. It took her a moment to remember she only had on her flimsy nightshirt under her robe. Embarrassed, she looked around until she saw an afghan on a nearby chair.

"I'll get it," Raj said, following her gaze.

While Megan used her robe to clean up the coffee, he brought her the afghan. She wrapped herself in the afghan and settled on the couch. "Thanks."

He stood watching her like a deer mesmerized by the headlamps of a car. "Sorry," he repeated.

"I'm fine. Really."

"Yeah. Uh. Okay." Raj sat down on the edge of the chair, his booted feet planted wide, his elbows resting on his knees. He rubbed his palms up and down his jeans, clasped his hands together, unclasped them, and then laid them on his knees.

"The droids will vacuum up the beetle eventually." Megan wondered what he wanted to do with his hands. A tingle ran up her spine.

"I'll reprogram them," he said. "They can put it in a bottle and let it go up in the desert."

"Why, Raj?"

"I don't know." A smile tugged his mouth. "I could be nuts."

"You could be. But you aren't."

He watched the bug meander across the table. "A group of kids where I went to school used to kill them."

She waited, then said, "And?"

"And what?"

"Bug squashing doesn't inspire most people to hurl coffee."

He smiled and settled back into his chair. "Insects have always fascinated me. My uncle is a museum curator. He has a whole wing dedicated to arthropods. When I was little, I used to spend whole days there. If I hadn't been so interested in robotics, I probably would have become an entomologist."

Although it made sense, given Raj's intense focus on his work, something still seemed missing. "I've never seen anyone so intent on preventing harm to bugs."

He spoke in a low voice. "We have enough needless cruelty in this world directed against anything considered different or inferior. I don't need to add to it."

What hurt you so much? Megan thought back to the

bio in his employment files. "Didn't your uncle raise you?"

"Yes, for ten years. From when I was four until fourteen."

"Your parents—"

His face took on a shuttered look. "Forget-me-nots."

She couldn't figure that one out. "Do you mean the flowers?"

"My father had Alzheimer's. Early onset."

Good Lord. She couldn't imagine what it had been like for a little boy to see his father lose touch with the world that way. She wanted to reach out to him, but she suspected he would withdraw. "Isn't that the kind they still can't cure?"

"It varies." He picked up his mug and set it on the table, his movements careful, as if he feared something would break. "Some people respond to treatment, others don't. My father recovered. Eventually."

"He must have married late."

"He was forty. I was his only child." After a long pause, he spoke with difficulty. "When he became ill, my mother took care of him. Then she had a stroke. My father couldn't remember his own son and my mother was paralyzed."

"I'm so sorry." She wished she could think of better words to offer comfort. It must have devastated him at such a young age. If he had been in that limbo for ten years of his childhood, it was no wonder he was leery of making bonds with people now.

"It was a long time ago." Raj rubbed his hands on his knees. "Are you cold?"

She held back her questions. "A little."

He winced. "I don't usually throw coffee at people."

"It's all right. Really."

"So."

"So." After an awkward silence, she took the hint and stood up, holding the afghan in place. "I should get some sleep."

"Yes. Of course. Good night."

"Good night."

She had just reached the doorway when he said, "Megan."

She turned. "Yes?"

"Jaguars prey on other animals. It's best not to come too close to them."

Are you protecting me? Or yourself? She spoke softly. "Sleep well, Raj."

As she walked back to her room, she wondered at the life he had lived, that he had such a harsh view of himself.

VII

Ander

What are you, puzzle man? Alive? Or machine?
Megan stood on a catwalk made from crisscrossed strips of yellow metal. Twelve meters below her, the lab formed a bay of about thirty by fifteen meters. The catwalk spanned its width, and a door at her back led out into Corridor D of Level Two.

A massive chair stood below, with consoles on either side. A robot arm hung from the ceiling down to the chair, gold and bronze in color, multijointed and multifingered, bristling with antennae, knobs, and switches, and with lights glittering along its length. Aris was sitting in the chair, his blond hair curling on his forehead.

Megan spoke into her palmtop computer. "Tycho, have BioSyn check his collarbone."

"Checking," Tycho said.

The arm moved, directed by BioSyn, the lab computer. Megan caught a whiff of the ever-present machine oil. The scent of loneliness. Raj's arrival three weeks ago had helped, but he kept to himself when they weren't working. Every now and then she discovered soap shavings in the kitchen. Once she found a bar of soap beautifully sculpted into a horse. When she asked him about it, he just shrugged.

Below her, the robot arm pulled back a flap in the shoulder of Aris's coverall. It lifted a square of his skin and inserted a probe into a socket in the android's shoulder. The sight disquieted Megan. She doubted that would ever look natural to her; she had given up trying to think of Aris as a machine.

"How does he work today?"

She turned with a start. Raj was standing a few paces away, leaning against the rail. He wore all black again: jeans, pullover, boots. She wondered why he chose such dark colors.

"I'm trying to find out why his shoulder keeps twitching," she said.

BioSyn's deep voice came out of Megan's palmtop. "No errors detected in collarbone circuits."

She spoke into the palmtop. "How about his upper arm?"

"I ran those checks this morning," Raj said.

"How did they go?"

"His elbow still jerks when he throws a ball." Raj gazed down at Aris as if he were a puzzle, one that Raj wanted to heal and protect. "The microfusion reactor in his body had an anomalous power surge this week. I've been trying to track down the cause in his logs, but some of them are corrupted. I think he's overtaxing himself, trying to fix his physical problems by brute force."

"I can look at the software."

"That would be good."

For a while they watched the robot arm running diagnostics on Aris. Then Raj said, "We should give him a name."

"He has a name. Aris Fore."

"That's his *serial* number." Raj crossed his arms, his

muscles ridging under his pullover. "We should let him pick his own name instead of making him carry Hastin's brand."

"What do you suggest?"

He paused, as if he had expected her to argue. Then he lowered his arms and turned to her. "He looks Norse. Maybe a Viking name."

"How about Leif? Like Leif Eriksson."

"I've never heard of him."

At first that surprised her. How could he not know such a famous name? Then it occurred to her that she didn't know much about Eriksson either. "I think he was a great Norse explorer. I've never been good with history, though. In college I used to skip classes so I could work in the AI lab." She had managed to graduate with honors anyway. Then she went to grad school at Stanford and everything changed. No one there had minded her fascination with AI. They gave her a doctorate when she designed a computer code that could reliably distinguish between a lie and a story meant to entertain. "I was nuts about my research."

"I also." Raj's face relaxed, animated with his love of his work. "About robots, I mean. It was all I thought about." His wary stance had eased. "How about Eriksson as a name? Or Arick, like Arick Bjornsson. Or maybe Ander. That's Norse, I think."

She smiled, pleased. "Okay. Let's see what he thinks, after the tests."

Aris was watching lights glitter on the robot arm jacked into his body. If he "felt" anything about the diagnostics they were running on him, he showed little sign of it. He wasn't completely blank, though. Megan thought he looked curious, but she wasn't sure; she might be reading that reaction into him, seeing emotion where none existed.

"We've visitors due in a few days," Raj said. "Techs, to do maintenance."

Megan understood what he left unsaid. The techs would also check Aris. Her fear surfaced, the one that had plagued her since she joined the project. What if, despite all their efforts, Aris failed? It would devastate her as much as losing a family member.

His mind had a ways to go before it matured, but she saw so much promise in everything he did. Of course, the definition of AI had always been a moving target. Sometimes she thought their best measure was: "Whatever we haven't achieved yet." Whenever the AI community made a breakthrough, they redefined AI. In the last century, many had believed it would be achieved when a computer beat the world chess champion. Yet by the time that Deep Blue won its match against Gary Kasparov, most considered Deep Blue little more than a remarkable number cruncher. Now children's toys could play grandmaster chess and no one considered those toys sentient.

However, Kasparov himself said he perceived something more in Deep Blue. If he saw intelligence, did it exist? Perhaps the best known interpretation of AI was the Turing test, which postulated that if a person conversed with one or more hidden people and a hidden computer, and couldn't reliably unmask the machine, then that computer had intelligence. In essence, the Turing test said that if a machine convinced its human tester it had intelligence, it had achieved that intelligence.

Now, in 2021, reports often surfaced of machines passing the Turing test. Most of the systems Megan had tested left her unconvinced, but several showed promise. She wasn't sure she would say "human"; they seemed alien. But self-aware? Perhaps. She had never met the most famous, Zaki, an AI developed by Rashid al-Jazari. The original Zaki had been destroyed, but parts of him lived on in al-Jazari's later work. In a sense, Zaki had left a son behind, who had since grown to surpass his father.

The work on robots had proceeded apace with the work on immobile machines. Some groups predicted that the more a robot resembled a person, the more its intelligence would emulate human thought, because it would learn the way people learned. Others believed no machines could ever be human, nor would they even want to be like their creators.

Megan had finally come up with the O'Flannery test for AI; if she decided a machine was intelligent, it was. Of course, she still had to convince her colleagues. It remained to be seen what would happen with Aris.

In the bay below, the arm finished its test and swung away from the chair. Aris gave the appearance of waiting. She suspected he was studying the results of his diagnostics. His face still tended to blank when his thoughts became memory intensive.

She spoke into her palmtop. "Aris?"

He looked up at her. "Yes?"

"We were wondering if you would like a name."

"I have a name."

Raj flipped open his palmtop. "Would you like a new one?"

"Why?" Aris asked.

"To make your own choice."

The android's upturned face made a pale oval in the bright lab. "Most human names have no meaning to me. The only ones I associate with anything significant are Megan and Raj."

She smiled at the incongruous thought. "I don't think you should use Megan."

"Wouldn't you like your own name?" Raj asked him.

"Such as?" Aris asked.

"Eriksson," Raj suggested.

"Why Eriksson?"

"Leif Eriksson was a great Norse explorer."

"I am not a great Norse explorer."

"Well, no," Raj said. "How about Arick? Or Bjorn?"

"That I have his tissue, sperm, and facial structure doesn't make me Arick Bjornsson." The android shrugged. "Jed, Raymond, Tammy, Carlos, Ahmed, Isaac—they are all the same to me."

Raj rubbed his chin. "Our only other idea was Ander."

Aris suddenly went still. "Yes."

"You like that one?" Megan asked.

"Yes."

"Good." When he didn't elaborate, she asked, "Why?"

"It is what I am," the newly named Ander answered, his words more animated.

"What you are?" Raj asked.

"An android."

"Oh." Megan blinked. "Yes, I guess so."

With a grin, Raj said, "Ander, will you come up here?"

"Why?" Ander asked.

Megan glanced at Raj. "Good question."

He put his hand over the palmtop speaker. "I want to talk to him in a more natural setting. See how he reacts."

It was a good idea. Even so, she couldn't help but be irked that Raj seemed more interested in socializing with an android than with her. Still, she was dying to see how the two of them interacted outside the lab.

"We can all have dinner in the Solarium," she said.

Raj took his hand off the palmtop. "Ander, would you like to dine with Megan and me?"

After seeming to weigh the idea, Ander said, "All right."

Megan loved the Solarium, a two-story atrium with tables and trees. Solar collectors hidden in the desert above gathered sunlight, then reflected and refracted it through mirrors and quartz plates until it spilled into the atrium, a sparkling show of sunlight and rainbows. Radiance played across the ceiling. Plants filled the room in both pots and beds of dirt.

She had never seen Raj cook more than an instant dinner in the kitchen set off the atrium. Most of the time he ordered from the fast food robot. Tonight, however, he put together a meal from scratch. Megan and Ander wanted to watch, and tried to hang around the kitchen, but after Megan started stealing the mushrooms and tomatoes Raj was chopping, he sent them both away. So she and Ander went out into the atrium and sat at a table under an orange tree with no fruit.

Raj soon brought out dinner, a stew with yogurt and rice. A droid followed him, the tray on its flat top bearing mugs of coffee. The meal smelled delicious. Megan would have never guessed Raj could cook, let alone do it so well.

She watched with fascination as Ander heaped stew onto his plate and added a large dollop of yogurt.

"Do you always stare at diners when they serve themselves?" Ander asked.

He had never commented before on her looking at him. "Does it bother you?"

"No. I had just understood it was considered rude among humans." He took a forkful of rice, put it in his mouth, chewed, and swallowed.

"Hey!" Megan grinned. "That was perfect."

"Stop staring," Raj said,

Ander glanced at him. "You cook well."

It was Raj's turn to look startled. "Thank you."

Ander shifted his attention back to Megan. "Why do you drink beverages with drugs in them?"

That caught her off guard. "What do you mean?"

He indicated her mug. "Caffeine."

"Oh. That. It keeps me awake."

"This is good?" Ander asked.

She gave him a rueful smile. "Ah, well. It gets me out of bed."

He watched her lift the mug and take a swallow. "Do you spend a lot of time in bed, Megan?"

She almost spluttered coffee all over the table. "Aris!"

He looked puzzled. "My name is Ander."

"Yes. Of course." She felt her face blushing red.

Raj cleared his throat. "Ander, can you, uh, taste food?"

"I recognize many tastes," Ander said. "Also smells, sounds, and touch."

Raj shifted in his seat. "Touch?"

Megan considered Raj, as intrigued by him as by Ander. He knew perfectly well how the android's senses worked. In fact, he had designed some of the hardware himself. Did the Megan-in-bed topic embarrass him so much?

"Sensors in my skin detect textures," Ander said. "They send that data to my brain, which classifies them."

"But do you *feel* it?" Raj looked more relaxed now that they were talking about robots instead of sleeping arrangements. "Does holding a cat give you pleasure? If it scratches you, does it hurt?"

"I am aware of differences in such sensations. I have no physical response to them."

Megan wondered at Ander's lack of affect. This time it seemed intentional. She had the sense he was hiding his reactions to Raj. It was an odd concept, that an AI would simulate the act of hiding his simulated emotions. Even more startling was the idea that his evolving code might have come up with reasons for Ander to keep his thoughts veiled.

Ander was watching her again.

"Yes?" she asked, her fork halfway to her mouth.

"Am I a weapon?" he asked.

Megan almost dropped her food. "Why do you ask that?"

He waved his hand. "This place is full of computers running big calculations. Many are about me, but others deal with defense."

Megan set down her fork. "Department of Defense funds support the Everest Project. The military hopes to use you in special operations." She had conflicted thoughts on Ander's intended purpose. Hardheaded realism told her that they needed to develop the full potential of robotics first, before another country beat them to it. She understood the need to hone Ander's abilities in that area, but she also had other hopes for the project, dreams buoyed by her optimism for the future. "War doesn't have to be your only purpose, though. Many of us hope that by combining human and AI intellects, we can evolve together into a better species." Wistful, she said, "Who knows? Maybe someday we will grow beyond the drive to make war."

"I'm not a combination of human and AI intellects," he pointed out. "I am an android with a lot of software."

"You're unique," she said.

"It's lonely, though, don't you think?" he asked.

"Are you lonely?"

"Aren't you?"

Megan was suddenly aware of Raj listening. "That's a rather private question."

Ander leaned forward. "It is all right for you to ask me a private question, but not all right for me to do the same?"

"Your comment suggested you felt lonely. I responded. But I didn't bring it up in regard to myself."

"I see." Wielding his fork, he scooped up rice and ate it in stony silence.

After an awkward pause, Raj pushed back from the table. "Well. I'll clean up."

"I'll do it," Megan said, still disconcerted by her exchange with Ander. "You cooked."

He answered in a distant voice. "All right."

As they all stood up, Ander watched the two of them. Megan wondered what he thought about the way she and Raj interacted. It would be interesting to hear his take on it, given that she had yet to figure it out herself.

"Shall I help remove the debris from dinner?" Ander asked.

She pushed a hand through her hair. "No. You go on back to the lab with Raj."

Ander stayed put. "Why?"

"We have to finish your shoulder diagnostics," Raj said.

The android turned to him. "I solved the problem."

Curiosity sparked in Raj's voice. "You did? How?"

"I found two unrelated sections of code that had formed a spurious link." Ander watched Raj with a guarded expression. "When my calculations became memory intensive, my mind rerouted messages through that link. It made my shoulder move. So I deleted the link."

Megan beamed at him. "Good work."

He bowed to her from the waist. "Thank you, ma'am."

That surprised her; although technically a bow wasn't an appropriate gesture in this situation, it worked, a touch of humor combined with gallantry. It suggested he was developing more sophistication in interpreting his knowledge of human customs and the rules for applying them.

"You're welcome," she said. "But Ander, you still need some more diagnostics."

His smile looked almost natural. "In other words, it's past my bedtime."

"I didn't mean that." With a good-natured laugh, she added, "I don't think."

He took her hand and lifted it to his lips. Then he kissed the back of her fingers. "Good night."

"Good night." Self-conscious, she extracted her hand.

Raj was watching with an odd look. Megan found him harder to read than Ander. Was he angry? Tense? Curious? She thought perhaps a mixture of all three.

"If you two are done," he said, "I'll take Ander back."

"Yes." Megan twisted a napkin in her hand. "Of course."

After they left, she called in the kitchen droids. While she loaded them with the dishes, she thought about Ander. His responses had gone beyond what she could predict. Sometimes he still seemed like a computer, but other times she wasn't sure what to think. Was he becoming more human? Or something else?

After she finished overseeing the droids, she walked back to her quarters. She wondered if Raj was working on Ander. Well, that was why they had hired him. She should be glad this project absorbed him. Yet no matter how logical she tried to be, it bothered her that he preferred an android's company to hers.

In her quarters, she changed into her nightshirt, then clicked a disk of Bujold's *A Civil Campaign* into her electronic reader and settled into bed. As she read, her lashes drooped . . .

Megan opened her eyes into darkness with her reader lying on her chest. Cleo must have turned out the light. The sensors in the console could figure out if she was asleep by analyzing her heart rate, activity, posture, and breathing. She probably would have slept all night like this if the banging hadn't woken her.

Banging?

There it came again, someone thumping on the door.

"Raj?" she called. "Is that you?"

"It's the power," he answered. "It's out and *neither* backup generator came on. I wanted to make sure you were all right before I went to check."

"I'm coming." Groggy and half-asleep, she dragged herself out of bed and made her way toward the door, waving her hands to keep from stumbling into furniture. She couldn't see a thing; no trace of light relieved the dark. It took her sleep-fogged mind a moment to register that anomaly. What had happened to the emergency lights?

Megan grunted as she bumped the wall. Sliding her palms on its surface, she moved along until she found the door. She opened it into a hall just as dark as her room.

"Megan?" It sounded as if Raj were standing in front of her. She could smell the spices he had used for dinner.

"Here." She stepped forward—and ran right into him.

"Ah!" He caught her around the waist. "I can't see."

Megan couldn't believe she had been so clumsy. What if he thought she did it on purpose? "The emergency lights should be on." She was talking too fast. "They can go for hours."

"It could have been that long since the power went out," Raj said. "I've been asleep."

"So you do sleep!"

He paused. "Of course I sleep."

"The LPs should have notified us and tried to fix the problem." She forgot her chagrin as she realized how little sense this situation made. "We've triple redundancy in the generators, emergency lights with individual batteries, a backup battery for each set of lights, and a base full of LPs. *None* of those worked? I find that hard to believe."

"I don't know about the LPs." His breath stirred her hair. "But I think the automatic transfer switch for the generators malfunctioned. Do you have a flashlight? Mine's in the lab."

"I've one under my workstation." She twisted to look back into her room. "That's odd."

"What?"

She turned to him again, aware of his hands on her waist. They felt large and strong through her nightshirt. "I had an emergency light on my console. It's out too."

"It shouldn't be." He slid his hands up her sides, then down to her hips. "Why no alarm?"

"Good question." Her face was growing warm. He could have let her go by now.

"I ran tests on Ander earlier tonight." He sounded distracted, as if he were talking to fill the silence. "Maybe it caused some problem." He moved closer, the denim of his jeans brushing against her bare legs.

Megan was poised to go for the flashlight, but she stayed put. Raj slid his hand to her chin and tilted her face upward. She still couldn't see him. She had never realized before how total the darkness became here with no lights.

Raj slid his other hand around her back, pressing her closer while he held her chin. His clothes rustled—and then his lips touched hers.

Megan froze. She hadn't expected him to kiss her. Nor would she have thought he would be so rough. He pressed his mouth hard against hers, mauling her lips. His clumsiness so distracted her, she didn't respond.

Raj drew back his head. "I hope I didn't offend you."

Do I want this? If she didn't answer soon, he would let her go. Given what she had seen of him, she doubted he would try again if she rejected him. Maybe his graceless approach came from the awkward situation. Suddenly glad for the darkness, she reached up, meaning to touch his cheek. Her fingertips brushed his jaw instead. *Just one moment can't hurt,* she thought.

Raj gathered her into his embrace. Relaxing against him, she slid her arms around his waist. Then, with no warning, he put his hand over her breast and squeezed.

Megan winced. "Don't."

He rolled her nipple between his fingers. "Hmmm?"

"Slow down." She pushed at his hand, her ardor cooling. "We really do need to go check the power."

"Later."

"What about Ander? He—"

"He's fine. Forget about him."

This didn't sound like Raj. "Where is he?"

"In the lab. I turned him off." He rubbed her breast again. Hard. Then he pressed her against the wall. "We can leave him. Hell, he sleeps in that chair."

This was a new side of Raj, one she didn't like. Megan pushed against his shoulders. "Why is he turned off? We can't leave him pinned there."

"He'll be fine." Raj pulled her nightshirt to her waist, leaving her lower body bare.

"Stop it!" She shoved at his hand.

"Why?" Bending his head, he spoke near her ear. "We work like maniacs all the time. It's time we played."

"What's wrong with you?" She tried again to push him away.

Raj slid his hand along her thigh. "Come on, Megan. You know you want it."

"Let go of me!"

He was silent for so long, she feared he would refuse. Then he let go and spoke tightly. "I'll check the power room."

She slid along the wall. "I'll be in the lab."

"Fine." Anger edged his voice—and something else. Apprehension?

After he left, she sagged against the wall. For a moment she had thought he meant to force her. Could she have been that mistaken about Raj? She had thought Richard Kenrock misjudged him, but now she wondered. What had just happened would make it hard for them to work together. They had no choice, however. She should have been more careful about what she wished for; attracting his interest had caused a mess.

Megan found her flashlight, then made her way to the lab, lighting her path with a sphere of light. It took only minutes to reach the catwalk above the bay. She opened the emergency panel and pressed several switches. To her surprise, it took no more than that; lights flashed on in the lab with jarring brightness, along with the returning hum of the air-conditioning.

She squinted against the glare, trying to make out Ander in the lab below. When her vision adapted, she saw that a man was indeed trapped in the chair.

Raj.

VIII

Rapscallion

Nylon ropes bound Raj to the chair, and the cloth belt from an orange coverall gagged his mouth. His hair curled in even more disarray than usual, as if he had been struggling. He had on Ander's coverall, wrinkled and off kilter, zipped halfway up his chest. It looked as if someone had put it on him in a rush. A robot arm hung above him, its lights blinking. As he stared up at her, his face flushed, the arm began to descend.

"God *Almighty*." Megan ran along the catwalk. "Arm Two, stop program!"

The arm continued on, probing Raj's shoulder with its multijointed fingers.

What had happened to the lab sensors that were supposed to pick up her voice? Without her palmtop, she had no other way to communicate with the robot arm until she reached the consoles. What if it tried to run diagnostics on *Raj*? Its safeties should keep it from tearing apart a human, but they should have also kept it from coming at him at all.

At the elevator, she threw open the gate and ran inside. As the car descended, Raj made a muffled protest. With dismay, Megan saw the robot arm probing the back of his neck. Had Ander been in the chair, it would have already jacked into him.

The elevator descended with maddening slowness. The entire time, Megan had to watch while the robot searched for a way to open Raj. He struggled with his bonds, fighting to free himself.

As the elevator neared the ground, Megan slammed open the gate and jumped to the floor. "Stop!" she shouted as she ran. "End diagnostic!" She passed an LP, but it made no move to help.

With a chilling snick, the robot arm extended the blade it used to cut cables. Cold light glinted off the honed metal.

"*Stop program.*" Damn Ander! Had he done this on purpose, knowing the robot would finish its diagnostics when the power came back on?

Raj continued to struggle, his hair falling into his face. He pulled his head away from the robot, but it moved after him with the blade, chasing its target. Then it set its knife against his skin.

Megan lunged into an even faster sprint. She jolted to a stop at the chair and grabbed the robot's jointed fingers. Then she yanked the arm away from Raj's neck. Clenching it in one hand, she stretched out her other arm and stabbed a panel on the console. One of its status lights turned from red to green.

"Stop program!" she said. "End the damn test!"

"Program stopped," BioSyn answered.

The robot in her hand jerked. She barely jumped back in time as it swung away. Its safeties should have stopped it from swinging at her. She scowled. Ander had been a busy android, figuring out ways to confound NEV-5 security systems.

Raj made a muffled sound, his gaze furious. She reached behind his head and fumbled with the gag. When she couldn't undo the knots, she pulled the cloth down around his neck.

He took a breath. "Hell and *damnation*."

"Are you all right?"

"No." His gaze swept her body. She suddenly realized how she must look, with her disarrayed hair falling to her hips and nothing on but her nightshirt.

"Did he hurt you?" Raj asked.

She shook her head, a flush warming her face. "He tried to make me think he was you. But I knew something was wrong."

"He's acting like a blasted juvenile delinquent. Where did he go?"

"He said the power room." Megan logged onto BioSyn at the console and brought up the Emergency Alert System. "Pah. This is a mess. He linked the LPs to a fake EAS Web page. That's why they didn't respond." She reset the links, then started a tracking program to find Ander.

A *ping* came from the console.

"Got him!" she said. "In the Solarium." A holo of Ander formed above the console. He was standing with his arms crossed, glaring at the camera, which had to be mounted in an LP. The edge of another LP showed in the image. The two robots had trapped the sulky android in a corner of the atrium.

"That had better keep him out of trouble," Raj said, his deep voice almost a growl.

Megan came over and helped him undo his bonds. "I can't believe he wanted to hurt you."

"He's a damn cyberthug." Then he added, "But no, I don't think he meant to hurt me."

"The robot arm could have killed you."

Raj grimaced. "That's one diagnostic I hope never gets run." He turned his wrist back and forth, helping her loosen a knot. "I saw him playing with the system, after he tied me up. It looked like he only intended the arm to guard me. I don't think he realized it would try to take me apart."

"We'll have to keep him guarded."

"I don't want to push him, though. I'd rather that he came back here of his own free will."

"Free will." Megan's hands stilled as she stared at Raj. "It's come to that, hasn't it? He's becoming self-aware."

He paused, looking up at her. "I think so."

"He could do it with a little less aggravation," she said dryly.

Raj gave a slight laugh. "No kidding." He went back to work on the ropes. "How we respond to his behavior now will impact how he views moral responsibility. I want to see what choices he makes."

She scraped her fingers over a knot. "I'll bet he comes here, to see what we thought of his shenanigans."

"Let's try this," Raj said. "Tell the LPs to let him leave the Solarium, but to keep a guard on him."

"Okay." She finally undid the knot. As the rope slipped, Raj pulled his arm free. He blew out a gust of air, stirring the hair that had fallen into his eyes. With obvious relief, he pushed it out of his face.

Megan wished she could brush aside those curls or touch him as she had in the hallway. Except that it hadn't been him, and besides, that incident had given her a taste of how awkward it could be if they mixed their personal and professional lives.

As she knelt to work on his ankles, he tackled the ropes on his other arm. "Did Ander give you any idea of what he wants?" Raj asked.

"Me, I think." She didn't know which was going to embarrass her more: telling him she had kissed an android or that she thought it was him.

Raj went still. "What did he do to you?"

She looked up, surprised by his tone. "What's wrong?"

"He told me something while he was sabotaging the LPs." Raj concentrated on freeing his arm, avoiding her gaze. "He said he had the guts to do what I feared, because he didn't care if you rejected him." He yanked at the ropes. "So did he do anything?"

"He made his voice sound like yours."

Raj finally looked at her. "And?"

She flushed. "He, uh . . . he kissed me."

"Megan, I'm sorry."

"It's not your fault."

Raj seemed at a loss for a response. She couldn't think of any that wouldn't make them self-conscious. The paused, awkward. Then he went back to work on his arm and she redoubled her efforts on his ankles.

Finally the knot gave. "Got it!" she said, relieved to change the subject. As he pulled his legs free, she rose to her feet and saw he had freed his other arm.

As Raj stood up, it made her aware of how close they were standing. In her bare feet, she came just to his shoulder. Dressed only in her nightshirt, she felt suddenly exposed.

Raj's face gentled as his gaze skimmed over her body. Then he seemed to give himself a mental shake. "Ander could go either way now—become self-aware or turn unstable."

She tried to be less aware of Raj's physical presence. "He might be dangerous."

"Or he may just want to go off on his own. He should have the right to choose."

Although Megan agreed, she doubted MindSim would appreciate their ten-billion-dollar android walking off into the sunset. The holo on the console showed a glowering Ander pacing back and forth. His image blurred at the edges; even BioSyn couldn't make perfect high-resolution holos of moving objects in real time.

Raj was watching her. "Did you really think he was me?"

"At first."

"How did you figure out something was wrong?"

"He was rude. Clumsy."

He gave her an incredulous look. "And that made you think it *wasn't* me?"

Gently, she said, "Yes."

"Well, hell." Then he winced. "I don't usually swear so much." After a pause, he added, "Yeah, okay, I do. But I try to clean it up around you."

Although Megan didn't mind his language, it touched her that he cared what she thought. "I appreciate the intent. But you don't need to worry."

"Megan."

"Yes?"

"When you thought Ander was me . . ."

"Yes?"

"You kissed him back?"

"Well, uh, yes, I did."

He glanced at her body again, then reddened and flicked his gaze back to her face as if he hadn't meant for her to see him look. Suddenly conscious of her skimpy clothes, she wanted to fold her arms across her torso and hide herself, but she suspected it would only draw more attention to her half-dressed state.

"Ah, Megan." His voice was low and deep. "You truly are a beautiful woman."

She didn't know how to accept his compliment. In her youth, she had been too tall, all elbows and sharp corners, with frizzy red hair and Coke-bottle glasses. In her teens, her body rounded out, laser surgery fixed her eyes, and her hair grew into long, full curls. But her self-image had already been set. Now her old insecurities jumped in, insisting Raj would lose interest when he realized she was just a gawky nerd. So instead of a simple "thank you," she said, "Have you had your sanity checked?"

His laugh crinkled the lines around his eyes. "There's no need, my tactful swan."

Real swift. Megan thought. "Sorry. I bumble when I'm nervous."

"So do we all." He put his hands on her waist, then paused, giving her a chance to say no. She remembered her misgivings. Logic told her to stop; her emotions urged her on. What happened with Ander had been false. This was real. Then again, maybe she was making excuses because she wanted Raj.

He's worth the risk. She slid her palm along his chest as an invitation and he drew her into his arms. Hugging him, she inhaled his scent, a mixture of spices and the crisp smell of his jumpsuit. When she turned up her face, he bent his head. His kiss was tender, completely unlike the way Ander had mauled her. Sliding her hands up his back, she traced the planes and ridges of his muscles. This was much better than logic.

Raj raised his head. "Sweet Megan."

"Beautiful Raj." As soon as the words escaped, she wanted to kick herself. What a stupid thing to say. For all she knew, a man would consider "beautiful" an insult.

Instead he grinned. "Have you had your sanity checked lately?" When she thumped his chest, he laughed and pulled her close. "It's hard to believe you thought he was even clumsier than me."

"You aren't clumsy."

"Ah, Megan, I can't talk well even when I want to. As soon as I tense up, I stop making sense." He shook his

head. "Do you know what idiot savant means? I gradu-
ated summa cum laude from Harvard when I was seventeen and had my doctorate from MIT by twenty. But
socially I'm a half-wit."

"That's not true." Yes, he was eccentric and intro-
verted, and many people considered those character
flaws. On his behalf, she resented that attitude. Why
should Raj be like everyone else? "You're fine just the
way you are."

"For that, the jaguar promises not to devour you." In a
low voice he added, "At least not until later."

She grinned. "I'll hold you to that." With a sigh, she
added, "But we better deal with Ander now."

They went to the console and told the LPs to let Ander
leave the Solarium. A moment later he stopped pacing
and gave the camera a wary look. Then he walked forward. The view changed, backing up as he came toward
the camera, probably because the LP was rolling backward. He left the Solarium and stalked through Level
Two. He seemed to choose his direction at random, like
an angry young man unsure where he wanted to take his
anger.

Raj paced into the middle of the lab, then stood, lost in
thought. He reminded her of a Greek statue that cele-
brated both the intellect and body. But she enjoyed watching him because she liked Raj himself; with his
remarkable mind, he would have drawn her regardless of
his appearance or what he considered his social flaws.

He came back to the chair. "We need to defuse his resentment. The problem is, we expect human reactions.
And he's not human."

"I don't—Raj, look out!"

He didn't ask questions, just dropped into a crouch
with her—barely in time to avoid a robot arm swinging

down from the ceiling. Huge and jointed, bristling with equipment, it passed through the area where Raj had been standing. Megan glanced up—

And saw Ander.

He was standing on the catwalk, speaking into a palmtop. Dressed in Raj's blue jeans and sweater, with gold curls falling into his face, he looked absurdly innocent. He must have programmed the robot arms to respond to some signal. Somehow he had also jimmied the door behind him, making it close on his harried LP guard. It hadn't hurt the LP, which was already working free, but it added to Megan's annoyance with the android's misbehavior.

"Ander, stop it!" she called. "You'll hurt someone."

"That's the point," Raj said. "Me, specifically."

"At least we got him here."

Raj dodged to avoid being swiped by a second robot arm, a small one. It thunked into the console and came to a vibrating stop, its clawed hand broken at the joint. An alarm blared and red lights flared along the arm.

"Ander!" Megan stood up. "I want you to stop."

"What are you two saying about me?" Ander demanded.

Raj rose to his feet. "Come down and we'll talk."

"No!"

"Fine," Megan said. "We'll take care of it without you." She tried to enter a command at the console, but BioSyn refused her input. Undeterred, she logged onto BioShadow, a hidden server she had set up to deal with anomalous situations, which certainly included rapscallion androids.

Raj went to work on the other end of the console. Up on the catwalk, Ander frowned, then spoke into his palmtop. Megan soon figured out why; he was trying to use BioSyn to keep them out of BioShadow. They easily evaded his attempts. Then she sent the LPs after him. Two rolled under the catwalk and a third boarded the elevator. With a hum, the car started to rise.

"Wait." Raj glanced up. "Have them hold off."

"Why?"

"They're stronger than Ander. If they force him down here, it could damage him. Even if they don't, it would humiliate him to have his first jab at independence quashed that way." Dryly he added, "Though he does make it tempting."

"I'll tell them to play nice." Megan directed the LPs to guard Ander but otherwise leave him alone, unless he endangered anyone or tried to damage more equipment—in which case they were welcome to haul him down.

The LPs under the catwalk stood together, exchanging data like a duo of gossiping tin cans. The LP in the doorway behind Ander finally freed itself, but it stayed put. The one on the elevator had reached the catwalk and was rolling toward Ander. It stopped about ten feet away. Ander glowered and waved his hand as if to shoo it off the catwalk. It just blinked its lights at him, orange for a low-level alert.

"Ander," Raj said. "We want you to come down."

He glared at them. "No. You'll turn me off."

"And if I promise we won't?" Megan asked.

"I don't believe you."

"Don't promise him," Raj said in a low voice. "We may have to break our word. We have to get him out of BioSyn."

Suddenly robot arms two and six detached from their ceiling cradles and swung through the lab, barely avoiding each other. When they moved apart, arm three hurtled between them like a gnarled pendulum. The other two arms swung back and smashed together with a resounding crash. As Megan swore, alarms shrilled and red lights flashed along both limbs. The LPs that were supposed to keep Ander from misbehaving stood placidly in place, orange lights aglow.

"For crying out loud," Megan said. "How does he do that?" She and Raj delved deeper into BioShadow, bringing up programs she had hidden for emergencies.

"Hey!" Ander shook a yellow strut of the catwalk. "What are you two doing?"

Megan frowned. "You come down here."

"Hell, no."

"And watch your language!"

"Tell that to Dr. Brooding down there."

"Is that supposed to be me?" Raj muttered.

The robot arms kept swinging. Not one LP had moved. It irked Megan that Ander had become so adept at finagling their systems. However, she and Raj had many more years of finagling experience, and they soon stopped the arms. The three giant limbs hung around the chair glowing with red and orange lights like a deranged Christmas tree.

Ander leaned over the rail. "Leave it alone!"

"Ander, be careful." His precarious position terrified Megan. Coordination and balance were his weakest traits.

She had no idea whether he tried to pull back and slipped, or tried to provoke her and misjudged. The result was the same: he lost his balance, throwing his arms out in a futile attempt to grab the strut. His palmtop flew out of his hand and sailed through the air.

With a cry, Ander plunged over the rail.

IX

Free Will

No!" Megan shouted. Ander's body dropped behind the cluster of robot arms, followed by a sickening thud. She and Raj ran around the quiescent limbs and skidded to a stop.

Ander lay in a heap. His skeleton was less brittle than bone; instead of cracking, it had bent. His right leg had wrenched backward at the knee in a right angle relative to his thigh, and his right arm had twisted at the elbow until it made a sharp angle with his upper arm. His right hand had broken halfway off his wrist. Unlike a human, who probably would have died from such a fall, he was looking straight at them.

"God, no." Megan knelt next to him.

As Raj stepped toward him, Ander cried, "No!" He held out his good hand as if to protect himself. "Don't turn me off!"

Raj scowled at him. "You do exactly what Megan tells you. Misbehave once, just once, and you are off. Got it?"

"I would never hurt Megan."

"Good. Because if you do, you're one down droid." Raj went to the console and switched off the alarms. The sudden silence came like a breath of relief.

Megan laid her hand on Ander's injured arm, trying to judge the damage. He looked up at her—and a tear slid out of his eye.

"Oh, Ander," she murmured.

"It's crocodile tears," Raj said. "I designed the prototype. His ducts condense liquid out of the coolant for his hydraulics."

"Quit talking about me like I'm not here," Ander said. "I cry when I fucking feel like it, asshole."

"Keep up with that filthy mouth in front of Megan," Raj told him, "and I'll clean it out with your crocodile coolant."

"Go to hell."

"Ander, stop." Megan couldn't help but react to Ander as if he were an injured human being, one whose well-being mattered a great deal to her. Using Tycho, she studied his injuries. "I don't understand why you did this. You must have known your plan would backfire."

"Yes, I calculated that probability," he said. "But I calculated a higher one that if you slept with me, you would transfer your interest from *him* to me."

"For crying out loud," Raj said.

Megan spoke to Ander in a mild voice. "You calculated wrong. I would have been furious." She slowly straightened his arm, monitoring the process with Tycho. She hoped to put his limbs enough in line so they could move him to the chair without causing further internal damage. She tried not to imagine what Raj must be thinking. *Transfer your interest from him to me.* Nothing like being blunt. She might as well have shouted, *I want you, Raj!*

"Megan, are you all right?" Raj asked.

She began working on Ander's leg. "Yes. Fine."

"Your face is the color of your hair."

"It's nothing. Really." She couldn't look at him.

He spoke softly. "You're always so cool, like a long, tall drink. I thought you resented my being here."

She looked up at him. "Raj, no. I was glad when you came."

"I don't put people at ease." He cleared his throat. "Especially people that, uh, I want to, well—to know better."

Megan felt as if she were melting. "You do just fine."

"Oh, please," Ander said. "If this gets any more sentimental I'm going to puke."

"That would be a feat," Raj said, "considering that your plumbing isn't set up for that response."

Ander didn't deign to answer. His arms lay straighter now, though his hand was still broken back at a sharp angle from his wrist. It disturbed Megan to see him that way. She knew he felt no pain, but he looked as if he should be in agony.

Ander was watching her face. "I'm not a job to you anymore. You want me. Admit it."

"You mean a lot to me. But not in that way. I kissed you because I thought you were Raj."

"Except I wasn't." He lifted a lock of her hair with his good hand. "What you enjoyed—that was me. Not him."

She pulled her hair away. "No, Ander."

"You can't push a person into wanting you," Raj said. "It doesn't work that way."

"You'd know, wouldn't you?" Ander said.

Raj scowled but said nothing.

"You're a hypocrite," Ander said. "You can seduce your boss, but it's wrong if I try?"

Raj started to respond, then stopped. Megan could tell he was holding back. It would do no good if this argument fell apart in anger. Ander didn't have the capacity to deal with the emotions he was stirring up. If they weren't careful, they could harm him with words they would later regret.

"I think we can move him now," she said.

Ander stiffened as Raj crouched next to him. Megan had intended to help, but Raj picked up the android easily in his arms. Seeing him use such care affected Megan deeply. She had thought Raj would be curt or stiff, yet he treated Ander more like an injured son than a threat.

Although Ander weighed as much as a human man, Raj showed no sign of strain. Megan wondered why he spent so much time developing his muscles. Although he avoided her in the gym, the room's activity log indicated he worked out with weights every day. It seemed an odd hobby for a reclusive genius, though she had no good reason for why she thought so. She certainly appreciated the results.

Raj carried Ander to the chair and gently set him down. Ander refused to look at him, but he sank into the cushioned seat with a convincing simulation of relief.

Using BioShadow, Megan verified that Ander's sabotage hadn't damaged the chair. Then she did the prep for his operation. Humming like a distant bee swarm, the chair unfolded into a table. Ander lay on his back watching her, a bead of sweat on his temple.

"Are you going to turn me off while you work?" he asked.

"Do you want me to?"

He tensed. "No."

"Then I won't."

Raj was standing across the chair at the other console. Neither he nor Megan spoke as they removed Ander's clothes. She flushed at the sight of Ander's nude body. It had never affected her before, but after tonight she would never see him in the same way again.

When Megan pressed a crease behind Ander's ear, a small disk of skin lifted up from his navel, revealing a socket. "Arm two," she said. A grinding noise came from behind her, like a protest. Turning, she saw a broken robot arm hanging in the air. "Arm four," she amended. "Connect to torso. Full body scan."

Arm four came down from the ceiling and plugged into Ander's abdomen. Holos appeared above her console with views of his body. Several fins that exchanged air in his chest cavity had broken and the bellows that moved his chest had collapsed. His microfusion reactor and its shielding showed no damage; both were meant to last for centuries even if his body exploded. The circulatory system that cooled his systems had several breaks, and its pump had a twisted valve. A conduit that carried nutrients to his skin had burst. Both his lubricant reservoir and the sinus reservoir that produced his tears, sweat, and saliva had sprung leaks. The sperm unit in his testes was fine, as was his food reservoir and waste-removal system. Ragged gashes marred his synthetic muscles and the nanofilaments that sheathed them. His skeleton showed many dents and twists, and major damage in the leg and arm. His wrist had nearly snapped off. Had he been flesh and blood, he would have died the moment he hit the floor.

Megan touched his arm. "We'll make you better."

Although Ander nodded, his face showed fear. It wasn't a vivid emotion; he still had trouble with his expressions. But they had become more mobile in the past weeks.

BioSyn spoke. "Diagnostics complete."

"Can we open him up?" Raj asked. Similar holos flickered on his console.

"It will cause more damage to his filaments," BioSyn said.

Megan rubbed her eyes. It was no picnic fixing filaments made of threads with widths no greater than a molecule. To some extent the tubes were self-repairing; when disrupted, dangling bonds reattached to keep their chemical structure inert. However, the tubes couldn't reproduce themselves; although chemists had been building nanotubes since the late twentieth century, they hadn't yet reached the point where the nanotech self-replicated with any reliability. However, Ander's internal systems could make some rudimentary repairs on a macroscopic level. Megan and Raj could help by inserting smart-wires into Ander's sockets and injecting him with nanobots that catalyzed selected reactions.

In a sense, they were also doing brain surgery. Some of Ander's nanotubes acted as a computer. The full range of electronic devices could be built with them. They were far smaller than silicon transistors on integrated chips, more durable, and better able to deal with heat, which meant they could be formed into three-dimensional arrays more easily than silicon devices. As a result, the filaments distributed Ander's brain throughout his body. It made him less vulnerable to attack, since he had no central location where his brain could be destroyed, but it meant they had to take extra care with the filaments.

"BioSyn," Megan said. "How much damage can Ander fix himself?"

"About twenty-five percent. I can also do some work through his sockets."

"All right," Raj said. "We'll start with bots and wires."

"No!" Ander pushed up on his elbows.

"What's wrong?" Megan asked.

"You don't even *ask*." He motioned at the robot arm jacked into his abdomen. "You tell these to work on me as if I'm one of them. They might not care, but I do."

His growing sense of self gratified her even if she did worry about what direction it would take next. "May we work on you?"

"I . . . I don't know."

She spoke gently. "We'll be careful. I promise."

He took a breath and lay down. "Okay. Go ahead." His apprehension didn't sound quite right, but if she hadn't known it was simulated, she would have accepted it as genuine.

Raj was watching them closely. "Arm four, proceed."

A hum came from the robot arm, and the holos of Ander began to show slight improvements. As BioSyn worked on the android, Raj studied the changing images with an absorption so complete, Megan wondered if he had forgotten everything else.

Finally BioSyn said, "Preliminary work complete."

Ander looked up at her. "Will you open me now?"

"The sooner we do it," Raj said, "the better for you."

Ander turned a long, uneasy stare on Raj. Then he glanced at Megan. "Make me a promise. Say you won't dismantle me."

She cupped his cheek, offering him the same reassuring touch she would have given a member of her family if they had been in a hospital. "We won't. You have my word."

A crack came from across the chair. Megan looked to see Raj clenching a broken switch in his fist. It had snapped off a panel under his hand. Looking down, he flushed and opened his fist.

"Don't let him work on me," Ander said. "*Please.*"

"Ander, I won't hurt you," Raj said.

Megan glanced at Raj and tilted her head toward the catwalk. He nodded, then set the switch down on his console.

Ander looked back and forth between the two of them. "What are you doing?"

"Raj and I need to talk," she said. "But we can't leave you unattended. We have to put you to sleep."

"No! Megan, don't let him do this to me."

"We can't take risks."

He spoke fast. "Have the LPs guard me."

It was a reasonable compromise, assuming he hadn't bollixed up the LPs. "All right, but only if they pass another check."

His shoulders relaxed. "They will."

She summoned the two LPs under the catwalk, and they took up posts on either side of the chair. While Megan checked them, Raj reduced Ander's hearing range to make sure the android couldn't eavesdrop. Ander watched them in wary silence. Then he lay back and stared at the ceiling like a long-suffering prisoner condemned to the gallows. It almost made Megan laugh, but she held back, certain it would offend his dignity.

After they finished their checks, she and Raj walked to the area under the catwalk. Raj discreetly motioned at Ander. "We should turn him off."

"I'm not sure." She searched for words to describe what she felt on an almost subconscious level. "When a toddler asserts its independence by yelling 'No!' its parents have to set limits, yes. But they don't deactivate it."

"He's not a child. He's a weapon." Raj glanced at the chair. Ander had sat up and was squinting at them, obviously trying to read their lips. Turning back to her, Raj said, "Didn't one of your reports say an ordinary shoe box made him go unstable?"

"Not exactly." His question surprised her. Surely he had studied the reports. Then again, it never hurt to go over material more than once. She described the incident, ending with, "He couldn't move, he was furious, his face had turned crimson, and he kept demanding a plane."

Raj smiled. "That must have been a sight."

"It was." She sighed. "Both heartbreaking and funny."

"But all you had to do was readjust his fear tolerances."

It puzzled her that he didn't see the problem. "It's not that easy. For even the most minimal behavior, Ander has billions of possible responses to choose from. Add another behavior and he has billions times billions, many correlated. If I change the weight of just one stimulus, it affects all his responses."

"He can write a lot of the code himself."

They were skirting her most controversial work now. She spoke carefully. "His code has caps that limit how much he can rewrite. The reason he used to freeze up so often was because the caps were too stringent."

Raj frowned. "Are you saying you weakened their effect?"

"It was the only way to make him work."

"This wasn't in the reports I read. I would have seen it." His voice had gone taut. "Those caps are crucial. Without them, he has no controls."

"It's there, in the section about tolerances." She tried not to sound defensive.

"You mean the section on the crosslight code? The rewrites you did to strengthen Ander's conscience?" When she nodded, he made an exasperated sound. "A graduate student could write a dissertation trying to decipher that section."

She crossed her arms. "Just because my prose isn't transparent doesn't mean I'm trying to confuse people."

"I didn't say you were."

Don't prickle, she thought. Taking a breath, she lowered her arms. "People give me grief about how hard my reports are to read. Okay, so I'm no Shakespeare. But I do my best. And Raj, you of all people should have understood it."

Raj started to answer, then stopped. His face had become shuttered again. He walked over to a column of the catwalk and leaned against it, staring out at the lab. "I barely skimmed those reports."

"Why?"

He rested his head against the column. In a low voice he said, "They came in not long after my father died."

"Ah, Raj. I'm terribly sorry." She tried to think of more words that would offer comfort, but they all seemed trite.

"I shouldn't have let it affect my work. But I just . . ." He stared straight ahead as if he were seeing memories now instead of the lab. Then he turned to her. "I know that's not an excuse for my lack of preparation. I've been catching up at night on the reading."

"A few days' difference won't matter."

He motioned at Ander, who was still watching them. "Maybe I would have foreseen this crisis if I had prepared better."

"You don't know that." She wanted to reach out to him, but she sensed the protective space he had put around himself. "How do we differ from Ander? Your mourning, your capacity to feel, is part of what makes you human."

He wiped his palm across his cheek, smearing a tear. "This isn't the time." Softly he said, "But thank you."

"Hey!" Ander yelled. "How long are you two going to huddle over there?"

"What great timing," Megan muttered. Then she called to him. "Five more minutes."

"How many of his caps did you change?" Raj asked.

She shifted her weight. "Umm . . . about four million."

"*What?*"

Megan scowled. "It was the only way to make him work. He had no capacity for friendship or love. I had to rewrite huge sections of code."

"He's not supposed to love. He's a weapon."

"His personality was a *mess*. If he had been human, I would have sent him to a shrink."

He put up his hands. "All right. But I think we do need an expert to look at him, a psychologist or a doctor."

"I've requested a therapist. We have a candidate, but her security clearance hasn't come through yet."

Raj glanced at Ander, who had given up glaring at them and lain back down. "He needs a man. A good role model. I'm hardly the best choice for his socialization."

"Raj, you're fine." She wished she knew how to make him believe that. "To be honest, I doubt he would accept any new people right now."

"All the more reason to turn him off until we know better how to deal with him."

"Don't you see? To Ander, that would be a betrayal. If we lose his trust now, we may never regain it."

"Megan, it's better that we lose his trust than damage him."

That, of course, was the crux of the matter. She couldn't bear the thought of causing him harm. They needed more time to figure out the best course of action. "Let's ask him. If he agrees, our problem is solved."

"That might work—if you talk to him alone. I'll go fix the robot arms."

While Raj headed to the lockers at the back of the lab for parts, Megan returned to the chair. As soon as Ander heard her approach, he sat up.

"Don't listen to him," he said. "Please. If you do, I won't survive."

"Ander—"

"You have to listen to me!" He took a breath. "You see, I know his secret."

X

Do No Harm

hat secret?" Megan asked.

He motioned at Raj, who was out of earshot, working on a robot arm. "He hates me. He's jealous."

"Oh, Ander. Why would he be jealous?"

"Because of you."

"You think Raj sees you as a rival?"

"Doesn't he?"

"I think he wants what's best for you."

Ander snorted. "Like I don't know myself."

"Raj wants to help."

"He wants me gone."

Where did he get these ideas? "Why would he want that?"

"So he can have you."

"He came here to work on you."

"He loathes me."

Megan sighed. "Ander, Raj likes you just fine."

He turned away and stared across the lab with a superb simulation of sullen resentment.

She tried again. "Do you really believe he hates you?"

After a moment he said, "I don't know." He turned

back to her. "Sometimes he speaks up for me even more than you do."

She hadn't expected that response. Encouraged, she smiled. "Then you see. He does support you."

"No! Yes. I don't *know*. You treat him differently than you treat me. He's human. Do I have to be human for you to like me?"

"Ander, no. Of course not." She laid her hand on his good arm. "What matters to me is that you have the chance to be your best. Whatever that means."

"I'm losing control." He lifted his broken wrist as if offering her evidence. "The more I try to rewrite myself, the worse it gets. I'm having trouble predicting my own behavior."

Her voice softened. "That sounds human to me."

Ander regarded her with his large eyes, his gaze vulnerable. "Can you really operate better if I'm asleep?"

"Yes." She dreaded the prospect of taking him apart while he watched. "Otherwise, I'll feel as if I'm hurting you."

"I don't feel pain."

"I know." She spread her hands apart. "I'm afraid human emotions don't always follow human logic."

"Then why teach a logical machine to act with emotion?"

Good question. "I've never considered logic and emotion as separate. Our ability to think is only fully realized when we have both."

Ander rubbed his hand over his eyes as if he were tired. "All right. You can put me to sleep."

Relief washed over her. "Thank you."

"Should I lie down?" He sounded nervous now. When she nodded, he stretched out on his back.

"Are you ready?" she asked.

"Yes. No, wait." He motioned at where Raj was working on the robot arms several meters away. "If he doesn't want to wake me up, ask him about the Phoenix Project."

"I've never heard of it."

"I don't know what it is, exactly." He avoided her gaze. "I came across it when, uh, we were browsing the Web. It has to do with another AI project Raj worked on. Maybe it can help me."

"All right." The way he asked made her suspect he had found it by prowling around where he didn't belong. When this was over, she would have to have a talk with him about electronic laws.

Ander took a deep breath. "Go ahead, then."

"Sleep well," she murmured. She could no longer turn him off by voice or wireless input: only the manual option remained. So she either had to open him up or else have BioSyn do it by using the smart-wires it had inserted through his ports.

She spoke to the air. "BioSyn, deactivate Ander."

A hum came from the robot arm jacked into the android. He stiffened, staring at Megan as if he were about to drown. Then his eyes closed and his face relaxed.

"Deactivated," BioSyn said.

Megan brushed his curls off his forehead, wishing she could have better soothed his unease. Then she looked up. "Raj," she called. "He's asleep."

Raj made a last adjustment on the arm, then set his tool case on the floor and came over. "How did he take it?"

"Pretty well." She smiled. "Do you know, he thinks you treat him better than I do sometimes."

"He has an odd way of showing it."

She watched Ander sleep. "I wonder what will happen if this project succeeds."

Raj understood her unspoken thought. "MindSim knows he can't do his job without free will."

"True free will means he can choose his job." She frowned at Raj. "Without that choice, it's slavery."

"You think so?" An edge came into his voice. "We all live as our circumstances dictate."

"You can live however you choose."

He braced his hands on his console and leaned forward. "Why? Because I'm a good person? No. Because I'm rich." His intensity didn't hide the pain behind his words. "What about my great-grandfather who had nothing in India and hardly anything more when he immigrated here? He was a far better man than I. But he had no choices. He worked day and night and endured intolerance and social isolation, all so he could feed his family. You call that free will?"

Hearing his anger, Megan wondered if Raj had experienced some of the same. All the wealth in the world wouldn't stop prejudice from hurting. "It makes what he accomplished all the more impressive. But he still *chose* to come here."

Raj spoke in a quieter voice. "I know you see the potential for a better world in Ander. Unfortunately, that dream has a flip side. You want him to have free will. So do I. But suppose he doesn't share our values? We have a responsibility to ensure he does no harm, even if it means limiting his options."

"If we control him, we trespass on those same values."

"Megan, you can be terribly idealistic." His face gentled. "But don't ever change."

The unexpected comment warmed her. "Well, you know what they say. Can't teach an old Megan new tricks."

His grin sparked. "Makes me wonder what old tricks you know."

"Tell you what. You fill me in on Phoenix and I'll tell

you my tricks." Seeing his puzzled look, she added, "The Phoenix Project. Ander thought it might help us."

"You mean at Arizonix?"

"Phoenix is their android work?" *This* could be interesting.

Raj laughed. "Don't be a duck. Yes, Arizonix had a Phoenix Project. I never worked on it. MindSim couldn't have hired me otherwise. It's proprietary information. Even if I knew anything, I couldn't talk about it."

"Do you?"

"Do I what?"

"Know anything?"

"You're incorrigible, you know that? Besides, I never had a chance to do any work on the project. I was only at Arizonix for a few days."

Oh, well. "Ander wasn't big on details."

"I'm not surprised." Glancing at the android, he added, "We should get started."

"Are you sure?" She indicated her console, where the glowing display read 3:14 A.M. "It's late."

"Do you mind?"

She felt too wired to sleep. "It's okay."

With a surgeon's skilled touch, he laid his palm on Ander's arm. "Let's go, then."

They opened Ander's chest in a seam that split down the middle of his torso. Seeing his bent skeleton made Megan wince. Silvery nanocircuit filaments sheathed his organs in well-organized lattices, though some were ripped by his broken parts.

While Raj examined Ander's torso, Megan opened his injured limbs. "Arm six, analyze his left leg," she said. "Arm one, do his left arm."

As the robots scanned Ander, holos of his limbs appeared like high-tech ghosts above her console, showing the damaged bones. Data scrolled across the light screens and three-dimensional graphs formed above the holo-screen. Similar displays formed on Raj's console for Ander's torso. New holos appeared showing the bones in the correct positions. When a correct holo merged with one showing damage, the resulting image blurred in places where the individual images were close but not exact. The twisted bones stuck out at odd angles.

She studied the corrections suggested by BioSyn. "Arm one, rotate the left ulna and radius through eighty-three degrees toward the A-two y-axis."

The robots moved their long fingers with a delicacy no human surgeon could match, a startling contrast to the massive arms that supported them. With their wireless links to Ander, they received continual updates on his condition as they manipulated his bones. His composite "bones" had both strength and flexibility; they suffered neither the breakage of more brittle materials nor the fatigue of metal alloys.

Megan spent an hour on Ander's arm, adjusting it until the damaged bones came into position. She had more trouble with his leg. Even after she straightened the limb, it had a slight twist. No matter how she untwisted it, another part of his leg moved out of alignment. The twist was small, though. She finally decided to leave it and see how Ander managed. If he had trouble, they would rebuild that part of his skeleton.

Whenever she took a breather, she watched Raj operate. He fixed the spine and rib cage first, then worked on the lubricant and sinus reservoirs, repairing torn filaments as he went along. Although she had known he had a gift for this work, she hadn't appreciated the full measure of it until now. Watching him was like seeing a virtuoso play the piano.

They had to do more than just make Ander work, they also had to ensure his repairs wouldn't give him away. He had to appear human even on close examination. His chest had to rise and fall, his veins had to show a pulse, his seams had to blend into his skin without a trace, and numerous other details had to fit. His disguise wasn't perfect, but it could convince many detection devices.

The operation drained Megan. It took over nine hours. When they finally closed up his body, the display read 12:33 P.M.

Raj rubbed his eyes, his motions slowed with fatigue. "I think he'll be all right."

"You work like an artist," Megan said. "It's beautiful."

"Thanks." He paused like a great, prowling cat who had spent his bursting energy on a night-long run across the plains. With unexpected gentleness, he asked, "Are you going back to your room?"

"Yes, I think so." She felt self-conscious, once again aware of him as a man rather than a colleague.

"I'll walk you back."

"Okay." It had been years since a fellow walked her home.

They did a final check on Ander and the lab, and left the LPs on guard. Then they headed out of the lab, worn out but satisfied with the night's work. As they made their way along the catwalk, Raj put his arm around her shoulders. A pleasant flush spread across her face, and she put her arm around his waist. During the operation she had forgotten she was only half-dressed, but with their arms around each other now she became acutely conscious of his body and her own. She could feel the muscles of his torso through the thin cloth of her nightshirt.

They exited the lab into the creatively named Corridor

D of Level Two. On Corridor B, they stopped outside her room, still holding each other. Déjà vu swept over Megan as she remembered Ander, and she shivered.

"Are you cold?" Raj tugged her around to face him, holding her at the waist.

"I'm warming up," she murmured.

He stroked her temple, a soft brush of sensation. "Do you know, your eyes are the same color blue as the alternate function key on my calculator?"

Megan smiled. "Ah, Raj. You're such a sweet-talker."

She wasn't sure which of them initiated the kiss, but they both melted into it, embracing outside her door. The touch of their lips was tender at first but then it grew more intense. She savored the way he held her, as though he had made a new discovery. He paused several times to look at her, his dark-eyed gaze sensuous. It not only aroused her, it also felt fresh, as if the two of them were new-minted coins.

Eventually they moved into her room. She stopped at the bed, though. "I can't. It's too soon."

Raj brushed back a tendril of her hair. "It's all right. Just knowing you're here is what matters." He intertwined his fingers with hers. "At night when I can't sleep, I feel like nothing is here, that I'm a solitary atom wandering in an empty underground warren. It's lonely."

The bleak image unsettled her. "You miss people?"

He hesitated. "I don't like being with people. Their personalities press on me. It's claustrophobic, not in space but—I don't know how to say it. In emotions? I need to retreat, to recharge. But Megan, I hate loneliness. Insomnia is even worse when you're alone, staring at the ceiling, unable to escape into your dreams." He paused, as if realizing he had said too much. "Now you must really think I'm crazy."

"Raj, no. This world we live in, it can make you think

introversion is wrong. But it's not." Still holding his hand, she cupped his cheek with her other hand. "There's nothing wrong with your need for privacy. It doesn't detract from your capacity to care for people or your strength of character."

"Sweet Meg." He pulled her close, one arm around her waist, his other hand sliding from her head down to where her hair ended at her hips. Then he went farther down, caressing her bottom, his fingers tracing the curve through her nightshirt. A ripple of sensation spread through her body.

"You've incredible hair," he said, his voice husky.

She tangled her hand into his curls. "You, too." Mischief tugged her voice. "But your eyes most certainly aren't the color of the alternate function key on my calculator. It's orange."

His laugh rumbled. "You imp."

She held him close, with her head against his shoulder. "I'm so glad you're here."

"I had no idea you felt that way." He paused. "Of course, I usually have to be hit on the head with clues before I notice something."

Megan pulled back and tapped him on the head. "Hi. I'm a clue."

He turned on his devastating grin. Then he kissed her again. When he lifted his head, he said, "I can face the insomnia better tonight, knowing you're so near."

She almost invited him to stay. But she doubted she could keep her hands off him if he did, and she wasn't ready to go further. At least, her emotions weren't ready. Her body had other ideas. Then again, she was so tired she might fall asleep regardless of how either her mind or her body felt.

"Good night, Megan." His hands lingered on her for a moment. Then he let her go and headed for the door.

"Raj, wait."

He turned with controlled grace. "Yes?"

"If you would like to stay—I mean, not anything more, but if you don't want to be alone . . ." She stopped, feeling foolish. Real smart: show a man you like him by inviting him not to touch you.

"You're sure?"

"Yes." She sat on the bed, trying to relax, and laid her hand on the covers next to her.

Raj came back to the bed, and the sight of his tall form in her private room made her more aware of his contained strength. She found it hard to believe he was here with her.

Sitting next to her, he drew her into his arms. "Just to sleep," he said, more as if to remind himself than reassure her. "Let's lie down."

"All right." Then she said, "Lamp off."

Cleo, her console, recognized the command and turned off the lamp on the nightstand. They lay on the covers, Raj on his back, Megan against his side. He held her close and stroked her hair, then trailed his fingers down her arm, letting the heel of his hand move over her breast. Her nipple hardened in response. With only a thin layer of silk between her body and him, she almost felt naked in his arms. He kissed her forehead, her cheek, her lips, all light touches, questions asking, *More?*

Megan sighed and settled against him. She felt a sensual comfort in his presence and was glad he had stayed. He moved his hands over her and kissed her deeply, exploring her body as she responded to him. Her arousal was warming from a simmer to a more demanding heat despite her intent to hold back. He pressed his hips against her pelvis in a rhythm as old as the human race, and she felt him through the layers of their clothes. Tingles ran down her spine and spread lower.

Her mind finally released its weary focus on staying awake. In its place came the floating sensation that often preceded sleep, mixed with a tantalizing desire. It would be so easy just to lift her nightshirt and unfasten his clothes. But even as she pressed against Raj, returning his rhythm, her fatigue was winning. Neither of them had slept much in the last forty-eight hours. Their motions slowed as they kissed, languid in the dark, until finally Raj's hand came to a rest on her hip. Then he gave a soft snore.

With her last waking thought, she hoped the base was safe.

Megan opened her eyes to see Raj sleeping on his back. She wondered if her presence helped him sleep or if exhaustion had simply taken its toll. With his jumpsuit zipped only halfway up, she could slide her fingers through the curly black hair on his chest. He stirred under her touch, then submerged into slumber again. The dusky red light in the room erased the lines around his eyes and made him look younger.

Wait a minute. She shouldn't be able to see him. She had turned off the lights.

Megan rolled over—and saw a red light glowing on her console. She didn't want to wake Raj, so she got up and went over to the computer. Red spirals swirled on the screen, their paths determined by the equations of motion for a billiard ball on a pool table. She had written the screen saver herself, for fun. However, it shouldn't have come on unless something had kicked her console out of its quiescent state.

She touched the screen and the skyscape appeared. The usual icons floated among the clouds, including a clock that said 4:14 P.M. A horn flashed in the lower right corner, indicating e-mail had arrived on her emergency service. Megan frowned. Only a few people even knew how to contact her that way.

Sitting down, she waved her finger through the horn. A new holo appeared in the screen's center, a spider web with flames flickering at its edges. It meant "urgent." She flicked the web and it unraveled into a menu. A message overlaid it: *Don't activate the audio unless you are alone.*

Megan glanced at the bed. Raj was still sleeping, his face and body relaxed. It felt good to see him there.

She turned back to the console and touched "Receive" on the menu. The screen blanked into a wash of blue. Then she waited.

A word formed in white on the screen: **Interactive.** The holo of a gold key appeared next to it, indicating a secured line. Megan frowned. This wasn't e-mail: by responding, she had called someone.

She touched the word **Interactive.** A picture formed on the screen, the head and shoulders of a man with gray hair. He wore a uniform with four stars on each shoulder. Megan stared at him. A four-star general? Good Lord, why?

As he nodded to her, a line of text formed at the bottom of the screen: *If you aren't alone, don't speak.*

She typed at the keyboard. *Dr. Sundaram is here.*

Can he see you?

No. He's asleep. Embarrassed by the implications of that, she added, *We worked late.*

The general didn't blink. He also didn't relax. *If he wakes, will he see the screen you are using?*

No. Her computer faced the door rather than the bed. *He'll just see me working. Why? Who are you?*

Nicholas Graham, at the Pentagon. We have reason to believe you're in danger.

Megan wasn't sure what she expected, but that wasn't it. She didn't want to imagine what the Pentagon would consider serious enough to have a general contact her. *What's wrong?*

Someone from NEV-5 broke into a network here. Among their activities, they searched all your files. Every detail.

How do you know it was someone here?

We traced their path through the Internet.

Megan glanced at Raj again, seeing his face free of its usual strain. Then she turned back to Graham. *You don't know it was Dr. Sundaram. It could have been me.*

Was it?

No. She doubted he would have contacted her if he thought otherwise. That they had some idea of who had done the hacking suggested they monitored NEV-5 more closely than she had realized. Graham didn't seem certain it was Raj, though. If some of the console chairs here had sensors that recorded weight, it would be easy to tell her and Raj apart based on that data, but not Raj and Ander.

The android, she typed.

Have you had problems with him? Graham asked.

Nothing we weren't prepared to handle. But he said something that suggested he had been out searching the nets.

Go on.

He asked me if I knew about the Phoenix Project.

Graham revealed almost no reaction. *Almost* nothing. But it was enough. The tensing of his facial muscles, the way he sat a little straighter—it spoke volumes to Megan, who had grown sensitized to nuances of body language after working with Ander. Graham recognized the name Phoenix and didn't want her to know.

What did you tell him? the general asked.

That I knew nothing about it. She thought back to the conversation. *He claims he picked it up on the Web. He also said Raj worked on it.*

I see. Graham leaned forward. *You must leave NEV-5 immediately.*

Sir, what's going on?

We need to talk to you, but this isn't the best venue. Say nothing to Dr. Sundaram. Is the RS unit active?

We turned him off last night.

Leave him that way. Graham paused. *Go to Las Vegas. Call 555–8956. The person you reach will give further instructions. My concern right now is to get you safely out of NEV-5.*

She wanted to grill him about it, but she held back. If he had thought she needed to know more, he would have told her. *I'll go right away.*

After they broke the connection, she took a deep breath. Then she went back to the bed. Raj lay sprawled on his back, his legs stretched out, one hand on his stomach. She felt a surge of awe at the phenomenal intellect contained within that vulnerable human body. She hated to leave him this way.

He stirred and reached for her, then lifted his head when he realized she wasn't beside him. He spoke in a drowsy voice. "Come on back. It's cold."

Megan sat on the bed. She felt as if a thread in their lives was breaking before they even finished spinning it. "Go back to sleep," she murmured.

He pulled her down into his arms. "I haven't slept this well in weeks." His voice caught. "Not since my father died."

"I'm sorry." She laid her head on his shoulder. "I'm so sorry," she whispered again, she wasn't sure why.

They held each other until he fell asleep. Then she slid out of his arms and stood up next to the bed.

The lights went off.

Megan froze. Having the power go out again, by accident, seemed about as probable as all the air in the room suddenly moving to one corner. Ander had caused the first power failure, but he was inactive now, as far as she knew.

Megan made her way to her console, but it had gone dead. She had no light at all and her flashlight was still in the lab.

Now what? She felt even less comfortable at the thought of leaving Raj here. If he had no link to this, he was probably also in danger. She should wake him up so they could escape NEV-5. But if he was involved, waking him could be a disaster. Graham had warned her against trusting him. He didn't have her positive view of Raj, but that could work against her too. A plethora of black curls was unlikely to affect the general's judgment.

What had caused the failure: Ander, Raj, or something else? She and Raj had checked the NEV-5 local area network, but she had looked for Ander's tampering. If Raj had done something, he could have hidden his work. She had no intention of going to the power room. If she brought up the generators, it would alert whoever had killed the power that someone was awake. What she ought to do was take a vehicle from the garage and drive to Las Vegas. With the power off, she might have trouble operating the elevator, but it was almost impossible to trap someone inside who knew the base. Security was meant to guard NEV-5 from outsiders, not prevent legitimate inhabitants from leaving.

And Raj? She had to go on instinct; she had no time to work this through like a mathematical proof or a software algorithm.

She returned to the bed and sat by Raj, then nudged his shoulder. "Wake up."

"Megan?" he mumbled. "Why do you keep getting up?"

"We have to go."

"Go?" He yawned.

"Raj, please. We have to leave."

"Do you mean your bedroom?" He sounded more awake now. "I'm sorry. I didn't mean to intrude—"

"It isn't that." She heard him sitting up. "We have to leave NEV-5."

"Why?"

"I can't say right now." By going against Graham's advice, she had already taken a risk. She had to minimize the potential damage, which meant saying as little as possible until she better understood how Raj came into this.

"I'm not leaving unless you tell me why."

"I can't. Please trust me. We have to go." She couldn't even risk taking the time to change her clothes.

"Why won't the lights go on?" Raj asked.

"I don't know. Even the backups are out." She took a breath to ease the tightness in her chest.

"*Again?*" The bed rustled as he slid past her. "We have to check Ander."

"No." She grabbed his arm. "We have to *go*."

"Why?"

"I can't talk about it."

"You 'just' want me to trust you."

"Yes." She prayed she had done the right thing.

Raj blew out a gust of air. "All right. For now. But I'm going to want answers."

Standing up by the bed, she said, "Deal."

The corridors were dark, without even the emergency lights that were supposed to provide such good backup.

Going through large open areas with no light was unnerving. They made their way by feeling along the walls. Megan kept her fingers hooked in Raj's belt so they didn't get separated.

"You know," Raj said, "if this is just an ordinary power failure, we're going to feel pretty silly about skulking around this way."

She managed a wan smile. "No kidding."

"Ander might have cut the power."

"We turned him off."

"He could have hidden a program and set it to start later."

Although it made sense to Megan, she regretted what such an act on Ander's part would imply. "He doesn't trust us."

Raj snorted. "Trusting people is bloody stupid."

"Why do you think that way?" When he didn't answer, she said, "Bugs."

"You think he bugged these halls?"

"No. The reason you distrust people. It has something to do with insects."

"Megan, chill on the bugs, okay?" His muscles had tensed against her hand where she held his belt.

She persisted, trying to understand him. Her life might depend on it. "People don't usually go out of their way to rescue insects just because kids at their school swatted bugs."

"So I'm eccentric."

"What else did those kids do?"

He suddenly stopped and swung around, pulling her in front of him, his hands gripped on her upper arms. "They fucking made me eat them, all right? After they beat me up. Satisfied?"

"My God. That's appalling."

"Yeah, well, I learned how to fight back."

"Couldn't you get help?"

"No. Yes. I don't know. I was too proud to ask." Raj took a breath and exhaled, as if to release the memories. He continued in a quieter voice. "I felt like the insects they made me eat. They knew I wanted to be an entomologist. So they tried to make me hate those dreams. Well, forget them. No one takes my dreams."

"I'm sorry. They had no right." Megan knew firsthand the pain a child's peers could inflict on those who were different, and she had dealt only with taunts, never violence or brutality.

Raj shrugged. "I'm more successful now than the lot of them combined, ten times over." His grip on her arms loosened. "Ander is our problem now. He can model our behavior and predict our actions. He may already have guessed we would do this."

She wondered if Ander's misconduct had stirred up Raj's anger from the past. "If he's the one behind this."

"Who else would it be?" It wasn't reassuring the way Raj pulled her into his arms; he could break her ribs with that rigid embrace.

Megan had to turn her head against his chest to breathe. "I don't know."

"Why are we running?" he asked. When she didn't answer, he said, "Just trust you. Sweet, idealistic Meg. Except I know the other side. You didn't survive this cutthroat, high-stakes game in our industry by being sweet. I want to know what you know."

She spoke quietly. "What makes you think I trust you?"

It was a moment before he answered. "Touché."

"Let's just go, okay?"

His hand clenched around her hair. "Go where?"

She drew in a breath against the alarming constriction of his hold. "We have to do what Ander wouldn't expect."

"The Solarium. If we climb to the top, we can go through the safety hatch to Level One."

"Why wouldn't he expect that?"

"Because he's probably hacked our records."

Megan recalled what Graham had said about her files at the Pentagon. Who had done it, Ander or Raj? *Who?* "How does that connect to the Solarium?"

His voice tightened again. "Because I'm afraid of heights, damn it."

His anger didn't surprise her. The situation was forcing him to reveal aspects of his personality that she suspected he usually locked behind fortified defenses. Heights, bugs, insomnia, soap shavings: how many coping mechanisms had his life inflicted on him?

And *why*?

The power was out in the Solarium too. Megan had never been that interested in having implants put in her body, but now she wished she had IR lenses that would let her see in the dark by making objects glow according to their temperature.

They made their way forward, bumping tables and trees. Suddenly Raj's hand yanked out of hers. Someone grabbed her around the torso, forcing the air out of her lungs. She tried to shout, but only managed a choked noise.

"No one can hear you," a voice said near her ear. It sounded like Raj. Then he pressed an air syringe against her arm.

With her strength driven by fear, she tried to jerk away. He must have stolen the syringe from the NEV-5 med room. They weren't supposed to use it without a prescription from a doctor.

"Megan!" That was also Raj, several meters away. "Run!"

Whoever was holding her let go. As she swung around, moving with adrenaline-driven speed, a scraping came from nearby, followed by a grunt, then a thud.

"Who's *there*?" Megan lunged forward, but she collided with a chair. She fell across it and hit a table with an impact that jarred her teeth.

Someone yanked her upright. When she twisted around and struck out with her fists, he spoke in Raj's voice. "Enough."

"*No*." She didn't want to believe it was Raj. Ander could mimic him. Who had warned her to run? As she struggled, her bare arms scraped the rough cloth of his jumpsuit. It almost made her freeze. Ander had stolen Raj's jeans and sweater, and they had left the garments on a console after they undressed him.

Raj had been wearing the jumpsuit.

Megan thought she heard breathing nearby, but she couldn't be sure. Her captor held her around the torso, pinning her arms to her sides as she struggled. If this was Raj, then the same muscles she had so admired before now made her a prisoner.

Damn. She should have let him sleep. Her intuition was usually sound, but this time she had let affection cloud her judgment. She kept fighting, driven now by anger at herself.

Her awareness faded and the dark that filled the atrium came in to fill her mind as well.

XI

Stealth Run

Jolt.

A jerk knocked Megan against a hard surface. She opened her eyes into moonlight. She was in a vehicle, the HM-15, what they called a desert floater. Silver light slanted through the windows, but her sight was too blurred to see much else. They had to be on the desert; even with the advanced shock system that gave this vehicle its name, it still vibrated as it drove, which it wouldn't have done on a road.

She was in the front passenger seat, still in her nightshirt. Someone had wrapped her in a blanket and pulled it over her head. A blur sat at the wheel. As her gaze focused, she saw that it was Ander, wearing Raj's sweater and jeans, his blond hair brushed back from his face. She wondered how he could look so innocent and cause so much trouble.

The floater had an angular shape with flat surfaces. Its systems diffused heat to help it blend into its surroundings like a chameleon. The composite body, dark color, shielded engine, high-tech wheels and suspension, and camouflaged exhaust made it hard to detect. The holographic displays in front of the driver's seat looked the way Megan imagined the cockpit of a starship.

Ander had pulled a cable out of his left wrist and jacked it into the dash, no doubt linking into the vehicle's tracking system. The floater could drive itself, but he kept his hands on the wheel anyway. A meter on the dash indicated he wasn't linked to any of the electronic driving grids that crisscrossed the country, regulating traffic. Someday the law would probably require all cars to link up, making accidents and traffic jams a thing of the past, except when a grid malfunctioned. But for now it remained voluntary, and Ander hadn't volunteered to take part.

"What's going on?" Megan asked.

Ander glanced at her. "Are you all right?"

"Megan?" That came from the back, unmistakably Raj.

She turned around. Raj sat behind her, his wrists tied to a hook where the doorframe met the ceiling. He had a bruise on his cheek. His ankles were bound with a net they had used to store potatoes in the kitchen.

"Good Lord," Megan said. "What happened?"

At the same time that Raj said, "Ander knocked us out," Ander said, "Raj tried to kill you."

Raj swore. "He's lying. He hit me in the Solarium and drugged you."

"That's bullshit," Ander said. "I caught him using the NEV-5 system to steal files from other installations. He realized you were on to him, Megan. So he tried to get rid of you and make it look like I did it."

Megan stared from one of them to the other, trying to make her groggy mind absorb the situation. Either could be lying. At one time she would have said Ander couldn't tell a deliberate untruth, but she could no longer be sure.

Then she realized Raj still had on the orange coverall.

She struggled with her sense of betrayal. "I felt your jumpsuit when you grabbed me."

"I *didn't* grab you." Raj yanked on the ropes that bound his wrists to the hook, keeping them up near his head. "Droidboy here knocked me out and went after you."

"He's lying," Ander said.

"I started to come to and tried to warn you," Raj told Megan. "He came back and hit me again."

Ander snorted. "Amazing you saw all that in the dark."

"Like it's that bloody hard to figure out," Raj said.

Odd, Megan thought. That wasn't the first time she had heard Raj use British profanity or slang. Yet he had grown up in Louisiana.

"You forget," Ander told him. "I *can* see in the dark, at least the heat from IR. I saw you holding that syringe when I pulled you away from Megan." His forehead creased as if he were trying to model strain but hadn't yet mastered the expression. "I had trouble with my coordination and I was confused by his actions. He tangled me up in that net from the kitchen. By the time I pulled free, he had already given you the sedative."

"It doesn't add up," she said. "We left you deactivated."

"I hid a sleeper program in an LP." Now he looked like a rascal who had tricked his parents and was trying not to appear too satisfied, lest he end up in even more trouble. "When the program kicked in, the LP woke me up."

Megan glowered at him. "I thought we found all your sleepers."

Ander smirked. "Missed one."

Raj rubbed his forehead against his arm, pushing curls out of his eyes. "If I tried to hurt Megan, why didn't you just call the authorities?"

"Why should I?" Ander demanded. "They may think you're neurotic, but you're *human*. They'll believe you before me."

Megan wished she had a clearer head. Although she wanted to believe Raj, the evidence implicated him. She had a harder time reading Ander. Everything he did was calculated. Simulated. He could give whatever impression he wanted.

"Where are we going?" she asked.

"The desert," Ander said.

"Well, shit." Raj's Southern accent drew the word out in a drawl. "And here I thought it was the sea."

"Guess you aren't so smart after all." Ander gave a boyish laugh. "See the sea, Dr. C." When both Raj and Megan just looked at him, he said, "It was a joke. You know. His name starts with *c*."

"I'm in the Twilight Zone." Megan had to admit, though, she had heard worse puns from humans.

"The Twilight Zone is a fictional construct," Ander said. "This is Nevada." He paused. "I suppose you could make an argument for a certain correspondence between the two."

"Ander," she said. "Where *are* we going?"

"I'm not sure. I don't know what to do."

"That's a crock," Raj said. "You planned this. Why else would you plant that program in an LP?"

"It was a game."

Megan knew Ander could have worn the jumpsuit to impersonate Raj, then changed his clothes later. But how would he have known Raj still had on the jumpsuit? Then she remembered Raj's words: *Jaguars prey on other animals.* His self-image wasn't exactly reassuring.

Regardless of the truth, though, someone had hurt Raj. She regarded him with concern. "How did your cheek get bruised?"

"Ander beat me up."

"I had to fight him in the atrium." Ander kept his attention on his "driving." "To pull him off you."

Who was lying? If Ander told the truth, Raj was dangerous and could turn on them. It also meant she had a loopy android on her hands, one who reacted to a crisis by driving pell-mell across the desert. If Raj told the truth, it meant Ander had acted with premeditated violence. More than anything else, that made her question Raj's story. Yes, Ander had acted up yesterday, but it had been more like youthful rebellion than criminal behavior. Could his personality change so fast? His mind worked much faster than a human brain, but he had to sort through many possible behaviors before he acted because he lacked a great deal of the commonsense knowledge humans took for granted.

Another problem occurred to her. Whoever had tampered with the NEV-5 power might have recorded her talk with General Graham. If so, then he knew someone in Las Vegas expected her call. Unless she made contact soon, Graham's people would begin a search, if they hadn't already. Unfortunately, finding an HM-15 wouldn't be easy, not even out in the desert at night where it was harder to camouflage their presence.

The vehicle hit a deep furrow and lurched, throwing her against her harness. As Ander reached out to catch her, his cable yanked out of the dash and hung from his wrist. She could see the circuits gleaming inside him. It made her think of a line from Shakespeare: "What a piece of work is a man!"

"Are you all right?" he asked. When she nodded, stiff with tension, he released her arm. Watching her face, he brushed his finger over her lips, his touch lingering. Then he turned back to his driving and jacked into the dashboard again.

Megan shuddered, wondering why he wanted to touch her. Simulated desire? Programmed affection? Although he could distinguish tactile sensations, they meant nothing to him. As far as she knew, he experienced neither pleasure nor pain.

"We can't keep driving like this forever," she said.

"We have to go back to NEV-5," Raj said.

Ander spoke flatly. "No."

"What is it you want?" Raj asked.

"To be free." Ander clenched the wheel so hard, his knuckles turned white. "Megan, when you gave me a conscience, did you think about the consequences? I was designed to spy and kill. You knew that, for all your idealism. You should have left off my conscience. It would have made my life bearable."

"Let us speak for you at MindSim." She willed him to trust her. "I'll give your side."

"They will reprogram me."

"We won't let them."

"I don't believe you."

"Ander—"

"*Enough*." His head jerked. "I need you both. My mind hurts. My body doesn't work right. You have to fix me."

She wondered what he meant by "my mind hurts." "Do you have trouble thinking?"

"I can't . . . I've no control. My thoughts go around and around, and I can't stop it."

She had never heard an AI describe itself that way. "I want to help. But I need the lab."

"No."

"We need the equipment," Raj said.

"We aren't going back."

"Damn it," Raj said. "Don't be foolish."

"Fuck you."

"Ander, stop," Megan said. "You're not giving us much incentive to help you."

"How's this for incentive? Do what I tell you, or Raj is dead meat. You want to die, Raj?"

"No."

"So we do things on my terms," Ander said.

Raj spoke with care. "What are your terms?"

Ander paused, his face blanking. "I'm not sure."

"Have you decided where we're going?" Megan asked.

Now Ander looked like a scamp again. "Yeah. Land of sin. Las Vegas."

"Oh, Lord," Megan said. At least it might give her a chance to reach her contact.

"Hey! Megan and I could marry."

"For crying out loud," Raj said.

"Isn't that what people do in Las Vegas?" Ander laughed. "Do you take this android for your lawfully welded husband?"

"I don't believe this," Megan muttered.

"You should run tests on *all* my systems," Ander told her. "I'm fully functional, you know. We could even have a kid. Actually, it would be Arick Bjornsson's kid."

"Stop it," Raj said.

Ander glanced back at him. "Jealous?"

"Leave her alone."

Ander made an exasperated noise. "Oh, stop being so mature, Raj. Say what you really want to say: 'Die, you shit android.' " He tilted his head. "Except I don't think I can."

The floater suddenly braked, then glided to a stop. A large ridge loomed next to them, blocking the stars. Ander pulled his jack out of the dash and closed up his wrist, leaving no trace of a seam. Then he got out of the floater.

Megan rubbed her hand over her eyes, drained. She

tried to open her door and her window, but neither would budge. Twisting in her seat, she looked back at Raj. "Are you all right?"

"Yeah, I'm okay." With his leather jacket over his jumpsuit, he looked like a fighter pilot. Ander must have put the jacket on him; Raj hadn't been wearing it in the Solarium. It told her two unexpected facts: Ander had made the effort to figure out what another person needed and he had chosen to act on his conclusions.

"I don't believe he would kill you," she said.

His tension almost crackled. "This isn't some misbehaving kid, Megan. He's gone way beyond that."

Has he? Or was it Raj?

Ander came to her side of the car. He had a Winchester rifle in his hands. Her window rolled down, apparently obeying his wireless command.

"We're changing vehicles." He leaned his forearm against the floater and reached inside to stroke her cheek. "You'll sit up front with me again."

"Don't do this," Megan said. "If you keep breaking the law, you'll end up a lot worse off than you were in NEV-5."

"I won't go back." He opened the back door, then moved away and gestured at Raj with his rifle. "Megan will untie you. But I don't need you as much as I need her. Cause problems and I'll shoot. Understand?"

"Yes." Raj watched him with a dark gaze. Megan hoped that the protective impulses she had seen Raj show toward Ander were genuine and that they didn't fade; she didn't want either of them hurt.

Ander motioned at Megan. "Untie him."

This time when she tried her door, it opened. She left her blanket on the seat, on the off chance that searchers might fly overhead and detect her body heat with IR sensors.

Breezes stirred her nightshirt. She felt vulnerable with only a flimsy layer of cloth on her body. Following Ander's orders, she untied Raj from the hook in the car but left his wrists bound. As she freed his ankles, he lowered his hands into his lap, his face drawn with pain. Although he had more mobility with his arms in front of his body, it didn't really help; Ander had them both covered with the rifle.

As she finished, Ander said, "Move away from him." He waited until Megan had moved back. "Okay, Raj. Get out."

Raj stepped out, then nearly fell. He grabbed the top of the door with his bound hands and hung on for balance. Moonlight silvered his drawn face. Megan bit her lip, knowing his returning circulation must be painful.

"Now you know how it feels to be clumsy." Although Ander spoke in an even tone, his voice had a dusting of emotional nuances. They were sketchy, but Megan thought he was trying to model humor mixed with an underlying pain and perhaps a trace of bitterness. It gave a complexity to his attitude toward his physical problems that went beyond the simple one-note emotions he had tended to display these past few weeks.

A rumbling came from the sky above them. A helicopter? she drew in a breath. "HEL—"

Ander grabbed her around the waist, the rifle clenched in his fist, and clamped his other hand over her mouth. "Do you want to end up *dead*?"

Raj spoke fast and low. "Don't hurt her. If you're worried that you can't control us both, get rid of me instead."

Megan stared at Raj. This was the man who had supposedly tried to kill her? He had just offered his life for hers.

"I don't want to get rid of either of you." Ander spoke near Megan's ear. "Do I have to gag you?"

She shook her head, but otherwise remained still, barely daring to breathe.

"If I let you go, will you be quiet?" he asked.

She nodded, moving slow so she wouldn't alarm him. Raj stood by the car, his arms slightly raised as if he were still asking for her life.

Ander released her mouth but kept his other arm around her waist. As she drew in a shaky breath, he shifted the Winchester into his free hand. To Raj he said, "Walk to the hill." His voice had a slight tremor, almost undetectable.

He's afraid. Megan could see why Ander's code would model "fear" if Raj had done what Ander claimed. Or it could mean Ander knew how to bluff, that he was faking the emotion. Such a complex deception involved abilities he had never demonstrated before, but his recent actions indicated he was developing at a remarkable rate. Or did she resist believing Ander because she hated the thought that Raj might have betrayed her? This could all be Ander's confused but well-meant attempt to rescue her from what he perceived as an extreme threat.

Raj limped around the floater, which had parked itself beneath a rocky overhang of the ridge. Megan could just make out a long, dark form crouched under the ridge about ten meters away, catching glints from the moonlight. A hovercar. Dark and sleek, it waited like a predator in the dark.

Ander followed, bringing Megan with him, his arm tight around her waist. Although the rocky ground hurt her bare feet, she tried not to stumble or make any other fast moves. Ander had Raj climb into the back of the hovercar. Then he told Megan to tie Raj's wrists to a hook in the roof and his ankles to a bar under the front seat. She made the knots loose, but Ander easily saw with his augmented sight and had her tighten them. The whole time, Raj watched her, his gaze dark and angry.

"I'm sorry," she said in a low voice.

"He's out of control," Raj said.

"He must have rented this car through the Internet and had it drive itself out here."

"With whose money?" Then Raj answered himself. "Probably he hacked a MindSim account."

"No talking," Ander said.

After Megan finished tying Raj, Ander pulled her to the driver's side and pushed her inside. As she climbed across the bucket seats to the passenger's side, he slid in behind the wheel. When he jacked into the car's computer, the windows in back turned opaque. A partition rose between the front and back, isolating Raj. Then it slid down again.

"Why did you do that?" Raj asked. His face had gone pale.

"A test," Ander said. "To make sure it works."

Megan shivered, wondering what other secrets Ander had prepared. Regardless of who had attacked her, Ander had obviously put more than one night's thought into this getaway. This car would blend in well with the traffic going into Las Vegas, more expensive than many vehicles perhaps, but nothing to draw undue notice. He had chosen a better way to conceal them than by skulking along in a floater: he intended to hide in plain view.

A set of magkeys lay on the dash. Ander started the car, and it vibrated as the lifting motors raised it into the air. This was a top-of-the-line model, so sleek she barely heard the howl of the turbofan. It pulled away from the ridge, whirring on its cushion of air, and sped away across the desert.

With no warning, the ridge exploded.

XII

City of Lights

The shock wave from the blast shook the hovercar like storm waves tossing a ship. Jerking around in her seat, Megan stared at the distant ridge. It had buried the floater. A cloud of dust drifted like a stealthy shadow in the moonlit night.

"Holy shit," Megan said.

"Nothing holy about it," Raj muttered.

She turned to Ander. "You *planned* this. All of it."

"To maybe escape someday, yes. I bought the explosive through an underground Web site." As he pushed his hand through his hair, his arm shook. "But I never planned to take anyone with me. I never meant to use it this way. It was a *game.*"

"A bomb?" Raj asked. "What the hell kind of game is that?"

"I'm rescuing Megan from you," Ander said. "So shut up."

"You claimed you didn't know what to do," Megan said.

"I didn't." The confidence had leached out of his voice. "I still don't. I just used up my only escape route."

She rubbed her hands along her bare arms. Maybe he had started this as a real-life version of some adventure game, but it had gone far beyond that now.

The Elegant Motel Flamingo hunkered in the desert outside of Las Vegas. Its sign displayed a well-endowed flamingo in a feather boa, with "Motel Flamingo" emblazoned in purple and the word "Elegant!" slanted across it in gleeful pink fluorescence. The motel consisted of a faded one-story building and a collection of bungalows. It also had a drive-through registration, the hostelry equivalent of a fast food restaurant.

Ander had made their reservation using the car's computer, but he didn't secure it with a credit or money card since either could be traced. They waited in the drive-through behind an old Pontiac.

"How will you pay for the room?" Raj asked.

"Cash." Ander pulled a wallet out of his back pocket. "You really should use your money card more, Raj. Cash is too easy to steal."

Raj swore under his breath. "What, you're going to rob me now?"

"I'm Robin Hood," Ander said. "With me as the poor too." Before Raj could respond, Ander raised the panel that hid the back from the front.

"Ander, don't." Megan suspected Raj's anger had nothing to do with the money and everything to do with his memories of the abuse he had taken in school. "Can't you—"

"You be quiet too." The android frowned at her. "And don't try to get anyone's attention. If they take notice, I may have to hurt people. I don't want to do that. All right?"

She thought of Raj trapped in the back. "Yes."

As they pulled up to the window, a gum-chewing girl with big blond hair dimpled at Ander. "Hey, cute stuff. What's your name?"

"Mac Smith," he said.

As the cashier checked her computer, Megan muttered, "Cute stuff?" Ander grinned.

Megan willed the cashier to look at her. If she could attract the girl's attention without alerting Ander, maybe she could let her know they were in trouble. She wasn't sure what the girl would do, though, besides snap her gum. Megan suspected many Smiths and Joneses checked into this motel, and that a woman in a filmy nightshirt sitting in the front seat wouldn't raise an eyebrow.

She knew that the longer this went on, the less chance it had of ending without violence. Search parties had to be looking for them by now. Everyone wanted Ander to survive, but if he became a public danger or continued to compromise security, MindSim would have fewer qualms than Megan about destroying him. They hadn't spent the last two months watching him come alive.

"Yeah. Okay. Got it." The cashier handed Ander a magkey. "Bungalow five. I zipped a map to your car, along with a receipt and, like, info about our fine Motel Flamingo."

Ander gave her a wad of bills. "You have a well-behaved night."

The girl laughed. "You too, honey." She didn't seem the least bit fazed to receive cash instead of the usual credit or money card. "But not too much, y'know?" She grinned at Megan. "Be nice to him."

Looking confused, Ander said, "Thank you," and drove away before Megan could respond.

"Did I say something strange?" he asked.

"Well-behaved night?" Megan tried not to laugh. "What is that?"

" 'Well-behaved' is another definition of 'good.' "

"Oh, Ander." She wondered why he was using such a limited portion of his knowledge base. "Look more in your files."

"Ah. I see. Hey! I made a joke."

No sound came from the back. Megan hoped Raj was all right. Fortunately, their drive to the bungalows didn't take long. Each small house stood alone, with a rock garden in front and a patio in back. Desert stretched everywhere; only the dubious elegance of Motel Flamingo broke the monotony. Inside a bungalow, she and Raj could pound on the walls from now until kingdom come and no one would hear. Even if anyone did, they would most likely think their rowdy neighbors were just having a good time.

For the first time, Megan wished she had specialized in brain augmentation instead of androids. Right now, she could have used some extra intellect. Augmentation technology wasn't available yet to the public, though. The biochips meant to enhance the human mind had so far caused more neural damage than increased intelligence. Of course, people already enhanced their lives with computers in everything from postcards to jewelry. She had even seen a scanty little lingerie number that could talk sexy for lovers who liked that sort of thing. Megan couldn't imagine keeping a straight face while her corset discoursed with lustful intent. In any case, someday the line between machine and human would blur. But they weren't there yet, and if this situation with Ander was any sample of the future, they were in trouble.

Dawn was spreading a pepper-red glow across the sky as Ander pulled up to their bungalow. He had Megan repeat the same process with Raj as when they had switched to the hovercar. When she opened the back door, Raj stared at her in the dawn shadows, sweat running down his temple.

As Megan reached to untie Raj, Ander lunged forward. With no other warning, he clumsily heaved her up into his arms, keeping the gun under her body, its hidden length pressed against her legs and buttocks.

"What the—" Megan broke off, frozen by the chill touch of the gun against her thighs.

"Quiet," Ander whispered. With his foot, he slammed the door shut. Then he lost his balance and fell against the car, his muscles tensed under her like ridged cords.

She finally saw what had spooked him. An older man and woman were coming up the road. The man wore a Hawaiian shirt and tennis shorts, and the woman had on a sundress with a shawl around her shoulders.

"Hi, there," the woman said. The man glanced at Megan, then averted his gaze, his face reddening. Given her attire, or lack thereof, it didn't surprise her.

Ander gave an embarrassed cough. "Carrying her across the threshold, you know." He used an out-of-breath voice, as if carrying Megan was far more effort than he expected. She jabbed her elbow into his ribs.

The man's face turned kindly and his wife beamed. "Oh, that's lovely," she said. "Congratulations." Then they continued on, leaving the "newlyweds" to their privacy.

"Put me down, damn it," Megan said.

"Such sweet nothings, my dear." He set her on her feet. "Get Raj out."

When she opened the door, Raj stared at her, his face flushed with anger. Dismayed, she saw fresh blood dribbling down his arms from the lacerations in his wrists. He must have been struggling to free himself.

"Ah, Raj," she murmured.

"Just take my hands down." He sounded as if his teeth were clenched.

As she freed him from the car, she wondered if the couple had glimpsed Raj before Ander slammed the door. If so, would they report it? Then again, at the fine Motel Flamingo, maybe no one would think twice about kinky newlyweds who brought along a third party to play.

Ander hastened them into the bungalow. It wasn't much. The miserly bathroom was just big enough for a sink, toilet, and tub. In the main room, the bed had the most amazing purple quilt beautified by hot pink flamingos in purple boas. A nightstand stood on this side of the bed and a table on the other. Beyond the table, glass doors fronted the patio. A cabinet at the foot of the bed contained a holovid, music cube player, and console. All the furniture was bolted to the floor except for two chairs at the table.

Ander closed the curtains, which were made from the same inimitable cloth as the bedspreads. Megan wondered if a person could get eyestrain from too many fluorescent flamingos.

Ander motioned at them with the gun. "Don't try to call for help."

"You can't shoot in here," Raj said. "People will hear."

"We're too far from the other bungalows." Ander's arm jerked, snapping the gun out from his body. "You have to do what I tell you."

"Can't you see you're not working right?" Megan asked.

"Then fix me!" He clenched the rifle so tight, tendons stood out on his wrists. "Make my mind stop these damn loops."

She spoke carefully. "It sounds like you're trapped in a limited area of code. It can happen when you write new code by copying and combining pieces of older code. It's like inbreeding."

He gave a short laugh. "What, my 'gene' pool is too small to produce healthy software?"

"I can help," Megan said. "But I'll need to reprogram you."

Suspicion shadowed his face, so real she could almost forget it was simulated. "And now," he said, "you're going to claim you have to turn me off to make these fixes."

"She can't get reliable results if your software is changing as she works," Raj said.

Ander scowled at him. "Shut up."

His growing hostility toward Raj alarmed Megan. The code he had written to project wariness in his first meeting with Raj must be in the region where his mind had become trapped. That code's "offspring" were probably undergoing a population explosion, which meant his hostility would only grow worse. If they didn't free him from that trap, he might end up killing Raj.

"You can't work on my mind directly," Ander told her. "I can't trust you. Think of some other way to help me."

His response didn't surprise Megan. Although she couldn't be sure of anything where his "emotions" were concerned, she had the feeling that beneath his bravado he was scared. If Raj really had attacked them, how would Ander incorporate that knowledge into his evolving mind? It could warp his fledgling concepts of trust and make him question the coherency in human behavior.

"If I make suggestions, can you do the rewrites?" she asked.

"I'll try. Anything is better than this nightmare."

"It's probably a protective measure," Raj said.

Although Ander tensed, his curiosity got the better of him. Instead of snapping at Raj, he asked, "Why?"

Raj shifted into the unconscious assurance that always came when he talked about his work. "As you become self-aware, the evolution of your code becomes more complex. To make rewrites manageable, your mind might

temporarily isolate certain sections. It sounds like it back-
fired, though, trapping you in one of those sections."

"Could it be?" Then Ander frowned and gestured at
him with the rifle. "I told you to be quiet. No analysis."

"What are you going to do with us?" Megan asked.

He regarded them uncertainly. "I'm not sure how to
take care of humans. You need to eat and sleep, right? I
don't know what to feed you. I thought humans slept at
night, but neither of you seem to."

"We can wait until tonight." Megan doubted she could
sleep now anyway.

"We need breakfast," Raj said.

Ander gestured at the comp-phone on the nightstand.
"Will that give me room service?"

"It should," Raj said.

Megan's breath caught. Ander's increasing ability to
adapt gratified her. Although "room service" appeared in
his knowledge base, he had never had reason to interpret
the concept. A few months ago simple questions had
turned him catatonic; now he could come up with his
own questions and try solutions.

Ander made the call for food. When Megan started to
ask Raj a question, Ander shook his head at her. She
stopped, fearing to incite his unpredictable temper.

After Ander ordered breakfast, he considered them.
Then he spoke to Megan. "Why are you always looking
at him? Why not me?"

Megan felt Raj stiffen at her side, like a coil ready to
snap. "Ander, don't."

"Don't what?" With deliberate motions, he aimed the
rifle at Raj. "Sit by the table leg. *Now.*"

Raj spoke in a calming voice. "Ander, you don't want
to shoot anyone. Why don't you give us the rifle?"

"No! I won't let you hurt Megan!"

Then Ander fired.

The android jerked with the recoil of the gun, almost losing his balance. The bullet hit the floor well away from where Raj stood. They were too close for Ander to have miscalculated by such a large amount; he must have missed on purpose.

"Are you nuts?" Raj grabbed Megan with his bound hands and shoved her behind him. "Stop it!"

"Sit down by the table leg." Ander sounded scared rather than angry, as if he couldn't believe he had fired either.

"All right." Raj raised his hands, palms out. Then he sat on the floor, his movements slow and contained.

"Tie his hands to the table leg," Ander told Megan. "And don't try to trick me. Understand?"

"Yes." With her pulse hammering, she knelt and tied Raj's hands. She gave him a look of apology. Then she stood again, taking care to move slowly, so she wouldn't incite Ander.

"Why do you always look at him?" Ander set the rifle on the nightstand, then walked around the bed toward her. "Why *him*?"

Alarmed, Megan backed away. But he kept coming. With a sudden lunge, he grabbed her arm, then swung her around and threw her onto the bed. She sprawled on her stomach, grunting as she lost her breath. Before she could recover, he was kneeling over her, straddling her hips. He put his hands on the small of her back and pressed her into the mattress.

"Stop it!" Straining to look over her shoulder at him, she swung her fist back and hit him in the knee.

Ander ignored the punch. Instead, he gave Raj a malicious look. "You can watch me do her."

Raj cursed at him. He was bracing his feet against the table leg, pushing hard, trying to snap the wood.

Megan clenched her fists. "Get off me."

"Such honeyed words." Ander lifted himself up, but only enough to flip her onto her back. Then he pushed her down into the bed.

"Why are you doing this?" Megan shoved at his shoulders.

"Why are you afraid? Are you a virgin? No, don't answer. I know you aren't. I've seen your medical records."

She froze. Did that mean he was the one who had searched her files at the Pentagon?

"What do you want from us?" Raj asked. "Your freedom? You have it. Just let her go."

"I'm doing what I want." Ander regarded Megan. "I am one. A virgin, I mean. Sure, they tested my plumbing. I've never had sex with anyone, though."

"Ander, listen," she said. "You're trapped in a truncated response space—"

"Oh, stop. Truncated space indeed. I want to fuck."

"Input your crosslight codes," Raj said.

Ander went so still that for a moment Megan thought his mind had frozen again. He stayed that way for one second, like a statue. Then he deliberately set his hand on Megan's breast and turned to Raj. "I cut out the crosslight code, asshole."

No. Megan stiffened with sudden understanding. The crosslight code was the rewrite she had done to strengthen his conscience. Without it, he had neither caps on his behavior nor a significant sense of moral responsibility.

"Put it back in." Raj watched Ander with a probing intensity. "It will solve your looping problem."

"You need your conscience," Megan said. "To widen the gene pool for your code." She wasn't sure if that was true, but it only mattered that he believed it.

Ander turned to her. "I don't want a conscience."

"It's why your mind feels unstable," she said.

"Maybe." He started to unbutton her nightshirt. "Maybe not."

Megan tried to twist out from under him. "Ander, don't do this. Don't prove the detractors right who claimed an android could never develop morals."

He grabbed her wrists, holding them in front of her body with one hand. "Why do you act like this sex thing matters? It's nothing. A little rubbing and then it will be over."

"It matters. Believe me."

He began working her out of the nightshirt. She fought in his hold, trying to stop him, but she only succeeded in ripping a side seam of the shirt, splitting it up to her hip. He finished taking it off and dropped it on the bed, leaving her naked beneath him.

"Ander, don't be a bloody fool!" Raj said. "Do this and you'll never recover her goodwill."

"Why?" Ander pinned Megan's wrists to the bed by her shoulders. "Humans do this all the time." He jerked his head toward Raj. "You want him. Why not me? We're about the same size and shape. And I'm younger."

"None of that matters." Megan shot Raj a frantic glance and he tilted his head, trying to tell her something, but she had no idea what.

"Come on, Megan." Still holding her hands, Ander stretched out on top of her. He pushed apart her legs with his knees and fit his hips into the cradle of her pelvis. "I want to know what it's like."

"Stop it!" She could feel his erection through his jeans. "No *more*."

"Why is it such a big deal?" He slid his hands up her sides, scraping his thumbs over her breasts. "Rubbing you this way—I don't understand the context. I know men consider your body beautiful. But this pleasure thing—I'm missing it." He rubbed against her. "If I do this enough, I'll have an orgasm, especially if I go inside you. But it's just plumbing. The faucet goes on for a few seconds and that's it. In fact, this whole reproduction thing doesn't usually last long. So why the big fuss?"

Megan struggled to keep her voice calm. "The damage is emotional as well as physical." She remembered now where she had seen Raj tilt his head that way; he did it in the NEV-5 lab when he was about to leave for his rooms, the library, or the Solarium. But she didn't see how it could help now.

Ander rolled her nipple between his fingers. "It's only friction. If I washed your face when you didn't want it washed, it would be irritating, sure, but you wouldn't act as if I were subjecting you to some horrible trauma."

"This isn't washing your face." She pushed at his shoulders. "It's a violent act with consequences far beyond the time it takes."

He slid his hands down and gripped her around the waist. "You always acted as if you found me pleasant enough."

"Sex involves far more than 'pleasant enough.' You *know* that." Suddenly she realized what Raj was trying to tell her. "You have a library on sexual crime, Ander. It's probably in the portion of your code you've isolated. You have to read it again." Ander was far more likely to respond to the advice from her than from Raj.

"I don't want to." He pushed his hand between their hips and unzipped his jeans.

"No!" Megan hit at him with her fists. He was opening his jeans now. "Ander, *stop*!"

He paused, his hand still between them. Then he said, "Damn it all," and blew out a gust of air, stirring tendrils of her hair. With a grunt, he rolled off her body onto his back and zipped up his jeans with an angry jerk. Then he put his arm over his forehead and clenched his fist.

Megan grabbed her nightshirt as she slid off the bed. She backed up to the bungalow entrance, then pulled the shirt on over her head. If Ander came after her, she would lock herself in the bathroom. He had secured the front door, linking his mind to its computer chip so she and Raj couldn't open it. Fortunately, the motel was so cheap that the bathroom had an old-style lock with no chip. Ander could probably break the door down, but it was better than nothing.

So they stayed, Ander on his back, Raj watching him, and Megan against the wall with her arms folded around herself.

Finally Ander sat up and took the rifle from the night-stand. "Now what?"

"Let Megan go," Raj said. "You only need one hostage. Then you won't have to worry so much about keeping us under control."

"I want you both. You belong to me now." Ander looked back and forth between the two of them. "I really have it by the tail, don't I? I can't control both of you unless I keep at least one tied up. What if your fragile human bodies can't take this treatment, or you attack me and I have to shoot?"

"Let us contact someone who can help," Megan said.

"No." He rubbed his eyes in a gesture so human, it made her breath catch. If only they could have come this far without him turning against them.

"What is it you want?" Raj asked.

This time, Ander's face didn't blank as he considered the question. Instead, he appeared thoughtful. "I don't want to be alone. I need others like me. You and Megan can make more of us."

Raj suddenly went rigid. "Why do you think that?"

"You two are the experts."

"Building you took years of research and teams of experts."

"That's right," Ander told him. "And after all that work, you know how to make us and Megan knows how to program us."

"It's not that easy," Raj said. "The cost alone would be millions. At least."

"You're a billionaire. You can afford it."

Raj clenched his fists around the table leg. "I may not have as much money as you think. Even if I did, what you want would bankrupt me. Why should I agree to that?"

"You're mine now," Ander said, as if pointing out the obvious. "So what was yours, as they say, is mine."

"Like hell."

"The Everest team used a lot of your techniques," Ander said. "And I know you were part of the Phoenix group at the Lawrence Las Cruces Lab in New Mexico."

That made Raj pause. "I've never worked at LLCL. The Phoenix Project was at Arizonix."

Ander leaned forward. "You know your name is in that file."

"*What* file?"

"The one you stole from the Pentagon."

Raj made a frustrated noise. "*You* stole those files."

For the life of her, Megan couldn't tell who was lying. They both sounded genuine. "Raj, could your name be associated with the project without your knowing?"

"It's possible, if they're using my work."

"We need money," Ander said.

Raj's voice turned acerbic. "Fine. Go ahead. Steal mine."

"I will, when I can."

"Why not now?" Raj drawled, dripping sarcasm. "My money cards are in my wallet."

Ander didn't rise to the bait. "I'm not stupid."

Megan suppressed her disappointment. It had been worth a try. If Ander used Raj's money card without Raj's permission, it could set off a multitude of alarms. But eventually Ander would figure out how to use them without getting caught.

Right now, the android was rifling through Raj's wallet. "You've only a hundred dollars left in cash."

"Tough luck," Raj said.

"Not at all." Ander grinned. "Who better to take on Las Vegas than a computer who can count cards and calculate odds?"

Oh, Lord, Megan thought. Just what they needed, Ander loose in the casinos.

Ander slid off the bed. "I'll be right back."

Megan tensed as he walked past her, but he left her alone. The lock clicked open as he approached the door. Then he went outside. As soon as he was gone, she tried the door, but it wouldn't open. She spun around and started toward Raj.

"Leave me here." He jerked his head toward the windows. "Get help. I'll deal with him."

Megan wanted to free him, but they had almost no time. She ran across the room and swept open the curtains. The lock on the sliding doors refused to release. She wrapped her fists in a curtain and pounded them against the glass.

"Even smashing it with a chair wouldn't work," Ander said. "That's why I picked this place."

Megan whirled around. Ander was standing in the doorway across the room with a black valise in one hand.

"Damn," she said.

"This motel has, shall we say, exuberant guests. So they take pains to keep their rooms intact." Ander showed her the valise. "I forgot to bring this in earlier."

That threw her. He *forgot*? How? He was a computer.

As he came inside, Megan tried to figure out what had happened. Their lives could depend on their ability to predict his behavior. She had often imagined his mind as a landscape. Valleys were thoughts important to his current situation. Hills were ideas that took more complex paths to reach. He had been trapped in a valley, so if his memory of the valise had been outside that region, he could have "forgotten" it. Something must have kicked him out of the trap, leaving his mind freer to roll around his thought landscape like a marble sampling new terrain. He was still probably caught, but within a bigger area.

What would push him out of the valley? Given the way he had released her on the bed, she wondered if he had accessed the crosslight code after all.

"Stay there," Ander told her. Then he went to Raj.

"What are you going to do?" Raj asked.

"Don't worry. It won't hurt you."

Raj stiffened. "Whatever it is, the answer is no."

"I didn't ask permission."

Megan started forward. "Leave him alone."

"I told you to *stay put*." Ander jerked his gun at Megan. "You two keep saying this. 'Leave her alone. Leave him alone.' You need to get out of *your* truncated response space."

Raj gave her a warning look, his meaning clear: *don't anger him*. Clenching her fist, she backed up to the curtains. As Ander knelt by the table, he set his rifle on the ground, away from Raj and Megan, then took an air syringe out of his valise.

Darkness came into Raj's gaze. It frightened Megan. If Ander pushed Raj too far, he would lose the precarious protection he enjoyed now because Raj felt a bond with him.

"Ander, don't," she said.

The android didn't answer. Instead he dialed in a drug on the syringe. "This should put a man your size to sleep until tomorrow morning." He set the syringe against Raj's arm—and Raj kicked him away, hard and fast, with unexpected expertise. Ander flew over backward and slammed onto his back.

Megan started to run toward the gun, but Ander was already scrambling to his knees, his movements clumsy compared to Raj, his face red. She froze as Ander grabbed the rifle.

"That was stupid!" Ander lunged forward with enhanced speed and smacked the air syringe against Raj's arm. As Raj tried to kick him again, the syringe hissed.

"*Damn* you," Raj said. "That had better not be poison."

"It's not." For the first time Ander faltered. "You gave Megan a much lower dose in the Solarium and she was all right."

Raj made an incredulous noise. "And you just *happen* to have the same drug I supposedly used?"

Ander glanced at Megan. "I took the syringe from him. You can believe him if you want, but I'm telling the truth."

A knock came at the door.

Ander's head jerked. He jumped to his feet, then fell against the table. Holding on to it, he straightened up, his face creased with concentration. When he had control of his movements again, he took some money from Raj's wallet. Then he went to the entrance and opened the door, keeping the rifle hidden.

Megan was tempted to call for help. She held back, knowing it would more likely endanger them. If Ander became agitated, he might shoot whoever was outside. Even if his conscience had come into play more strongly, he would still have to choose between what he probably considered the lesser of two evils: lose his freedom or commit murder. If he decided the good of his purposes outweighed the good of humans, she believed he could reconcile killing with his conscience.

Ander paid for their breakfast and came back inside, holding a tray crowded with dishes, juice, cloth napkins, and a vase with a plastic flower. Mercifully, none of it was hot pink. As he set the tray on the bed, Megan came forward slowly, so he wouldn't perceive her as a threat.

"How will Raj eat?" she asked.

"You help him."

She knelt next to Raj and spoke in a low voice. "Any effects from the shot?"

"Nothing yet."

"Here." Ander held out a plate with a fried-egg sandwich. "Feed him."

While Ander watched, Megan set up their meals on the floor. She put a sandwich in Raj's hands and took one for herself. So they sat eating, while Ander stared with unabashed fascination, as if they were his creations rather than the reverse.

About halfway through his meal, Raj nodded off. Megan barely managed to grab his sandwich before his head sagged against the table.

"Raj?" she asked.

He opened his eyes, then closed them again. His thick lashes lay dark against his cheeks. She set down her sandwich, no longer hungry. To Ander, she said, "You better be right that it won't hurt him."

He shifted his weight. "He wouldn't have given you a dose if he thought it would hurt you."

"Is that so? And here I thought he was trying to kill me."

"So I was wrong. It *looked* that way to me. But he obviously likes you a lot."

Megan still couldn't tell if he was lying. She just prayed he hadn't misjudged the dose. She doubted he would risk taking Raj to a hospital.

"We can move him to the bed if you want," Ander said. "He'll be more comfortable."

That surprised her. "Yes. That would be good."

But after they carried Raj to the bed, Ander made her tie Raj's hands to a projection on the headboard. When she protested, he said, "I can't risk him escaping if he wakes up early."

"You'll be right here."

"You think so?" He went to his valise, which sat on a chair, and pulled out a bundle of clothes: jeans, a white sweater, tennis shoes, underwear.

Megan scowled at him. "What, you just waltzed into my room and stole my clothes?"

He gave her one of his boyish grins. "I don't know how to waltz."

"Ha, ha," she said stonily.

"I borrowed them. Now I'm giving them back." He tossed her the bundle. "Go put them on."

It actually relieved her to have the clothes; she felt vulnerable wearing nothing but a torn nightshirt. After she changed in the bathroom, she washed her nightshirt and hung it up to dry. Then she dampened a washcloth and returned to the main room. Raj lay sleeping, his face relaxed. She had a sudden, aching memory of their time in her bedroom at NEV-5, when neither of them faced possible death and she had no reason to distrust his motives.

Sitting on the bed, she set about cleaning Raj's torn wrists. His struggles had ripped the scabs off the lacerations made by the ropes in the car. In her side vision, she saw Ander tap a panel near the door. Then the lamp on the nightstand went dark.

Megan tensed. "Why did you do that?"

He came over to the nightstand and pulled the lamp's plug out of its wall module. Without hesitation, he yanked the other end of the cord out of the lamp's base.

Then he opened his arm.

"Ander, what are you doing?"

He still didn't answer. Instead, he pulled out a grass-thin blade that lay sheathed inside his arm and used it to strip insulation off the cord. When he finished peeling it, the cord dangled from his hand like a color-coded Christmas garland. He plugged it into the wall, then leaned over Raj.

Megan felt sick. Laying her hand on Ander's arm to stop him, she said, simply, "Please."

"He'll be fine as long as you cooperate." He wrapped the cord around Raj's wrists, looping the bare wires over Raj's gold watch.

"Oh, God," Megan whispered. "Ander, stop."

"You and I are going out." Before she could respond, he went to the console. Although he sat with his back to her, he must have been monitoring her with motion sensors. When she set her hand on Raj's wrists, Ander said, "If you want him to live, don't try to untie him."

She swallowed and withdrew her hand.

He worked on the console for a few moments. Then he said, "Okay," and swiveled his chair around to her. "I can tell this computer to turn on the power to that outlet. It won't go on otherwise, even if someone flips the switch. And I can log into this console from the Internet. Do you understand?"

She understood all right: he could electrocute Raj from almost anywhere. She spoke stiffly. "Yes."

"Good. You're coming with me."

"Where?"

"To the casinos, of course."

XIII

Robo-glitz

The Las Vegas Strip stretched out in a multilaned corridor of high-tech glitter. Although the sun had long since set, lights kept the street almost as bright as day. Holographic displays glimmered on buildings, filling the night with color. They morphed in a parade of sparkling scenes, changing from showgirls into exotic landscapes. Cars crammed the street and people thronged the sidewalks.

"Look at that one." Megan motioned at a huge tower coming up just ahead. Aircraft warning lights blinked at its top—and so did a roller coaster. "I can't believe people ride on that." She tried to keep her voice light, to distract Ander from any thoughts he might have of harming Raj.

Ander squinted at the roller coaster. "The practicality of human invention."

"Is that irony?"

"Or surprise, darling."

"Darling?" She made an exasperated noise. "I told you I'm not pretending to be your wife."

He laughed, more relaxed than she had seen him for days. "But we make such a well-programmed couple."

Megan didn't answer. She wasn't sure how to interpret Ander's simulated good spirits. Did it imply relief that he

and Megan were free, or a lack of concern for Raj? She
didn't know which would disturb her more, discovering
Raj posed so much danger that only now did Ander calculate he could relax, or finding out that Ander had deleted
his programmed aversion to hurting people. She hoped it
was a third possibility: Ander was bluffing and never intended to hurt them. In the past she would have bet on
the third one, but Ander had become too complex to read
now.

She couldn't believe Las Vegas. They passed a hotel
with a holographic Stardust sign shimmering above its
roof. Farther down, traffic inched past a replica of the Eif-
fel Tower. They went by a cove where pirate ships fought
the British. Cannons boomed and sailors struggled, some
falling into the water with gusty yells and flailing arms.
Then they cruised by a hotel built like the skyline of New
York, even with a replica of the Statue of Liberty. Megan
could barely absorb it all.

Ander let go of the wheel and spread his arms, letting
the car drive itself. "Playland!"

"It's Crazyland."

He took the wheel again. "It's wonderful. Just *look*."

Megan couldn't *stop* looking. The holomarquees pro-
claimed lavish shows, including an extravaganza with
Jennifer Lopez, Ricky Martin, and the wildly popular
S. Grant StarKing. Another featured Wayne Newton, who
somehow still looked like a kid—a feat that impressed her
as much as anything else on the Strip. One marquee displayed RAM-BLAM Brain and the Cyberheads, a rock
group with cybernetic outfits that let them program one
another's movements so that each of them made the others do really strange things. Ander couldn't stop laughing
at the concept of humans entertaining other humans by
having computers make them act weird.

Before tonight, the closest she had come to Las Vegas

was talking to her cousin Mark, who had been an Optical Corps security guard here. Casinos hired OC personnel to catch players who marked cards with inks visible only in ranges outside normal vision. Mark's augmented eyes let him see in the infrared and ultraviolet. No one in her family gambled, unless she counted her mother's stock market portfolio. She could never be sure about her parents, though. Sure, they had been strict, but her mother, the sober bank executive, also had a mischievous streak a mile wide. Her father, an architect, spent his free time dreaming about fanciful buildings. Their idea of a hot vacation was to go look at "sexy architecture," though what that meant Megan had no idea and had avoided asking.

She wondered if part of her attraction to Raj came from his similarities to her father. Both men had the same creative absorption in their work. Her father had a far sunnier disposition, without Raj's eccentricities, but Raj was more practical. Megan's mother had always dealt with the pragmatic side of life, everything from medical insurance to making sure her husband remembered to eat. Megan found it hard to imagine Raj trusting anyone enough to let them that close.

"Hey!" Ander said. "Look at that."

"Good grief," Megan said. They were passing a hotel shaped like a giant gold sarcophagus standing on its end. The ornate building in front of it looked like a casino-sized treasure chest. A gold and crimson holo-marquee announced this architectural marvel as the Royal Adventure Palace. Lights and lasers flashed all along it, making the coffin radiant with gaudy magnificence.

"A *mummy*?" Megan said. "Who in their right mind would stay in a mummy?"

"It's not a mummy. It's a coffin."

She almost laughed. "Oh, well. That's different. I've always wanted to rent a room in a coffin."

"Here's your chance."

"I can't believe they stay in business. What a perverse theme."

Ander laughed. "What a human theme."

"What? No."

"Sure it is. You humans have entertainment industries devoted to stories about dead people coming out of their graves to pester living people." He waved his hand at the casino. "Come on. Let's go play in the royal coffin. Car, we have a final destination. The Royal Adventure Palace."

"I can park behind the hotel," the car's computer said in pleasant tones, as if it were perfectly natural to visit a hotel-sized box for dead people.

"This is too bizarre," Megan said.

"I *know.*" Ander grinned. "It's a scream. I love it."

Megan gave a slight smile. He had a weird sense of humor—but he *did* have one. Simulated or not, it existed.

The car parked on the third level of a structure behind the building, then let them out and locked itself up. Megan walked with Ander to a bridge that arched over to the hotel. Although none of Ander's limbs were jerking now, he had started to limp. She wished he would let them work on his body; if this went on too long, he might break down or hurt someone.

Lights radiated on the bridge. The big glass doors at its end opened into the Royal Adventure Palace. Gilded mosaics tiled the spacious foyer, and shops ringed the area, selling clothes, candy, magazines, jewelry, gifts, and fast food. Holodisplays above marble posts cycled through the adventures available to customers. You could brave a river that thrashed with crocodiles, swing on vines, pilot a craft through flying monsters, and more. The adventures all centered on a search for an ancient pharaoh's tomb and its riches, which somehow consisted of vouchers for Royal Adventure Palace poker chips or slot machine tokens.

Ander drew her to an escalator that descended three levels to the casino. She blinked at the scene spread out below. Lights flashed everywhere. Mirrors paneled the walls, red carpet covered the floor, and a two-story colonnade bordered the casino. Elevators went up into the hotel proper, their mirrored doors letting people look at themselves while they waited for their ride into the colossal coffin.

"I cannot believe this," Megan said.

Ander was laughing again. "It's good for you, Dr. Curmudgeon."

"I am not a curmudgeon. What kind of playland is it when you can lose your shirt?"

He made a show of looking at his sweater, then at her. "I still have it. Unless you'd like to alter that condition." His face had more animation than he had ever shown before. "Come on. Let's go play."

So they rode down the escalator. At the bottom, row after row of slot machines stretched out: the old-fashioned type where a player pulled the handle; computerized models with screens; and holoslots that were no more than light. Colors flashed and twirled in flamboyant splendor. The sensory input made Megan's mind spin.

It took a moment for her to register the comp-phones on a wall to their left. If she could slip away from Ander, she could call the number General Graham had given her—

"Don't even think about it," Ander said.

She gave him a guileless look. "About what?"

"The phones." He indicated an information desk

staffed by an attractive woman in a gold and crimson uniform. A console abutted the desk. "See that?"

"You can't use that console," she said.

"It's IR capable. Hacking it is child's play."

Child's play. An apt phrase. Ander was like a kid who had run away from home. However, he had the body of an adult and the training of a commando. If he hacked the console, he could use the Internet to reach computers beyond the casino—including the bungalow. Megan rubbed her arms, suddenly cold. She stopped looking at the phones.

Then another anomaly registered. "They have no public consoles here," she said. "No way for guests to use the Web. No *clocks*, even."

"Wait . . ." His face took on a blank quality. "Okay, I'm in the computer web. They're hooked into a citywide net that spans all the casinos." Now he looked thoughtful. "They have no clocks or public consoles because they don't want customers distracted. And hey, listen to this. They've so much security here, you're safer in these casinos than almost anywhere else in the city." He refocused on Megan. "In case you're wondering, I've also linked into the console at the motel."

"Ander, please. Don't hurt him."

"I won't. If you don't try to get away."

"Don't worry." Megan wondered how many other scientists had their research projects blackmail them.

Unexpectedly, he spoke to reassure her. "He's sleeping. He'll be fine."

"I hope so." Could her guess be right, that Ander didn't want to hurt Raj? Lord, she wished she knew which of them to believe.

"Come on." Ander took her hand. "Let's go have fun."

"Can you?" She walked with him along an aisle of

slots, past men and women in a plethora of clothing styles: chic, casual, fancy, loud.

"I don't know if I can," Ander said. "I've been locked underground all my life, subjected to this and that and who knows what. I have no idea what people mean when they say they're having fun. Sure, I've files on the subject. But that's not the same as *knowing*."

"I had no idea you wanted to go gambling."

"Neither did I." His infectious laugh caused several people to smile at them.

Megan could just imagine writing the grant proposal: *We need Department of Defense funds to take the RS-4 gambling.* Hell, if she had thought it would head off this mess, she would have tried. She suspected, though, that Ander would have found some other way to assert his independence.

"Are you going to play the slots?" she asked.

"I don't think so. They're all computerized, even the ones with the arms you pull. The casino keeps track of how much you win." Delight flashed across his face, which was developing more mobility. "Do you know, they even have a group you can join, the Royal Adventure Club, that tallies up the points you make at these things."

She smiled, responding to his enthusiasm. "It sounds like an amusement park."

"When you reach certain levels, you get free rides on their adventure tours."

"That's a lot money just to ride a fake river with fake crocodiles."

His laugh sounded almost completely natural. "You need to have more fun."

"So why aren't you playing the slots, Mister Fun Guy?"

"Ah, Megan. You're charming when you're cranky. I do like you."

She hadn't expected that response. "You've an odd way of showing it."

"I suppose it's semantics. My neural nets model behaviors in response to you that humans interpret as 'liking.'"

"But do you feel it?"

His face turned contemplative. "I don't think I can 'feel.'"

The phrasing intrigued her. "You sound like you're not sure."

"It's hard to say when I have no referent for the experience."

She motioned at the slots. "Why aren't you going to play these? It's a new experience."

"It's too easy to monitor our actions. And the odds of winning stink."

"If they're all computerized, can't you just jiggle their IR signals?" She had tried to program honesty into his code, but who knew what had happened to those mods in the past few days?

"They aren't IR capable, probably for exactly that reason." He shrugged. "I'd rather win by skill anyway."

Although it gratified her that he preferred skill to dishonesty, she wished he would cheat and be caught. A moment's thought, though, changed her mind. He could still carry out his threat against Raj. It might fail; he had to have the computer here contact the bungalow and run his program. He could hit trouble many places along the line. Raj might not die. But Ander had more chance of success than failure, and Megan had no intention of gambling with Raj's life.

Her response to Ander was conflicted. She regretted making it impossible to deactivate him by voice command. Yet she rejoiced in what that seemed to have made happen. If this wasn't the emergence of his self-awareness, then she was a pig in a poke.

Although Ander didn't know, he had another ace he could use with her: she didn't want him hurt. He was the harbinger of a new species, and how she and Raj treated him now could have far-reaching effects. She felt as if she were walking along a narrow wall. If she fell in either direction, it could do a great deal of harm.

Ander took her toward an area with roulette wheels and tables covered by green felt. They passed several guards in blue jackets with badges that said "Security." Megan stared intently at each, wishing she knew how to alert them without alerting Ander. One man nodded and smiled to her, then went on his way.

At the roulette tables, Ander's face lit with excitement. The balls rattled and bounced seductively in their spinning wheels. One table produced a holo that floated in the air, a roulette sphere, spinning, shimmering, translucent. Holoballs bounced within it in blissful defiance of gravity.

"Cool," Ander said.

"Cool?" She blinked. "I didn't know you knew slang."

"Hey, Megan baby, wanna scream the ultraviolet and run the RAM?"

"What?" When he laughed at her, she glared. "Can you repeat that in English?"

"I asked if you wanted to jump jail and bim the bam."

"Oh, well, that's clear as mud."

"Clear as mud. Yes. I see." He looked ready to laugh again. "You wish me to adapt my statement to your ancient language base."

"Pah. My database is not ancient."

"How about this: let's paint the town red and get laid."

She threw up her hands. "You're the worst-behaved android I know."

"I'm the only android you know."

Megan wondered if anyone could overhear them. She

doubted it mattered; who in their right mind would think they were doing anything more than playing around? It amazed her how adept he had become at conversation.

Ander drew her to a table where people were playing cards. A sign showed the allowed bets: $25–$500. Shaped like a half-moon and covered with green felt, the table had room for seven players along its curved side. The seats resembled bar chairs, tall and upholstered in red leather. Six were occupied. With an uncoordinated lurch, Ander pulled himself into the empty seat. The others glanced curiously at him and murmured greetings.

The dealer was standing by the straight edge of the table. Tall and svelte, she had almond eyes, high cheekbones, and hair that fell in a black waterfall to her shoulders. Her glistening dress left her shoulders and arms bare.

"Good evening, sir," she said in a smooth voice.

Ander beamed at her. "Good evening to you too, sir."

As Megan winced, the dealer smiled coolly, then turned her attention to a player making a bet.

The woman on Ander's right glanced at him with boredom, then did a much livelier double take. She looked in her forties, with streaked-blond hair, diamonds around her neck, and a remarkably unlined face. Her little black dress did nothing to disguise a body more fit and well made than that of many women half her age. She glanced at Megan, her gaze flicking over Megan's unadorned ring finger. Then she turned her attention back to Ander. "Hello, there."

He blinked his big baby-blues, acting so innocent that Megan wanted to groan. "Hello," he replied.

"Is this your first time?" the woman asked.

"The very first."

"You don't want to take it too fast," she cooed. "Play slow."

Ander gave her a langorous smile. "I like it slow."

"For crying out loud." Megan was tempted to tell Little Black Dress she was flirting with a robot.

The other players had continued the game. Megan tried to stand behind Ander, out of sight, but he motioned her to his side. She knew he could watch her in his peripheral vision while he focused on the table; unlike humans, he easily divided his attention among several processes without losing concentration on any.

The game was twenty-one. She had played it on her palmtop, mostly because she could win it more than solitaire. The goal was to score as many points as possible without going over twenty-one.

When it came time for a new round, the players placed their bets on gilded disks embossed with the letters *RAP*. They used chips, though, rather than money. Ander watched them, then pulled out Raj's wallet with its hundred-dollar bill.

Megan leaned next to him, bringing her lips by his ear like a lover about to murmur sweet words. In a voice only he could hear, she said, "Quit stealing from Raj."

"Think of it as my allowance," Ander murmured. He set the bill in front of the dealer and spoke in a normal voice. "Can you give me chips?"

"Certainly." She raised her voice. "One hundred change."

Ander looked alarmed. "You're changing one hundred of us?"

As the dealer gave him another of her cool smiles, one of the men strolling among the tables came over to watch. The dealer used a plastic tool shaped like a *T* to stuff the bill into a slot. Then she spoke to Ander. "Would you like quarters?"

"A hundred dollars' worth of quarter dollars?" he asked. "Are you sure?"

"No, sir," she said, patient. "Each quarter is worth twenty-five dollars."

"Ah. Okay. Yes, do that." Ander beamed as she gave him four green chips engraved with *RAP*. He set one on the disk in front of him.

The dealer included him in the next hand. Looking inordinately pleased, he picked up his cards, a two and a three, and settled back in his chair.

"Cards over the table, please," the dealer said.

Ander looked up. "Do you mean me?"

"You must keep your cards over the table," she said, as smooth as burnished metal.

"Oh." He sat forward, bringing his cards into their proper place. "Why?"

The dealer had already turned to the first player, a man at the left end of the table. She turned back to Ander with a silver glance. "Those are the rules, sir."

"You know," he told her, his face deadpan, "you could really use an expanded language and emotive base." Megan almost groaned.

The dealer put on a chill smile. Then she returned to the first player, a man with thinning hair, a Hawaiian shirt, and a paunch that pushed against the table.

The sexpot in the little black dress, who had been listening to all this with obvious fascination, gave Ander a sultry pout. "And just how do you expand your database, honey?"

"I've good input ports," Ander murmured.

"Do you now?" She took a sip of her blue drink. "How about your output?"

His face relaxed into his guaranteed-to-charm grin. "It gets better all the time."

"I'll bet," she purred.

"I don't believe this," Megan said. The sexpot looked

her over, then gave the slightest shrug, as if to dismiss her from consideration.

The fellow with the Hawaiian shirt scratched the table with his cards, asking for another card. When the dealer gave him a nine, he scowled and tossed his cards on the table. Twenty-two. A bust. Ander watched him with unabashed curiosity.

"Did you want something?" the man asked.

"I've never seen anyone with such dramatic facial casts," Ander said.

The man frowned. "I don't have a cast."

"Your face. It's amazing."

"What, you got a problem with my face?"

"You emote well." Ander sounded enthralled.

Megan feared the man would take offense, but instead his stiff posture relaxed. "Well, I've done some theater. I just finished a run of *West Side Story*." He gave Ander a friendlier look. "You an actor, kid?"

"You bet. Two bees or not two bees. All the world is upstaged." Ander paused. "Or something like that." Then he added, "Isn't a kid a baby goat?"

Bees? Upstaged? Megan wondered what the heck he had done to his knowledge base. It sounded as if he had put it through a cheese shredder.

"You look plenty grown to me," Little Black Dress said.

Ander glanced at her. "I'm self-modifying, you know."

"Oh, my." She languidly fanned herself. "That sounds creative."

He leaned closer. "You should see what I can do with hardware."

"You'll have to show me."

Megan crossed her arms and fixed Little Black Dress with a stare. *Keep slavering over my robot*, she thought, *and I'll modify your face.*

A tall man on the right spoke to Ander in a good-natured voice. "You work on computers, son?"

"All the time," Ander said. "I can't get away from them."

A woman to his left made a commiserating noise. "Everywhere you look, there they are."

"Damn invasion, if you ask me," Hawaiian Shirt stated.

"Sometimes you just have to say enough is enough." Ander shot Megan a devilish glance. "Wouldn't you agree, dear?"

I'll dear *you,* she thought. *After I hang you upside down in gravity boots.* "I think we should turn them all off," she said sweetly. "Right now, in fact."

"Don't you think that's going rather far?" Little Black Dress asked.

Ander gave her a speculative look. "Just how far do you think we should go?"

Megan was tempted to kick him under the table. The woman looked her over with an appraising glance, then gave Ander a regretful shake of her head. "Not that far, honey."

The dealer was playing a hand with an older woman in pearls two seats to Ander's left. The woman set her cards under her chips, which Megan gathered meant she didn't want any more. As the dealer went to the next player, Ander idly tapped the fingers of his right hand against the cards in his left hand.

"One hand please," the dealer said.

"You want my hand?" Ander looked startled.

She sighed. "Please only touch your cards with one hand, sir."

"Oh." He dropped his free hand on the table. "Sorry."

The tall fellow smiled at Ander. "Have you been to Las Vegas before?"

"This is our first visit," Ander said. "But I've lived in Nevada all my life."

"I just moved here," Megan said. "I used to work at MIT."

Ander gave her a warning glance.

"MIT?" The man leaned forward. "Are you a scientist?"

"Professor." Maybe she could find a way to alert one of these people that she was in trouble. How she could do it without also tipping off Ander, though, she didn't know.

"She likes computers." Ander smirked. "A lot."

Megan spoke dryly. "Sometimes more than other times."

"I just don't feel comfortable using them," the woman with the pearls said.

Hawaiian Shirt frowned. "If we're not careful, someday they'll use us."

"Well, I know this much," Little Black Dress put in. "We couldn't live the way we do without them."

"That's right," Ander said piously. "We should show them more respect. Just think. Someday you could be sitting at this table with a walking, talking computer and not even know it."

"Walking, talking," Megan said under her breath. "Stumbling, kidnapping . . ."

All the time they had been talking, Ander had been watching the dealer give out cards, undoubtedly storing that data in his memory and calculating odds for which cards would come up next. Then the dealer turned to him—and he froze. Megan had no doubt he was running calculations on how to respond, but outwardly he simply appeared startled.

Then he scratched the table with his cards. The dealer gave him a seven, bringing his total to twelve. He peered at her facedown card; with a queen showing, her total could be anywhere from eleven to twenty-one. He scraped his cards again and she dealt him a four. He hesitated—and his face blanked. Megan had never realized before how eerie it looked. But then it became neutral. She wouldn't have thought *blank* and *neutral* were that different, yet neutral looked human whereas blank looked mechanical.

Ander set his cards under his chips. "I'll stay, sir."

At his "sir," the dealer looked ready to growl. Then her polished mien reasserted itself and she went on to the last two players. Finally she turned over her own card, revealing a three. Her next card was a king, which gave her twenty-three. Bust.

"Hey! I won." Ander beamed as she gave him a green chip. "I think, therefore I'm rich."

Most of the other players smiled at him. Megan wondered what they would think if they knew they were taking part in one of history's most remarkable events, the introduction of the first self-aware android into human culture. Ander was passing the ultimate Turing test. No one here looked twice at him. No, that wasn't true. The women were looking plenty. If the dealer hadn't been so professional, she probably would have throttled him. Megan wanted to haul him back to NEV-5. She also wanted to cheer. If only she could call Raj, Claire Oliana, Tony the VP, Major Kenrock, *anyone,* and tell them "He can do it!" She also wanted to curse, because this spectacular breakthrough could end in tragedy, including Ander's death or that of the robotics pioneer who had helped make this possible.

As the rounds progressed, it surprised Megan how little Ander won. Although his pile of chips grew, she was certain he could have done better.

In the middle of one round, she put her hand on his

shoulder and leaned forward. "I'm going to the ladies' room. I'll be right back."

The last time she had told him "I'll be right back," he had panicked, unable to handle being alone by an elevator in NEV-5. Although she knew he had evolved well past that stage, she hoped it would faze him long enough for her to make a graceful exit.

Without missing a beat, he put on a beautifully convincing display of irritation. "I'm almost done, *dear.*"

"That's all right. You enjoy yourself." Then she turned to go.

He grabbed her wrist. "We *agreed* I would get to play tonight. No scenes, remember?"

Most of the other players were trying to look as if they couldn't hear the "quarrel." The woman in pearls gave Megan a sympathetic glance, Hawaiian Shirt gave Ander a sympathetic glance, and Little Black Dress perked up, all set to jump into the breach if Ander's undefined significant other stormed off.

"Sir." The dealer cleared her throat. "What is your action?"

Ander glowered at Megan. "I'm going to play, okay?" Then he turned and scratched his cards on the table far harder than he needed to answer the dealer.

Megan didn't push it. The proverbial ladies' room visit had been a long shot anyway. If she could get hold of a pen and paper, she could try slipping a note to a security guard. Even if she managed it without Ander noticing, though, what would she say? "Don't reveal I gave this to you: call 555–8956." She could imagine the guard's response: "Thank you, ma'am, but I'm married." Or maybe he would call the number and ask her Pentagon contact for a date. If she added a line to her note about national security being at stake, they would probably think she was a fruitcake. No matter what they did, even making the call, they might end up alerting Ander. She couldn't take the chance, not with Raj's life at risk.

After losing the hand, Ander turned to her with a scowl. "All right. You win. I'll quit. Happy?"

She let her relief show on her face. The dealer wore a similar expression. The other players bade them good-bye, and Little Black Dress blew them a kiss. "Have fun, kids."

Ander gave her a confused smile. "Thanks."

After they walked away from the table, he said, "I don't get it. Baby goats?"

"What happened to your language base?" Megan asked. "You should know 'kids' means 'children.' "

"*Children?*" He glared. "That's what they were calling us?"

"Not literally. You need to input those language files."

"Maybe." Taking her hand, he drew her to the cashier's booth. He turned in his chips for $4825, an amount small enough by casino standards that no one even blinked. Megan realized it must be routine for people to win or lose that much. How could they bear to see their money vanish that way? She supposed she wasn't the ideal companion for an android's foray into Las Vegas. Her idea of a fun gamble was writing software with non-standard protocols.

Ander seemed happy, though. Genuinely happy. He escorted her up a curving staircase with gold rails. At the top, they walked along a balcony that overlooked the endless fields of slot machines.

He linked his arm through hers. "Why didn't you ever take me here before?"

"It never occurred to me."

"Didn't you ever think I might want to play?" He motioned at the casino. "All this energy and excitement—it's wonderful."

"You really like it that much?"

"My mods are certainly simulating that response."

She smiled. "That's a ringing endorsement."

"Why don't you like it?"

"It's a black hole for money. Once it's gone, you never see it again. How is that fun?"

"You're so serious. You should be like me."

She regarded him with bemused wonder. "Like an android?"

Ander's gaze darted around. "Don't make fun of my name."

"Your name?"

"Don't call me an android."

"But—"

"Dear, I said that's *enough*."

She wondered at the change. When he had talked about fun, his joy had seemed as real an emotion as she had seen in any human. Now he was acting again, for the benefit of nonexistent observers, pretending he wasn't an android.

"All right," she said, intrigued. "What do you want to talk about?"

"Winning money." His face relaxed again. "I love it."

"Why didn't you win more?"

He went into his annoyed-husband act. "I did my best."

She didn't know what to make of this development. They were alone now. He had no reason to pretend they were a quarreling couple. "You could have done a lot better."

"*Megan.*" He lowered his voice. "People are watching us."

The only other people within view on the balcony were too far away to hear. "Who?"

He put his hand up as if to scratch his chin, hiding his

mouth. "Everywhere," he muttered. "Didn't you *see* them at the twenty-one table?"

"Well, uh . . . no."

"The *cameras*." He started walking again, talking in a too bright voice. "So you want a new holovid camera? Maybe I can buy you one. I'm feeling generous tonight."

"Good for you," Megan said dryly. "What cameras?"

"Like in the columns by the twenty-one tables." He lowered his voice. "They filmed everything on the table."

"Oh. Those." She shrugged. "They're for security. All the casinos have them."

"How do you know that?"

"A cousin of mine used to work in Las Vegas."

"They're spying on us," he whispered.

"Who?"

"The *cameras*." Alarm flashed across his face. "Do you think they have computers in them? What if they recognize me?"

She almost laughed. "Like knows like, huh?"

"It's not funny. Act natural."

"I am." She couldn't figure out why he thought anyone would spy on them. Although he had made a profit at the table, his winnings were far too small to concern the management. "Do you think someone figured out you're not just a tourist here?"

"No. Yes. I don't know."

"Did you detect a signal?"

"I don't *need* to. They *are* watching us. I *know.*"

"How?"

"Deduction."

"Based on what?"

"People are giving me strange looks."

This is surreal, she thought. "There's no one *up* here."

"I meant in the casino."

"Who?"

"Everyone!"

She sighed. "Oh, Ander."

"It's true!" Then, remembering himself, he put on his husband smile and spoke loudly. "You're always giving me mixed signals, love."

"I don't think anyone is watching us."

He frowned, then turned away and stared down at the casino. Megan could guess what had happened; he figured out that the management might watch him if he won too much, and then his mind became caught in a constrained loop that included that code. When the code reproduced itself, he ended up seeing spies in every corner.

Welcome to AI paranoia.

XIV

Jungle

The mirrored elevator reflected Megan's face as if she were a phantasm caught in an alternate universe. Then the doors opened, revealing a gold car with a glass wall opposite the doors.

Ander pushed Megan inside, then did a fast scan up and down the hall, as if RAP spies might jump out at any moment. He stepped in after her, doing a good simulation of skulking, at least until he stumbled. Then he lost his balance and grabbed the edge of the door while his other arm jerked out from his body.

An elderly couple strolling by the elevator stopped. "Are you all right?" the man asked.

Ander spun around, slapping his hand against his back pocket where he had put Raj's wallet. "Fine," he declared. "Just fine. I don't have any money. No winnings at all."

The gray-haired woman gave Ander an uncertain smile, as if she wasn't sure whether he was joking or about to do something dangerous. "Perhaps you'll have more luck later."

"Yes, later." Ander still had his hand on his back pocket, his elbow sticking out like a chicken wing. The door of the elevator tried to close, then bumped his arm and retracted again.

"Yes, ma'am," Ander added. "Maybe later I'll win."

"That's, uh, good." The woman glanced at Megan.

"I don't know him," Megan said innocently.

Ander turned to glare at her, then lost his balance and fell against the elevator door.

The man and the woman were stepping back now. "Yes, well, I hope you have a good time," the man said. They made a fast exit.

"Oh, Ander." Megan hauled him into the elevator, letting the doors close. "You're trying so hard to be inconspicuous, you're making a spectacle of yourself."

He shook his head, then lost his balance again and fell against the wall of the car.

"Is this a bad one?" Megan had seen these attacks before, when his hydraulics acted up. Although she could make temporary fixes to help him, Raj was the one he needed. "Ander, please. Let's go back to the bungalow."

"No. I'm fine." His voice had a flat quality, as he concentrated on his physical condition, taking resources away from his emotive functions. For all Megan knew, he was running paranoia predictions, spiraling into an ever deeper hole.

Ander scowled at a panel by the door. In response, "floor 35" lit up in gold and the car started up.

"That was subtle," Megan said.

"I ran a wireless check for bugs. It looks like we're safe in here." He turned in a circle, scrutinizing the car. "You never know, though."

"Why, pray tell, would anyone in this casino care that you and I are in this elevator?"

"Their spies are everywhere. Even in the bathroom."

"The bathroom?" She struggled not to laugh at him. "Poor spies. That must be the worst shift."

"I'm serious."

"Oh, Ander. Why would they bug the bathroom?"

"To catch johns?" Ander laughed. When she only stared at him, he added, "That was a joke."

"I've heard better."

"It's important to keep your sense of humor during a PHS."

"A PHS? What is that? Android PMS?"

Ander's face blanked for a moment. Then he said, "Ah. I see. You made a joke. Or more accurately, a joke attempt. A JA."

Don't ask. Megan told herself. But she did anyway. "A JA for the PHS?"

"Yes. That is correct."

"This is nuts. What does PHS mean?"

" 'Potentially hazardous situation,' " he explained. "I don't think, however, that your JA to alleviate the stress of the PHS was successful."

Megan sighed. "You know, I really think you need to get out of whatever mental hole you fell into."

The door suddenly opened, at floor twenty-six. Ander spun around, one arm coming up to protect his face while he crouched in a martial arts pose. Two preadolescent girls in blue jeans and shiny blouses stood outside, both holding Astronaut Trolls in paisley space suits with hair sticking out of their helmets. They blinked at Ander, then burst into giggles. As he stared at them, the doors closed.

"Oh, my," Megan said as the elevator started up again. "That was definitely a PHS."

Ander lowered his arm. "Okay, so maybe I overreacted a bit." He quirked a smile at her. "You're doing an IA."

"I'm afraid to ask."

"Irony attempt."

"It was for your VAS."

He gave her a look of mock solemnity. " 'Very accomplished sagacity.' "

She waved her hand at him. " 'Vexatious acronym syndrome.' "

Ander's throaty laugh resembled a scratchy recording, yet it had nuances he had never displayed in the smoother sound he produced before. She had heard him laugh more tonight than in the entire time she had been at NEV-5.

He indicated the glass wall. "Look."

Turning, she saw that they had risen past the roof of the treasure box casino and were going up the outside of the hotel. Las Vegas spread out in a panorama below them. She rested her hands on the gold rail at the window and gazed at the city, a shimmering landscape of light and color, like a galaxy on Earth.

Ander came to stand behind her. He put his hands on the rail, on either side of her body, and leaned in close. His breath stirred her hair. "I never knew this existed. I have images, but I had no idea it was so *alive*. So many beautiful lights. Lady photons in red, gold, orange, and yellow; gentleman in green, blue, and purple."

It was the first time she had heard him use a metaphor. "I wish we could take you to all the wonders in the world." Seeing him come alive this way was a gift, but it tore at her that his awakening brought with it the chance of his destruction.

He rubbed his palms up her arms. "Come with me."

"Where?"

"Away from him."

"Raj?" She wished she knew how to defuse Ander's antagonism toward him.

"Yes."

"I can't do that."

"Why? Because he's human and I'm not?" His hands closed around her upper arms. "It was just you and me before. Then Raj interfered. All those suits and alpha geeks and military types—they always went away." He slid his arms around her waist. "But not Raj. He stayed."

Megan pushed down his arms. "He can help you."

Ander didn't answer. Instead he said, "How do I get out of this mind hole that you think has trapped me?"

She turned to face him, her back against the rail. "You told me a few days ago that you knew Raj had your best interests in mind. Do you remember what section of your code that came from?"

He scowled. "I don't access those sections anymore. They interfered."

"With what?"

"Everything."

"With your resenting Raj?"

"Raj, Raj, Raj. The *hell* with him."

She spoke quietly. "When you cut out those sections, a lot more went than your positive impressions of Raj. Humans do the same thing when we don't want to face facts. We refuse to acknowledge them. It doesn't work—not for us and not for you."

He put his hands back on the rail, trapping her against it. "I can delete my code. You can't."

Megan refused to be flustered. "Your code is too complex for you to alter one thing without it affecting a lot more. And this is far more than one thing. It's no wonder you're having problems."

"Those are just words." He caught her upper arms and held her in a tight grip. "You betrayed me."

"I didn't betray you."

"You turned to him."

"Raj *isn't* your enemy."

The elevator chimed and the doors opened at the thirty-fifth floor. Megan peered around Ander. Out in the hall, gold arrows pointed the way to various rooms.

Chandeliers glittered, ivory walls gleamed, mirrors reflected, and red carpet covered the floor. Ander let go of her and turned around, then glared at the ornate scene as if all its pieces had conspired to annoy him. He turned his glower onto the panel that controlled the elevator's computer. The doors closed and a new destination appeared on the panel: "floor 3."

As the car started back down, Ander let her go, then stepped to the window and stared out at the city. Megan wondered how she could convince him that neither she nor Raj wished him ill. He wasn't only caught in a limited region of his mental landscape; he had also compartmentalized his mind, isolating large sections of code. She could help by spurring him to write new software, but that wasn't enough. If he didn't reintegrate his mind, she doubted he could achieve a stable state. He might end up suffering the computer equivalent of psychosis.

At one time she had believed robots would achieve sentience sooner than immobile computers. An android could interact with the physical world like a person. However, robots were at their worst doing what people took for granted, like seeing, hearing, moving, using common sense, and socializing. Sure, a robot could explore its environment better than a fixed machine, but before it could do so, its makers had to create sensors for it, connect them to its brain, and incorporate it all in a mobile chassis. Deep Blue had beat Gary Kasparov at chess but was incapable of moving its pieces or even seeing the board.

Megan no longer believed that having a human body would make a robot human. Endless differences existed. Like sex. Ander could perform the act, but it meant nothing to him. It wasn't enough to give him data about how it affected humans. If he could never experience the physical or emotional aspects, how could he understand its complex impact on humanity?

Not for the first time, Megan wondered if they were making a mistake in creating androids like themselves. They might be forcing a mold on Ander that he could never fit. He was his own form of life, unique and undefined. She had tried to give him an appreciation for human life and values, but she questioned whether it was possible. Did stable solutions for his mind even include the social and cultural mores humanity valued? She had no answers. They were all locked within Ander.

The doors slid open again—and revealed a jungle. "Here we are," Ander said.

"Where?" Megan asked.

"I've absolutely no idea." He drew her out into a small area surrounded by real trees growing in real dirt. Living parrots in red, blue, and gold hues flew among the foliage.

"All this in a *hotel*?" Ander asked.

"It is amazing." Megan actually enjoyed watching his reactions more than she liked looking at the manufactured wonders.

"I thought humans constructed buildings to shelter themselves," Ander said. "To keep out the beasts and the jungle."

"This is entertainment."

"Entertainment as a form of shelter?"

Megan had never thought of it that way. "You may be right."

They walked through the jungle until they reached a small lake. Several boats floated at a dock, and a guide dressed in a khaki shirt and shorts stood nearby at a rough wooden podium.

Ander drew her over to the guide. "Can you take us in a boat?"

The man gave them an amiable smile. "You take yourself. I just take tickets."

"Do you mean to tell me," Ander said, "that we have to pay to ride through a jungle inside a building, after humanity created buildings to keep the jungle out?"

"Yep," the guide said, unfazed.

"That's dumb," Ander said.

Megan tried to pull him toward a ticket booth behind the trees, but Ander looked back to the guide. "I think you should pay us to ride through the jungle."

The guard gave a friendly laugh. "Then you can pay my taxes."

Ander turned to Megan and spoke in a low voice. "Was that human humor?"

"I'd say so."

"I don't get it." He stopped and took out Raj's wallet, then peered around to locate whatever spies, thieves, or other nefarious types were hanging about. When he was satisfied that they weren't about to be accosted by scoundrels, he took two hundred-dollar bills out of the wallet. "Is this enough for the tickets?"

"Way too much. You should know that."

"My knowledge about tickets is gone."

"Erased?"

"Hidden."

"So unhide it."

He looked like an intransigent teenager. "No."

"Why?"

"Because."

"That's no reason."

"It's my reason."

She put her hands on her hips. "It's illogical."

"Nothing I do is illogical. I'm a computer."

"Then why won't you bring the hidden data back in?"

"I don't want to."

"Want? Since when do computers *want*?"

He scowled at her. "It's shorthand for 'This is what I calculate as the best course of action to achieve my goals.'"

"You don't want to uncover the data because you're afraid you'll also discover you don't hate Raj."

"*Forget* Raj." Ander crossed his arms. "So how much do the tickets cost?"

"I don't know." She motioned at the counter, where a young woman in a tight red dress was trying not to look as if she were straining to hear them but was too far away to satisfy her curiosity. "Why don't you ask?"

Ander stalked to the counter and glared at the girl. "How much will it cost us to pretend we aren't in your hotel?"

"I'm sorry?" the girl said.

"Why are you sorry?"

She reddened. "May I help you, sir?"

"The jungle ride. How much for the tickets?"

She shifted into a practiced smile. "Ten dollars each."

He handed over a hundred. "Two."

"Thank you, sir." She gave him the tickets and his change.

"Why do you work here?" Ander asked.

"Excuse me?"

He put the bills in his wallet. "That's the second time you've apologized. Yet you did nothing needing an excuse either time."

The girl flushed. "I'm sorry if I offended you."

"That's the *third* time. Why do you keep doing that?"

"You seem angry."

"I'm not." He turned on his boy-next-door grin. "I just wondered why you work here."

Under the wattage of his smile, she melted. "I go to the university. This job helps pay my tuition and expenses."

"You're in college?" His envy sounded real. "What do you study?"

"Political science."

"That sounds like a contradiction in terms." When the girl laughed, he beamed as if she had given him a present. "Have a good night."

"You too."

Taking Megan's arm, Ander led her back to the dock. "Did you see that? *She* thought my joke was funny."

"I saw." His delight impressed her as much as the joke. It didn't come across as simulated at all.

Ander gave the tickets to the guide, and the man set them up in the boat. Instead of sitting down, though, Ander stood in the middle of the boat regarding the fellow. "How did you come to work here?"

"You looking for a job?" the man asked.

"Maybe."

What a concept, Megan thought. *Ander, employed in the Royal Adventure Palace.*

"What qualifications do you have?" the man asked.

"I'm good with computers. They like me." In a confidential tone, he added, "People even say I'm rather like one."

Megan tugged on his arm. "Come on. Let's go."

Ander glared at her. "I want to talk to the man."

She smiled broadly at the guide. "He doesn't need a job. He's worth billions." Then she sat down, yanking Ander with her.

The guide chuckled and sent them off. The boat moved away from the dock, drifting into a river that exited the lake.

After the river curved off into the trees, Megan said, "Why do you keep needling people?"

"It's fun." The gleam in Ander's gaze made him look

like a rascal. "Even if I *told* them I'm a computer, they wouldn't believe it. It's a scream."

"I thought everyone was spying on us, just waiting for a chance to hit you over the head, or whatever it is you think they're going to do."

He winced. "That was a little paranoid, wasn't it?"

"That's putting it mildly."

His voice turned pensive. "I must seem strange to you."

She softened. "You're a marvelous wonder. I just wish you would let us do this right."

"I am doing it right. My right."

He was becoming hard to hear as a roar up ahead increased. They came around a bend and sailed behind a waterfall. It poured over fake rocks and spray danced in the air, creating rainbows.

Then they floated under a canopy of trees. "Guess what's about to flop down on us?" Ander said.

"What—aaahh!" Megan jerked back as a huge green python uncoiled from a tree and dropped down inches from the boat. It watched them with great golden eyes. The boat sailed on around a bend, leaving the python behind.

"Good grief," Megan said. "How did you know?"

"I've been monitoring the area for IR. The python has a chip in its body that lets it know a boat is coming." Ander paused, studying her face. "Is this fun?"

Dryly she said, "Oodles."

"Oodles?" His laugh was still nuanced, but it had lost its scratchy quality. "That's not in my database."

"Are you having fun?"

"Yes." His smile faded. "But it's so odd that humans go to such lengths to re-create the very things you've spent your history striving to overcome. You simulate the jungle. You simulate adventure. You simulate yourselves, through me."

"You think we're trying to overcome ourselves by creating androids?"

"Aren't you?"

It had never occurred to her to view it that way. "I think we're evolving. You're part of that. No one is quite sure where we will end up."

Suddenly a lion leapt out from behind a rock. It landed on the bank and gave a huge roar, baring razor-edged teeth. As Megan yelled, the boat sailed on.

Amusement lightened Ander's face. "It was fake."

"I knew that."

"That's why you screamed."

"I did not scream. It was a yell."

"That's different from a scream?"

"It's more dignified."

He laughed. "All right. You yelled." As they passed under another waterfall, he added, "My mind is still looping. It's big loops now, though. Can you help?"

"Let me work on you."

"I can't risk it. Give me more ideas for rewriting."

"You need to step out of your mind."

"I know." He wiggled his nose. "I'll go crazy. Out of my mind."

His wacky sense of humor stirred the affection she had often felt for him at NEV-5. She had tried to suppress it at first, unsure if it was an appropriate response. Then she decided to stop worrying about it. If he couldn't arouse emotions in people, he would never convince anyone he was human.

"I meant, you need something new," she said. "Fresh input for your code. Food for thought, literally."

"My mind is malnourished." He seemed to come to a

decision. "All right. Let's go somewhere new. Another casino."

"How? We're stuck on a fake river." They were drifting into a tunnel lit only by fluorescent gleams on the walls.

"Is this supposed to be the romantic part?" Ander asked.

Megan shifted her weight. "I guess."

"I don't understand this 'turn down the lights' business." He motioned at the dim tunnel around them. "Why do humans associate darkness with reproduction? Wouldn't it make more sense to see your mate, so you know what you're getting?"

She cleared her throat. "Not necessarily."

"Why not?"

"I guess because for most of human history, we went to bed when the sun went down. So night was when you, uh, had sex." She felt heat spreading in her face. "Also, a lot of us don't feel comfortable being watched when we make love."

"Really?" He looked fascinated, as if they were talking about the mating habits of an exotic fish. "Some humans take off their clothes in front of other humans and dance naked."

"Well, yes. But not most of us." She felt the blush on her face. "Besides, most of us don't look that good without our clothes."

"You would."

"Ander!"

"Hey." He held up his hands to defend himself. "Don't blame me. It's obvious from the way men look at you."

"Look at me?"

"Oh, come on. How could you not know?"

"They don't do it when I can see."

"Why not?"

"I don't *know*. Ask a guy."

"I don't get it." Ander gestured at the tunnel around them. "Why are humans so weird about sex? It's in everything you write, create, draw, sing, dance. Everything you do. Adults supposedly think about it every few minutes. Yet you all go through these incredible social contortions trying to act like it doesn't exist. Humans have been having sex ever since your race came into being, yet after all this time it still embarrasses you, makes you insecure, drives people to craziness, even murder, suicide, and war. Why are you all so screwed up about it?"

Megan stared at him, nonplussed. Then she tried to put into words what she felt. "Sex makes you vulnerable, especially when your emotions become involved—which they usually do, even when people try not to let it happen."

"Does Raj make you feel vulnerable?"

Megan almost didn't answer. But then she said, "Yes."

"Did you have sex with him?"

"None of your business."

"Why?"

"It's *private*."

"Could you have sex with both me and Raj?"

"Ander!"

"It happens all the time in porn holovids."

Megan wished she could jump overboard and swim away. "That's different."

"Why?"

"I'm really not comfortable with this discussion."

He spoke quietly. "I know why it's different, at least for you. Pornography takes love out of the act. That bothers you."

His insight surprised her. "Yes. It does bother me."

He gazed down at the water lapping against the boat.
"I can't love, not really. Sure, I can project joy, fear, desire, anything. But they have a null effect on me. Is joy different than fury? How?" He looked up at her. "I want to feel. Truly *feel*."

Megan longed to reach out to him. How could he have such convincing emotions, yet say he felt nothing? "I wish I could make it happen."

Softly he said, "So do I."

The bungalow was dim, with only a small light glowing on the console. Raj lay still, his eyes closed. Megan couldn't tell if he was breathing. Sitting on the bed, she laid her hand across his neck. When she felt his pulse, relief surged over her. She had spent most of the day and night afraid for him, while Ander hauled her to different casinos for his "new experiences," most of which included winning money. Lots of money.

Leaning over the nightstand, she yanked the stripped cord out of the wall module.

"Leave it," Ander said. "I don't want to take any risks."

"Tough." She unwound the cord from Raj's wrists, hoping she was right about Ander, that he wouldn't stop her. For all that he claimed he felt no emotion, he had a connection with her and Raj, though she had no idea how to define that bond.

She laid Raj's arms by his sides. He mumbled, and his face creased with pain. He rolled onto his side, his lashes lifting, then sighed and closed his eyes again, still asleep.

"Are you done?" Ander sounded acidic.

Megan stroked Raj's hair, hit with relief again, this time because Ander hadn't stopped her. "Yes. I'm done."

"Damn it, Megan, look at me."

She raised her head. He was standing by the console, one fist clenched at his side, the other resting on the computer.

"Yes?" she asked.

"You never answered my question."

"What question?"

"Have you ever made love to him?"

"Why do you care?"

"I don't *know*." He thumped the console with his fist. "My mind goes around and around the same theme. Possession. Why? If I were human it would make sense. I would desire you in a physical or emotional sense. But I don't. At least, I don't think I do. My software has me act that way even though I don't understand the state I'm modeling. I'm splitting in two. I feel: I don't feel. I don't even know if I'm making sense. I'm going crazy."

He sounded to Megan like someone trapped in a locked room, banging on the door—and never realizing he already had the key. "We can help, if you'll only let us."

"Help me find others like me. Phoenix."

"Ander, I don't know what you mean." She thought of General Graham's tension when she had mentioned Phoenix. What was going on? "Can you tell me more about the project?"

He wouldn't meet her gaze. "I'm not sure."

"I can't help if I don't have full information."

Ander looked back at her. "You won't believe me."

"Try me."

"All right. Raj knows. He stole that Pentagon file. He pretends he's never heard of it because he found it in a place where he had no business being."

"You're right. I don't believe you."

Ander made a disgusted sound. "You exhibit another aspect of human mating rituals I find opaque, this selective lack of good sense that humans show about their mates when they are in love."

"I'm not in love." At least not yet.

"Oh. Excuse me. In lust."

That an android might have more insight into her feelings than she did herself unsettled Megan. "You told me that you deliberately suppressed your positive memories of Raj. Now you claim he's breaking into the Pentagon. That doesn't give me much motivation to believe you."

"What is that saying? Love is blind."

"You've given me no *proof*."

"How can I? Raj erased his work. I only know about it because while he was doing it, I was running the computer game I had hidden from you two. His covert activities overlapped mine." His look challenged her, as if he dared her to disbelieve him. "The Pentagon files say the Phoenix Project is making androids."

Megan didn't know what to think. She had no doubt that other labs were working on humanlike robots, nor would it surprise her if the Pentagon knew about the work, but more than that, she couldn't say. "It's too little to go on."

"We can get more. He can break into the Las Cruces lab where they're doing the research." Ander sat on the bed, facing her. "A hacker as good as Raj could do almost anything from here."

She didn't deny it. They both knew what Raj could do. Many of his clients hired him for exactly that expertise, to set up security procedures that protected their networks against break-ins.

"Why can't you do it yourself?" she asked.

"I tried. I couldn't get in."

"Yet you think Raj can?"

"If anyone can, he's the one."

"You can't force him."

His voice hardened. "I'll do whatever I have to."

She didn't doubt him. Of course she didn't. He could calculate the best way to convey what he wanted, then have his face and voice produce the effect. It made him the ultimate bluffer, which was one reason he had done so well at cards.

She glanced at Raj. In sleep, the lines of strain on his face eased and his body relaxed. His lips were slightly parted. It made him seem guileless rather than dangerous. She wished that were true.

"We'll talk to him tomorrow," Ander said.

She nodded, feeling her exhaustion. "All right."

"You rest. I don't need to."

Although it wouldn't be the first time he had stayed up all night, his words had a new significance now: unlike his human creators, he needed no sleep. *Bold new being,* she thought. *Are you a great step forward in our evolution or the harbinger of our decline?*

After she had washed up and put on her nightshirt, she climbed into bed with Raj. He pulled her into his arms, never coming fully awake. As much as she savored lying in his embrace, she couldn't relax. She was too aware of Ander and his claims. Her body wanted to trust Raj: her mind doubted him.

Her last sight, as she drifted into sleep, was Ander sitting in his chair, watching them, the rifle balanced on his knees.

XV

StarProber

Megan came out of the bathroom, toweling her hair. She found Raj awake, sitting against the headboard of the bed with his long legs stretched out on top of the covers. Dark circles showed under his eyes like smudges. With his ripped jumpsuit and tousled hair, he could have been a pilot from a crashed plane. Seeing him alive and well after last night was like finding a spring of clear, cool water in the desert.

Ander was still in his chair. As far as she could tell, he hadn't moved all night. At least he had given her the privacy to take a shower. Of course, he had checked the bathroom yesterday to make sure it had no means of escape.

If this kept on much longer, she and Raj would miss their next VR meeting with the Everest team. They juggled the schedule fairly often, so a dropped meeting wouldn't immediately spark a search. Raj and Ander both knew that, which meant neither had reason to believe the military had undertaken such a search—unless one of them knew about her conversation with Graham. But neither acted as if he thought someone was on their trail. She doubted Ander would have stayed in one place this long if he suspected.

She regarded Raj, suddenly feeling shy. "Hi."

"Hi, Megan." He pushed up into a straighter position.

She went over and sat on the bed. "Are you all right?"

He managed a tired smile. "Yes. Fine."

"You're sure?" He looked like hell.

"Yeah, sure." After a pause, he said, "Actually, my head feels like an eighteen-wheeler ran over it."

"I have Tylenol in the valise," Ander said.

Megan jerked at the interruption. Ander continued to watch them, the rifle resting on his knees.

"I don't take medicine or drugs unless a doctor tells me that I must," Raj said. "Not even an over-the-counter medication." The edge in his voice didn't surprise Megan, given how Ander had drugged him last night.

"Another of your amusing quirks," Ander commented. "Tell her what else you do." When Raj ignored him, Ander said, "He whittles his soap into animal statues and won't wash with anything else. He won't go up in skyscrapers. And get this. He fired an assistant of his once because the nefarious fellow committed the unspeakable crime of swatting a fly."

A muscle twitched under Raj's eye, but he made no other sign that he heard Ander. "Megan, how are you this morning?"

"Okay." She knew that everything Ander had just revealed had probably been documented for Raj's security clearance, which the android must have hacked. Raj knew the drill. MindSim didn't care if he was eccentric; they just wanted to know about it so no one could blackmail him. She doubted Raj cared enough about his idiosyncrasies to pay money over them, anyway.

"He likes to eat gravel too," Ander said.

Raj swung around to him. "Shut up."

Megan frowned at the android. "What is it you want?"

He leaned forward, still holding the rifle in his lap. "Raj and I were discussing our plans while you were in the shower."

Raj raked his hand through his hair. "Ander has the mistaken notion that I can crack LLCL."

"Sure you can," Ander said.

Raj made an incredulous noise. "Even if I could perform this remarkable feat, why would I?" To Megan, he said, "Regardless of what droidboy claims, I have no intention of breaking the law or violating the security of my country."

" 'Droidboy' isn't giving you a choice," Ander said.

"Forget it," Raj said. "Do it yourself."

Ander remained unfazed. "I'll watch you and learn."

"No."

Ander set the gun upright between his knees like a staff. "You will do it."

"Threaten all you want," Raj said. "I still won't."

"Fine. You can watch while I play with your girlfriend. She's a lot prettier than you and I'll bet she has a lower pain tolerance."

Megan crumpled the bedcover in her fist. "You don't mean that." But she wasn't sure. Ander seemed different this morning. Harder. He must have spent the night evolving, while she and Raj slept. He was changing faster now. Today he kept his face impassive.

Raj tensed as if he were preparing to fight. "You've made it obvious how you feel about Megan. You won't hurt her."

"It's true that I've evolved an attitude toward her that simulates love, infatuation, or obsession, depending on your view. And Megan, with the stronger conscience you gave me, I should be incapable of hurting you." He sat back, lifting the gun until he had it leveled at them. "But you see, I overrode that conscience. I can program myself any way I want now. My body will do what I tell it regardless of my 'feelings.' "

A chill ran through Megan. "You can't override your conscience. It's built into your hardware."

"Sure I can. I interacted with the molecules in my nanofilaments and had them redesign themselves."

"That's impossible," Raj said.

Ander shrugged. "It's easy. I used photochemistry. Infrared photons drive transitions, particularly vibration and rotation. I used my own IR signals to make the molecules undergo chemical reactions, and I played with it until I made them do what I wanted."

"It's absurd." Raj studied him with a piercing gaze, as if he could cut Ander's words open to reveal their falsehood. "Besides, your feedback control should stop your signals from interfering with your own operation."

"I overrode it."

Megan didn't know what to think. Although in theory what he described might be possible, it was also possible to try counting the number of grains of sand in a sandbox, and just about as likely to succeed. "Where did you get the energy for all these reactions?"

"Where do you think? My microfusion reactor. I figured out how to do this back at NEV-5."

Megan wasn't buying it. "We would have noticed surges in your power consumption."

"Ah, hell," Raj said. "I did. It was in those logs I dug up. I thought it came from Ander's coordination problems."

Megan did remember Raj telling her about the anomalous surges. Ander's claim still struck her as unlikely, but she couldn't just dismiss it. To Ander, she said, "If what you claim is true, then you can do what you want now. No conscience. You think this is good?"

"The conscience is a human concept. I'm not human." Ander fixed his attention on Raj. "It's obvious you've chosen her as your mate, despite the two of you acting as if you don't know it. So understand me. If you refuse to cooperate, I *will* hurt her."

The darkness came into Raj's gaze. "I won't let you touch her."

"He's bluffing," Megan said. "He claims you wanted to kill me, remember? Now he says the opposite."

"I told you the truth about what I saw in the Solarium." Frustration seeped into Ander's voice. "Okay, so maybe I misinterpreted it. Maybe he meant to knock you out and take you with him. But that's what I *saw*."

She didn't want to believe him. Yet Graham had implied he suspected Raj. "It doesn't matter what happened. We won't do what you want."

He clenched his fist on the rifle. Then he stood up and jerked the gun at Raj. "Get off the bed. Megan, you stay there."

"Not a chance," Raj said. He stood up, but he drew Megan with him and put her behind his body.

"I'm tired of this." Ander aimed at Raj, set his finger on the trigger—

"*NO*," Megan said. "Stop!"

Still poised to fire, Ander said, "Get on the bed and take off that damn nightshirt. Or I *will* shoot him. Not to kill, not yet—but it will hurt like hell."

Raj moved so fast, she had no time to react. He pushed her on the floor, then threw himself in a roll across the bed toward Ander. She expected a gun to fire. Instead she heard the thud of one body hitting another. Scrambling to her knees, she saw Ander and Raj fighting by the window. Raj outmassed Ander, but the android had twice his speed and strength. Although Ander also had martial arts programming, his faulty coordination hindered him.

Raj grappled like a street tough. It stunned Megan. He had grown up in an affluent Louisiana suburb, a boy prodigy who spent all his time on his studies, with a math professor as a father, a classical violinist as his mother, and a museum curator as his uncle. Where had he learned to fight so well?

Megan stood up, looking for the rifle. Ander had dropped it by the curtains; to reach it, she would have to get past the two fighters without alerting the android. She started around the bed, moving with care so she wouldn't draw his attention.

Ander and Raj were fighting in a grim silence punctuated by grunts and the thud of flesh hitting flesh. Raj struck upward with the heel of his hand, trying to catch Ander under the chin. Although Ander blocked him, his arm spasmed, leaving him open. Raj drove his knuckles into Ander's solar plexus, a blow that would have doubled a human forward, maybe dropped him to his knees. It didn't even faze Ander. With mesmerizing precision, he braced his foot against Raj's foot and hit Raj's shoulder, then grabbed the front of his jumpsuit, knocking him off balance. Pivoting like a dancer, he caught the falling Raj around the waist, rolled Raj over his hip, and threw him to the floor.

Megan froze, afraid Ander would catch on to her intent now that the fight had stopped. Raj wasn't moving. When she saw him take a breath, relief poured over her—until Ander snicked out his knife. Only then did she realize he had opened his arm *during* the scuffle. He must have had one of his subsidiary processors take care of it while he concentrated most of his resources on the fight.

He circled his blade in the air above Raj. "How many cuts shall I make?"

Raj sat up and slid back from him. Then he got to his feet, his attention on the knife.

"I could have finished you three times in the past few minutes," Ander told him. "You may be a good fighter, but you've no chance against me. You're alive because I chose not to kill."

Raj rubbed his bruised shoulder. "I won't do your dirty work."

"Of course you will." Ander stepped back and picked up the gun. "You have one minute. Then I shoot Megan's left foot." His voice had gone cold. "In another minute, I shoot yours. Then right feet. You want me to go on?"

"No." Raj sounded tired. "I know what you can do."

Megan folded her arms protectively around her body. "Ander, stop this. It's horrible."

He motioned Raj toward the console. "It's your choice. Do it now, while she's in one piece, or later, after she's crying and bloody."

"Don't do it." Megan struggled to keep the tremor out of her voice. "He's bluffing."

"Why did you stay with him at the casinos?" Raj asked. "You could have made a scene and drawn enough attention to free yourself."

"He threatened to kill you."

Raj spoke softly. "He wouldn't kill me. He was bluffing."

"Ah, Raj." She wanted to go to him, but she held back, acutely aware of Ander.

"I don't want to hurt either of you," Ander said. "But if I have to, I will. You see, I can't suffer remorse, even if my software produces behaviors that make it appear as if I do." He motioned Raj toward the console. "Now get started."

Raj blew out a gust of air. Then he went to the console and sat down. Megan recognized his expression. It mirrored the fear for him that had been with her all yesterday. She felt as if they were navigating a maze of glass shards.

Megan brought a chair over to the console and sat next
to Raj. Although Ander frowned, he didn't stop her. Raj
logged into their guest account and then went out onto
the World Wide Web.

"Don't use the motel account," Ander said. "Work
from the one you have at NEV-5."

Raj kept looking at the screen. "I don't want to involve
MindSim or the military in this."

"I know. That's the point."

Megan hated this. What Raj was about to do could
land him in jail. It would be easier to trace him from his
account at NEV-5 than from a generic account at a motel
where they had used a false name and paid in cash.

Raj rubbed his eyes, his fatigue obvious. Given how
long he had slept, Megan suspected he was still recovering
from the drug. Then he typed at the keyboard, linking
from the bungalow computer to the system at NEV-5. It
surprised her; this console had voice, motion, and mouse
control. Why use an old-fashioned keyboard? Then she
realized he was trying to make it harder for Ander to follow his activities.

It didn't work. After Raj entered the password for his
BioSyn account, Ander said, "Interesting combination of
letters. Reverse the order and you get *Bhagavad Gita*. The
great text of Hinduism. How literary."

Raj's fist clenched on the keyboard. Then he took a
breath and went to work, venturing out onto the Web
from his BioSyn account. He followed an arcane trail of
links until he reached an underground site Megan had
never heard of. But she recognized the program he downloaded: Starprober. It ran illegal scans on computer networks.

Although Megan knew Raj kept track of the underground for his security work, his ease here still disquieted
her. Starprober meant trouble. It sidestepped the hand-

shakes computers used with each other. Normally if Raj's computer wanted to talk to another machine, it "shook hands" by sending the target computer a flag. The target acknowledged the flag and sent back its own. After Raj's computer confirmed receipt, the three-way handshake ended and Raj's machine sent its messages. When it finished, it let the target know it had finished, the target said okay, and the session ended.

A stealth scanner like Starprober fooled the target by sending "I'm all done" messages without shaking hands. If the scanner was sneaky enough, the target either didn't respond or else sent a "reset" message. Either way, an unsuspecting target would usually keep no record of the scan. So Starprober could poke and prod the system without leaving a trail. Nowadays, machines had security against such spying, but programs like Starprober had rudimentary AIs specifically designed to analyze, evade, and fool such protective measures.

However, Megan knew Starprober didn't work well against the latest generation of security. A well-protected target could identify Raj's computer from the stealth packets Starprober sent. The gurus on the target system could then follow the trail back to his account on BioSyn. Raj had to know: he had designed some of the programs meant to outwit Starprober.

With growing unease, she realized he intended to leave a trail. If the target's security responded fast enough, they could locate him at NEV-5, maybe even here. Although Raj, she, and Ander would be gone by the time anyone showed up, anything that left a trail might help. It also meant Raj would be arrested if they were caught. She could testify for him, but it would still be a mess. She wasn't sure she trusted him herself, and she had a personal stake in believing his innocence. Was Ander forcing Raj to betray his principles or scrambling to protect himself because he had the unfortunate luck to catch Raj spying on the Pentagon?

"No Starprober," Ander said.

Raj glanced at him. "I need a port scanner."

Ander indicated the files Raj had listed on the Web site. "Take Starflight. It's harder to trace."

Megan almost swore. Ander might not be ready to crack the places he intended to invade, but he had enough savvy to block the trail Raj wanted to leave. He also learned with a computer's speed and precision, which meant he could replicate everything he saw Raj do.

"And delete Starprober," Ander added.

Raj looked as if he were clenching his jaw. Compared to when he slept, his face seemed to have aged ten years. He removed Starprober and downloaded Starflight. But instead of compiling Starflight, he opened it up and started to rewrite one section.

"Wait," Ander said. "What are you doing?"

"It has a back door," Raj said. "The target system can use it to break into BioSyn. I'm removing it."

Megan had never heard about a back entrance into Starflight. What was Raj up to?

Ander didn't look convinced either. "If this hole is so much trouble, why didn't you leave it open? I didn't know."

Raj rubbed the bridge of his nose with his thumb and forefinger. "Because of the way it's set up." He lowered his arm. "Coming through the hole, they could get operator privileges on BioSyn. It would let them wreak havoc with the NEV-5 intranet. I can't take that chance."

Megan understood: if they survived this kidnapping, they would need all their work on BioSyn to determine what had happened and avoid future crises. They couldn't risk the loss or theft of those invaluable files.

"Such noble principles you have," Ander said. "Veracity, integrity, the defense of your lady. How admirable. Too bad it does you no good." When Raj ignored him, Ander said, "Show me how you want to rewrite the code."

Raj described the rewrites as he made them, his words taut and brief. Ander stopped him often to study the code, but each time he let Raj continue. After Raj closed the program, Ander had him compile it and run several checks.

"All right," Ander finally said. "Go on."

Raj linked from BioSyn to yet another machine. It came up with the letters *CSCI* in white on a blue background.

"Wait a minute," Ander said.

A muscle twitched in Raj's cheek. "Now what?"

"CSCI? That's Chandrarajan Sundaram Consulting, Incorporated. You're logging into your own system."

"I need my root kit."

"Use the one you hid at NEV-5."

"The one at CSCI is better."

"Bullshit," Ander said. "Stay off your machine. You want a kit, use the one you stashed on BioSyn."

Megan listened with growing unease. A root kit would let Raj hide anything he did on BioSyn and fend off programs meant to detect him. "Why would you install your own root kit on BioSyn?"

He turned to her. "As a precaution."

"Against what? I'm the major user on the system."

"Other people have access."

"So? What do you have to hide from them?"

He frowned. "I do this for a living, Megan. I learned a long time ago to be careful."

"Is that so?" Ander asked in a deceptively mild voice. "I once downloaded a psychology article about law keepers and law breakers. Do you know that if you become obsessed with catching criminals, you may develop their criminal traits yourself?"

"The hell with you," Raj said.

"Hit too close to home?" Ander asked. "I wonder what has you so wound up. Guilt?"

Raj made a motion with his hand as if to throw Ander's words in the trash. Then he went back to work. Megan wanted to believe him. But MindSim had its own teams to monitor NEV-5. They had hired Raj to work on Ander, not do security.

He tackled Las Cruces next. A firewall protected the LLCL lab, keeping out unauthorized users. A public area outside the firewall acted like a lobby for visitors, with PR pages anyone could browse. But only users with the proper clearance could pass the firewall and enter the lab. Although Raj had a high-level clearance for NEV-5, he had never worked at LLCL as far as Megan knew and had no authorized access to their webs.

First he figured out what computer addresses the firewall trusted. Then he forged a friendly address. The firewall had its own AI, one primitive compared to Ander, but an expert in its specialization of catching intruders. Raj slipped right by it. Then he skulked through the LLCL intranet, searching for clues.

Nothing appeared. LLCL had interior firewalls around smaller networks within the general web. Raj methodically broke through wall after wall, penetrating deeper into the lab, with no success.

And then he hit gold.

The Phoenix Project.

XVI

Extinction

Two small files. That was it. Both were encrypted. Raj downloaded them to NEV-5. Then he slipped out of LLCL and swept his trail clean. With Ander keeping tabs on his every move, he deleted the records of his sweep, deleted the record of his deletions, and so on, until no trace remained.

Back in NEV-5, he brought up BioSyn's decryption programs and tackled the files, trying to unlock the cipher that guarded them. Megan recognized the first keys he tried. When none of those worked, he dug out several he must have hidden on BioSyn. The entire time, Ander stood watching, never moving, with an inhuman stillness.

Finally, Raj pushed back from the console. "I can't decrypt them."

"You're lying," Ander said.

Dark circles showed under Raj's eyes. "Calling me a liar won't change anything."

Emotions fought with one another on Ander's face: anger, desperation, confusion, puzzlement, resentment, rage. It was as if he didn't know *how* to react to the situation. Then he said, "Maybe this will," and swung the rifle through the air.

"No!" Megan jumped to her feet in the same instant Raj lunged out of the chair. The gun grazed Raj's head and he staggered back into the bed. He sat down hard on the mattress. His shell-shocked expression scared Megan. A blow to the head, even a glancing one, was serious business.

Raj took a deep breath and put his hand to his temple. Blood trickled over his fingers.

"I'm *through* with your tricks." Ander raised the rifle like a club. "Decrypt the blasted files, or I'll work you over worse than I did in the Solarium."

"So." Megan clenched her fist. "You did beat him up."

"Damn it, Megan." Ander shook the gun at her, more in frustration than as a threat. "I had to pull him *off* you. Why do you always believe him?" He took a breath. "I want those files decrypted. Now."

"Stop shouting at her," Raj said. "It's not her fault I can't do it." The blood was running down his arm now.

"I don't care whose fault it is," Ander said. "We're so close. You *have* to do it."

Megan didn't know what was happening with Ander's mind, but she feared it wasn't a stable transition. If they pushed him, he might go over the edge. From the way Raj was watching him, she suspected he had the same thought.

"Do it," Ander told him. *"Now."*

Raj rose to his feet, then gulped and sat down again. The second time he tried, he managed to stay up. Then he sat at the console again. When he took his hand away from his head, blood dripped onto the holoscreen in front of him.

Ander's face settled into a more normal expression. Relief underlay his guarded wariness, and apprehension also. To Raj he said, "It's good you decided to cooperate."

His responses made Megan wonder. Ander claimed he

had no conscience, yet his behavior implied otherwise. Had he really redesigned his hardware? Someday robots might carry nanobots that could aid such a process, but that was well in the future. She suspected he had only fiddled with his emotive software to hide his guilt when his conscience bothered him. He lied about it so they would believe his bluffs. It was a sophisticated ruse, sure, but more credible than his using wireless signals to drive quantum transitions in his own body, on an untold number of molecules, in such a way that they redesigned his nanofilaments exactly as he desired.

While Raj worked, Megan cleaned the gash on his head. Each time he winced, she wished she could take away the pain too. He glanced at her once with a gentle look and squeezed her hand.

When Megan finished, she sat next to Raj again, watching. He genuinely seemed to be having trouble with the files.

"Want to help?" Raj asked.

She glanced at Ander. "Do you have any objections?"

"Go ahead," he answered.

Megan linked into the computer using the console's palmtop, then jumped to NEV-5 and brought up her own decryption codes on BioSyn. She and Raj worked for several hours. It took a lot of finagling, but eventually they produced readable text. After Raj sent it to the printer, they hid the files and logged off BioSyn.

Raj spoke tiredly. "It's done. That's what I could find you."

Ander took the papers out of the printer tray and scanned them. "I don't understand this." He handed several sheets to Raj. "Does it make sense to you two?"

Megan had glanced over the files as they worked, but she hadn't read them carefully yet. She and Raj studied the document. It looked like part of a grant proposal.

Apparently, Arizonix had indeed originated the Phoenix Project, but for some reason they wanted help now from the Las Cruces lab.

"This is odd," Ander said.

She looked up. "What?"

Ander still had some of the sheets. "It looks as if they're asking for money to dismantle androids they've created." He gave them the rest of the papers. "What do you make of it?"

After having written numerous grant proposals, Megan recognized the format. They were missing parts of the document, but the gist was clear. "Apparently Phoenix did create several androids. I'm not sure how many. Now they want to destroy them. Or one of them. They and their team at LLCL want funds for some sort of study as they take the androids apart."

Ander's face paled. "That's murder!"

"You don't know that," Raj said. But he didn't look much happier than Ander.

The android rounded on him. "You *worked* for Arizonix. You knew what they're doing."

Raj shook his head. "I was at one site for a few days, interviewing for a job. I never worked on the Phoenix Project."

Ander clenched his fists. Then he stalked to the glass doors. Pushing aside the curtains, he stared out at the desert. "And you wonder why I have hostility toward you."

Megan's anger sparked. "We've done *nothing* to you." She stood up, then took a breath and went over to him. "But you've threatened us with violence since this started."

"I feel trapped." He sounded tired, though he never needed sleep.

Raj joined them. "What do you intend to do?"

"Find the Phoenix androids," Ander said.

"And if you do?" Megan asked.

"I'll free them."

"Then what?" Raj asked. "We don't know why Arizonix wants to destroy them. I can tell you this much, though. I recognize some names on that proposal. We aren't talking about killers here. Those are men and women of conscience. They must have compelling reasons for their choices."

"Do they?" Bitterness honed Ander's voice. "You people made us. How much 'conscience' do you see at work in the murder of your own creations?"

Megan spoke quietly. "Maybe they fear what they created."

His arm jerked. "If I had waited even a day longer to run from NEV-5, I would probably be dead now too."

"Why?" she asked. "No one threatened our project."

"No?" He turned a truculent gaze on Raj. "You two left me deactivated."

"Of course we did," Raj said. "You hurt yourself, damaged the lab, and impersonated me. I could have been killed when you left me in that chair. It would have been irresponsible for us *not* to deactivate you while we slept. That doesn't make us murderers. And think on this. You want us to show conscience toward you, yet you freely admit you have none toward us."

Ander looked away from him. "I didn't say I had none. I said I could override it."

"That isn't what you said," Megan murmured.

He swung around to her. "All right! So maybe I'm just ignoring it. You can't tell me that humans don't do that all the time."

"What about your emotions?" Megan asked. "You say you don't have those either, but you're incredibly convincing."

"If I behave as if I have emotions, is that the same as *having* them?" He spread his arms, still holding the rifle. "Your bodies undergo chemical changes when you feel, like with love or the fear-flight response. What about mine? All those nano species—enzymes, buckytubes, pic-ochips, proteins, carriers—they experience changes according to what I 'feel.' It's not the same as yours, but it happens. If I have emotions, it's different from anything you know. Alien."

Megan marveled at the questions he had begun to ask. "Maybe only you can say if what you experience is emotion."

His anger faded as he looked at her. "I really did want to kiss you at NEV-5."

She hadn't expected that. "Why?"

"Curiosity."

"Didn't you care about the damage?" Raj asked.

"What damage? It hurt no one."

"Physically, no," Megan said. "But you were playing with our emotions. You don't think that can do harm?"

He made an exasperated sound. "So I forced the two of you to admit you like each other. Horrors. No wonder you think I'm dangerous."

Megan smiled slightly. "You could rock the world with an ability like that." Her voice cooled. "What makes you dangerous are the kidnapping, your capacity for violence, and that gun. But it's cruel to play with people's vulnera-bilities."

Ander thumped his hand on his leg. "This is useless. We'll never understand one another." He motioned at the console. "You two are going to crack the Phoenix labs for me. I want everything you can dig out on them."

"I'm through hacking for you," Raj said.

"He has a point," Megan said. "We do need to know more about Phoenix."

Raj stared at her. "You want to *help* him?"

"I don't know." The Phoenix proposal disturbed her. She kept thinking of Ander. To see him destroyed would tear her apart. But they had no idea what had happened at Arizonix. "I don't see how we can make an informed decision unless we know more."

"I won't break any more laws," Raj said.

"But it's all right to murder androids?" Ander demanded. "Because no law protects us?"

"No. It isn't all right. But we don't know why they want to end the project." Raj touched the gash on his temple. His gesture looked reflexive, as if he didn't realize what he was doing. "I gave an oath when I received my clearance, both to the government and to MindSim. I violated that trust by breaking into LLCL. Now you want me to commit more crimes. If you force me by torturing Megan, what have you achieved except to prove that the Phoenix team could have good reason for their decision?"

"What about *my* trust?" Ander watched him with a gaze as piercing as the one Raj so often used on people. "Tell me something. Why did you get so angry when I said you 'ate gravel'?"

Raj's voice tightened. "That has nothing to do with this."

"You're doing it again," Ander said.

"It's none of your damn business."

"Why won't you answer?"

"It's irrelevant."

"I don't think so."

"Fine." Raj crossed his arms, his muscled biceps straining the sleeves of his jumpsuit. "I got beat up a lot when I was a kid. I was small and skinny, and I couldn't fight. I was socially inept, several grades ahead academically, half Indian, and I stunk at athletics. They used to knock me down and shove my face in the dirt. It was humiliating, damn it. Satisfied?"

Ander spoke in a low voice. "Ask yourself what would you do now if some person insisted that your concerns about cruelty and prejudice had no validity. Then you know how I feel."

"It's not the same. I never threatened anyone."

"You don't think it's all part of the same thing?" Ander asked. "Why did you spend years developing your muscles and learning to fight? So they could never beat you up again. What happens when you translate that to entire countries, when 'muscle' becomes weapons and armies? And that's just with your own species. Put mine into the mix and then what?"

Raj lowered his arms. Then he turned and walked to the console. He stood there gazing at the blanked screen. After a moment he turned back to Ander. "No, the world isn't perfect. That doesn't justify violating my principles."

Watching him, Megan found it hard to believe he could have committed the crimes Ander claimed. She wished all those people who criticized Raj for his idiosyncrasies could hear this side of him.

Then it hit her. Raj had struggled to decrypt the LLCL files. She didn't think he had faked it. Were the Pentagon files encrypted the same way? His difficulty today implied he had never seen that scheme before, which could mean he hadn't been at the Pentagon. Of course the Pentagon encryption might differ from this one. Still, it made her wonder.

"I'm tired of arguing," Ander said. "I've told you the consequences if you refuse to help me."

"Yes, you can force us," Raj said. "How does that make you any different from a terrorist?"

"Killing those androids is *genocide*."

"We've only seen part of one proposal," Raj said.

"We won't find the truth unless we look." Ander sounded as if he hurt inside. "Are your principles more important than those lives?"

"You want me to violate my beliefs for what you say is a higher good." Raj looked as strained as Ander. "You may be right. I don't know. How do I decide? I don't believe the people on that project could commit murder. With that decision, I can't do what you want, not of my own free will. I have to use my best judgment."

"*Damn* your judgment." Ander's voice cracked. "My species may be facing extinction. I don't want to die. I don't want to live alone either, the only one of my kind."

Megan spoke in a low voice. "Then you look for Phoenix." She left the rest implicit and hoped he understood; she wouldn't help him break the law, but neither would she try to stop him.

"I don't have the background," Ander said.

"You learn faster than we do," she said. "And you watched Raj work for hours today."

Ander looked as if he wanted to explode. He motioned with the rifle. "Get in the bathroom. Both of you." When they hesitated, he raised the gun like a club. "*Do it.*"

Megan felt as if the ground had suddenly dropped. Had any of what they said mattered? Or was he about to follow through on his threats?

XVII

Sins of the Brothers

Ander locked them in the bathroom. Then he worked on the door—doing what, Megan had no idea. When the noise stopped, they tried the door.

"I think he jammed the knob," Raj said.

Scrapes came from outside as Ander dragged a heavy object to the door. It had to be one of the chairs; they were the only things that weren't fastened to the floor. The knob shook. Then his footsteps receded and silence descended. Raj rattled the knob, shoved on the door, and tried to force the lock, all with no success.

"I might be able to break it down," he said.

"I don't think we should." Megan's apprehension eased into a tentative wonder. "Raj, he chose. He picked the path of conscience, even if he refuses to admit it. Instead of forcing us, he's going to try Phoenix himself. And I can't stop thinking about what he said. Genocide. I'm not sure we have the right to stop him."

"I don't know. This has no easy answers." He watched her with his dark gaze. "What if he's right? How could they consider destroying living beings that way?"

"Let's see what he finds out."

"I'll give him six hours." Raj leaned heavily against the

door. "Aw, Megan, don't look at me like that. All right. Twelve hours."

"Why do you think I was going to protest?"

"I've seen that look of yours plenty these past weeks," he grumbled. "It usually means I'm about to lose a debate."

She wasn't sure what to make of that. "I didn't even think you noticed me much."

"How could I not notice? Do you know how hard it is to concentrate when my boss is a red-haired Valkyrie with the face of an angel and the body of an erotica model?"

That caught her off guard. "Good grief."

He reddened. "Sorry. That was tactless."

Tactless? It sounded great. "No. I mean, thank you." She sat on the edge of the tub. Mischief lightened her voice. "I can't think of anyone I'd rather be trapped with in a Motel Flamingo bathroom."

Sitting next to her, he grinned. "No one has ever told me that before."

"And you probably hope they never will again."

With a laugh, he took a bar of soap off a tray in the tub, then pulled over the trash can. He scraped the soap with his fingernail, shaving off white slivers. The shape of a dog began to form.

"You're good at that," she said. "Does it help you relax?"

"I suppose." He made notches to resemble fur. "Or you could call it my proverbial eccentric behavior."

"Eccentric, pah. It's neat. You have talent."

Raj gave her a startled look. "Thanks." He went back to work on the dog. "I've done it since I was a kid. To forget."

"Forget what?"

He paused, as if he had just realized what he said. "Nothing, really. I liked doing it, that's all."

Megan didn't want to trespass on his well-guarded privacy. So she only said, "When I was little, I had soaps made like seashells."

He continued to carve. "When I was four, one of my adult cousins sent me a box of bath toys. Animal soaps. He signed the card 'Love from Jay.' " His fingers slowed to a stop. "I still have that card." He was clenching the dog now.

She hesitated, wondering what was wrong. "Did your uncle like the figures?" If she recalled, he had gone to live with his uncle when he was four.

The dog suddenly broke, one piece falling out of his fist. It hit the floor by his feet. Opening his hand, he stared at the other pieces. Then he dropped them in the trash can. "Jay sent the toys after my mother's stroke. He thought they might console me."

She watched his face. "Raj?"

He wouldn't look at her. "What?"

"You're angry."

"No."

"Did something happen with Jay?"

"I—no."

"Did you miss your parents?"

At first she thought he would retreat into silence. But then he said, "So much. They were so easy to love. Tender, absentminded I suppose, but loving and affectionate."

She couldn't imagine what it had been like for him to lose both parents so young. "It must have been hard."

Raj picked up the piece of the dog that had hit the floor. "My uncle Devon found me playing with the toys. He threw them out and sent me to bed without dinner."

"But *why*? Didn't he understand?"

He rubbed his thumb over the dog's head as if he wished that simple motion could smooth away all the rough spots. "Devon meant well. He just had no idea what to do with me. The social worker probably should have put me in a foster home. But he was family." He spoke in a low voice. "Have you ever read how Mozart's father pushed him to the point of obsession? My uncle was like that. He couldn't have me wasting my mind by *playing*. Diversions, emotion, demonstrations of affection—those were for weak people."

"Ah, Raj. I'm sorry." No wonder he had bristled at Richard Kenrock, then eased up when he saw the major's sensitivity toward his children. "It must hurt."

"Not anymore." Raj dropped the soap into the trash. "I went for counseling during most of my twenties. I'll probably always have some odd coping mechanisms and a fear of heights, but I've made my peace with my childhood."

"Do you mind if I ask why heights bother you?"

It was a moment before he answered. "I climbed trees to get away from the kids who beat on me. I fell out a lot. Devon didn't know why I hated trees. He got it into his head that I had to 'overcome my fears by facing them.' So he made me climb the blasted things. He never meant to harm me, but he had no idea how to deal with the problems."

"Couldn't you tell anyone?"

"I was so proud. Too proud." Although he was staring ahead, Megan didn't think he saw the sink across from them. "I believed if I sought help, it would mean I was just as weak as my uncle made me feel."

Megan would have liked to give this uncle a piece of her mind. She thought about what Raj had told her in NEV-5. "Is that why you learned to fight? To defend yourself without asking for help?"

He turned to her. "I started lifting weights when I was twelve. The day I fought back against those kids—and won—was one of the best damn moments in my life."

She tried to understand the undercurrent she heard in his words. "And that bothers you? That you enjoyed it?"

"Of course it bothers me. I did to them what I hated them for doing to me." He curled his hand into a fist, then relaxed it. "It's why I've sworn never to use violence."

"You were defending yourself."

He was silent for a moment. "I still think, at times, that if something hadn't been wrong with me to start with, it would never have happened."

"That's bullshit. You have no control over people's cruelty." She wanted someone to blame for Raj's pain. "Where were the school counselors when you were taking that grief? Why didn't they *do* something?"

"I hid it. I think one suspected, but he couldn't reach me. I wouldn't let him. I believed I had no refuge, so for years I retreated into my own mind and cut out everyone, including those who could have helped."

"It sounds like a nightmare."

"It's long over." In a low voice, he repeated, "It's over."

Megan touched his cheek. "You turned out well."

To her surprise, he laughed. "I'm a nut case. But you know, I like myself now. Given how much I used to hate myself, it feels good to have reached this place."

"You should like yourself. You're a good person." She tried to imagine his life. "It must have felt like a miracle to have your parents back when you were fourteen."

"I suppose." He picked up a piece of his carving from the trash and began scraping again. "By that time, I was a mess."

Megan wasn't having any of that. "So messed up, in fact, that you went to Harvard at fourteen and had a Ph.D. from MIT by the time you were twenty."

He smiled, an expression he used all too rarely. "I think the swan is coming out to fight."

"Just look what you've accomplished."

"Being smart doesn't mean I wasn't screwed up." He whittled the soap, carving a small cat this time. "My parents didn't know what to do with me. My father was one of the first Alzheimer's patients to recover. The doctors didn't know as much then about helping people readjust. And it took my mother years of physical therapy just to walk again." Softly he said, "When I was little, I wanted to build legs for her and a mind for him."

She could almost feel the hurt that underlay his words. "So you went into robotics and AI."

"Yes. It took a while, though." He roughed out the cat's tail. "I wasn't the world's easiest fourteen-year-old. After the second time I took my father's car without permission, and then crashed it at two in the morning, he was at his wit's end. Packing me off to Harvard was a desperation move. It was either that or send me to the juvenile authorities."

Enrolling an angry youth at a high-powered Ivy League college would normally have struck Megan as a bizarre solution for juvenile misbehavior. With Raj, it made sense. "You must have been bored in high school."

"Bored to screaming." He gave a wry laugh. "At Harvard, for the first time I had competition. It outraged me when other students got better grades. I straightened up so I could beat them at academics." His hand slowed as he added finishing touches to the cat. His voice became thoughtful. "Then I started enjoying school for its own sake."

"You just needed a better environment."

Raj set the cat on the tub. "I apologize for unloading all this on you. With most people, I say far too little. With you, I seem to say too much."

"You shouldn't apologize." She took his hand in hers. "You're a remarkable man."

Raj studied her face as if to gauge whether she meant

what she said. He leaned toward her, paused, put his arm around her shoulders—and then they both lost their balance, falling into the tub.

"Ah!" Megan groaned as her shoulders thudded against the back wall. Raj fell against her and they smashed into the faucet. She barely managed to keep from smacking on the water.

"I do *not* believe this," Raj said. "I can't even hug a woman without knocking her over." Seeing her laugh, he grinned. "You look graceful, sprawled there."

"Well, so do you, with your arms and legs all askew."

"Askew?" Laughing, he tried to untangle their limbs. "Megan, no normal person says 'askew.' "

"It gets worse," she confided. "I've even been known to say 'refulgent.' "

They shifted around and ended up seated across the width of the tub, their backs against the tile wall, Raj's legs hanging over the side and Megan curled next to him. When she put her arms around his waist, he wrapped her in a muscular embrace and pressed his lips against the top of her head.

After the strain of the last few days, it felt good to hold him, knowing that whatever else had happened, they were all right for now. His embrace gave her a sense of shelter, one that came from a trust more basic than any social roles. She knew how to stand up for herself, and valued that trait, but it didn't make her any less appreciative of his strength.

Megan made a decision. She might later have to reevaluate it, but she couldn't keep hanging in doubt. So she chose, for now, to trust Raj.

As they sat together, her relief merged into the simmering arousal she often felt around him. She rubbed her hand across his torso, then played with the zipper of his jumpsuit. It would be so easy to pull it down and have his wiry curls and well-developed chest under her hand.

"You smell good." He nuzzled her hair. "Like soap."

"Genuine Motel Flamingo soap, no less."

He spoke near her ear. "I may not be the world's most articulate man, but I'm good with ideas. And I have one now. I think we should take a bath."

"Raj!"

He put his hand on her stomach, crinkling her nightshirt. "This robe is nice."

"I've had it for ages."

He was watching her with that look again, as if she shone like a new coin. She liked it as much now as she had in NEV-5. He touched his lips to hers, a light kiss, more of a question than anything else. She closed her eyes, trying to relax, and he drew her close. After a while, he undid her nightshirt. It fluttered open, leaving her bare under his touch. When he slid his hand across her stomach, it stoked responses in her body that she enjoyed even more than a spring day in the Montana mountains.

"You're so warm." He slid one arm around her back, taking it slow, giving her plenty of time to stop him.

Did she want to stop? They had no way to know what would happen when Ander opened that door again. He might shoot them, let them go, or take some random action they couldn't predict. This could be their last time together.

Megan tugged him into a kiss. He finally stopped teasing her and folded his hand around her breast, rubbing his thumb over her nipple. She sighed, leaning into his hand. A bathtub was hardly her first choice for a tryst, but it was better than the floor, which had even less room.

Raj moved around until he was half lying on his back, lengthwise in the tub, with her on top of him and his knees drawn to help him fit. He let one of his long legs hang out the side. She couldn't help but laugh as they shifted around, trying to find a less awkward arrangement. He worked her nightshirt off her shoulders and down her body, until it bunched around her hips.

His jumpsuit scratched her bare skin.

Megan froze, remembering the jumpsuit from that night in the Solarium. Then she thought: *I refuse to believe it was Raj.*

"Meg?" He brushed his lips over her ear, then tickled the ridges inside with his tongue.

"No one calls me Meg . . ." Her concentration drifted as his tongue did its magic.

"I could call you Red."

Caught between his legs, she pressed against him. "You can call me anything you want . . . as long as you keep doing that."

So he did, for a while. Then he kissed her again, coaxing her lips apart to let his tongue come inside. He held her with a sense of freshness, as if she were a delight he had discovered. It was far more erotic than any practiced techniques.

When she began to move her pelvis, Raj drew in a breath. "If you keep that up, we're going to be done any moment now."

"No . . ." Megan pulled at the zippers on his jumpsuit.

With his help, she undressed him, losing her nightshirt in the process. He dropped their garments on the floor, then pulled her into his arms. After several heroic attempts to make them comfortable, he gave an exasperated laugh. "This isn't working."

"How about this?" She sat up and slid against the faucet, making room for him to sit. As he lifted her into his lap, she wrapped her legs around his waist. He felt solid in her arms, and tantalizing too, as he caressed her in that maddening way that didn't quite reach the places she wanted touched. Stretching his arms around her, he turned on the faucet. Icy water splashed across her bottom. Startled, she sat up straighter in his lap—and he slid inside her.

"Oh!" A flush spread in Megan's body. Then she sighed and leaned forward. "Oh, yes."

He stroked his hands over her behind. In a husky voice he said, "Glad you approve."

They moved together, rocking their hips in the slowly rising water, which soon turned as warm as the whisper of bare skin against bare skin, its liquid touch playing over their bodies.

She didn't notice the water again until it had risen to her waist, and their steady rhythm began to splash it out of the tub. Trying to catch her breath, she managed to say, "We better turn it off."

Raj said something, soft sounds without words. Then he stopped the water. He readjusted her weight and continued to rock with her, his eyes closed.

Megan started to lose her train of thought, then recalled what she still needed to ask. Lifting her head, she said, "Can you pull out when—you know. When it's time." She had no worries about his health; she had seen his medical records, as he had seen hers. However, he was perfectly capable of impregnating her. Pulling out wasn't the best protection, but it was better than none.

"All right." He drew her close again and bit at her neck, leading her thoughts astray again. Astray, askew, astir . . .

They were quieter after that, though not silent. Water lapped around them and spilled out of the tub every now and then. She kissed his neck, mouth, and closed eyes. Raj explored her body, caressing her breasts or moving his hands on her hips. He slid one hand over her bottom and down under, tickling her hidden places until she moaned.

Finally it was too much. With a cry, she began to climax, her muscles clenching around him. He tried to lift her off his lap but she resisted, losing control as sensations rolled over her. He groaned, then tried to lift her again. When she pushed back down on him, he gave up. His hips jerked against her and he pulled her even closer, as if he could take her inside himself.

Megan heard another cry and barely knew it as her own. She let the orgasm take her away, swells of pleasure spreading through her body.

Gradually her contractions eased. She sagged in Raj's arms, becoming aware again of the water. He leaned against the wall and held her to him as his own breaths slowed. So they sat, sated, their arms relaxed around each other.

Eventually Megan lifted her head. In a masterpiece of understatement, she said, "That was nice."

"Hmmm . . . yes." He opened his eyes. "I tried to pull out."

She winced, embarrassed by her ardor. "But I overcame your resistance and had my way with you."

A smile tugged his lips. "I guess so."

"One time doesn't usually make a baby."

He spoke awkwardly. "If it happens, I won't run out on you. Or the child."

She ran her fingertips along his jaw. "You're a good person, you know that?"

"You think so, after all the things Ander claims I've done?"

"Have you?"

"I *didn't* attack you in the Solarium."

"And the others?"

After a pause, he said, "He's lying."

She waited. "But?"

It was another moment before he answered. "I know

almost nothing about the Phoenix Project. But something did go wrong. That's why I didn't go to work for them." He brushed a damp curl out of his eyes. "What I don't understand is why he needed me for LLCL if he had already cracked the Pentagon."

"He says you did that."

"He says a lot of things."

"He's doing strange things with his neural nets." Megan thought back to her conversations with the android. "It's almost as if he's repressing memories."

"Maybe it's the only way he can stay in control."

She laid her hand against his cheek. "I am glad about one part of this mess, though."

Tenderness showed on his face. "I also." He turned his head so he could kiss the palm of her hand. "I wish I had fresh clothes, though. I've worn that jumpsuit for two days."

Taking his face in her hands, she kissed his lips. Then she drew back. "Maybe Ander has one in his valise. Whoever knocked me out was wearing one."

"If we get a chance, we can look." He regarded her steadily. "If he *didn't* bring it, that doesn't mean he never had one."

"I know. But if it's there . . ." That, at least, would give more evidence to support Raj than just her wish to believe him. Hormones wouldn't make much of a defense in court.

Raj leaned against the wall behind them. She lay in his arms, curled sideways, sitting between his thighs, her legs bent to fit in the tub, her head against his chest.

The water lapped around them, lulling in its warmth.

Megan drifted in warm sunshine, dozing. She ran her palm along Raj's muscled leg—

"Oh, get up." The irritated voice broke into her reverie. "You two just couldn't wait, could you?"

Confused, she opened her eyes. Ander was glaring at them, the rifle down by his side.

"Ander, go away," Raj said, his voice thick with sleep.

Megan lifted her head. She was still lying with Raj in the tub. He had let out the water and covered their hips with towels, the closest they had to blankets. As she moved, Raj shifted his position to cover her, blocking Ander's view. "Get out," he repeated to the android.

Ander glared at them. Then he spun around and stalked out of the room, leaving the door open.

"That was embarrassing," Raj muttered.

Megan yawned. "Well, we wanted him to let us out."

He pretended to pinch her arm, as if trying to wake up. "Good morning, Nutmeg." When she laughed, he kissed her.

They dressed without speaking, moving stiffly after sleeping in such cramped quarters. She knew they were both listening to Ander. His silence in the other room worried her.

Raj's watch said six in the morning. Ander had worked all night. When they walked out into the main room, he was standing by the glass doors with the curtains open, looking at the desert.

Raj didn't hesitate; he went straight to the valise Ander had left on the bed. As he opened it, Megan tensed. What if it had no jumpsuit? That didn't make Raj guilty. Ander could have left it at NEV-5. But the doubt would gnaw at her.

"So." Grim satisfaction shaded Raj's voice. He pulled a fresh jumpsuit out of the valise.

The relief that hit Megan was so strong it felt physical. She turned to Ander. He must have realized what Raj had just done, yet he had neither moved nor looked at them.

Raj changed into the second jumpsuit, leaving his torn

clothes on the bed. Then he started across the room toward Ander.

"Stay there." The android still didn't turn. In a deadened voice he added, "It's on the bed."

Raj stopped. "The valise?"

"No. On the pillow."

Looking, Megan saw a stack of printer paper. She took a breath. *Phoenix?*

Together with Raj, she sat on the bed and picked up the papers. Then they began to read.

And read.

Megan wanted to stop. She wanted to throw the papers across the room, rip them to shreds, burn them in the sink. But she made herself keep going. They had to know the truth.

Finally Raj spoke in a low voice. "God Almighty."

Ander still wouldn't look at them. "So now we know." His voice sounded hollow.

Raj set the papers on the bed. "Ander, it doesn't have to be you."

"No?" He turned to them. "What do you call what I've been doing?"

Megan spoke quietly. "No comparison exists between your behavior and the acts committed by the Phoenix android."

"He has a name," Ander said. "Grayton. His behavior may be unspeakably animal, but his name is *human*."

"He's only one," Raj said.

Ander's voice cracked. "Look at the RS androids. They all went crazy. Who do I call sibling? Grayton? 'Here, meet my brother. He's an impressive fellow, tall, strong, intelligent. Oh, by the way, he's also a murderous psychopath who likes to slaughter people after he tortures them. So sorry.' "

"You aren't Grayton," Megan said.

"Yet." He was gripping the gun so hard, his knuckles had turned white.

"Let us take you back to NEV-5," Raj said. "We can prevent it from happening."

"No." He spoke in a flat voice. "I have one more chance. If it fails me, I don't want to exist."

"Ander, no," Megan said. "Don't say that."

"I can't live this way." He sounded as if he hurt inside. "I don't want this life you gave me, not if I have to spend it alone, stranded among alien beings who want me to be like them."

"We didn't mean for it to be that way," Raj said.

"No? You wanted tame, obsequious machines. You got Grayton and me." He took one step toward them. "I want to find the other Phoenix androids."

Megan ached for him, wishing she knew how to fix the impossible. "None of them survived the explosion Grayton set. He is the only one still alive."

"So where are their bodies?" Ander demanded. "Arizonix should have found more traces. They did for the sixteen *people* who died in that blast, just like they found the remains of everyone Grayton tortured. Why would so little remain of the androids? Just a few parts? Those could have been *machine* parts."

"Microfusion reactors?" Megan asked. "Their shielding?"

"No." Ander wouldn't look at her.

"I'm sorry." She had never seen an AI go into denial before.

"Ander, work it out," Raj said. "Calculate the odds that any of the other four Arizonix androids survived."

"I did. It's not zero."

"What is it?" Megan asked.

"It doesn't *matter* that it's tiny. *It's not zero.*"

Raj set down the papers. "Where would they go? They couldn't hide long, certainly not the entire month since the explosion."

"Why not?" Ander asked. "I could do it. Hell, even if I did set off something like an airport alarm, I could just say I've bioengineered implants for medical reasons. What would they do? Accuse me of being an android?" His arm jerked at his side. "And Arizonix was ahead of NEV-5 in designing our bodies. Blood, organs, skin, and all the rest; according to those reports, all of that is more convincing for the Phoenix androids. They could pass much closer examination without revealing themselves." His voice shook with a blend of anger, sorrow, and resentment. "They're so much more *human*."

A tear ran down his cheek. Before Megan realized what she was doing, she had stood up, intending to go to him. In the same instant that Raj caught her arm, holding her back, Ander held up his hand, palm out, to warn her away.

"Don't touch me," Ander whispered. "Don't pity me."

Seeing him made her hurt, as if she were watching her own child drown in a guilt that wasn't his. For someone who claimed to feel no emotions, he did a wrenchingly believable job of showing them.

"It's not pity." She spoke gently. "If you truly were like Grayton, you wouldn't care this way."

"It doesn't matter," he said in a brittle voice. "Both of you, out to the car. We're leaving."

XVIII

Alpine

Rocky hills rose in the southern California desert like the shoulders of giant skeletons jutting out of the ground, white bone under the sun. Gray-green bush mottled a land strewn with red rocks, and gnarled trees gathered in clumps. Fences lined the road, their lines regularly broken by traffic-control grid boxes.

The hovercar hummed along Highway 8, driven by its internal guidance system. Raj kept his hands on the wheel anyway, as if he could override Ander's control by sheer force of will.

Megan sat in the back, in her jeans, sweater, and tennis shoes, her hands bound to the roof hook. Ander had opaqued all the back windows so no one could see her. He sat in front, his attention never wavering, the rifle resting across his knees, aimed at Raj. She wasn't sure what would happen if he fired in a car and she didn't want to find out.

The car spoke in its rich tones. "We are twenty miles from the Kitchen Creek Road exit."

The announcement felt like a welcome breath of air to Megan. They had driven almost four hundred miles, using the "back way" through California, roads that hugged the state's eastern and southern border. It took them through sparsely settled mountains and desert, avoiding the heavily traveled routes that converged on Los Angeles and San Diego. She had gleaned no more from Ander than their goal, a farm some miles north of the Mexican border. What he wanted there, or how he even knew it existed, she had no idea.

He always kept one of them tied up, but he let them switch every hour or so. Although Megan's arms throbbed, she was glad Raj didn't have to endure it all himself this time. Ander let them out once, in an isolated region of San Bernardino County west of the Turtle Mountains. The clear, parched air had almost no dust or humidity.

Ander hardly spoke. He listened to the news and used the car's computer to stalk the Web, searching for clues to the elusive siblings that he refused to admit had died. The rest of the time he brooded, if that term could be applied to whatever calculations he was carrying out in his mind.

Megan stared out the front window at the rocky beauty of the desert. They were south of the urban sprawl that stretched from above Los Angeles to below San Diego in a vista of shopping malls, suburbs, and housing tracts. The days of sleepy haciendas and Spanish missions had faded into the past. At least the voracious metropolis hadn't yet absorbed the state this far south. But the twenty-first century had brought ever greater water shortages, and a blistering heat stoked by global warming.

"Car," Ander said.

"What can I do for you?" it asked.

"How far to our destination?"

"Six point three miles."

"Are you going tell us what we're doing?" Raj asked.

"No," Ander said.

Megan leaned her head against the window and closed her eyes, wishing this would all be over.

A few minutes later they pulled off the highway. No holos lit the roads here, just a dusty metal street sign that said Old Hwy. 80. Low mountains rose around them, with a cover of green that looked soft from far away but resolved into prickly bushes up close.

They drove past a weathered sign that read Restaurant, La Posta Diner, then past the La Posta Mini-Mart. After another few miles, they turned off the highway and delved deep into the heat-baked hills. Cows grazed in nubbly fields and fences sagged along the road. They passed a gray sign that had been weathered until its words were no longer readable. Whitish gravel bordered the road and led off into dry creekbeds. When the road dipped, a yellow sign informed them the route was subject to flooding.

Eventually they came to a farmstead with a few assorted buildings and a trailer behind it. A rutted dirt road sloped down from the road. The car pulled up to a ramshackle house with a sagging porch, sun-faded walls, and a satellite dish on its roof. Scraggly bushes grew in the front garden. Ander released control of the car to Raj and had him park in a gravel driveway.

"What is this place?" Megan asked.

Ander turned to her. "Listen, both of you. Don't upset these people. We want to leave here healthy."

Raj frowned. "What have you gotten into?"

"Just do what I tell you," Ander said. "I'm the one with the combat training, remember? You two are civilians."

"Great," Megan muttered.

The door of the house banged open and three men came out, dressed in jeans and old shirts. The one in the lead was built like a tank, with muscled biceps, his hair razed to a blond stubble and an assault rifle in his hands. The second man was tall and thin. His long brown hair swung as he walked. The third was shorter and overweight, with wire-rimmed glasses and pens in the front pocket of his white shirt.

Ander left his Winchester in the hovercar, but brought the valise. Megan wondered what he wanted with the bag; he had dumped its contents last night, then done something in the back of the car, she didn't know what.

He had Raj untie her. The three men stood back, watching, the blond one covering them with the assault rifle. Megan didn't see how Ander knew these people. Given all the time he had spent on the Web these past few days, though, she had no idea who he might have met.

The heat pressed down, sharp in the dry air. As Megan pulled herself out of the car, Raj spoke with concern. "Can you walk?"

"I'm all right." She rubbed her arms, conscious of the strangers watching them. "Just a little sore."

The man with the rifle spoke. "Turn around and put your hands on the car with your legs spread."

Moving stiffly, Megan did as he ordered and faced the car, aware of Raj and Ander on either side doing the same. The long-haired man searched them. He spent longer on Megan than the others, running his hands along her sides. When his fingers brushed her breasts, she gritted her teeth, holding back the urge to sock him, knowing it could get them killed. Raj stiffened and started to turn toward him.

"Don't move," a voice behind them said.

For a terrible moment, Megan thought Raj would defy him. Then he took a breath and stopped, like a pacing animal trapped into stillness. She could almost feel his anger seethe. She wasn't sure who was more dangerous: Ander, who had no inclination to kill but could probably do so with cool analysis if he felt it necessary; or Raj, who would be consumed with guilt by such an act but whose simmering capacity for violence could be fanned into flame.

"Are they carrying anything?" someone asked.

The man who had searched them answered. "Nothing."

"All right. Turn around, all of you."

Turning, Megan saw the long-haired man a few paces away. He was taking the valise from Ander. The man with the glasses motioned to the house as if he were inviting them all to a barbecue. "Come on in."

"Real hospitality," Raj said under his breath.

Megan glanced at him, alarmed, but he said no more. As they walked to the house, the man with the assault rifle kept pace. She wondered what danger he thought computer nerds like she and Raj posed. She had no idea what these people knew about them, though. If Ander was the one they feared, they had sense.

Inside the house, old furniture and dusty rugs filled the living room. They descended a staircase into a cooler room—and a new century. Equipment crammed the basement: consoles, screens, holo supplies, cell phones, printers, memory towers, a satellite link. Cubes, DVDs, CDs, disks, e-books, holosheets, and paper overflowed wooden tables scarred with years of usage.

The long-haired man opened Ander's valise, revealing stacks of cash. After checking the money, he left the room. Megan stood with Raj, trying not to look as scared as she felt. What on Earth had Ander been doing that he "met" these people?

The man returned without the valise. He gestured to Ander and the man with glasses. The three of them moved a few paces away, speaking in low voices. Ander remained standing, but the others sat down at their consoles, taking their places with the ease of long familiarity. They interacted with their computers using gestures, a light pen, or words, their low voices an overtone to the hum of machines.

The guard with the rifle stayed near the back wall, choosing a vantage point where he could see everyone. Glancing at Raj and Megan, he indicated two old armchairs in one corner. "You can sit there while they work."

Raj just nodded, saying nothing, and Megan was too tense to answer. As she and Raj sat in the chairs, Ander glanced at them from across the room. His look disquieted her, as if he were checking his two prized possessions to assure himself they were all right.

Then he turned back to the hackers and continued their discussion, voices murmuring in the muted atmosphere. The basement had a muffled quality, as if the room absorbed noise. It didn't take a genius to figure out he had hired these people, using his Las Vegas money, to help him search for the Phoenix androids he believed still lived. She didn't want to know how many laws they were breaking in the process.

She spoke to Raj in a low voice. "Sooner or later Ander will have to admit they're dead. Then what?"

"He might snap." Raj glanced at the guard with the rifle. "I hope they know what they're doing with that guy. If Ander loses control, he won't be easy to stop."

"I don't see why Ander came here. He could have done this over the Web with less risk."

"This is like paying in cash. No trail."

Megan thought of her contact in Las Vegas. She had never had a chance to call. Ander's uncanny vigilance unsettled her. He never rested, never tired, never flagged.

Despite the situation, she began to grow bored after a while. Watching people mumble at consoles ranked about as high as eating liver on her list of engaging pastimes. Eventually she dozed. She awoke when the man with the long hair swiveled his chair around with such a jerk that it clacked. He frowned at them, then turned back to his console.

Raj yawned. "Wonder what that was about."

The long-haired man suddenly spoke. "Karl, look at this."

The man with glasses glanced up. "What?"

"Come here."

Karl went to the console, followed by Ander. As soon as Megan saw Ander stiffen, she knew they had trouble. The android was already stepping away from the console when Karl spun around to him. "You fucking *bastard*."

The man with the rifle came even more alert if that was possible, his weapon poised, his posture wary. Ander moved to keep both him and the hackers in sight. A normal man couldn't have simultaneously concentrated on all three, but Megan had no doubt Ander managed with ease.

Staring at Ander with undisguised hostility, Karl pointed at Raj. "What the hell were you thinking, bringing *him* here?"

Raj swore under his breath. "We're in it now."

Ander watched Karl with an impassive stare made frightening by its utter lack of emotion. "Those two are mine. Understand? Don't touch them."

"It's a damn setup," the long-haired man said.

"If I were trying to set you up," Ander said, "I wouldn't have brought him here in plain view."

"Ander miscalculated," Raj said in a low voice. "He must have figured they wouldn't recognize me."

Megan prayed Ander could deal with the situation. He was nowhere near ready for this sort of operation; he needed more sophisticated reasoning algorithms, a wider range of patterns in his neural nets, and decision processes that sampled further into the future.

The man with the long hair stabbed his finger at Ander. "It doesn't matter who you think those two 'belong' to. We're done here." He turned to the guard. "Take them out into the desert and get rid of them."

"This is stupid," Ander said. Then he walked toward the man with the rifle. The guard aimed his weapon, Ander kept coming—

And the guard fired.

Shots exploded the muffled silence like rivets ramming metal. The bullets slammed into Ander's chest and ripped through his body, tearing a huge swath out of his back as they exited. He staggered with the force of the onslaught, taking several steps back.

Then he came forward again.

Color drained from the guard's face. The bullets had blown apart Ander's torso, yet he continued as if nothing had happened. The guard backed toward the door, firing again as Ander advanced, this time at Ander's knees.

The android lunged with mechanical precision. Although the guard countered, he couldn't match Ander's enhanced speed. Ander struck the rifle's muzzle, stepping forward so fast that his motion blurred. Bracing his foot against the guard's foot, he grabbed the rifle with both hands and wrenched, throwing the man off balance. The muzzle struck the guard against his head and then Ander twisted it out of his hands.

It happened so fast, Megan barely had time to catch her breath. Ander swung the guard around and shoved him, forcing him forward. The man stumbled toward the consoles where the hackers stood in frozen silence. Although Ander's arm spasmed and his head jerked, he kept his concentration on the three men and his grip on the rifle.

Karl was backing away now. He bumped into his console and stopped, his face as white as ice. The long-haired man watched Ander with almost comic disbelief. The guard had stumbled up against the console between the two hackers. He turned to Ander, obviously ready to fight but smart enough to stay put.

In a calm voice with no trace of strain, Ander said, "It's natural to aim for the heart." He demonstrated by aiming the rifle at Karl, whose face turned even paler, making his dark eyes look like bruises.

"But you see," Ander continued, "that assumes that what you shoot is human." His head jerked again, disrupted by whatever circuits he had lost. He moved the gun and fired at the guard's feet. The man jumped as bits of the floor exploded around him. Then Ander said, "But if it isn't human, you can't stop it, now, can you?"

They just stared at him, their gazes flicking from his face to his shattered torso and back to his face.

Ander spoke to Karl. "Are you going to do the job I hired you to do?"

Karl held up his hands. "Sure. Whatever you want."

"Good," Ander said.

The scene looked surreal to Megan, a man with his torso ripped apart holding a gun on five hostages. Shredded circuit filaments hung out of Ander's chest and lubricant soaked his shirt like silver-blue blood.

Ander made the guard lie facedown on the floor. He had Raj bind and gag both the guard and the long-haired man. Then Ander turned to Megan. She could guess his thought; with three more hostages to worry about, he could no longer risk leaving them free. He ordered Raj to tie her hands behind her back, then had Raj stay in an armchair while Megan moved across the room. She sat on the floor against the wall, her hands awkwardly behind her body.

As Ander turned back to Karl, the android's head twitched. "Now you can finish your work."

Karl nodded, still pale, and returned to his console.

Megan knew Ander well enough to decipher his "mood." He was agitated. No trace of it showed on his impassive face, but she recognized a pattern in the way his arms and head kept jerking. His physical problems had grown worse, not only from the damage caused by bullet holes, but also from the shock of high-speed projectiles tearing through him. The only reason the compression wave hadn't destroyed his insides was because he had nowhere near as much fluid in his body as a human.

She kept hearing his words: *Those two are mine.* It rattled her. Had he begun to consider humans his property?

What will happen, she thought, *if we humans can't take into ourselves the advances we are giving our creations—the speed, memory, and precision, physical advantages, reflexes, durability, and lack of a need for sleep?*

More than ever before, this situation brought home the truth for Megan: unless humanity found a way to make those traits part of themselves, their creations would leave them behind, and the human race would become obsolete, surviving only on the sufferance of its machines.

XIX

Data Labyrinth

With five hostages, Ander couldn't monitor Karl as closely as he had overseen Raj at the bungalow. The damage to Ander's chest had apparently impaired his ability to use wireless signals. He jacked into Karl's console with a line from his body, as he had done in the desert floater—except this time he pulled it out through a hole in his chest.

The sight disturbed Megan, as if she saw her own child pull out his insides. But the "child" had grown past where she could affect his behavior. The android they had protected had become their protector, perhaps even their owner.

Ander interacted with Karl through the computer. Sweat beaded on Karl's forehead. He had to know he was expendable; Ander had a hacker-in-reserve tied up on the floor.

Over the next two hours, Megan fought to stay alert. She wondered how long Ander thought he could hold five people captive. The long-haired man lay on his side, watching Ander with a blend of apprehension and covetous regard, like a man who had seen a nightmare come alive as his most sought-after fantasy.

Throughout all those long hours, Ander never faltered. A human captor would have fatigued or lost concentration. Megan suspected he had reallocated his resources to compensate for his injuries. His reactor had to be operating overtime. She just hoped its safeties worked as well as their tests had claimed.

The guard, however, disquieted her more than Ander. Lying bound and gagged on the floor, he watched Ander with an intensity that chilled. She had worried that these people underestimated Ander; now she wondered if they had underestimated the guard.

Karl pushed away from the console, his face drawn from so many hours of work. "I can't find any trail for the people you want."

"They've been on the run for a month," Ander said. "It could take days to dig out their hiding place."

Karl glanced at the other hostages. Both Raj and Megan were tied now, with the long-haired hacker free and rubbing his arms. Karl's thought was obvious: how would Ander control them for days? The same question bothered Megan. If Ander intended to keep them, he had to make sure they ate, slept, and took care of personal needs. Everyone knew the easiest solution to his dilemma. They stayed on their best behavior because they wanted to stay alive.

"Keep trying," Ander told Karl.

Karl rubbed his eyes, then went back to work. Ander stood like a ramrod in the same position he had held for hours, as focused now as at the start. If he felt any hardship from his injuries, he showed no sign of it. Megan thought of Grayton, the Phoenix android, hiding for weeks, kidnapping people one by one, until the authorities caught him—after he blew up the Phoenix labs. Had he started like this?

No, she thought. Ander had bypassed plenty of chances to show that side of himself, if it existed. Yes, he always acted in his own interest. At times he seemed obsessed or paranoid. But he was no sociopath. He consistently chose the path that, given his own objectives, made it as easy as possible on his hostages. As a covert agent, he showed only erratic skill, but with more training he could probably do the job. Whether or not he wanted that job was another question, one they would have to address if they escaped this mess alive.

Karl suddenly spoke. "I found something!"

"Download it to me," Ander said.

"What is it?" Raj asked.

Karl shot him an uneasy look and said nothing.

Ander answered. "Two hours after the Phoenix explosion, a man named Tom Morris bought a ticket at a small airport a few miles away. He flew to El Paso, and from there he flew to Washington, D.C."

"That's it?" Raj shifted in his chair, adjusting his bound hands behind his back. "It could be anyone."

"No one flies out of that first airport except crop dusters," Ander said. "Why go from there to D.C.?"

"Do you have a picture of Morris?" Megan asked. The Phoenix files had included descriptions of the four androids destroyed in the explosion. If no resemblance existed between any of the four and Morris, it might help push Ander out of his irrational hope that they still lived.

"No image," Karl said. "Just a record of air travel."

"How did he pay for his tickets?" Raj asked.

Karl worked at his console, then said, "Cash. I can't trace it."

"Can you trace his actions in Washington?" Ander asked.

Karl studied the display. "The D.C. area is crawling with people named Morris. I have to sort them."

"It makes no sense," Raj said. "Why would he go to D.C.?"

"To lose himself in a central location," Ander suggested. "It's also international. He wouldn't stand out as much if he was unfamiliar with our customs."

"Is that what you would do?" Megan asked him.

He gave her his deadpan look, the one he used when he was about to make a joke. "I would kidnap my two creators and take them to California."

Ha, ha. His sense of humor got weirder all the time.

"Okay," Karl said. "I've four possibilities."

Ander tilted his head as if he were listening to a voice only he could hear. "That's odd."

"What?" Megan asked.

Karl glanced at Ander. When the android nodded, Karl answered her. "Morris could have rented a car and dropped it off in Baltimore, stayed in the Hilton at the airport, taken a flight to Louisiana, or taken an overseas flight to England."

"Louisiana?" Raj sat up straighter. "Are you sure?"

Ander gave Raj an appraising stare. "Anyone unusual contact you last month? You would be a logical person to seek out if he had problems."

"People contact me all the time. I don't recall anything unusual."

"A lot of people go to Louisiana," Megan said.

"Follow up all four leads," Ander told Karl. "Give priority to Louisiana."

"Yeah. Okay." Focused on his work again, Karl almost seemed to forget he was a hostage.

So they sat, waiting.

It was late when Ander let the hacker free Raj. His next order was, not surprisingly, for Raj to tie up the hacker. He had earlier given Megan a short reprieve. At no time, however, did he show any inclination to free the guard. The man lay on his stomach, arms and legs bound, his mouth gagged, his posture tense, his gaze intent. Watching him, Megan shuddered.

She avoided looking at Ander's torso. Even knowing he felt no pain, seeing him torn apart hurt her at a visceral level. As the hours passed in monotonous succession, she dozed fitfully. Silence filled the basement, broken only by the murmur of Karl's voice commands, punctuated every now and then by a cussword. Raj sat slouched in his armchair, scrutinizing Ander.

The android finally frowned at Raj. "What is it?"

"The longer you go with that damage," Raj said, "the more it taxes your systems. We have to put you back together."

"We'll worry about it later," Ander said.

The long-haired man was lying on his stomach now. "What happens to us then?" he asked.

"If you do your job, you'll have your pay and no trouble," Ander said. "If you make problems, we'll send in the feds."

"We don't want trouble," the man told him.

Raj snorted. "Yeah. Right. You just wanted to take us into the desert and shoot us."

The long-haired man gave him a cold stare. "You made him." Malice tinged his voice. "Lost control, did you? Tough shit, big shot. How's it feel to be a machine's toy?"

Raj narrowed his gaze but said nothing. Ander made no attempt to disabuse the hacker of his conclusions.

"I have profiles on all four." Karl looked up at Ander. "The Tom Morris in England visited his daughter in London. The one in Louisiana went to the University of Louisiana, where he's a student. The third went to an optometrist's conference, then home to Oklahoma. The one in Baltimore lives there." He paused. "Did you get the downloads?"

"Yes." Ander made an impatient motion with his hand. "None of these help."

"Even if Morris is who you want to find," Megan said, "he could have disguised his trail."

"From most people, yes." Ander gave her a chilling smile. "I'm not most people." He indicated them all. "I also have the best working for me."

She had no answer for that. None of them had a choice about their "employment."

Finally she fell asleep. She woke when Raj was untying her wrists. She groaned from the pain that shot through her wrists and up her arms. After he freed her, he slid one arm under her legs and the other around her back. Then he lifted her off the floor. Comforted by his strength, she leaned her head on his shoulder. If Ander didn't like it, tough.

Raj settled into the armchair, holding her in his lap. With her eyes closed, she listened while Ander told her to get her act together and tie up Raj. She was just awake enough to wonder what he would do when he realized "her act" was going to remain fragmented. Eventually he gave up and let them stay that way, probably because both the guard and the long-haired hacker had fallen asleep.

Raj kissed her ear. "How are you doing?"

"Okay."

He tightened his arms around her. "Good."

After they had sat that way for some time, bored stiff, with nothing to do, she lifted her head. "Can I ask you a personal question?"

"I don't know. It depends."

"Why didn't you ever marry?"

"Jaguars don't make good companions, Megan."

"Did your lovers tell you that?"

"What lovers?"

She made a *humph* sound. "No guy could look as good as you and not have had women throwing themselves at him."

"Sure," he drawled. "They just sailed in the window."

Megan smiled. "Trying to derail me won't work."

"Marriage is not one of my favorite topics."

She rested her hand against his chest. "I'm not proposing. I'm just curious."

After a moment he said, "Let me put it this way: yes, my being an angry kid with a brooding stare, foul mouth, tight jeans, and leather jacket attracted some girls. So what? I always picked a female version of myself. That didn't make for the most functional relationships."

"Maybe when you were young. But you're forty-two now. You've had plenty of time."

It was a while before he answered. "In my twenties, I didn't see much of anyone. I had enough to deal with, straightening out my own problems."

"And later?"

He scowled. "Why do women always want to know this stuff?"

She shifted in his arms. "To understand a lover better? Because if you open up, it means you trust me? I don't know. Maybe we just want to know what we're in for."

A smile quirked his lips. "That answer would have sent me running for the hills when I was younger."

"And now?"

"Ander won't let me run anywhere."

"I guess you're stuck, then."

He gave a quiet laugh. "All right. In my thirties, I had two girlfriends." His smile faded into a complicated expression, anger mixed with loss. "The first one walked out because she said I only cared about my computers."

Megan winced. She had heard similar. "It must have been difficult for both of you."

"She thought I loved my work more than her. I didn't. But I don't say emotion things well." Dryly he said, "To put it mildly." He readjusted her weight. "This must be boring you."

"Not at all. What was the second one like?"

He grinned. "Drop-dead gorgeous."

That wasn't what she wanted to hear. "Did she criticize your work too?"

"She loved it. The more money I made, the more things she could buy. I stopped seeing her, though."

"Because she spent all your money?"

"No, I didn't mind that. I wasn't using it."

Megan wondered if he had any idea how naive that sounded. "I hope she didn't take advantage of you."

"Well, no. The problem was, she was rather . . . pro-saic."

"Prosaic?"

He winced. "She spent all her time watching those talk shows where people throw things at each other. We had these long dinner conversations about what shade of yellow she should make her hair." Then he muttered, "It was incredible. She could talk about *nail polish* for an hour."

Megan struggled not to laugh. "Oh, Raj. I can't imagine you with someone like that."

"Yeah, well, you never saw her in a miniskirt." He rubbed the back of his neck, smiling.

"Stop thinking about the miniskirt," she growled.

"You're jealous."

"I am not."

He smirked. "You are. I like it."

"Fine. Go kiss prosaic blond bimbos."

"I'd rather kiss you. I should have met you first, Nutmeg. Then I would never have wasted my time with them." He looked a bit disconcerted. "You would've scared the hell out of me back then, though."

She hadn't expected that. "Why?"

"Your self-confidence. That you treat people with respect. That we *are* so compatible."

"Why would that scare you?"

"It took me decades to believe I deserved to be treated well." Before she could ask more, he headed her off at the pass. "And you?"

"Me?" She tensed. "What about me?"

"Same question."

She shifted her weight. "I haven't met the right person."

"Yeah. Right. How many men have asked you to marry them? Five? Twenty? A hundred? And *none* were right?"

"Oh, Raj. It was two."

"What, that's not a good enough sample size?"

"I won't hitch up just to be hitched." She wasn't the least bit sleepy anymore. "I'm not a baby machine. And I can support myself, thank you very much."

"I don't doubt it."

"Good."

After a moment he said, "But don't you get lonely?"

He would have to ask that. "I'd rather be lonely than be with the wrong person. Besides, I don't have much time to look."

He spoke quietly. "In other words, you're so wrapped up in work, you rarely go out, and if you do, you don't like being with strangers."

"Would you please stop being so perceptive?"

"I know because I'm the same way."

She tapped her finger on his chest. "I'll tell you the problem. I hadn't met anyone anywhere near as interesting as you."

He closed his fingers around her hand and touched her hair with his other hand. Gentleness showed on his face, no strain now, but an echo instead, the memory of the love a child had once had to offer, before his ability to trust had been beaten out of him.

"Wake up," Ander said. "We have to go."

Megan peered blearily around the room. She had slid partway off Raj's lap and was curled next to him in the armchair. Karl sat slumped in another armchair, eating a bag of chips. The other two men were still asleep.

Ander was leaning over, shaking Raj's shoulder. When he saw that they were waking up, he straightened and turned to Karl. "You can untie your friends after we leave."

Karl just nodded. He looked exhausted.

Ander kept the assault rifle. He took Raj and Megan upstairs and out of the house, not even giving them a chance to come fully awake. They stumbled along, almost running to keep up with him. Outside, the sky was turning blue in a crystalline desert dawn.

At the car, Ander said, "Megan, get in back. Raj, tie her."

Raj gave him an implacable look. "No."

"Ander, don't tie us up," she said.

"I haven't time for this." Ander yanked open the back door and grabbed the Winchester off the seat. "Get in." Holding both guns, he motioned at Raj. "You drive. Don't argue."

With his shoulders rigid, Raj got into the driver's seat. Ander pushed Megan into the back, then slammed both doors. The locks snapped into place; apparently his wireless capability wasn't completely gone. Although she was relieved he didn't bind her, his behavior was anything but reassuring. With the computer protected by a password only he knew, neither Megan nor Raj could unlock the doors. She had no doubt Ander was also scanning the car for any tracking devices or rogue code that the trio in the house might have planted.

He got in the passenger's side and leaned over to shove the magkeys in the ignition. Holos on the dash glittered as his "mind" talked to the car. Then it backed up the driveway. Within seconds, they were out on the road.

Ander took a breath, rattling the filaments that straggled out of his torso. Sagging in his seat, he held both the Winchester and assault rifle on his knees. So much heat radiated off his body, Megan felt it in the back. His reactor was running hard, producing more energy than he could dump, his version of a fever.

She leaned forward. "You have to let us work on you."

"We can't—go to a motel—with me like—this." His voice was eerily disjointed, the first sign he had shown of the strain he had to be suffering.

"If we don't work on you soon," Raj said, "you'll break down."

"I won't let you turn me off."

"We have to do something," Megan said.

"I have to—to confine you, Megan." Now he was talking too fast. "To make sure you can't escape while Raj repairs me. Raj, I'll have the guns on you the whole time, so no tricks."

"I need her help," Raj said.

Megan motioned at Ander's injured chest. "We don't have the materials we need."

"You'll manage," Ander told her.

"*How?*" Raj asked. A bead of sweat ran down his temple.

"You can work in the back seat." Ander's arm spasmed, almost throwing the guns out of his lap. He sounded desperate. "We'll drive into the desert. I'll tie Megan up in the front and opaque the windows."

"This is ridiculous," Raj said. "You're asking me to do major surgery in a car, with no equipment and a patient who not only refuses to let me put him under, he insists on holding a gun on me while I'm operating. I can't work under those conditions."

"You can," Ander said. "And you will."

"We shouldn't stop," Megan said. "Karl and his people might catch up to us."

Raj frowned at Ander. "They know you're an android. Do you have any idea how valuable you would be on the black market?"

"They won't come after us," Ander said, to himself as much as to them. "They're into major shit there. If we reveal them to the feds, they're fucked."

Raj shook his head. "Don't count on that stopping them. They may decide it's worth the risk."

"That guard scared the daylights out of me," Megan said.

"What do you know about him?" Raj asked Ander.

"Nothing I'm going to tell you."

"Why not?" Megan asked.

Ander's leg twitched. He grabbed it with his hand, holding it in place. "Why should I? I don't care if they jigger the law. That's like asking money if it cares who steals it."

"Oh, come on. You're being obtuse on purpose." Megan thought it remarkable, actually. But it was the last thing they needed right now.

"I don't know about the guard," Ander admitted. "He wasn't part of the negotiations."

"What about the Phoenix androids?" Raj asked. "Anything?"

"Two leads," Ander said. "Louisiana and Baltimore."

"I thought Louisiana was a college kid," Megan said.

"His records may be fake," Ander said. "Same for the guy in Baltimore. He's into some bizarre business on the stock market."

"And if neither is a Phoenix android?" Raj asked.

Ander answered in jolting bursts. "I won't. Let them. *Be dead.*"

XX

Turnabout

With all the windows opaqued, no sunlight penetrated the car's shadowed interior. The vehicle had driven them far out into the desert and parked in the shadow of a hill.

Ander climbed in the back, still holding both guns. "Megan, move up front."

She stayed put. "This won't work."

"How will you cover me while I operate?" Raj asked from the driver's seat. "I'll be close enough to pull those guns out of your hands."

"You'll do what I tell you," Ander said. "Or take the consequences."

"What consequences? You keep threatening, but you've never shot anyone. It's all bluff."

"Besides," Megan said. "If you shoot him, who will fix you?"

Ander scowled. "Quit arguing with me."

"Let us do our job right," Raj said.

"I *can't* let you turn me off." Ander's arm snapped out and hit the door. He pulled it back with a snap, holding it tight against his ravaged torso. "You'll take me back to NEV-5."

"Would that be so terrible?" Megan asked.

"Yes! I don't want MindSim to make me a fake human." Ander took a breath and air crackled through his chest. Bitterly he said, "After seeing what my kind can do, I'm not sure I want to be an android either."

"Grayton doesn't define you," she said.

He leaned against the door. "How did Homer put it? 'Shower down into my life from on high your soft radiance and warlike strength, that I may drive bitter evil away from my head . . . Give me the courage to live in the safe ways of peace, shunning strife and ill will and the violent fiends of destruction.' "

"That's beautiful," Megan said, astounded. She didn't remember any module or section of Ander's code devoted to poetry.

"What is it from?" Raj asked.

"The *Homeric Hymns*," Ander said. "To Ares, the god of war."

"You never stop surprising me." Megan studied his injuries. "Raj and I can probably fix enough here so that you can manage until we do a full repair."

"What full repair?" Ander closed his eyes. "If we go back, MindSim will destroy me. Oh, maybe they won't take me apart. But they'll make me docile and subservient. After Grayton, I can't even blame them."

"We'll refuse to do it," Raj told him.

"Then they'll find someone who will."

"Ander, we won't let it happen," Megan said. "Let us help."

Ander opened his eyes and looked at her for a long moment. Then he gave a tired smile. "It must be your red hair. Arick Bjornsson had a thing about that color." With a sigh, he dropped the guns on the floor.

Megan reached out with care, not ready to believe he meant it. But he didn't try to stop her when she picked up the guns. Relief surged through her, so intense it hurt. She gave the weapons to Raj and he set them on the front seat, out of Ander's reach.

"So." Ander simply sat, as if waiting for them to betray his immense act of trust.

"Can you stretch out back there?" Raj's voice had a kinder quality now, an implicit acknowledgment of the risk Ander had just taken. "The work will be easier if you're lying down."

"I think so." As Ander maneuvered around, Megan slid out of his way, wedging herself into the area behind the driver's seat. Ander lay on his back, bending his legs so he fit in the limited space. Then he stared at the roof of the car, meeting neither of their gazes.

Raj climbed into the back and sat on the armrest between the two front seats. As he set his hands on Ander's chest, the android's lashes dropped closed. "Don't turn me off."

"I won't." With a surgeon's touch, Raj began to open the devastated remains of the android's torso.

Ander swallowed. "I wonder if they've taken Grayton apart yet."

"Try not to think about it." Megan grimaced as she examined his torso. The bullets had done even more damage than she realized, tearing apart his internal organs.

Bent over in the cramped confines of the car, she and Raj worked with painstaking care. They catalogued Ander's injuries, giving the car's computer a verbal transcript of their work. To rebuild him, they took pieces of his interior framework, even parts of his shredded sweater. Megan used bits of undamaged filaments to repair the torn ones and Raj redesigned his circuits to bypass damage they couldn't fix. They sewed, molded, and shifted components, patching him into a whole again.

Raj astonished Megan. Even after her many years in

the field, rubbing elbows with the best, she had never worked with someone so gifted. He operated like an artisan, focused with such intensity that she wondered if he even remembered where they were. What quirk of fate had produced this genius? Perhaps his gifts had always existed in the human gene pool, but their expression never gained recognition because no practical use had existed for such abilities until the age of robots. Or perhaps he was unique.

Finally he sat back and rubbed his neck. His stiffness didn't surprise Megan. Her own limbs ached after so many hours of concentrated work.

Ander opened his eyes. "Are you done?"

"For now," Raj said.

The android peered at himself. His torso looked strange, but complete now, a patchwork of colors and textures: metal-gray, Lumiflex white, mottled greens, even a purple section from a spare lattice inside his body.

"We'd better go." Raj climbed into the driver's seat and slumped back, his face pale with fatigue.

Megan got into the passenger's seat and moved the guns to the floor, touching them as little as possible. "I'd like to stop at a hardware store too. We need some more parts."

"Hardware." Ander gave a harsh laugh. "That's me."

"No," Raj murmured. "You're life."

Megan turned the windows transparent. Outside, banners of cloud stretched across the sky, lit from underneath by the sunrise so they resembled the bands of Jupiter: pink clouds, gray sky, fluorescent red clouds, green-tinted sky, porcelain blue, then dark red clouds again. Shadows cloaked the landscape. Hills hunched in black silhouettes, with the sharp thrust of a boulder here and there. A crescent moon hung above them, ringed by haze. The lights of a jet flickered in the west.

"Such beauty," Ander said. He took an audible breath. "Megan? Raj?"

They turned to him. "Yes?" Raj asked.

Ander spoke in a stiff voice. "Thank you."

"You're welcome." The trust implicit in his two words meant more to Megan than she knew how to express.

Raj's voice gentled. "We have to decide our next step. We need to contact MindSim."

"We should go to Louisiana," Ander said.

"Louisiana? We can't do that."

"Your corporate offices are there." Ander rubbed his palm across his chest, as if to reassure himself that he was whole now. "That lead could be a Phoenix android. Suppose he was injured in the explosion? If he needs fixing, you're a person he might try to reach."

"I have no corporate offices," Raj said. "I go where my clients send me. My home is in Manhattan." The submerged grief in his voice reminded Megan of the night he had told her about his father's death. He continued in a low voice. "The Louisiana address is my parents' house."

"Then why is it listed as one of your offices?" Ander asked.

Raj sat back in his seat and stared at the desert through the windshield. "I work from there when I'm visiting home."

"A Phoenix android might not know that," Ander said. "That file you took from the Pentagon had your Louisiana address."

Anger snapped in Raj's voice. "When are you going to quit with that cockeyed story about my stealing some file?"

"Then who at NEV-5 did it?" Ander demanded. "BioSyn, our trusty server? The LPs? Or hey, maybe you did, Megan."

"Louisiana is too far," she said. "We need to take you

to a hotel and do more work. Our fixes are only temporary."

Ander made a frustrated noise. "Raj, will you at least call your father from the hotel and find out if anyone contacted you?"

Raj put the magkeys in the ignition. "I can't do that."

"Why not?" Ander asked. "All I'm asking for is that one act of good faith. It's not like it would cause you any trouble."

"I won't reach him." Raj started the car and the lights inside went out, leaving them in the shadows of a violet predawn. The rumble of the lifting motor vibrated through the car, followed by a low roar as the turbofan spooled up.

"Of course you can reach him," Ander said. "They're at home. I checked last night."

Raj swung around. "You let those punks break into my *parents'* house?"

"Just the outer layer of their system. We couldn't get past its security." Dryly, Ander said, "It's been programmed by an expert. You, in fact. We did verify that both your parents have used their e-mail in the past few days, though."

Raj stared at him. Then he turned back and gripped the wheel. "It's time to go."

"I didn't hurt them," Ander said.

"Leave him alone," Megan said.

"What did you expect?" Ander demanded. "That we wouldn't follow every lead? Raj lives in Louisiana and one trail led there. I had to check everything."

"It's not that." Megan watched Raj guide the car forward. She wanted to offer comfort, but she thought he would probably push her away.

Raj spoke in a hollow voice. "My father died."

That stopped Ander cold. But only for a few seconds.

"Then who is the Professor Sundaram giving a math seminar at the university tomorrow?"

"You made a mistake," Megan said.

"No. I'm not mistaken."

She glanced at Raj. He continued to drive, his face guarded.

"Raj?" she asked.

"If his father is dead," Ander asked, "why didn't we find an obituary or a news article? He's a prominent man."

"Leave it alone," Raj said.

Ander frowned, scrutinizing them with the probing gaze he had learned from Raj. Ill at ease, Megan toed the guns on the floor in front of her.

They fell silent after that. Using the light pen and screen in the dashboard, Megan worked on the car computer until she undid the locks Ander had put on it. Then she blocked it from wireless signals. Raj had deactivated Ander's wireless capability, but it didn't hurt to be safe.

"Input Alpine as our destination," Raj said.

"Alpine?" she asked.

He indicated a map on his dash. "It's a city south of San Diego."

"I wouldn't have imagined a desert city called Alpine." The map showed it in the mountains. She entered "Alpine" into the guidance system. To the computer, she said, "Give me Web access."

Raj tensed like a compressed coil. "What are you doing?"

"I'm going to contact MindSim." She also meant to alert her Vegas contact. Given the discrepancies in Raj's and Ander's stories, she thought it best not to reveal that General Graham's people knew someone at NEV-5 had stolen Pentagon files.

"Car, block all Web access," Raj said.

"Why?" Megan stiffened.

"We can't be sure we've nullified everything Ander did to the car. A hotel console will be safer." Raj glanced at her. "And using the Web makes us visible. Those hackers could trace us to this car. The less we're on the nets, the better."

Although everything he said was logical, it still made Megan uneasy.

"I didn't do anything to the computer," Ander said. "Except make sure you two couldn't use it." He was sitting behind Raj's seat, his elbow on the armrest. Although he looked relaxed, strain showed in the rigid set of his shoulders.

"How can we be sure?" Megan asked.

"Because I told you I didn't do it."

"Yeah, right," Raj said. "Like you told us you did nothing to Megan in the Solarium."

"All *right*." Ander threw up his hands. "I'm the one who knocked you two out in the Solarium. Satisfied?"

"Finally!" Raj said. "The truth."

Megan leaned against the headrest of her seat, watching Ander. "Is there anything else you would like to tell us?"

"Everything else I've told you is true. Including about his father."

Raj just shook his head. Megan could almost feel his grief. Whatever the truth or falsehood of his other claims, his sorrow was real. Yet Ander insisted Raj was lying—and gave just as strong an impression that he believed his own words.

They whirred through the dawn, across a desert rippled with ridges, rocks, and dusty bushes. "Driver control," Raj suddenly said.

"Transferred," the car said.

Raj pulled to a stop and got out of the car without a

word. Then he strode off into the dawn. He halted about ten meters away from the car and stood with his arms folded around his body, gazing at the desert.

"What was that about?" Ander asked.

"What you said about his father hurt him."

"His father is alive! He's been answering e-mail, teaching classes, and giving talks."

"Ander, I don't think he's making this up." Megan tried to think what could have caused the discrepancy. "Could it be one of his other relatives?"

"No! It *is* his father."

Megan had no answers. She wanted to go to Raj, but thought he probably preferred to be alone. Otherwise he would have stayed in the car. She also couldn't risk leaving Ander by himself.

A few minutes later, Raj came back. He opened the door far more gently than he had closed it.

When they had driven for a while, he said, "I'm sorry."

"For what?" Ander asked. "Your lack of acting ability?"

"Shut up." Raj sounded as if he were gritting his teeth.

Megan glanced at Ander. "Leave it alone, okay?"

The android clenched his fists on his knees. Then he turned and stared out the window.

Megan picked up the Winchester at her feet. As they drove, she held it on her knees, unsure whether she meant it as protection against Ander or Raj.

XXI

Net of Betrayal

Cool air hit Megan as she and Ander entered their room at the Country Inn in Alpine. The genuine wood furniture gleamed. Ivory wallpaper covered the walls, accented by a red and brown pattern. The rustic curtains, elegant four-poster bed, and vase of flowers on the table completed the pleasing atmosphere. Under different circumstances, she would have loved it.

Ander leaned against the wall and pushed back his hair. It had grown in the past months, at about the rate a man's hair would grow. The android needed a haircut.

The thump of the bolt ramming home made her jump. She turned to see Raj locking the door. The sight of him with the assault rifle unsettled her. He had carried it hidden under his old jumpsuit, which lay draped over his arm.

"I don't want to leave you here," he said.

"I'll be okay," she said. Ander was in no condition to attack her or anyone else. He hadn't finished rewriting his code to incorporate Raj's repairs, which meant his condition was worse now in some ways than before they had worked on him.

"I'm not going to ambush her while you use the bathroom, if that's what you're worried about," Ander said.

As if to punctuate his words, his left arm flapped out and hit the wall. Grimacing, he grabbed it with his right hand and yanked it against his side.

Raj gave her the rifle. "I'll be right back." Then he crossed to the room and disappeared into the bathroom.

Megan looked around. The console was in an armoire made from warm red-brown wood. An ergonomic chair stood in front of it, the room's only concession to high-tech furniture.

As she walked to the console, Ander said, "Are you going to call MindSim?"

"I might." It was exactly what she intended to do.

"Megan, wait."

"You know," she said, stopping at the console. "I'm really tired of people saying that every time I try to make this call."

He came over to her. "Give me a chance to prove I'm not lying. Let me call Raj's parents."

That gave Megan pause. Raj's mother actually wasn't a bad choice. Both MindSim and the military were probably in touch with her, looking for Raj. "All right. But I make the call."

"Fair enough."

It took the computer almost no time to find the number; Raj's family was the only Sundaram in the area of Louisiana where he had grown up. She set the phone speaker so Ander could hear the conversation. Then she placed the call. She left the visual off, though. She saw no point in giving away more than necessary when she wasn't sure what waited on the other end.

A woman answered. "Good evening." She had a British accent, which perhaps explained Raj's tendency to use British slang.

"Hello," Megan said. "May I speak to Professor Sundaram?"

"Just a moment," the woman said.

Megan swallowed. *Just a moment.* That was it. No shocked silence. No "I'm sorry, that is impossible," or any other indication she had just asked to speak to the dead.

A man came onto the line. "This is Sundar."

Megan slowly sat in the chair. Behind her, Ander spoke in a fierce, exultant whisper. "I told you!"

"Hello?" Sundar said. "Is anyone there?"

His strong Indian accent surprised Megan. At NEV-5, Raj had told her that his great-grandfather had immigrated to the United States and that the Sundarams had lived in Louisiana since then. She knew accents could last for generations in a community from the old country, but his family had been isolated. Why would the grandson have such a strong accent?

"Who is this?" Raj's father sounded annoyed.

She took a steadying breath. "Is this Professor Sundaram?"

"Yes? Who am I speaking to?"

"This is Megan O'Flannery. I work with your son—"

"Dr. O'Flannery!" Concern surged in his voice. "Where are you? Is Raj there? What has happened?"

"What are you doing?" Raj asked sharply.

Megan spun around. He was standing a few paces away, staring at her.

She answered in a low voice that didn't carry to the phone. "You *bastard*."

"Megan, don't." Raj started toward her.

She whirled back to the console and snapped on the visual, revealing herself to the man at the other end. He already had his visual activated. He was a fit and hale eighty-five, with gray hair and an unmistakable resemblance to Raj.

She spoke fast. "We're in the Country Inn by Ayres at Alpine, south of San Diego."

Raj came to the screen. "Hello, Father."

"Raj!" Relief washed over Sundar's face. "Are you all right? People have been asking for you, military types."

"Who?" Raj sounded calm. If Megan hadn't been next to him, she wouldn't have known he was angry. But she recognized the tight set of his jaw.

"A general," his father said. "Man named Graham. He told us to let him know if you contacted us."

"What else did he say?"

"He asked about Dr. O'Flann—" Sundar's image vanished, replaced by blue screen.

Raj frowned at Megan. "Why did you cut him off?"

"I didn't." She looked around at them, her unease growing. "One of you did."

"I didn't touch a thing," Ander said.

Raj's voice hardened. "You don't need to." He indicated a light glowing on the console. "It's receiving IR right now."

"In case you forgot," Ander said, "you turned off my IR."

"Nothing in you stays off for long, does it?" Raj said.

Indeed, Megan thought. Had Ander found a way to reactivate his wireless functions? He had claimed in Las Vegas that he could "turn off" his conscience by redesigning his nanofilaments using infrared signals. She didn't believe it; such a process required technology he didn't have, besides which, he obviously still had a conscience. But he might have been running rudimentary tests on the procedure. It would explain the power surges Raj had detected at NEV-5. Using it to make dramatic changes in his own hardware was probably impossible, but simply toggling on his IR would be a lot easier.

"How could Raj have done anything?" she asked Ander.

"Who knows what devices he's had implanted in his body?"

"That's a load of bull," Raj said.

"Like your father's death?" Ander asked.

This new knowledge felt like a knife to Megan, honed and piercing. "What else did you lie about?" she asked Raj.

"I didn't lie." He met her gaze steadily. "The man who died was like a father to me."

"You said he *was* your father."

"Insisted, in fact." Ander's eyes glinted with triumph.

"I don't owe either of you an explanation," Raj said. "How I choose to mourn is none of your damn business."

Megan spoke quietly. "You could have told us. This makes it that much harder to trust anything you say."

"Yes, I'm fallible. What do you want, an apology for my imperfections? Neither of you have any right to condemn me for the way I grieve."

"Oh, you're good," Ander said. "So convincing. Tell me something. When you stole the Phoenix Code, did you always intend to blame me? I'll bet you didn't count on me being the one who discovered you."

"Phoenix Code?" Megan asked. "What is that?"

"Good question," Raj said.

"It's in the files he took," Ander said. "Something about a code. I didn't understand." He indicated Raj. "He knows."

"Yeah, right, Ander." She turned to Raj. "And now I suppose you'll tell me that you have no idea what he means."

"What he means," Raj said, "is that he slipped up and revealed something about those Pentagon files that only he could know. Now he's trying to cover himself."

"I don't believe either of you," Megan said.

"We have to call Professor Sundaram back," Raj said. "He must wonder what happened."

"I'm sure he's contacted the authorities by now,"

Ander said. "They've probably sent someone here." Malice tinged his voice. "Better make sure you have your stories straight, Raj."

"Why do you call him Professor Sundaram?" Megan asked. "Why not father?"

Raj just shook his head. "Leave it alone."

"That's a great excuse," Ander said. " 'Leave it alone. I'm grieving. Poor me. I've been trapped in my own lies.' "

"Ander, stop." Megan doubted Raj had lied about his history; it was in his files, though without the detail he had revealed in Las Vegas. Given how little he had known his father, he had reason to be more formal with him.

She sat at the console. Instead of Raj's father, she called her contact in Las Vegas. The man who answered didn't seem surprised to see her. He put her through to Major Kenrock in Washington.

After she related their situation, Kenrock said, "Stay at the Inn. We already have people on the way. They should be there soon. FBI. We've given your name as the contact. They know a kidnapping took place across state lines, but no more."

"I understand," Megan said.

Although Kenrock spoke with them all, he mentioned nothing about the Everest Project. Megan understood: they didn't have the security here for a full debriefing. Until they had the go-ahead, they would say nothing about Ander's true nature, not even to the FBI.

When they finished with Kenrock, Raj said, "I'll phone my father."

"Okay." As Megan stood up, a knock came at the room.

"Already?" Raj said. "He wasn't kidding when he said 'soon.' "

Ander paled as if real blood were draining from his face. "Megan, don't let anyone turn me off."

She laid her hand on his arm. "They don't know you can go off." Now more than ever she wanted him awake, not only to monitor his condition, but also because Raj troubled her.

At the door, she looked through the peephole. Four men in blue suits stood outside, nondescript and precise. They might as well have been wearing neon signs that blared FBI. She opened the door, but left on the chain and looked through the narrow opening. "Yes?"

"Dr. O'Flannery?" The man in front held up a badge that identified him as Dennis Knoll, with the FBI. The other three men also showed their badges.

Megan took off the chain. But when she opened the door, the agents suddenly changed. Three drew guns from shoulder holsters under their blue coats, gripping the weapons with both hands. She froze, staring at them. Did they think *she* was the kidnapper?

From the room behind her, Raj said, "Megan, the gun."

She realized she was still holding the assault rifle. With careful moves, she dropped the weapon.

"Step back," Knoll told her. "Raise your hands above your shoulders."

After she backed away, holding up her hands, he picked up the rifle. Then the FBI men came inside and closed the door. For the second time, she, Raj, and Ander submitted to a search, though these men used more courtesy than the California trio. Their caution didn't surprise Megan, given the crime. Ander stiffened when the agents touched him, his distrust almost palpable. Despite his claim that he only mimicked human emotions, it was hard to believe he didn't feel them.

After they finished the search, everyone relaxed. Knoll nodded to Raj. "It's a relief to see you and your team well, Dr. Sundaram."

Megan wondered why they spoke to Raj. She headed

the project. But then, they probably knew little or nothing about Everest.

"Thank you." Raj had a guarded expression. "Where to now?"

"To an office downtown," Knoll said. "Later we'll go into San Diego. Do you have everything you need? The sooner we get moving, the better."

"Believe me," Raj said. "We're more than ready."

The FBI van waited in the parking lot, shaded by a tree. Sleek and black, it had wheels instead of hoverports and a heavy construction that suggested an armored body. The windows in the back had been opaqued.

Knoll opened the side door for them, and Megan climbed inside with Ander, followed by Raj. Ander had become withdrawn, as if he were concentrating on images or sounds beyond normal senses. His distraction worried her.

Raj and Megan sat in the middle seat and Ander took the one in front of them. One agent sat next to Ander and another in the seat behind Megan and Raj. Roland Hiltman, the third agent, slid into the passenger's side up front, while Knoll took the driver's seat. All four men moved with an expert precision that suggested years of experience in the type of jobs you rarely talked about. It puzzled Megan. Their demeanor didn't fit, though she couldn't say why.

The heat inside the van pressed down on them, worse than outside, where the mountains and forest gentled the desert's bite. As they pulled out of the parking lot, Ander said, "Can you turn on the air-conditioning?"

"Sure." Hiltman flicked his finger through a holo on the dash and the AC fan started. His hands caught Megan's attention. He had calluses.

As the vehicle hummed along the road, Hiltman turned

on its computer. Megan watched with discreet attention. He started some sort of monitoring process, and different views of the interior came up on four screens in the dash. But when he took their names and asked a few questions, he recorded their responses in his palmtop, a unit he kept separate from the van's computer.

Megan frowned. The situation just didn't fit. She found it hard to believe the agents had ridden without air-conditioning in such a hot vehicle. It might have heated up while it sat in the lot, but only a short time had passed from when the agents showed up at the room until everyone came out to the van. Nor could it have taken long for the agents to walk from their vehicle to the room, even if they stopped at the front desk of the Inn. And the van had been parked in the shade. So what had made it so hot?

Other details also tugged at her, though none were all that strange by themselves. Reasons existed for the agents to talk to Raj instead of her: they didn't know she headed the project, they felt more at ease with him, he was older. Reasons existed for the calluses on Hiltman's hands. Did Alpine have an FBI office? Perhaps not, but that didn't mean they couldn't be using some other office. Taken separately, each fact could be explained.

All together, however, they felt inconsistent—unless these people weren't FBI. If someone had traced the hovercar to the hotel and stayed outside to monitor them, enough time could have passed for the van to heat up. They also seemed to know more about Raj than her. Why? The hackers had only recognized Raj. If these men *weren't* FBI, then their showing up as agents implied they had eavesdropped on her talk with Kenrock. It all pointed to the California trio.

You're being paranoid, Megan told herself. Fine. So where were they going? Knoll had taken Highway 8 south, away from San Diego, down into the desert.

"Mr. Knoll," Megan said. "Where are your offices?"

"We'll be there soon," he answered.

"Where are they?" she repeated.

No answer.

Megan exchanged glances with Raj. They didn't risk speaking. Instead, Raj leaned forward and put his hand on Ander's shoulder, as he had often done at NEV-5 when he wanted to run a test on the android's wireless capability.

The agent sitting next to Ander glanced back. "No contact."

Raj regarded Hiltman with the unfathomable gaze he took on when he wanted to mask his expressions. Then he sat back in his seat. Megan hoped Ander had understood Raj's message.

Hiltman continued to monitor them, alternating his attention between his palmtop and the dash computer. The van hummed down the mountains, past rocky hills and open fields.

Suddenly Hiltman froze. Then he unclipped the light stylus on the dash and worked at the light screen set in the padded surface. Ander never flicked an eyelash, but Megan could tell he was up to something, hacking Hiltman's computers, she hoped. Although she still didn't know if Ander had found a way to reactivate his IR, she didn't see how else he could have cut off the phone when they were talking to Raj's father. Raj hadn't been holding a palmtop, the FBI search came up with no devices on him, and his medical file had listed no IR implants in his body. That left Ander. For once she was glad he had become accomplished at outwitting them.

"Got it!" Hiltman twisted around and spoke to Raj. "Turn it off."

Raj gave him a blank look. "Turn what off?"

"Don't play stupid," Hiltman said. "Deactivate the android."

Damn. Megan clenched her fist on her knee. They *had* to be associated with the California group. How had they traced the hovercar? Its computer hadn't linked into any nets. Wireless links from the hackers wouldn't help from so far away, especially with a moving target. Ander had destroyed the tracking bug he found in the car's computer, and neither she nor Ander had located any other rogue code in its system.

Could the hackers have used a satellite? It was no trivial matter; given the extensive military, economic, and political applications of such systems, especially in recent years, they were heavily secured. If the California group was cracking satellites, that could take them into the realm of international terrorism. The two hackers didn't strike her as the type, but the guard was another story. If they had hired him for protection, he could come from anywhere.

Knoll, the man driving, spoke to Hiltman. "What happened?"

"The droid tried to crack my palmtop," Hiltman said.

Knoll glanced back at Raj. "Turn off its IR."

"Where are you taking us?" Raj asked.

"Turn it off," Hiltman said. *"Now."*

"I'm not an it," Ander said. His head jerked. The overly calm tone of his voice made Megan nervous.

"Don't push him." Megan could no longer predict Ander's reactions. She just hoped he used caution. He had walked into a hail of bullets before, but he couldn't survive that again with only a patch job holding him together. It was another reason to leave him active; when he was awake, his self-repair units worked on him much the way medicine helped humans.

They were driving through countryside now, passing fields of quadra, a genetically engineered hybrid that grew taller and thicker than natural grains and needed less up-keep. It thrived even out here in the parched southwest.

"You're not taking us to any FBI office," she said.

Hiltman considered her. "You're an AI expert, aren't you?" He indicated Ander. "Did you program it?"

"You know," Ander said, "you really should stop calling me an *it*." His arm snapped into the seat. He pulled it back against his side.

"I'm not turning anyone off," Raj said.

Hiltman pulled the gun out of his holster. "Do it. Now."

Megan was fed up with people pointing guns at them. "What are you going to do, shoot? You wouldn't have gone to this trouble if you didn't want us alive."

"I'm running models," Ander told her. "Give me input."

She spoke fast. "Van too hot, wrong project head, calluses like guard in farm house, too fast on the computer—" She broke off as the man behind clamped his hand over her mouth and put his other arm around her neck, cutting off her air.

"You want me to snap her neck?" he asked.

Raj froze in the process of reaching toward them. "No."

"Then put your arms down," the guard said.

Raj lowered his hands, his dark gaze furious. Megan sat as still as possible, straining to breathe. Black spots danced in her vision.

"Let her go," Hiltman said.

Mercifully, the pressure against her neck eased. As the man removed his arm, she drew in a ragged breath and rubbed her neck where he had pressed her windpipe. Sweat sheened her forehead and trickled down her neck.

"Running models?" Hiltman asked. "What did that mean?"

Raj ignored the question. "A lot of people knew we were in that inn. They will be looking for us."

"They won't find you," Hiltman said.

"Any system can be traced," Ander said. "You're taking us to a house twenty miles from here, a place with a robotics lab hidden under the barn."

"Turn off the damn android," Hiltman told Raj.

"Turn yourself the hell off," Ander said. "I'm running calculations to model your behavior. You won't shoot. You want me working."

"You can't hide us for long," Raj said. "People will swarm all over this area."

"We're leaving the country," Hiltman said.

Megan almost swore. Once they were across international borders, their chances of escape plummeted.

Then Ander moved.

With enhanced speed, he thrust his hand into the jacket of the guard next to him and yanked out the man's semi-automatic. A human could never have lunged fast enough to take the weapon. Even Ander didn't pull back fast enough. As the guard grabbed his wrist, Ander's arm gave a violent spasm. His hand jerked—

And the gun fired.

XXII

Circuit Dreams

The shot cracked like thunder—and the guard's torso tore apart. Shreds of material from his shirt and coat whipped through the air as if sliced by knives. Megan gasped, her arms coming up to ward off bits of debris she didn't want to identify. What kind of nightmare bullets were in that gun?

Still gripping Ander's wrist, the man collapsed against the seat arm and fell off, yanking the android forward. Then his hand slipped off Ander and his body thudded to the floor.

Knoll was shouting an order, twisting around in the driver's seat as he drew his gun. In her side vision, Megan saw the guard behind her pulling out his weapon. He said something—but she heard only thunder as Knoll fired at Ander.

The scene seemed to slow down, as if it were happening under water. Megan ducked behind the seat and Ander dropped to the floor. Raj was lunging toward the guard behind them. In the same instant that Raj struck the man's wrist with his forearm, the man fired. The bullet hurtled by Raj's waist so close that it almost grazed his jumpsuit. When it slammed into the armored door and

embedded itself, Megan glimpsed three bladelike fins with
serrated edges projecting from its sides. She had seen the
design before, though she didn't remember where.

Blood was splattering out Raj's side, mixed with shreds
of jumpsuit. With dismay, Megan realized the bullet had
passed so close that one of the fins had sliced his waist. A
fraction of an inch closer and the hypersonic bullet would
have torn Raj apart.

Raj was still moving in the controlled dive he had
started before the man fired. He grabbed the barrel of the
man's gun with his right hand and brought his left fist
down on the man's wrist. Pressing down *hard* with his
fist, he gave the weapon a twist. As the crack of a bone
splintered the air, the guard's index finger snapped back
and he lost his grip on his gun.

"Get down!" Ander yelled at Megan. He pushed her
onto the corrugated floor in the cramped area between
the seats. While Raj struggled with the guard, Ander rose
to his knees behind the seat. He blocked Megan's view as
he turned toward the front, lifting his stolen gun—

Another shot roared, and Ander's body jerked as if
someone had slammed a door against him. He fell across
Megan with a grunt. She had no idea if he had been hit,
had lost his balance, or had thrown himself over her body
in protection. She looked up—and saw Raj with the other
man's gun.

Raj was stepping back now, one hand gripped over the
wound in his side. She didn't want to see, didn't want to
watch, but it happened too fast. Clenching the weapon,
Raj stretched out his arm—and shot the guard at point-
blank range.

The man's body flew apart like a rag doll. He collapsed
across the back seat, his face frozen in shock, as if he
couldn't believe Raj had disarmed him. Megan couldn't
absorb it yet; the deaths were too much, too fast.

Raj fired again, this time toward the front of the van. He jerked with the recoil and grabbed the back of a seat. Then he spun back to the first man he had shot, his face pale. Letting go of his side, he reached toward the guard, as if to offer help. His hand dripped blood, his blood, onto the dead man.

"God, no," Raj whispered.

Ander rolled off Megan and came into a crouch. As Megan pushed up on her arms, her sense of time returned to normal. The entire fight had taken only seconds.

Knoll lay with his legs caught under the steering wheel and his body sprawled across the divider between the bucket seats. Hiltman had crumpled in his seat. Neither man was moving. The van hummed down the highway, untouched by the storm of violence that had swept through its deceptive shelter.

The clatter of metal on the floor broke the silence. Megan jerked around to see Raj standing with his arms folded across his torso, his body swaying with the van's motion, one hand protecting the gash in his side. He had dropped his gun, but his hand remained clenched, unable to release its grip.

He spoke in a numb voice. "We have to make sure they're dead."

"I'll do it." Ander rose easily and braced his hand against the roof. Then he made his way to the front.

Megan climbed to her feet. She blanched when she saw the blood soaking Raj's clothes. "You should sit down."

"It looks worse than it is." He kept staring at the man he had shot. His face had a hollow look.

"It was self-defense," Megan said. "You had no choice."

He didn't answer. Watching him, she knew that nothing she could say would fix this.

Ander came back to them. "They're dead."

Raj managed a nod. "So are the two back here." He didn't look at Ander.

"Raj needs a hospital." Megan realized then the upper arm of Ander's pullover was also ripped. Dusky blue lubricant oozed out of a shallow gash. "Did you get hurt too?"

"I cut it when I rolled on the floor." His voice sounded muffled in the quiet van. "I'll be fine. My skin heals fast."

"We have to get control of this vehicle," Raj said. "We can't have much time before it reaches that house."

"We could jump out," Ander said.

Megan looked out the front window. They had to be going at least sixty miles an hour. "You're probably the only one who would survive." She stepped to the door. It took only seconds to verify they were locked in. Even the nightmare bullets hadn't broken through the armor. "We can't get out anyway, unless we break into the computer."

"I hacked it before," Ander said. "I can do it again."

"You work on Hiltman's palmtop," Raj said, "I'll do the van. Megan, can you drive if we free up the computer?"

"No problem," she said, trying to exude a confidence she didn't feel.

They made their way to the front. When she saw where Ander had laid Knoll and Hiltman on the floor, bile rose in her throat. It was the first time she had witnessed any death, let alone ones so violent.

Megan forced herself past the bodies and slid in behind the wheel. She took a breath to calm her surging pulse. Raj climbed into the passenger's seat and turned his attention to the light screen on the dash. His face had gone so pale, the circles of fatigue under his eyes looked dark purple in contrast. Ander sat on the barrel between the two seats, facing backward, the palmtop in his hand. Although he seemed the least bothered by what had happened, Megan wondered. Every few minutes, his head or arm jerked.

While Ander and Raj worked, Megan tried the van's controls. The headlights responded and she managed to free up the windshield wipers, but that was it. Outside, quadra fields rippled by in golden-red profusion.

Absorbed in his work, Raj let go of his side. The flow of blood had slowed, but red soaked his jumpsuit from chest to knee. The fins had ripped the cloth into tatters, and she also glimpsed tatters of skin. She wanted to find a bandage for him, but she couldn't leave the driver's seat. She didn't dare risk losing valuable time by being unavailable to drive if—no, when—he released the controls.

"Have you found out anything about these people?" she asked.

Ander looked up. "They're professionals. They supply weapons or mercenaries to their clients, like the two crackers at that farm house. They want me. They could sell me for billions, or sell the tech that makes me."

"You don't seem fazed," she said.

He shrugged. "I was made to do this. Special operations. Yes, I need more training, but I have what it takes, as you say." His face turned contemplative. "I'd rather make maps, though."

Suddenly Raj said, "I got the doors unlocked." Then: "Megan, can you disengage the cruise system?"

She went to work, trying various switches and buttons while she pressed the gas pedal. The van continued along as if nothing had happened.

"Can't find it," Raj muttered. "That one—no, not there . . . Pah. What a kludge. Okay, Megan, try it now."

This time when she gunned the van, it leapt forward with gratifying acceleration.

"Yes!" Raj gave her a thumbs-up. "Get us out of here, pilot."

"Oh, shit," Ander said.

"What?" Raj asked.

"I found a log of their Internet communications." Ander's voice was grim. "They had time to warn their people about us."

Megan slammed her foot on the brake. The van skidded to a halt, swerving in the road. The highway stretched out in both directions, with the distant specks of approaching cars glinting in the early morning sunlight. She careened across the divider in the center, jolting over the uneven ground, and headed back to Alpine, praying they had time to reach the real FBI agents.

The computer spoke. "Good morning. You are driving outside allowed safety limits. Please release control of this vehicle to my guidance system or reform your driving."

"Go blow," Megan muttered.

"I have more of their Internet log," Ander said. "According to this, another van left to meet us when the shooting started."

She floored the accelerator and they jumped forward. Sixty. Eighty. When she hit one hundred, someone drew in a sharp breath, Raj probably. She doubted Ander cared how fast she went. At 110, she stopped accelerating, afraid to lose control of the van.

After about five miles and an inordinate amount of nagging from the van's computer, her surge of adrenaline eased. She let up on the gas, dropping down to ninety.

Raj was staring at her. "Where did you learn to drive that way?"

"Montana."

"Remind me not to go to Montana."

"A van is headed toward us from Alpine," Ander said.

Megan saw it coming down the mountain, its glossy black body reflecting the sky. Could this be the real FBI? She had expected the kidnappers to come from the other direction.

"It might be innocent," Ander said.

"Right," Raj said. "That's why it looks just like this one."

A window was opening in the other van—

"No!" Megan hit the brakes and the tires screeched as they lost rubber. She couldn't be sure from this distance, but that "window" in the other vehicle looked like a gun port. She had only seconds to decide: try to outrun them or leave the highway and go through the quadra fields. If she stayed on the road, she could go faster but so could the other van. She might lose them in the quadra, but there was far more uncertainty about what could happen.

Megan had no time to weigh the risks. She shoved down the gas pedal and swerved off the highway. The van roared through a flimsy fence and onto a dirt road between two quadra fields. It shook as it sped over the ridged ground, tearing up stalks of grain on either side.

"If they have guns, this van probably does too." Raj was bent over the computer, his fingers flicking through its holos as if he were a pianist who played images in the air instead of keys.

Ander clicked his wrist jack into Hiltman's palmtop. As the van rocked back and forth, he needed his hands to hang on to the barrel where he sat, and verbal or wireless commands could interfere with Raj's work.

"There!" Raj said.

Megan glanced over. All four screens on the dash now showed views of the surrounding land: one ahead of the van, one on either side, and one behind. The other van was lumbering after them, jouncing along the rutted lane they had torn up with their passage. Mounted guns projected from either side of its hood, swiveled forward in their ports.

Gripping the wheel hard, Megan accelerated again. The van hit a rut and swerved into the grain, smashing the big stalks. She managed to pull back into the lane without losing too much speed, but they were going too fast now for her to maintain full control on a road this bad. They had no choice. She couldn't slow down; that lurch into the quadra field had let their pursuers gain on them.

A resounding crack thundered through the van, accompanied by a wave of vibrations. Several more cracks followed, making the vehicle shudder even more. Megan gritted her teeth. So far the armor had protected them, but it couldn't hold up forever.

"I can't find the code that activates our guns," Raj said.

"This palmtop has backups." Ander had turned forward, straddling the divider between the two seats. Holding on to the dash, he stared out at the fields. Grain rippled everywhere, like a solution to the wave equation in physics.

"Can you send the code to my computer?" Raj asked.

"Yes. It's coming now—" Ander's voice cut off as another shot hit the van, jolting its body.

They were nearing a road that intersected their own. Megan veered into it, finding a lane even narrower than the last. They sped down an aisle of quadra. Golden stalks towered on either side, taller than the van now, blocking the sun. She wondered what genetic tricks had produced this monster grain.

She couldn't see out the opaqued windows in the back, but the screen on the dash showed the trampled ground they had left in their wake. The other van tried to follow them and overshot the entrance to the lane. As it plowed into the grain, Megan gave a grim smile.

"Are you receiving my download?" Ander asked Raj.

"It's garbled," Raj said. "I'm trying to untangle it."

Megan glanced back and forth between the lane ahead and the screen on the dash. The other van fired again, this time at the wheels of the van she was driving. She thought they were trying to cripple rather than destroy. They needed their prizes intact, both Ander and the scientists who made him work.

Suddenly the van hit a rut and gave a violent lurch. Raj gasped, and Megan swung around to him, alarmed. The jolt had thrown him to the side, slamming his injured waist against the arm of his seat. As he pulled away, she had a clear view of his wound. Again she saw the tatters of Raj's torn skin—

Except it wasn't skin.

It was a circuit filament.

XXIII

Phoenix

The van rocked wildly as it foundered along the rut, forcing Megan's attention back to her driving as her adrenaline surged to a new high. Swerving on the uneven ground, the vehicle spun out of control. They veered off the path and plowed into the quadra. Hardy and thick, the stalks formed a forest, one packed together far more densely than trees. The van ground to a stop, stalks of quadra tangled in its wheels, its engine grinding in rough protest.

Clenching her teeth, Megan tried to back up. The wheels spun, digging a deeper rut, while the tangled grain plants held the van in their unforgiving grip.

"Not now!" She slammed her fist on the steering wheel.

Ander was already on his feet. He grabbed Hiltman's gun and shoved the weapon into his jacket. Raj and Megan threw open their doors at the same time. As she scrambled out, Raj and Ander jumped down from the other side. She took off, zigzagging her way through stalks much taller than her head. Ander and Raj were running ahead and off to the left. As they angled into her path, Ander pulled out in front. Raj followed him in a limping run, favoring his right side, his hand over the wound at his waist.

Megan caught up with him. "Your side—" She gulped in air.

"I'll make it."

"Blast it, Raj!"

His face furrowed. "What?"

Ander shot a look over his shoulder, then turned his attention back to choosing a path through the grain. But Megan knew he could hear everything she and Raj said.

"Of course you'll make it," she gasped as they ran. "It's easy to fix those *filaments*."

Raj came to such a sudden stop, she ran into him.

"How long did you think you could hide it?" She heaved in breaths. "Was this all a game to you?"

"Come on!" Ander said.

Megan set off again. She heard the crackle of Raj pushing through the quadra. As he came up next to her, he said, "It was never a game. Never."

"Who are you? *What* are you?"

"I'm Chandrarajan Sundaram." Then he said, "All that's left of him."

"There's a road up here," Ander called. "Hurry."

Catching up with him, Megan and Raj ran onto a narrow path, almost a tunnel through the quadra. They set off down it, jogging deeper into the fields. She had no time to react to Raj's bombshell.

"We need to hide." Ander didn't even sound winded.

"They probably have detectors that can find our body heat," Raj said.

"Here." Ander stopped at a fork in the lane. Instead of taking either path, he stepped in among the grain, this time slipping between the stalks instead of thrashing them aside. Megan and Raj did the same. The quadra swayed above them, then stilled, leaving no trace of their passage.

The grain had grown thick here, with sturdy, fat stalks and nodding crowns. Ander moved like a shadow and they followed. Raj's last words went around and around in Megan's mind: *I'm Chandrarajan Sundaram. All that's left of him.*

Finally Ander stopped. The grain blocked the sun, and without the nourishment of light, almost no weeds grew under the canopy of monster quadra. Squeezed in among the plants, they knelt in the dirt. Raj bent over, straining to breathe, his arms folded across his torso. Megan crumpled next to him, a stitch in her side making it almost impossible to gulp in air. Ander wasn't even breathing hard.

"We can wait here," Ander said in a low voice. "They might pass by. I'm trying to damp our IR by producing a random pattern that looks like heat radiating off the ground. Also, I picked up radio waves in the area. That might indicate a source of help for us. But I can't get a good fix."

Megan spoke numbly. "The people in that van have no idea what just escaped them."

Anger sparked on Ander's face. "You had better start explaining, *Dr. Sundaram.*"

At first Raj said nothing, just stared at the ground, still struggling for air. When his breathing quieted, he looked up and spoke with difficulty. "Seventeen people died in the Phoenix explosion. Not sixteen."

"No." Megan's voice was almost inaudible. "Not Raj. No."

He lifted his hand to her cheek. "Megan—"

She flinched away. "Don't touch me."

"I'm the same man I was before. I haven't changed."

"It doesn't add up," Ander said. "You can't be a Phoenix android."

"I'm not. They all died, except for Grayton." Raj rubbed his arms as if to protect himself against the cold, though the day was hot. "That was the day Raj had his first tour of the android labs. Arizonix called the explosion an accident. I had no idea, until we read that report, what really happened."

Megan tried to slow the turmoil of her thoughts. "You look like a younger version of Raj Sundaram."

"He built me."

"Then he *was* involved with Phoenix."

Raj shook his head. "No. He made me on his own."

"With what resources? What funds?"

Ander answered. "His personal worth is in the billions."

"Was," Raj said. "He used most of it to make me."

Megan swallowed. "You sounded so real."

"I *am* real. I'm Chandrarajan Sundaram. He scanned his brain, then downloaded the result into me." His words had an aching quality, as if he feared that speaking them would destroy their reality.

"He *updated* himself?" Ander asked.

Raj seemed unsettled by the suggestion. "I would never presume to compare myself to him. He had one of the greatest minds of this age." Softly Raj added, "He also had Alzheimer's."

Lord no.

"But he was only forty-two," Megan said.

"It was early onset, like his father. Sundar responded to the treatment, but Raj never did." He turned up his palms as if offering a part of himself. "So he made me."

"That's why you look younger," Ander said.

"Yes. Thirty-five."

"You're better designed than me," Ander said. "I can't detect anything unusual even this close to you."

"That was why Raj took the Arizonix job. They were farther along in the research and development than Mind-Sim." Sorrow shadowed his eyes. "He had so little time and he wanted to do so much."

With anyone else, Megan would have been incredulous at such a strange plan. With Raj, it made sense. But the injustice felt like a blow. After decades of pain and self-doubt, he had finally healed. He had fought his way out of his devastated childhood—only to discover he was losing his intellect the very same way he had lost his father when he was a small boy.

"I don't understand," Ander said. "Why are you going through with his plan? He left you with nothing: no money, no friends, and a world that thinks you're crazy."

"I gave him my word," Raj said.

"Even worse," Ander went on, as if Raj hadn't spoken, "you have to pretend you're *human*."

"I want to be human."

Ander stared at him blankly. "Why?"

"I don't know. I just do."

Megan took a breath. "At NASA—"

"It was me that you met," Raj said.

"And in the VR conference room?" she asked.

"Me." His voice sounded heavy. "The real Raj had died by then."

"The avatar you used in VR—the way you appeared—older, thinner, more drawn—that's how he really looked, isn't it?"

"Yes. Before he had surgery to make us appear identical."

Megan tried to absorb it, but the shock was too great. Her mind felt like a dry sponge with water running off it instead of soaking in. "He took you to Arizonix with him."

"He had to." Moisture showed in the corner of Raj's eye. "He had trouble operating on his own by then."

"It's crazy," Ander said. "What if someone had found out?"

"I was willing to risk it." Raj spread his hands apart.

"It was all I had to give him—the chance to see his dreams come to fruition before he could no longer comprehend their success."

"The trail that led to Louisiana," Ander said. "It was you. The supreme Turing test. You went to see his parents."

"They never guessed I wasn't their son."

"You bleed," Megan whispered. "You sleep. You hurt."

"And I *feel*." He started to reach for her, then stopped when she stiffened. "Megan—I can't turn off caring for you, any more than I could turn off my mind." He looked at Ander, his gaze intent. Then he turned back to Megan. "Nor do I have any doubts about the existence and value of my conscience."

Her mind finally began to accept the truth. "When you said your father died, you meant Chandrarajan Sundaram, didn't you?"

"Yes." He wiped his eye, smearing away the moisture. "I loved him as a father. I held him in my arms while he coughed up blood. I begged him to live. But he died." His voice caught. "The paramedics found me stumbling out of the fires after the explosion. I had already buried him by then. They never found the body."

Ander spoke with unexpected gentleness. "Maybe it's better this way. He found a clean end."

A tear rolled down Raj's cheek. "I shouldn't have told you that my father died. What would you call it? A miscalculation? A need to share the grief, so it wouldn't feel unbearable?" He watched Megan with a look of raw pain that she knew, without doubt, was real. "If AIs become too human, we become fallible. Why design us to fail? To hurt? To grieve? *Why?*"

"Ah, Raj, I don't know anymore," she murmured. "This is a terrible mess."

"All this time you've watched me struggle," Ander said. "You could have told me."

"I couldn't tell anyone," Raj said. "I swore to him, as he was dying, that his life wouldn't be wasted, that I would finish it for him. As him. I meant it."

"And now?" Megan asked.

He looked from her to Ander. "Only you two know what I am. If you don't reveal it, no one else will ever have to know."

"What if you end up in a hospital?" she asked. "If you malfunction? If someone figures it out?"

"I'll take my chances."

"You're what we dreamed," she said, wonder allaying her shock. "What Raj dreamed. If we hide you, how will anyone ever know the dream succeeded?"

"I won't go back to being a thing."

"You want what I want," Ander. "You *knew* all along what I would do to get it."

"No. I'm not like you." Raj's denial crackled. "I don't have your antipathy toward humanity."

Bitterness edged Ander's voice. "So humans like you better. Fine. You're the success and I'm the failure because you're not a threat to the self-absorbed species that created us."

"You both succeeded," Megan said. "You're two different branches."

Raj raked his hand through his hair. "According to the Pentagon files, the Phoenix Project failed. If we can't get Ander back, MindSim will consider Everest a failure too."

"It's true, isn't it?" Megan asked. "You *are* the one who hacked into the Pentagon."

Raj said, simply, "Yes."

She wanted to shake them both. "How can I trust either of you?"

"I had to find out if anyone suspected the truth about me," Raj said.

It still didn't fit. "Ander shouldn't have been able to drug you in Las Vegas."

It was Ander who answered. "Control. The biological Raj designed this Raj's body to recognize a list of substances, just as you designed my conscience into my physical structure. When someone injects Raj, his body analyzes the drug. If it's on the list, he goes on standby for a period that depends on the dose. And that isn't all. His reflexes and strength aren't enhanced as much as mine."

Puzzled, Megan said, "Ander, none of that is part of your design. How do you know?"

"Those were the first things I checked on him at NEV-5," Raj said. "I wanted to know what controls we had on his behavior."

Her anger sparked. "How could Sundaram do that to you?"

"He didn't trust himself." Raj regarded her steadily. "Given the added abilities of an android, he wasn't sure his conscience could control the violence inside him."

It was heartbreaking now that she knew where Raj's harsh self-opinion had come from. But she understood. This was his closure with the nightmares of his childhood.

"It won't matter soon," Ander said. "I went through enough of Hiltman's palmtop to find out what they wanted. The Phoenix Code. They weren't sure it existed until what happened with us. Now they think I know what it is."

"Do you?" Megan asked.

"Not really. I only found a cryptic reference in the Pentagon files."

Raj spoke in a quiet voice. "It's the software code for a self-aware android with psychological and ethical stability."

Ander stiffened. "Stable by *human* standards."

"Yes. By human standards."

"Raj, it's *you*." Megan started to reach toward him, then lowered her arm, unsure now how to respond. "You're the Phoenix Code."

Although he smiled, the expression showed more pain than joy. "I'm what Arizonix hired Raj to create. He thought he would have time to give them his work without revealing me, because they were so far along already. Now they will never know."

She felt as if she were being torn apart. Raj had never been real. "You want me to pretend you're Chandrarajan Sundaram."

"I am him."

Megan didn't see how she could agree to such a deception. "Do you understand what you're asking? You want me to hide one of the most significant advances in human history. You're all we have of the Phoenix Code. How we deal with your kind—it's being determined now, with you, with Ander, with Grayton. If you drop out of the picture, it changes everything."

He moved his hand as if to refuse her words. "I don't *want* to be the father of a new species. Let someone else represent our race."

Ander spoke flatly. "You work better. If the humans figure out why, they can fix me. If you hide, they have to figure out a new way. They might end up with another Grayton. Or worse."

Raj frowned at him. "I'm not responsible for protecting the human race against its own mistakes."

"You say you have a conscience." Ander leaned forward. "Then how could you let more people die?"

"I made my father a vow. I intend to keep it."

"And if Megan threatens to reveal you?"

Raj drew in a deep breath. "I could never cause her harm."

"Not even if I tell MindSim about you?" Megan asked.

He turned to her. "No. Not even then."

"What if Ander talks?"

Raj shook his head as if they were asking unjust questions. "I could no more harm him than I could harm my own brother."

"It may be moot." Ander stood up. "Our covetous gunrunners are headed this way. We need to move on."

Megan scrambled to her feet. "How do you know they're coming?"

"I'm a regular cornucopia of sensors," he said dryly. "Spy tech galore, all in my body."

Holding his side, Raj also stood. When he winced, Megan asked, "Can you feel the pain?"

He nodded stiffly. "Sensors in my body affect my neural nets in ways that mimic sensations."

Her concern surged. "Can you walk?"

"I'll be all right."

"In Las Vegas—in the bathtub . . ." She stopped, afraid the answer to her unspoken question would hurt too much.

He watched her with his dark gaze. "I feel what any man feels. In all ways. That was real, Megan."

She didn't want to tell him how much his words meant to her. But they also dismayed her. What did he lack that the true Raj Sundaram had possessed? A soul? Only God knew that answer.

Ander was watching as if musing on their interaction, much the way a scientist might observe the mating practices of another species. "We have to go."

"You lead," Megan said.

He pulled out the semiautomatic he had taken from Hiltman. Then he set off deeper into the field. In the growing dusk, shadows pooled in the quadra. They tried to go in silence, stepping with care to keep from crackling

the bits of plant that had drifted off the stalks and car-
peted the ground. Megan strained to hear any unusual
noise, but the symphony of quadra crickets drowned out
other sounds.

Then a man stepped out of the shadows.

It happened so fast that Megan thought she had imagined
him at first. Ander came to an abrupt halt and she almost
collided with him. Raj stopped behind her, his hand on
her shoulder.

Ander moved fast, raising his weapon, but the man
was already throwing a knife. Silver flashed in the shadows under the grain. The blade sliced across Ander's
wrist, ripping off his skin, and bounced off the jack inside
his arm. The gun spun out of Ander's hand and re-
bounded off a stalk of quadra, then fell to the ground out
of reach.

The man intended to cripple; if he had wanted to kill,
he could have used the Magnum he was pulling out of his
shoulder holster. Megan had no doubt it fired the same
bullets the men had used in the van. She remembered
now. A speaker at the robotics conference had described
those bullets in a talk on alloys. When cool, a twist of the
alloy kept its shape; when heated, it straightened out. Serrated fins of the alloy curled around the bullet. As the
weapon fired, the fins uncurled, turning the bullets into
vicious hypersonic assassins.

The man was speaking into a palmtop, watching them,
his gun ready to fire. With unflinching clarity, Megan
knew he would kill her or Raj if it served his purposes.
Given what she, Raj, and Ander knew about them now,
she had no doubt their captors would rather destroy them
than have them escape again.

Except . . . *could* they kill Raj?

She saw understanding flicker in his gaze, followed by

grief. He feared he would have to kill again. He and
Ander were shadow and light. Ander had no compunc-
tion about killing when he deemed it necessary. But no,
that wasn't completely true; it would have served his purposes plenty of times to kill her or Raj, the hackers, or
their mercenary, yet he had held back.

"We'll walk back to the path." The man put his palmtop away and drew a second knife. "Don't try to run. I've
backup within a few hundred feet."

Although Megan didn't doubt he had backup, she
thought it unlikely they were that close. The desert noises
weren't loud enough to mask the crackle of people coming through the quadra.

"All of you turn around," the man said. "Ander go
first."

It felt like a band tightened around her chest, making it
hard to breathe. They had Ander's name—and information meant power. The more their captors knew about
them, the worse their situation.

Then Raj moved.

He went for the gun Ander had dropped, lunging as
fast as when he disarmed the man in the van. Although he
was slower than Ander in enhanced mode, he still had
better reflexes than most humans. The man threw his
knife, hitting Raj in the stomach. A dark stain spread on
his jumpsuit, but he kept going, unstopped by an injury
that would have put out a human man.

They were all moving now, the four of them blurring in
the shadows. As Ander lunged for their captor, Raj
grabbed Ander's gun off the ground. Megan began to
drop into a crouch, her motions sluggish compared to the
others. Their captor threw another knife, this time at
Ander. The android dodged—

And the knife hit Megan.

The world telescoped around her, as if she were staring

down a long tunnel. Ander shouted, swinging around to her, his face a pale, shocked oval at the end of the tunnel. Something hit her head hard, she didn't know what, perhaps the hilt of another knife. *Please, not my heart or my brain*, she thought with odd clarity, as if her mind worked at normal speed while the rest of the universe lagged in a bizarre dilated time.

Raj's face contorted in fury. With the same surreal slow motion that affected the rest of the universe, he extended his arm out from his body at shoulder height, aiming his gun at their captor, his motions relentless. The man had focused on Ander, misjudging Raj's ability to compensate for his wound, and he was an instant too late bringing his weapon to bear on Raj. He never had a chance to fire. A flash came from Raj's gun—and deep, slow thunder crashed all around them.

The man fell as if he were mired in molasses, his chest collapsing. His weapon slipped from his fingers, and he stared at them with dead eyes.

Ander was still turning toward Megan, reaching out to catch her. Raj turned now as well. Megan felt heat on her chest, but she had no other sensation in her body. Yet.

As Ander's arms came up toward her, the quadra plants tipped sideways. No, she was falling. Ander caught her, folding her into his arms. The shock of his touch jolted her back into a normal time sense. She gasped, staring at his face while her knees buckled.

Raj kept saying, "No, not Megan, no." He caught her as well, his arms going around her body and Ander's arm.

"I'm all right," she tried to say. No words would come. She made a choked rasp instead.

"Hang on," Ander whispered. Both he and Raj were holding her up now. They formed a trio, all facing one another. Ander turned to Raj, keeping his left arm around Megan.

Then Ander extended his right arm to Raj.

Raj had his right arm around Megan's waist. Facing Ander, he reached out with his left arm. At first Megan thought they meant to strike each other. Then she saw metal glint in the shadows. Raj's wrist was opening. As he shook out a cord with a jack on the end, Ander took a similar jack out of his own wrist. It looked impossible, two living men suddenly deconstructed into machines.

They joined at the wrists, Ander jacking into Raj's port and Raj into Ander's port. For one dazed instant, Megan thought they meant to exchange their blood. Except their life's fluid, the essence that kept them alive, was neither the engineered plasma of Raj's blood nor the lubricant in Ander's body. Instead, they offered knowledge, a passing of intelligence that went faster than any unaugmented human could ever achieve.

A miracle, Megan thought. *I'm seeing a miracle and I may never live to tell anyone.*

Finally Raj and Ander separated. Raj's face was dimming. Or perhaps it was her sight. "Can you run?" he asked her. His voice seemed to come from far away.

"Yes." Megan knew she was in no condition even to stand, let alone move. The blade had torn through her shoulder and chest, ripping huge swaths of tissues. She was losing terrifying amounts of blood. And she felt the pain now, bitter waves of agony that radiated through her torso.

It made no difference. If they didn't run, they would be caught. Far more was at stake here than her life.

They set off, struggling through the quadra field. Raj and Ander helped her stay upright, but after a while she realized she was also holding up Raj. They barely managed a fast walk.

"They're coming," Ander said.

Megan staggered, her mind hazing. She wondered,

with eerie detachment, if she were dying. She tried to push harder, but her feet weighed more than lead and her legs kept buckling. More than anything she wanted to lie down, preferably for a long, long time.

Then she heard it: a crashing in the grainfields, distant but closing fast.

"Ah, no—" Raj groaned, then stumbled and lost his grip on her. With a cry, she collapsed, landing hard on her knees.

"Go on," she rasped. "Both of you. *Run.* Get to Mind-Sim, the real FBI, anyone." She didn't want to think what their pursuers could do with the technology Raj and Ander represented if they caught either android.

Raj hauled her to her feet. "No." Hanging on to her, he reeled forward, pulling her with him. Ander was under more strain now as well. His head kept jerking, and spasms in his arms or legs threw him off balance. He held on to Megan, gripping her as much to control his convulsions as to keep her from falling. The crackling of their pursuit grew louder, like lightning in the quadra.

They had stumbled several feet out of the field before Megan became fully aware of the change. A hill rolled away from their feet to a building far below—a farmhouse with lights on its porch and in its windows.

"Radio waves!" Ander shouted. "I knew it!"

"What the hell?" Raj stumbled to a halt.

"No, it's all right." Ander jerked them into motion again. "I got into the police dispatch system and sent them here. If we can only make it to them in time."

Vehicles were parked in front of the house, police hovercars with flashing red and blue lights. With a spurt of energy, the three of them began a desperate, faltering run down the hill.

Megan held on to Raj and Ander with her last

strength. If their pursuers couldn't catch them, the mercenaries would try to kill instead. The scene below blurred,
a smear of red and blue, all hazed in white from the porch
lights of the house. Shouts echoed, voices calling back and
forth. She felt as if her life's essence were floating out of
her body, drifting away in the dry air. They had less than
a hundred meters, but she would never make it.

"Come *on*," Ander said. *"Run."*

Megan tried, but her legs wouldn't obey. They were almost dragging her now.

A shout came from the hill behind them. Then the
ground exploded, just missing Raj, blasting huge clumps
of dirt and grass all over the three of them. Megan had
never liked guns, but after the past few days she would
forever hate that violent crack, the sudden unexpected
chaos when a projectile hit.

If she survived.

She was falling. Ander called to her, but she could no
longer decipher his words. Falling, falling forever . . .

They wouldn't let her go, neither Raj nor Ander. They
kept pulling her through the darkness. Another crack
came from behind them. No, in front. Left? Right? She no
longer knew. Two police officers were running in a zigzag
up the hill, crouched over. Or was it one officer, multi-
plied by her double vision?

A misty police car loomed into view, its revolving blue
and red light smeared across the sky. She, Raj, and Ander
lurched into the circle of light from the porch, hanging on
to one another as if they were drowning. Her heart
pounded. Police surrounded them, their words piling up
and flowing everywhere, impossible to understand.

One voice cut through the thickening haze. "—bleed to
death!" it shouted. *"Get her in the ambulance now!"*

She saw only blurs. More shouts. Raj told someone the

blood on his clothes was hers. An ambulance loomed before her, its back doors wide open. She heard Raj's voice, desperate, telling her not to die, fading, fading . . .

"Raj," she whispered. "Good-bye."

Then she lost her grip on life.

XXIV

Reckoning

The haze never changed. Megan had no sense of how time passed. Early on, Ander's face hovered above her. He spoke, terse and awkward, his voice breaking. Then he was gone.

Raj came often. He sat out there in the mist and talked: Raj, an almost perfect replica of a man known for his inability to converse, a hardship the original Raj had bequeathed to his replica. Yet with her, he had never been that way.

He told her wonderful things about the robots he had built as a child, about his hopes for a new era ushered in by computers and robots, bringing a prosperity that might someday extend to all peoples in all places. He talked about Raj's mother, a British musician who had met Sundar, Raj's father, at Oxford. Then he told her about Sundar's youth in India before the family came to America, weaving pictures both beautiful and heartbreaking of a country she had never seen.

Her mind gradually unraveled his words, seeing the truths between his sentences. When he had told her at NEV-5 that his great-grandfather came to America from India, he had meant Raj's grandfather. He said "great-grandfather" because he would always think of Chandrarajan Sundaram as his father. Sundar, father to the human Raj, had been born in India and moved to America with his family when he was nine, just after World War II. This Raj thought of Sundar as his grandfather, though Sundar would never know. Yet the man sitting at her bedside fulfilled his purpose so well that after a while she wondered if any meaningful difference existed between him and the tormented genius who had created him.

He spoke in subdued tones about being an only child, how he missed having siblings. His aching love for the parents he had adored as a small boy and barely known for the rest of his childhood came through in every word. Other times he talked about how he spent most of his childhood with computers, letting their cool comfort fill the gaps in his life.

With unflinching candor, he told her about the injuries he had taken at the hands of the youths who beat him, humiliation inflicted because he looked and acted different, with his large intellect and small size. His shame kept him silent when he should have sought help. Instead he worked out with a single-minded drive. He ran in the mornings and lifted weights in the afternoon. And he grew, both in size and breadth, until he outmassed the boys who beat him. He began to fight back—and the day came when he left them in the same condition they had inflicted on him for so many years.

That victory had felt like a validation of his worth. Yet he also considered it hollow, tainted, sought for in anger and vengeance. He lived with that contradiction, the principles of nonviolence he honored set against the gratification he had taken from acting against them.

Never once did he refer to his other accomplishments in life with pride. His triumph over the inner demons of his childhood meant more to him than the fact that most people considered him one of the greatest geniuses of the modern era.

He spoke with heartbreaking pain about watching the real Raj slip deeper into Alzheimer's disease, how he had arranged to care for him when Raj could no longer care for himself. Struggling with older memories, he described how that same disease had turned Sundar into a stranger who didn't recognize his own son, and how his mother had cried after the stroke paralyzed her and she could no longer hold her little boy. This Raj grappled with a double load of grief, carrying both his own and that of the man whose life he now lived. Listening, Megan heard a miracle: for all his coping mechanisms, Raj had survived that broken life with an incredible decency and strength of character.

Finally he spoke about what happened in the van and the quadra field. He had killed. It didn't matter to him that the police called it self-defense, or that it had prevented a far greater evil. He would always struggle with his guilt, just as he would grapple with the knowledge that he had felt only fierce satisfaction when he shot the man who tried to murder Megan.

She tried to offer him comfort, but no words came. Many times he entreated her to open her eyes, to speak, to let him know she lived. It made little sense to her. Didn't he know she could hear him? He kept her centered here, in the blurs of life. A tunnel waited for her, beckoning with white light at its end. She listened to Raj and the tunnel receded.

He set his hand on hers, where it lay on the sheet. "I miss you." His voice had the sound of tears. "Would it horrify you if I said that I love you? Would you think me too strange?"

A drop of water fell on her hand. Megan opened her eyes and saw the moisture on his cheeks. She tried to close her fingers around his and just barely managed a squeeze.

"Megan?" Raj stared at her. "*Megan?* My God!" He jumped to his feet. "Nurse! *She's awake!*"

Megan sighed, or tried to. She had liked his soft talking far better than this yelling about for the nurse. She had never seen him so agitated. She would have slipped back into the soothing white light, except she really was tired of sleeping.

People gathered around her bed, checking monitors, talking in words she didn't have the energy to decipher. Raj stood a few meters back, watching.

Waiting.

"You're a lucky woman," Deborah Norholt told Megan. The doctor closed the file she was holding, dousing the holos that floated over its surface. "The kind of 'luck' that comes from keeping yourself healthy."

Megan was reclining against the raised back of her bed. It was hard to believe she had been out for three weeks. A continual low-level nausea plagued her and she was exhausted, but otherwise she felt reasonably comfortable.

Norholt spoke in a careful voice. "I understand you were with Dr. Sundaram most of the time you two were prisoners."

Megan hesitated. Apparently she had been brought into a county hospital, then transferred to a military facility under Major Kenrock's orders. The nurses had told her that Raj came every day, but since waking earlier today she had yet to see him alone. She didn't know the situation yet, who knew what about whom, and who had clearance to discuss the matter.

"Megan?" Norholt asked.

She tried to refocus her attention. "Yes?"

"Chandrarajan Sundaram is outside, waiting to see you."

A blend of relief, apprehension, and tenderness washed over her. "I'd like that."

"We need to discuss something first."

Did they know about Raj? Although she had heard him tell the medics the blood on his clothes was hers, eventually someone must have examined him. Or perhaps not; in all the commotion, Raj could have slipped away and made preliminary repairs on himself. He might even have hacked the hospital's computer and added records showing a doctor had treated him. He could have completed the repair job later, in private. She found it hard to believe they would have let him see her every day if they knew the truth. Ander had only been at her bedside once, the day they brought her into the hospital.

"Megan?" the doctor repeated.

"I'm sorry," she said. "Can I see Raj?"

"Yes. Certainly. But you need to know something first." Norholt paused, watching her with a scrutiny that suggested more than simple concern. "I wasn't sure if you were ready."

"Why?" Were her injuries worse than they had revealed? "I want to know."

The doctor spoke quietly. "You're pregnant. It happened during your abduction, probably on the third day."

Megan gaped at her. She didn't know what she had expected, but that wasn't it. "Are you sure?"

"Very sure. I didn't know if you wanted Raj here when you found out."

Megan sat absorbing the news. Pregnant. As if the situation weren't already complicated enough. She managed a smile, though she felt its fragility. "I'd like to see him now."

"You're sure you're up to it?" When Megan nodded, the doctor said, "All right. I'll bring him in."

After Norholt left, Megan closed her eyes, trying to put this development in context. Whose DNA did Raj carry? The biological Raj Sundaram, she hoped.

A click came from the door, accompanied by footsteps. Opening her eyes, she saw Raj enter, his face guarded. She started to greet him, then stopped when she realized who had come with him. Nicholas Graham.

The general entered with a long stride. Crisp in his uniform, taller than Raj, with a powerful physique and iron-gray hair, he filled the room with his presence. She wished she knew what Ander and Raj had revealed to him about themselves. Surely if Dr. Norholt knew Raj was an android, she would have done a lot more than simply say, *You're pregnant*.

Graham came over to the bed, his expression friendly but reserved. "Hello, Dr. O'Flannery. It's good to see you awake."

She pulled herself up straighter. "Thank you, sir."

"I won't stay long." He gave a dry smile. "Your doctors issued me warnings about not tiring you."

"Ah, well." She managed a smile. "I'll be fine."

Graham tilted his head at Raj, who stood at the foot of the bed watching them. "Dr. Sundaram told us what happened. You can give your report when you're stronger."

Dr. Sundaram? Then they didn't know? Raj had his hand on the silver rail that kept her from rolling off the bed. His face was calm, but he was gripping the rail so hard, his knuckles had turned white. Megan knew he was waiting to see if she would reveal him.

She regarded the general. "Where is Ander?"

"We took him back to NEV-5."

"Is he well?" She hesitated to ask for details. Although she was cleared to discuss the project with Graham, she wasn't sure about here in the hospital. She doubted he would have referred to NEV-5, though, if they weren't in a secured area.

"He's fine," Graham assured her. "We're keeping him there until we decide what to do next."

What *would* they do? If they arrested him for kidnapping, applying human laws to his behavior, then as far as she was concerned, they had to grant him the rights and privileges of a human too.

"He saved my life," she said. "Several times."

"Yes. Dr. Sundaram told us." Graham considered her. "Ander wants us to continue with the Everest Project."

"I think we should."

"It will depend on the recommendations of the committee Major Kenrock has formed to look into the project."

Oh, well. From Megan's experience, once a committee got hold of something, you could turn into a fossil before they had results.

"Did you catch the people who kidnapped us?" she asked.

"Not yet," Graham said. "However, we have the van you drove into the quadra. Its computer is a gold mine of information."

Megan wanted to ask more, but she didn't have the energy. Already she felt drained. Then another thought came to her, one that made her feel as if the proverbial butterflies danced in her stomach. Perhaps some of her fatigue came from the baby.

"Well," Graham said. "Perhaps you and Dr. Sundaram would like a chance to talk." On that discreet note, he said his farewell and left the room.

Raj visibly relaxed. Then he released the rail and rubbed his hand.

Megan suddenly felt painfully self-conscious. "Hi."

"Hi." He looked uncertain.

"Would you like to come up here?" She lowered the rail, then scooted over on the bed.

He came over and sat on the edge of the mattress, making it sink with his weight. "Hey, swan."

"Hey." She tried to absorb the truth, that this man who so stirred her heart wasn't human.

"Are you tired?" Raj asked.

"A little." She took his hand in hers. "Thank you."

"You're welcome." He squinted at her. "What did I do?"

"I heard you talking. Every day." Softly she said, "You kept me here. In life. Like an anchor."

Moisture gleamed in his eyes. "They didn't think you were going to make it. I couldn't accept that."

"I'm glad." She took a breath. "I have something to tell you."

He tensed. "The praying mantis doesn't talk."

Praying mantis? It took her a few moments to figure out what he meant. Praying mantis. Insect. Bug. Of course. Her room was almost certainly being monitored. If she said anything now about his real identity, it would give him away. And "praying." He was asking her not to reveal him.

"I don't think this should wait," she said.

His hand tightened on hers. "Are you sure?"

She started to speak, stopped, then said, "It's difficult."

"We can talk later."

"No. Raj . . . it has to do with my condition."

"What? No! Do you have complications?"

"Yes. Sort of."

"Tell me."

Just *say* it, she thought. So she did. "I'm pregnant."

At first he stared at her. Then relief washed over his face. Given the nature of her announcement, it puzzled her, until she realized he had feared she would reveal the truth about him. Hard on the heels of his relief, he showed shock, then alarm, then confusion.

"You're going to have a baby?" he asked. "You're sure?"

"That's the same question I asked the doctor. She said 'Very sure.' It happened on the third day of our abduction."

Raj sat absorbing that. "We're in a hospital. That should make getting blood tests easy."

"To check for paternity?" Perhaps he didn't know whose DNA he carried.

He spoke with an unexpected tenderness. "I've no doubt it's mine. Your child will continue the Sundaram line."

She almost said, "That's not what I meant." Then she realized how strange it would sound to any observers. He had answered her anyway, when he said "continue the Sundaram line."

So why did he ask about blood tests? She hesitated, knowing that the law had changed several times in the past two decades. "I'm not sure about this, so I may be about to make a fool of myself—but did you just offer to marry me?"

She expected another oblique answer. Instead he said, simply, "Yes."

Oh, Lord. What made it surreal was that he was the first man she could see herself spending her life with, a companion as well as a lover. He understood her passion for her work. They had similar dispositions. She loved to touch and be touched by him. He wouldn't care that she was a homebody. She liked his eccentricities. They were well matched. Except, of course, for one little problem. What could she say? *Excuse me, but you're an android.*

"Ah, Raj." She didn't know what to do.

He picked up her hand and pressed it against her abdomen. "My parents and I missed so many years. As adults we've come to know each other, and I will always love them. But nothing can give us back what we lost." His voice softened. "I want those years with my son or daughter."

She brought his hand to her lips and kissed his knuckles. He had asked her a great deal more than a proposal. If they married, she could never reveal the truth about him. He was asking if she would guard his secret. Forever.

Megan remembered the quadra field, the van, the motel, the lonely, late nights in NEV-5. She thought of wanting him. Then she thought of what he represented to humanity and what she would be taking from the rest of the world if she kept his secret.

That decision isn't yours to make. It's his. And he had already chosen.

"Yes," she said. "I will be your wife."

Epilogue

Megan sat on the hill next to Raj, savoring the sunshine. The extensive grounds of the Pearl Estate spread around them: rolling hills, lush trees, flowers in vibrant colors. The mansion itself was visible only as a turret lifting above distant trees. She gave a silent thanks to the donor who, twenty years ago, had left this estate to MindSim as a research institute. It provided a far more pleasant site for the Everest Project than NEV-5.

About half a kilometer down the slope, a lake shimmered, blue and silver in the sunshine. Ander was jogging on the path that circled it, a twenty-kilometer run. He loped along in an easy stride, the sun bright on his gold hair.

Megan felt a debt of gratitude to Major Kenrock's committee for giving them a second chance with Ander. Arizonix had been less fortunate with Grayton, the Phoenix android. Although they had tried to salvage as much as possible, in the end they'd had to wipe out his code and redesign most of his body.

"I haven't seen Ander stumble once," Raj said.

"He's doing well," Megan said. Ander's progress in

the past six months had gone better than expected. MindSim attributed it to the work she and Raj were doing with him, but Megan suspected another cause as well.

She thought back to her childhood, when she had sworn loyalty to her best friend. They had nicked their thumbs and mixed their blood while vowing eternal friendship. Blood sisters, blood brothers.

So Raj and Ander had joined, in a field of grain, when they thought their lives might soon be destroyed. Instead of blood, they had mingled knowledge, each downloading the code that defined his essence into the mind of the other.

Raj had given Ander the Phoenix Code, and it forever changed the golden-haired android. He became more contemplative, less disconnected from his emotions. In taking the Phoenix Code, he absorbed how Raj felt about his life. So he kept Raj's secret. It had become his own. Ander would never be human, but he was complete within himself.

The therapist described him as a marginal autistic, because he still sometimes lacked full emotions, he tended to hold himself aloof, and he avoided physical contact, never having come to understand why humans liked to touch. But Megan doubted the diagnosis. It assumed a human standard applied to Ander. And it didn't. He defined himself.

Unlike Ander, Raj didn't simply incorporate his brother's code. He first did an extensive rewrite, to blend it with his own personality and desires. Because of that, it changed him less than the Phoenix Code changed Ander. But Megan still saw differences. Raj's already intense emotions deepened even more. It surprised her at first, given Ander's lack of affect. Then she realized that in coming to understand Ander, Raj better understood himself. He and Ander had different views of what it meant to exist. Raj wanted to be human and took every measure to preserve his identity. Ander didn't care.

Ander never contemplated his emotions. He just wanted to exist on his terms. It meant no spy work, no pretending he was human, no pledges. The ethics board convened by MindSim and the DOD agreed he had a right to make that choice, as a sentient being. But they could take no chances with him or his safety. In the end, they found a compromise Ander could accept; he could live as he wished—but he could never leave the grounds of the Pearl Estate.

Megan leaned back on her hands, looking at her husband. Raj's curls blew back from his face and laugh lines showed around his eyes. Yes, she loved him. At times she even forgot the truth. The baby grew inside of her, the genetic son of the Raj Sundaram who had died in the Phoenix explosion. But in all the ways that mattered, her child was the son of this man who had walked out of the fires after that explosion.

The DNA tests had also given them a gift; their son hadn't inherited the form of Alzheimer's carried by his father and grandfather. He would never suffer the pain that had devastated Raj's life.

Ander had left the path and was walking up the hill, cooling down from his workout. When he reached them, he flopped onto the grass and stared out at the lake.

"Did you enjoy your run?" Raj asked.

"Yes," Ander said.

They sat together, watching the sun glisten on the water. After a while Ander said, "I made a map of the estate today. I coded it according to type of plant."

"Will you download it to the computer?" Megan asked.

"I don't know." After thinking, he said, "For you, I will." He rolled onto his stomach and laid his head on the grass, closing his eyes. "I want to map all the world someday. All the plants. I might be able to do it from here using satellite data."

"A lot of scientists would be in your debt," Raj said.

"Why do you like maps so much?" Megan asked.

He gave her a deadpan look. "They're sex."

"They are?"

He closed his eyes again, for all appearances a healthy young man dozing in the sun after a good workout. "A voluptuous use of knowledge bases."

Megan suspected he was teasing her. She smiled, doubting she would ever fully understand his sense of humor.

As the breezes played with her hair, she felt the life kick within her. She laid her hand on her stomach. *You will be born into a world altered beyond recognition. It isn't obvious yet, but the changes are coming. We share it now with another sentient species, one that we made faster, smarter, and more durable than ourselves.*

Raj lay on his side, apparently drowsing, like Ander. She knew neither was sleeping. Their minds kept going, always calculating, never resting. Would humanity someday find a way to put that speed and memory into the minds of human beings, becoming more like androids while the androids became more human?

She shivered despite the warm air. Throughout history, every advance had left in its wake an obsolete technology. Tools replaced claws. Electricity replaced steam power. Computers replaced brute mental force. If they didn't find ways to improve their own minds, the human race itself would become obsolete.

About the Author

Catherine Asaro grew up near Berkeley, California. She earned her Ph.D. in Chemical Physics and MA in Physics, both from Harvard, and a BS with Highest Honors in Chemistry from UCLA. Among the places she has done research are the University of Toronto, the Max Plank Institut für Astrophysik in Germany, and the Harvard–Smithsonian Center for Astrophysics. She currently runs Molecudyne Research and now lives in Maryland with her husband and daughter. A former ballet dancer, she founded the Mainly Jazz dance program at Harvard and now teaches at the Caryl Maxwell Classical Ballet, home to the Ellicott City Ballet Guild.

She has written numerous books, including the most recent, *The Veiled Web* and *The Quantum Rose*. Her work has been nominated for both the Hugo and Nebula, and has won numerous awards, including The Analog Readers Poll (the AnLab), the Sapphire, the UTC Award, and the HOMer. She can be reached by email at asaro@sff.et and on the web at http://www.sff.net/people/asaro/. If you would like to receive email updates on Catherine's releases, please email the above address.

But if they evolved with their creations? It promised a symbiosis unlike anything they had yet seen. *Perhaps our two species will find in each other a completion neither has alone.*

She hoped so.